OPEN
SECRETS

190201

ALICE MUNRO

Chatto & Windus

LONDON

First published in 1994

1 3 5 7 9 10 8 6 4 2

Copyright © 1994 Alice Munro

The stories in this collection were originally published in the following:
The New Yorker: "The Albanian Virgin", "Carried Away",
"The Jack Randa Hotel", "Open Secrets", "A Real Life" (originally titled
"A Form of Marriage"), "Vandals", and "A Wilderness Station".
The Paris Review: "Spaceships have Landed".
Some parts of the journal section of "A Wilderness Station" are taken from the account
written by Robert B. Laidlaw in 1907.

First published in Great Britain in 1994 by
Chatto & Windus Limited
Random House, 20 Vauxhall Bridge Road
London SW1V 2SA

Random House Australia (Pty) Limited
20 Alfred Street, Milsons Point, Sydney
New South Wales 2061, Australia

Random House New Zealand Limited
18 Poland Road, Glenfield
Auckland 10, New Zealand

Random House South Africa (Pty) Limited
PO Box 337, Bergvlei, South Africa

Random House UK Limited Reg. No. 954009

A CIP catalogue record for this book
is available from the British Library

ISBN 0 7011 6145 0

Printed and bound in Great Britain by
Clays Ltd, St. Ives PLC

This book is for ever-faithful friends—
Daphne and Deirdre, Audrey, Sally, Julie,
Mildred, Ann and Ginger and Mary

CONTENTS

Carried Away 3

A Real Life 52

The Albanian Virgin 81

Open Secrets 129

The Jack Randa Hotel 161

A Wilderness Station 190

Spaceships Have Landed 226

Vandals 261

OPEN
SECRETS

OPEN SECRETS

CARRIED AWAY

LETTERS

In the dining room of the Commercial Hotel, Louisa opened the letter that had arrived that day from overseas. She ate steak and potatoes, her usual meal, and drank a glass of wine. There were a few travellers in the room, and the dentist who ate there every night because he was a widower. He had shown an interest in her in the beginning but had told her he had never before seen a woman touch wine or spirits.

"It is for my health," said Louisa gravely.

The white tablecloths were changed every week and in the meantime were protected by oilcloth mats. In winter, the dining room smelled of these mats wiped by a kitchen rag, and of coal fumes from the furnace, and beef gravy and dried potatoes and onions—a smell not unpleasant to anybody coming in hungry from the cold. On each table was a little cruet stand with the bottle of brown sauce, the bottle of tomato sauce, and the pot of horseradish.

The letter was addressed to "The Librarian, Carstairs Public Library, Carstairs, Ontario." It was dated six weeks before—January 4, 1917.

Perhaps you will be surprised to hear from a person you don't know and that doesn't remember your name.
I hope you are still the same Librarian though enough time has gone by that you could have moved on.

What has landed me here in Hospital is not too serious. I see worse all around me and get my mind off of all that by picturing things and wondering for instance if you are still there in the Library. If you are the one I mean, you are about of medium size or perhaps not quite, with light brownish hair. You came a few months before it was time for me to go in the Army following on Miss Tamblyn who had been there since I first became a user aged nine or ten. In her time the books were pretty much every which way, and it was as much as your life was worth to ask her for the least help or anything since she was quite a dragon. Then when you came what a change, it was all put into sections of Fiction and Non-Fiction and History and Travel and you got the magazines arranged in order and put out as soon as they arrived, not left to molder away till everything in them was stale. I felt gratitude but did not know how to say so. Also I wondered what brought you there, you were an educated person.

My name is Jack Agnew and my card is in the drawer. The last book I took out was very good—H. G. Wells, Mankind in the Making. *My education was to Second Form in High School, then I went into Douds as many*

*did. I didn't join up right away when I was eighteen so
you will not see me as a Brave Man. I am a person
tending to have my own ideas always. My only relative
in Carstairs, or anyplace, is my father Patrick Agnew.
He works for Douds not at the factory but at the house doing
the gardening. He is a lone wolf even more than me and
goes out to the country fishing every chance he gets. I
write him a letter sometimes but I doubt if he reads it.*

After supper Louisa went up to the Ladies' Parlor on the
second floor, and sat down at the desk to write her reply.

*I am very glad to hear you appreciated what I did in
the Library though it was just the normal
organization, nothing special.*

  *I am sure you would like to hear news of home, but
I am a poor person for the job, being an outsider here.
I do talk to people in the Library and in the hotel.
The travellers in the hotel mostly talk about how
business is (it is brisk if you can get the goods) and
a little about sickness, and a lot about the War. There
are rumors on rumors and opinions galore, which I'm
sure would make you laugh if they didn't make you
angry. I will not bother to write them down because I
am sure there is a Censor reading this who would cut
my letter to ribbons.*

  *You ask how I came here. There is no interesting
story. My parents are both dead. My father worked for
Eaton's in Toronto in the Furniture Department, and
after his death my mother worked there too in Linens.
And I also worked there for a while in Books. Perhaps
you could say Eaton's was our Douds. I graduated from
Jarvis Collegiate. I had some sickness which put me in
hospital for a long time, but I am quite well now.*

*I had a great deal of time to read and my favorite
authors are Thomas Hardy, who is accused of being
gloomy but I think is very true to life—and Willa
Cather. I just happened to be in this town when I heard
the Librarian had died and I thought, perhaps that is
the job for me.*

*A good thing your letter reached me today as I am about
to be discharged from here and don't know if it would
have been sent on to where I am going. I am glad
you did not think my letter was too foolish.*

    *If you run into my father or anybody you do not need
to say anything about the fact we are writing to each
other. It is nobody's business and I know there are
plenty of people would laugh at me writing to the Librarian
as they did at me going to the Library even, why give
them the satisfaction?*

    *I am glad to be getting out of here. So much luckier
than some I see that will never walk or have their sight
and will have to hide themselves away from the world.*

    *You asked where did I live in Carstairs. Well, it
was not anyplace to be proud of. If you know where
Vinegar Hill is and you turned off on Flowers Road
it is the last house on the right, yellow paint once upon
a time. My father grows potatoes, or did. I used to
take them around town with my wagon, and every
load I sold got a nickel to keep.*

    *You mention favorite authors. At one time I was fond
of Zane Grey, but I drifted away from reading fiction
stories to reading History or Travel. I sometimes read
books away over my head, I know, but I do get something
out of them. H. G. Wells I mentioned is one and Robert
Ingersoll who writes about religion. They have given*

me a lot to think about. If you are very religious I hope
I have not offended you.

One day when I got to the Library it was a
Saturday afternoon and you had just unlocked the door
and were putting the lights on as it was dark and raining
out. You had been caught out with no hat or umbrella
and your hair had got wet. You took the pins out
of it and let it come down. Is it too personal a thing
to ask if you have it long still or have you cut it? You
went over and stood by the radiator and shook your
hair on it and the water sizzled like grease in the
frying pan. I was sitting reading in the London Illustrated
News about the War. We exchanged a smile. (I didn't
mean to say your hair was greasy when I wrote that!)

I have not cut my hair though I often think about it.
I do not know if it is vanity or laziness that prevents me.

I am not very religious.

I walked up Vinegar Hill and found your house.
The potatoes are looking healthy. A police dog disputed
with me, is he yours?

The weather is getting quite warm. We have had
the flood on the river, which I gather is an annual
Spring event. The water got into the hotel basement and
somehow contaminated our drinking supply so that we
were given free beer or ginger ale. But only if we
lived or were staying there. You can imagine there
were plenty of jokes.

I should ask if there is anything that I could send
you.

I am not in need of anything particular. I get the tobacco
and other bits of things the ladies in Carstairs do up

*for us. I would like to read some books by the authors
you have mentioned but I doubt whether I would get
the chance here.*

*The other day there was a man died of a heart
attack. It was the News of all time. Did you hear about
the man who died of a heart attack? That was all you
heard about day and night here. Then everybody would
laugh which seems hard-hearted but it just seemed so
strange. It was not even a hot time so you couldn't say
maybe he was scared. (As a matter of fact he was writing
a letter at the time so I had better look out.) Before
and after him others have died being shot up or blown
up but he is the famous one, to die of a heart attack.
Everybody is saying what a long way to come and a lot
of expense for the Army to go to, for that.*

*The summer has been so dry the watering tank has been
doing the streets every day, trying to lay the dust. The
children would dance along behind it. There was also
a new thing in town—a cart with a little bell that
went along selling ice cream, and the children were pretty
attentive to this as well. It was pushed by the man who
had an accident at the factory—you know who I
mean, though I can't recall his name. He lost his
arm to the elbow. My room at the hotel, being on the
third floor, it was like an oven, and I often walked about
till after midnight. So did many other people,
sometimes in pajamas. It was like a dream. There
was still a little water in the river, enough to go out
in a rowboat, and the Methodist minister did that on
a Sunday in August. He was praying for rain in a
public service. But there was a small leak in the boat
and the water came in and wet his feet and eventually
the boat sank and left him standing in the water, which*

*did not nearly reach his waist. Was it an accident
or a malicious trick? The talk was all that his prayers
were answered but from the wrong direction.*

*I often pass the Douds' place on my walks. Your
father keeps the lawns and hedges looking beautiful. I
like the house, so original and airy-looking. But it may
not have been cool even there, because I heard the
voice of the mother and baby daughter late at night
as if they were out on the lawn.*

*Though I told you there is nothing I need, there is
one thing I would like. That is a photograph of you.
I hope you will not think I am overstepping the bounds
to ask for it. Maybe you are engaged to somebody or
have a sweetheart over here you are writing to as well
as me. You are a cut above the ordinary and it would
not surprise me if some Officer had spoken for you. But
now that I have asked I cannot take it back and will
just leave it up to you to think what you like of me.*

Louisa was twenty-five years old and had been in love once,
with a doctor she had known in the sanitorium. Her love was
returned, eventually, costing the doctor his job. There was some
harsh doubt in her mind about whether he had been told to
leave the sanitorium or had left of his own accord, being weary
of the entanglement. He was married, he had children. Letters
had played a part that time, too. After he left, they were still
writing to one another. And once or twice after she was released. Then she asked him not to write anymore and he didn't.
But the failure of his letters to arrive drove her out of Toronto
and made her take the travelling job. Then there would be only
the one disappointment in the week, when she got back on Friday or Saturday night. Her last letter had been firm and stoical,
and some consciousness of herself as a heroine of love's tragedy

went with her around the country as she hauled her display cases up and down the stairs of small hotels and talked about Paris styles and said that her sample hats were bewitching, and drank her solitary glass of wine. If she'd had anybody to tell, though, she would have laughed at just that notion. She would have said love was all hocus-pocus, a deception, and she believed that. But at the prospect she still felt a hush, a flutter along the nerves, a bowing down of sense, a flagrant prostration.

She had a picture taken. She knew how she wanted it to be. She would have liked to wear a simple white blouse, a peasant girl's smock with the string open at the neck. She did not own a blouse of that description and in fact had only seen them in pictures. And she would have liked to let her hair down. Or if it had to be up, she would have liked it piled very loosely and bound with strings of pearls.

Instead she wore her blue silk shirt-waist and bound her hair as usual. She thought the picture made her look rather pale, hollow-eyed. Her expression was sterner and more foreboding than she had intended. She sent it anyway.

I am not engaged, and do not have a sweetheart. I was
in love once and it had to be broken off. I was upset
at the time but I knew I must bear it, and now I
believe that it was all for the best.

She had wracked her brains, of course, to remember him. She could not remember shaking out her hair, as he said she had done, or smiling at any young man when the raindrops fell on the radiator. He might as well have dreamed all that, and perhaps he had.

She had begun to follow the war in a more detailed way than she had done previously. She did not try to ignore it anymore. She went along the street with a sense that her head was filled with the same exciting and troubling information as everybody else's. Saint-Quentin, Arras, Montdidier, Amiens, and then there was a battle going on at the Somme River, where surely there had been one before? She laid open on her desk the maps of the war that appeared as double-page spreads in the magazines. She saw in colored lines the German drive to the Marne, the first thrust of the Americans at Château-Thierry. She looked at the artist's brown pictures of a horse rearing up during an air attack, of some soldiers in East Africa drinking out of coconuts, and of a line of German prisoners with bandaged heads or limbs and bleak, sullen expressions. Now she felt what everybody else did—a constant fear and misgiving and at the same time this addictive excitement. You could look up from your life of the moment and feel the world crackling beyond the walls.

*I am glad to hear you do not have a sweetheart though
I know that is selfish of me. I do not think you and
I will ever meet again. I don't say that because I've
had a dream about what will happen or am a gloomy
person always looking for the worst. It just seems to me
it is the most probable thing to happen, though I don't
dwell on it and go along every day doing the best
I can to stay alive. I am not trying to worry you or get
your sympathy either but just explain how the idea I
won't ever see Carstairs again makes me think I can
say anything I want. I guess it's like being sick with
a fever. So I will say I love you. I think of you up on
a stool at the Library reaching to put a book away and
I come up and put my hands on your waist and lift
you down, and you turning around inside my arms
as if we agreed about everything.*

Every Tuesday afternoon the ladies and girls of the Red Cross met in the Council Chambers, which was just down the hall from the Library. When the Library was empty for a few moments, Louisa went down the hall and entered the room full of women. She had decided to knit a scarf. At the sanitorium she had learned how to knit a basic stitch, but she had never learned or had forgotten how to cast on or off.

The older women were all busy packing boxes or cutting up and folding bandages from sheets of heavy cotton that were spread on the tables. But a lot of girls near the door were eating buns and drinking tea. One was holding a skein of wool on her arms for another to wind.

Louisa told them what she needed to know.

"So what do you want to knit, then?" said one of the girls with some bun still in her mouth.

Louisa said, a muffler. For a soldier.

"Oh, you'll want the regulation wool," another said, more politely, and jumped off the table. She came back with some balls of brown wool, and fished a spare pair of needles out of her bag, telling Louisa they could be hers.

"I'll just get you started," she said. "It's a regulation width, too."

Other girls gathered around and teased this girl, whose name was Corrie. They told her she was doing it all wrong.

"Oh, I am, am I?" said Corrie. "How would you like a knitting needle in your eye? Is it for a friend?" she said solicitously to Louisa. "A friend overseas?"

"Yes," said Louisa. Of course they would think of her as an old maid, they would laugh at her or feel sorry for her, according to whatever show they put on, of being kind or brazen.

"So knit up good and tight," said the one who'd finished her bun. "Knit up good and tight to keep him warm!"

One of the girls in this group was Grace Horne. She was a shy but resolute-looking girl, nineteen years old, with a broad face, thin lips often pressed together, brown hair cut in a straight bang, and an attractively mature body. She had become engaged to Jack Agnew before he went overseas, but they had agreed not to say anything about it.

Louisa had made friends with some of the travellers who stayed regularly at the hotel. One of these was Jim Frarey, who sold typewriters and office equipment and books and all sorts of stationery supplies. He was a fair-haired, rather round-shouldered but strongly built man in his middle forties. You would think by the look of him that he sold something heavier and more important in the masculine world, like farm implements.

Jim Frarey kept travelling all through the Spanish flu epidemic, though you never knew then if stores would be open for business or not. Occasionally the hotels, too, would be closed, like the schools and movie houses and even—Jim Frarey thought this a scandal—the churches.

"They ought to be ashamed of themselves, the cowards," he said to Louisa. "What good does it do anybody to lurk around home and wait for it to strike? Now you never closed the Library, did you?"

Louisa said only when she herself was sick. A mild case, hardly lasting a week, but of course she had to go to the hospital. They wouldn't let her stay in the hotel.

"Cowards," he said. "If you're going to be taken, you'll be taken. Don't you agree?"

They discussed the crush in the hospitals, the deaths of doctors and nurses, the unceasing drear spectacle of the funerals. Jim Frarey lived down the street from an undertaking establishment in Toronto. He said they still got out the black horses, the black carriage, the works, to bury such personages as warranted a fuss.

"Day and night they went on," he said. "Day and night." He raised his glass and said, "Here's to health, then. You look well yourself."

He thought that in fact Louisa was looking better than she used to. Maybe she had started putting on rouge. She had a pale-olive skin, and it seemed to him that her cheeks used to be without color. She dressed with more dash, too, and took more trouble to be friendly. She used to be very on-again, off-again, just as she chose. She was drinking whisky, now, too, though she would not try it without drowning it in water. It used to be only a glass of wine. He wondered if it was a boyfriend that had made the difference. But a boyfriend might perk up her looks without increasing her interest in all and sundry, which was what he was pretty sure had happened. It was more likely time running out and the husband prospects thinned out so dreadfully by the war. That could set a woman stirring. She was smarter and better company and better-looking, too, than most of the married ones. What happened with a woman like that? Sometimes just bad luck. Or bad judgment at a time when it mattered. A little too sharp and self-assured, in the old days, making the men uneasy?

"Life can't be brought to a standstill all the same," he said. "You did the right thing, keeping the Library open."

This was in the early winter of 1919, when there had been a fresh outbreak of flu after the danger was supposed to be past. They seemed to be all alone in the hotel. It was only about nine o'clock but the hotelkeeper had gone to bed. His wife was in the hospital with the flu. Jim Frarey had brought the bottle of whisky from the bar, which was closed for fear of contagion—and they sat at a table beside the window, in the dining room. A winter fog had collected outside and was pressing against the window. You could barely see the street-lights or the few cars that trundled cautiously over the bridge.

"Oh, it was not a matter of principle," Louisa said. "That I kept the Library open. It was a more personal reason than you think."

Then she laughed and promised him a peculiar story. "Oh, the whisky must have loosened my tongue," she said.

"I am not a gossip," said Jim Frarey.

She gave him a hard laughing look and said that when a person announced they weren't a gossip, they almost invariably were. The same when they promised never to tell a soul.

"You can tell this where and when you like just as long as you leave out the real names and don't tell it around here," she said. "That I hope I can trust you not to do. Though at the moment I don't feel as if I cared. I'll probably feel otherwise when the drink wears off. It's a lesson, this story. It's a lesson in what fools women can make of themselves. So, you say, what's new about that, you can learn it every day!"

She began to tell him about a soldier who had started writing letters to her from overseas. The soldier remembered her from when he used to go into the Library. But she didn't remember him. However, she replied in a friendly way to his first letter and a correspondence sprang up between them. He told her where he had lived in the town and she walked past the house so that she could tell him how things looked there. He told her what books he'd read and she gave some of the same kind of information. In short, they both revealed something of themselves and feelings warmed up on either side. On his side first, as far as any declarations went. She was not one to rush in like a fool. At first, she thought she was simply being kind. Even later, she didn't want to reject and embarrass him. He asked for a picture. She had one taken, it was not to her liking, but she sent it. He asked if she had a sweetheart and she replied truthfully that she did not. He did not send any picture of himself nor did she ask for one, though of course she was curious as to what he looked like. It would be no easy matter for him to have a picture taken in the middle of a war. Furthermore, she did not want to seem like the sort of woman who would withdraw kindness if looks did not come up to scratch.

He wrote that he did not expect to come home. He said he was not so afraid of dying as he was of ending up like some of the men he had seen when he was in the hospital, wounded. He did not elaborate, but she supposed he meant the cases they were just getting to know about now—the stumps of men, the blinded, the ones made monstrous with burns. He was not whining about his fate, she did not mean to imply that. It was just that he expected to die and picked death over some other options and he thought about her and wrote to her as men do to a sweetheart in such a situation.

When the war ended, it was a while since she had heard from him. She went on expecting a letter every day and nothing came. Nothing came. She was afraid that he might have been one of those unluckiest of soldiers in the whole war— one of those killed in the last week, or on the last day, or even in the last hour. She searched the local paper every week, and the names of new casualties were still being printed there till after New Year's but his was not among them. Now the paper began to list as well the names of those returning home, often printing a photo with the name, and a little account of rejoicing. When the soldiers were returning thick and fast there was less room for these additions. And then she saw his name, another name on the list. He had not been killed, he had not been wounded—he was coming home to Carstairs, perhaps was already there.

It was then that she decided to keep the Library open, though the flu was raging. Every day she was sure he would come, every day she was prepared for him. Sundays were a torment. When she entered the Town Hall she always felt he might be there before her, leaning up against the wall awaiting her arrival. Sometimes she felt it so strongly she saw a shadow that she mistook for a man. She understood now how people believed they had seen ghosts. Whenever the door opened she expected to look up into his face. Sometimes she made a pact with herself not to look up till she had counted to ten. Few people came in, because of the flu. She set herself jobs of re-arranging things, else she would have gone mad. She never locked up until five or ten minutes after closing time. And then she fancied that he might be across the street on the Post Office steps, watching her, being too shy to make a move. She worried of course that he might be ill, she always sought in conversation for news of the latest cases. No one spoke his name.

It was at this time that she entirely gave up on reading. The covers of books looked like coffins to her, either shabby or ornate, and what was inside them might as well have been dust.

She had to be forgiven, didn't she, she had to be forgiven for thinking, after such letters, that the one thing that could never happen was that he wouldn't approach her, wouldn't get in touch with her at all? Never cross her threshold, after such avowals? Funerals passed by her window and she gave no thought to them, as long as they were not his. Even when she was sick in the hospital her only thought was that she must get back, she must get out of bed, the door must not stay locked against him. She staggered to her feet and back to work. On a hot afternoon she was arranging fresh newspapers on the racks and his name jumped out at her like something in her feverish dreams.

She read a short notice of his marriage to a Miss Grace Horne. Not a girl she knew. Not a Library user.

The bride wore fawn silk crêpe with brown-and-cream piping, and a beige straw hat with brown velvet streamers.

There was no picture. Brown-and-cream piping. Such was the end, and had to be, to her romance.

But on her desk at the Library, a matter of a few weeks ago, on a Saturday night after everybody had gone and she had locked the door and was turning out the lights, she discovered a scrap of paper. A few words written on it. *I was engaged before I went overseas.* No name, not his or hers. And there was her photograph, partly shoved under the blotter.

He had been in the Library that very evening. It had been a busy time, she had often left the desk to find a book for somebody or to straighten up the papers or to put some books on the shelves. He had been in the same room with her, watched her, and taken his chance. But never made himself known.

I was engaged before I went overseas.

"Do you think it was all a joke on me?" Louisa said. "Do you think a man could be so diabolical?"

"In my experience, tricks like that are far more often indulged in by the women. No, no. Don't you think such a thing. Far more likely he was sincere. He got a little carried away. It's all just the way it looks on the surface. He was engaged before he went overseas, he never expected to get back in one piece but he did. And when he did, there is the fiancée waiting—what else could he do?"

"What indeed?" said Louisa.

"He bit off more than he could chew."

"Ah, that's so, that's so!" Louisa said. "And what was it in my case but vanity, which deserves to get slapped down!" Her eyes were glassy and her expression roguish. "You don't think he'd had a good look at me any one time and thought the original was even worse than that poor picture, so he backed off?"

"I do not!" said Jim Frarey. "And don't you so belittle yourself."

"I don't want you to think I am stupid," she said. "I am not so stupid and inexperienced as that story makes me sound."

"Indeed I don't think you are stupid at all."

"But perhaps you think I am inexperienced?"

This was it, he thought—the usual. Women after they have told one story on themselves cannot stop from telling another. Drink upsets them in a radical way, prudence is out the window.

She had confided in him once before that she had been a patient in a sanitorium. Now she told about being in love with a doctor there. The sanitorium was on beautiful grounds up on Hamilton Mountain, and they used to meet there along the hedged walks. Shelves of limestone formed the steps and in sheltered spots there were such plants as you do not commonly see in Ontario—azaleas, rhododendrons, magnolias. The doctor knew something about botany and he told her this was the Carolinian vegetation. Very different from here, lusher, and there were little bits of woodland, too, wonderful trees, paths worn under the trees. Tulip trees.

"Tulips!" said Jim Frarey. "Tulips on the trees!"

"No, no, it is the shape of their leaves!"

She laughed at him challengingly, then bit her lip. He saw fit to continue the dialogue, saying, "Tulips on the trees!" while she said no, it is the leaves that are shaped like tulips, no, I never said that, stop! So they passed into a state of gingerly evaluation—which he knew well and could only hope she did—full of small pleasant surprises, half-sardonic signals, a welling-up of impudent hopes, and a fateful sort of kindness.

"All to ourselves," Jim Frarey said. "Never happened before, did it? Maybe it never will again."

She let him take her hands, half lift her from her chair. He turned out the dining-room lights as they went out. Up the stairs they went, that they had so often climbed separately. Past the picture of the dog on his master's grave, and Highland Mary singing in the field, and the old King with his bulgy eyes, his look of indulgence and repletion.

"It's a foggy, foggy night, and my heart is in a fright," Jim Frarey was half singing, half humming as they climbed. He kept an assured hand on Louisa's back. "All's well, all's well," he said as he steered her round the turn of the stairs. And when they took the narrow flight of steps to the third floor he said, "Never climbed so close to Heaven in this place before!"

But later in the night Jim Frarey gave a concluding groan and roused himself to deliver a sleepy scolding. "Louisa, Louisa, why didn't you tell me that was the way it was?"

"I told you everything," said Louisa in a faint and drifting voice.

"I got a wrong impression, then," he said. "I never intended for this to make a difference to you."

She said that it hadn't. Now without him pinning her down and steadying her, she felt herself whirling around in an irresistible way, as if the mattress had turned into a child's top and was carrying her off. She tried to explain that the traces of blood on the sheets could be credited to her period, but her words came out with a luxurious nonchalance and could not be fitted together.

ACCIDENTS

When Arthur came home from the factory a little before noon he shouted, "Stay out of my way till I wash! There's been an accident over at the works!" Nobody answered. Mrs. Feare, the housekeeper, was talking on the kitchen telephone so loudly that she could not hear him, and his daughter was of

course at school. He washed, and stuffed everything he had
been wearing into the hamper, and scrubbed up the bathroom,
like a murderer. He started out clean, with even his hair
slicked and patted, to drive to the man's house. He had had
to ask where it was. He thought it was up Vinegar Hill but
they said no, that was the father—the young fellow and his
wife live on the other side of town, past where the Apple
Evaporator used to be, before the war.

He found the two brick cottages side by side, and picked
the left-hand one, as he'd been told. It wouldn't have been
hard to pick which house, anyway. News had come before
him. The door to the house was open, and children too young
to be in school yet hung about in the yard. A small girl sat
on a kiddie car, not going anywhere, just blocking his path.
He stepped around her. As he did so an older girl spoke to
him in a formal way—a warning.

"Her dad's dead. Hers!"

A woman came out of the front room carrying an armload
of curtains, which she gave to another woman standing in the
hall. The woman who received the curtains was gray-haired,
with a pleading face. She had no upper teeth. She probably
took her plate out, for comfort, at home. The woman who
passed the curtains to her was stout but young, with fresh
skin.

"You tell her not to get up on that stepladder," the gray-
haired woman said to Arthur. "She's going to break her neck
taking down curtains. She thinks we need to get everything
washed. Are you the undertaker? Oh, no, excuse me! You're
Mr. Doud. Grace, come out here! Grace! It's Mr. Doud!"

"Don't trouble her," Arthur said.

"She thinks she's going to get the curtains all down and
washed and up again by tomorrow, because he's going to have
to go in the front room. She's my daughter. I can't tell her
anything."

"She'll quiet down presently," said a sombre but comfortable-looking man in a clerical collar, coming through from the back of the house. Their minister. But not from one of the churches Arthur knew. Baptist? Pentecostal? Plymouth Brethren? He was drinking tea.

Some other woman came and briskly removed the curtains.

"We got the machine filled and going," she said. "A day like this, they'll dry like nobody's business. Just keep the kids out of here."

The minister had to stand aside and lift his teacup high, to avoid her and her bundle. He said, "Aren't any of you ladies going to offer Mr. Doud a cup of tea?"

Arthur said, "No, no, don't trouble.

"The funeral expenses," he said to the gray-haired woman. "If you could let her know—"

"Lillian wet her pants!" said a triumphant child at the door. "Mrs. Agnew! Lillian peed her pants!"

"Yes. Yes," said the minister. "They will be very grateful."

"The plot and the stone, everything," Arthur said. "You'll make sure they understand that. Whatever they want on the stone."

The gray-haired woman had gone out into the yard. She came back with a squalling child in her arms. "Poor lamb," she said. "They told her she wasn't supposed to come in the house so where could she go? What could she do but have an accident!"

The young woman came out of the front room dragging a rug.

"I want this put on the line and beat," she said.

"Grace, here is Mr. Doud come to offer his condolences," the minister said.

"And to ask if there is anything I can do," said Arthur.

The gray-haired woman started upstairs with the wet child in her arms and a couple of others following.

Grace spotted them.

"Oh, no, you don't! You get back outside!"

"My mom's in here."

"Yes and your mom's good and busy, she don't need to be bothered with you. She's here helping me out. Don't you know Lillian's dad's dead?"

"Is there anything I can do for you?" Arthur said, meaning to clear out.

Grace stared at him with her mouth open. Sounds of the washing machine filled the house.

"Yes, there is," she said. "You wait here."

"She's overwhelmed," the minister said. "It's not that she means to be rude."

Grace came back with a load of books.

"These here," she said. "He had them out of the Library. I don't want to have to pay fines on them. He went every Saturday night so I guess they are due back tomorrow. I don't want to get in trouble about them."

"I'll look after them," Arthur said. "I'd be glad to."

"I just don't want to get in any trouble about them."

"Mr. Doud was saying about taking care of the funeral," the minister said to her, gently admonishing. "Everything including the stone. Whatever you want on the stone."

"Oh, I don't want anything fancy," Grace said.

On Friday morning last there occurred in the sawmill operation of Douds Factory a particularly ghastly and tragic accident. Mr. Jack Agnew, in reaching under the main shaft, had the misfortune to have his sleeve caught by a setscrew in an adjoining flunge, so that his arm and shoulder were drawn under the shaft. His head in consequence was brought in contact with the circular saw, that saw being about one foot in diameter. In an instant the unfortunate young man's head was separated from his body, being severed at an angle

*below the left ear and through the neck. His death is be-
lieved to have been instantaneous. He never spoke or uttered
a cry so it was not any sound of his but by the spurt and
shower of his blood that his fellow-workers were horribly
alerted to the disaster.*

This account was reprinted in the paper a week later for
those who might have missed it or who wished to have an extra copy to send to friends or relations out of town (particularly
to people who used to live in Carstairs and did not anymore).
The misspelling of "flange" was corrected. There was a note
apologizing for the mistake. There was also a description of a
very large funeral, attended even by people from neighboring
towns and as far away as Walley. They came by car and train,
and some by horse and buggy. They had not known Jack Agnew when he was alive, but, as the paper said, they wished to
pay tribute to the sensational and tragic manner of his death.
All the stores in Carstairs were closed for two hours that afternoon. The hotel did not close its doors but that was because
all the visitors needed somewhere to eat and drink.

The survivors were a wife, Grace, and a four-year-old
daughter, Lillian. The victim had fought bravely in the Great
War and had only been wounded once, not seriously. Many
had commented on this irony.

The paper's failure to mention a surviving father was not
deliberate. The editor of the paper was not a native of Carstairs, and people forgot to tell him about the father until it
was too late.

The father himself did not complain about the omission.
On the day of the funeral, which was very fine, he headed out
of town as he would have done ordinarily on a day he had decided not to spend at Douds. He was wearing a felt hat and
a long coat that would do for a rug if he wanted to take a nap.
His overshoes were neatly held on his feet with the rubber

rings from sealing jars. He was going out to fish for suckers. The season hadn't opened yet, but he always managed to be a bit ahead of it. He fished through the spring and early summer and cooked and ate what he caught. He had a frying pan and a pot hidden out on the riverbank. The pot was for boiling corn that he snatched out of the fields later in the year, when he was also eating the fruit of wild apple trees and grapevines. He was quite sane but abhorred conversation. He could not altogether avoid it in the weeks following his son's death, but he had a way of cutting it short.

"Should've watched out what he was doing."

Walking in the country that day, he met another person who was not at the funeral. A woman. She did not try to start any conversation and in fact seemed as fierce in her solitude as himself, whipping the air past her with long fervent strides.

The piano factory, which had started out making pump organs, stretched along the west side of town, like a medieval town wall. There were two long buildings like the inner and outer ramparts, with a closed-in bridge between them where the main offices were. And reaching up into the town and the streets of workers' houses you had the kilns and the sawmill and the lumberyard and storage sheds. The factory whistle dictated the time for many to get up, blowing at six o'clock in the morning. It blew again for work to start at seven and at twelve for dinnertime and at one in the afternoon for work to recommence, and then at five-thirty for the men to lay down their tools and go home.

Rules were posted beside the time clock, under glass. The first two rules were:

ONE MINUTE LATE IS FIFTEEN MINUTES PAY. BE PROMPT.
DON'T TAKE SAFETY FOR GRANTED. WATCH OUT
FOR YOURSELF AND THE NEXT MAN.

There had been accidents in the factory and in fact a man had been killed when a load of lumber fell on him. That had happened before Arthur's time. And once, during the war, a man had lost an arm, or part of an arm. On the day that happened, Arthur was away in Toronto. So he had never seen an accident—nothing serious, anyway. But it was often at the back of his mind now that something might happen.

Perhaps he did not feel so sure that trouble wouldn't come near him, as he had felt before his wife died. She had died in 1919, in the last flurry of the Spanish flu, when everyone had got over being frightened. Even she had not been frightened. That was nearly five years ago and it still seemed to Arthur like the end of a carefree time in his life. But to other people he had always seemed very responsible and serious—nobody had noticed much difference in him.

In his dreams of an accident there was a spreading silence, everything was shut down. Every machine in the place stopped making its customary noise and every man's voice was removed, and when Arthur looked out of the office window he understood that doom had fallen. He never could remember any particular thing he saw that told him this. It was just the space, the dust in the factory yard, that said to him *now*.

The books stayed on the floor of his car for a week or so. His daughter Bea said, "What are those books doing here?" and then he remembered.

Bea read out the titles and the authors. *Sir John Franklin and the Romance of the Northwest Passage*, by G. B. Smith. *What's Wrong with the World?*, G. K. Chesterton. *The Taking of Quebec*, Archibald Hendry. *Bolshevism: Practice and Theory*, by Lord Bertrand Russell.

"Bol-*shev*-ism," Bea said, and Arthur told her how to pronounce it correctly. She asked what it was, and he said, "It's something they've got in Russia that I don't understand so well myself. But from what I hear of it, it's a disgrace."

Bea was thirteen at this time. She had heard about the Russian Ballet and also about dervishes. She believed for the next couple of years that Bolshevism was some sort of diabolical and maybe indecent dance. At least this was the story she told when she was grown up.

She did not mention that the books were connected with the man who had had the accident. That would have made the story less amusing. Perhaps she had really forgotten.

The Librarian was perturbed. The books still had their cards in them, which meant they had never been checked out, just removed from the shelves and taken away.

"The one by Lord Russell has been missing a long time."

Arthur was not used to such reproofs, but he said mildly, "I am returning them on behalf of somebody else. The chap who was killed. In the accident at the factory."

The Librarian had the Franklin book open. She was looking at the picture of the boat trapped in the ice.

"His wife asked me to," Arthur said.

She picked up each book separately, and shook it as if she expected something to fall out. She ran her fingers in between the pages. The bottom part of her face was working in an unsightly way, as if she was chewing at the inside of her cheeks.

"I guess he just took them home as he felt like it," Arthur said.

"I'm sorry?" she said in a minute. "What did you say? I'm sorry."

It was the accident, he thought. The idea that the man who had died in such a way had been the last person to open these books, turn these pages. The thought that he might have left a bit of his life in them, a scrap of paper or a pipe cleaner as a marker, or even a few shreds of tobacco. That unhinged her.

"No matter," he said. "I just dropped by to bring them back."

He turned away from her desk but did not immediately leave the Library. He had not been in it for years. There was his father's picture between the two front windows, where it would always be.

A. V. Doud, founder of the Doud Organ Factory and
Patron of this Library. A Believer in Progress,
Culture, and Education. A True Friend of the Town
of Carstairs and of the Working Man.

The Librarian's desk was in the archway between the front and back rooms. The books were on shelves set in rows in the back room. Green-shaded lamps, with long pull cords, dangled down in the aisles between. Arthur remembered years ago some matter brought up at the Council Meeting about buying sixty-watt bulbs instead of forty. This Librarian was the one who had requested that, and they had done it.

In the front room, there were newspapers and magazines on wooden racks, and some round heavy tables, with chairs, so that people could sit and read, and rows of thick dark books behind glass. Dictionaries, probably, and atlases and encyclopedias. Two handsome high windows looking out on the main street, with Arthur's father hanging between them. Other pictures around the room hung too high, and were too dim and crowded with figures for the person down below to interpret them easily. (Later, when Arthur had spent many hours in the Library and had discussed these pictures with the Librarian, he knew that one of them represented the Battle of Flodden Field, with the King of Scotland charging down the hill into a pall of smoke, one the funeral of the Boy King of

Rome, and one the Quarrel of Oberon and Titania, from *A Midsummer Night's Dream.*)

He sat down at one of the reading tables, where he could look out the window. He picked up an old copy of the *National Geographic*, which was lying there. He had his back to the Librarian. He thought this the tactful thing to do, since she seemed somewhat wrought-up. Other people came in, and he heard her speak to them. Her voice sounded normal enough now. He kept thinking he would leave, but did not.

He liked the high bare window full of the light of the spring evening, and he liked the dignity and order of these rooms. He was pleasantly mystified by the thought of grown people coming and going here, steadily reading books. Week after week, one book after another, a whole life long. He himself read a book once in a while, when somebody recommended it, and usually he enjoyed it, and then he read magazines, to keep up with things, and never thought about reading a book until another one came along, in this almost accidental way.

There would be little spells when nobody was in the Library but himself and the Librarian.

During one of these, she came over and stood near him, replacing some newspapers on the rack. When she finished this, she spoke to him, with a controlled urgency.

"The account of the accident that was printed in the paper—I take it that was more or less accurate?"

Arthur said that it was possibly too accurate.

"Why? Why do you say that?"

He mentioned the public's endless appetite for horrific details. Ought the paper to pander to that?

"Oh, I think it's natural," the Librarian said. "I think it's natural to want to know the worst. People do want to picture it. I do myself. I am very ignorant of machinery. It's hard for me to imagine what happened. Even with the paper's help. Did the machine do something unexpected?"

"No," Arthur said. "It wasn't the machine grabbing him and pulling him in, like an animal. He made a wrong move or at any rate a careless move. Then he was done for."

She said nothing, but did not move away.

"You have to keep your wits about you," Arthur said. "Never let up for a second. A machine is your servant and it is an excellent servant, but it makes an imbecile master."

He wondered if he had read that somewhere, or had thought it up himself.

"And I suppose there are no ways of protecting people?" the Librarian said. "But you must know all about that."

She left him then. Somebody had come in.

The accident was followed by a rush of warm weather. The length of the evenings and the heat of the balmy days seemed sudden and surprising, as if this were not the way winter finally ended in that part of the country, almost every year. The sheets of floodwater shrank magically back into the bogs, and the leaves shot out of the reddened branches, and barnyard smells drifted into town and were wrapped in the smell of lilacs.

Instead of wanting to be outdoors on such evenings, Arthur found himself thinking of the Library, and he would often end up there, sitting in the spot he had chosen on his first visit. He would sit for half an hour, or an hour. He looked at the London *Illustrated News*, or the *National Geographic* or *Saturday Night* or *Collier's*. All of these magazines arrived at his own house and he could have been sitting there, in the den, looking out at his hedged lawns, which old Agnew kept in tolerable condition, and the flower beds now full of tulips of every vivid color and combination. It seemed that he preferred the view of the main street, where the occasional brisk-looking new Ford went by, or some stuttering older-model car with a dusty cloth top. He preferred the Post Office, with its clock tower telling four different times in four different directions—

and, as people liked to say, all wrong. Also the passing and loitering on the sidewalk. People trying to get the drinking fountain to work, although it wasn't turned on till the First of July.

It was not that he felt the need of sociability. He was not there for chat, though he would greet people if he knew them by name, and he did know most. And he might exchange a few words with the Librarian, though often it was only "Good evening" when he came in, and "Good night" when he went out. He made no demands on anybody. He felt his presence to be genial, reassuring, and, above all, natural. By sitting here, reading and reflecting, here instead of at home, he seemed to himself to be providing something. People could count on it.

There was an expression he liked. *Public servant.* His father, who looked out at him here with tinted baby-pink cheeks and glassy blue eyes and an old man's petulant mouth, had never thought of himself so. He had thought of himself more as a public character and benefactor. He had operated by whims and decrees, and he had got away with it. He would go around the factory when business was slow, and say to one man and another, "Go home. Go on home now. Go home and stay there till I can use you again." And they would go. They would work in their gardens or go out shooting rabbits and run up bills for whatever they had to buy, and accept that it couldn't be otherwise. It was still a joke with them, to imitate his bark. *Go on home!* He was their hero more than Arthur could ever be, but they were not prepared to take the same treatment today. During the war, they had got used to the good wages and to being always in demand. They never thought of the glut of labor the soldiers had created when they came home, never thought about how a business like this was kept going by luck and ingenuity from one year to the next, even from one season to the next. They didn't like changes—

they were not happy about the switch now to player pianos, which Arthur believed were the hope of the future. But Arthur would do what he had to, though his way of proceeding was quite the opposite of his father's. Think everything over and then think it over again. Stay in the background except when necessary. Keep your dignity. Try always to be fair.

They expected all to be provided. The whole town expected it. Work would be provided just as the sun would rise in the mornings. And the taxes on the factory raised at the same time rates were charged for the water that used to come free. Maintenance of the access roads was now the factory's responsibility instead of the town's. The Methodist Church was requesting a hefty sum to build the new Sunday school. The town hockey team needed new uniforms. Stone gateposts were being erected for the War Memorial Park. And every year the smartest boy in the senior class was sent to university, courtesy of Douds.

Ask and ye shall receive.

Expectations at home were not lacking either. Bea was agitating to go away to private school and Mrs. Feare had her eye on some new mixing apparatus for the kitchen, also a new washing machine. All the trim on the house was due to be painted this year. All that wedding-cake decoration that consumed paint by the gallon. And in the midst of this what had Arthur done but order himself a new car—a Chrysler sedan.

It was necessary—he had to drive a new car. He had to drive a new car, Bea had to go away to school, Mrs. Feare had to have the latest, and the trim had to be as fresh as Christmas snow. Else they would lose respect, they would lose confidence, they would start to wonder if things were going downhill. And it could be managed, with luck it could all be managed.

For years after his father's death, he had felt like an impostor. Not steadily, but from time to time he had felt that. And now the feeling was gone. He could sit here and feel that it was gone.

He had been in the office when the accident happened, consulting with a veneer salesman. Some change in noise registered with him, but it was more of an increase than a hush. It was nothing that alerted him—just an irritation. Because it happened in the sawmill, nobody would know about the accident immediately in the shops or in the kilns or in the yard, and work in some places continued for several minutes. In fact Arthur, bending over the veneer samples on his desk, might have been one of the last people to understand that there had been an intervention. He asked the salesman a question, and the salesman did not answer. Arthur looked up and saw the man's mouth open, his face frightened, his salesman's assurance wiped away.

Then he heard his own name being called—both "Mr. Doud!" as was customary and "Arthur, Arthur!" by such of the older men as had known him as a boy. Also he heard "saw" and "head" and "Jesus, Jesus, Jesus!"

Arthur could have wished for the silence, the sounds and objects drawing back in that dreadful but releasing way, to give him room. It was nothing like that. Yelling and questioning and running around, himself in the midst being propelled to the sawmill. One man had fainted, falling in such a way that if they had not got the saw turned off a moment before, it would have got him, too. It was his body, fallen but entire, that Arthur briefly mistook for the body of the victim. Oh, no, no. They pushed him on. The sawdust was scarlet. It was drenched, brilliant. The pile of lumber here was all merrily spattered, and the blades. A pile of work clothes soaked in blood lay in the sawdust and Arthur realized that it was the body, the trunk with limbs attached. So much blood had flowed as to make its shape not plain at first—to soften it, like a pudding.

The first thing he thought of was to cover that. He took off his jacket and did so. He had to step up close, his shoes squished in it. The reason no one else had done this would be simply that no one else was wearing a jacket.

"Have they gone a-get the doctor?" somebody was yelling. "Gone a-get the doctor!" a man quite close to Arthur said. "Can't sew his head back on—doctor. Can he?"

But Arthur gave the order to get the doctor; he imagined it was necessary. You can't have a death without a doctor. That set the rest in motion. Doctor, undertaker, coffin, flowers, preacher. Get started on all that, give them something to do. Shovel up the sawdust, clean up the saw. Send the men who had been close by to wash themselves. Carry the man who had fainted to the lunchroom. Is he all right? Tell the office girl to make tea.

Brandy was what was needed, or whisky. But he had a rule against it, on the premises.

Something still lacking. Where was it? There, they said. Over there. Arthur heard the sound of vomiting, not far away. All right. Either pick it up or tell somebody to pick it up. The sound of vomiting saved him, steadied him, gave him an almost lighthearted determination. He picked it up. He carried it delicately and securely as you might carry an awkward but valuable jug. Pressing the face out of sight, as if comforting it, against his chest. Blood seeped through his shirt and stuck the material to his skin. Warm. He felt like a wounded man. He was aware of them watching him and he was aware of himself as an actor must be, or a priest. What to do with it, now that he had it against his chest? The answer to that came, too. Set it down, put it back where it belongs, not of course fitted with exactness, not as if a seam could be closed. Just more or less in place, and lift the jacket and tug it into a new position.

He couldn't now ask the man's name. He would have to get it in some other way. After the intimacy of his services here, such ignorance would be an offense.

But he found he did know it—it came to him. As he edged the corner of his jacket over the ear that had lain and still lay upward, and so looked quite fresh and usable, he received a name. Son of the fellow who came and did the garden, who was not always reliable. A young man taken on again when he came back from the war. Married? He thought so. He would have to go and see her. As soon as possible. Clean clothes.

The Librarian often wore a dark-red blouse. Her lips were reddened to match, and her hair was bobbed. She was not a young woman anymore, but she maintained an eye-catching style. He remembered that years ago when they had hired her, he had thought that she got herself up very soberly. Her hair was not bobbed in those days—it was wound around her head, in the old style. It was still the same color—a warm and pleasant color, like leaves—oak leaves, say, in the fall. He tried to think how much she was paid. Not much, certainly. She kept herself looking well on it. And where did she live? In one of the boarding houses—the one with the schoolteachers? No, not there. She lived in the Commercial Hotel.

And now something else was coming to mind. No definite story that he could remember. You could not say with any assurance that she had a bad reputation. But it was not quite a spotless reputation, either. She was said to take a drink with the travellers. Perhaps she had a boyfriend among them. A boyfriend or two.

Well, she was old enough to do as she liked. It wasn't quite the same as the way it was with a teacher—hired partly to set an example. As long as she did her job well, and anybody could see that she did. She had her life to live, like everyone else. Wouldn't you rather have a nice-looking woman in here than a crabby old affair like Mary Tamblyn? Strangers might drop in, they judge a town by what they see, you want a nice-looking woman with a nice manner.

Stop that. Who said you didn't? He was arguing in his head on her behalf just as if somebody had come along who wanted her chucked out, and he had no intimation at all that that was the case.

What about her question, on the first evening, regarding the machines? What did she mean by that? Was it a sly way of bringing blame?

He had talked to her about the pictures and the lighting and even told her how his father had sent his own workmen over here, paid them to build the Library shelves, but he had never spoken of the man who had taken the books out without letting her know. One at a time, probably. Under his coat? Brought back the same way. He must have brought them back, or else he'd have had a houseful, and his wife would never stand for that. Not stealing, except temporarily. Harmless behavior, but peculiar. Was there any connection? Between thinking you could do things a little differently that way and thinking you could get away with a careless move that might catch your sleeve and bring the saw down on your neck?

There might be, there might be some connection. A matter of attitude.

"That chap—you know the one—the accident—" he said to the Librarian. "The way he took off with the books he wanted. Why do you think he did that?"

"People do things," the Librarian said. "They tear out pages. On account of something they don't like or something they do. They just do things. I don't know."

"Did he ever tear out some pages? Did you ever give him a lecture? Ever make him scared to face you?"

He meant to tease her a little, implying that she would not
be likely to scare anybody, but she did not take it that way.

"How could I when I never spoke to him?" she said. "I
never saw him. I never saw him, to know who he was."

She moved away, putting an end to the conversation. So she
did not like to be teased. Was she one of those people full of
mended cracks that you could only see close up? Some old
misery troubling her, some secret? Maybe a sweetheart had
been lost in the war.

On a later evening, a Saturday evening in the summer, she
brought the subject up herself, that he would never have mentioned again.

"Do you remember our talking once about the man who
had the accident?"

Arthur said he did.

"I have something to ask you and you may think it
strange."

He nodded.

"And my asking it—I want you to—it is confidential."

"Yes, indeed," he said.

"What did he look like?"

Look like? Arthur was puzzled. He was puzzled by her
making such a fuss and secret about it—surely it was natural
to be interested in what a man might look like, who had been
coming in and making off with her books without her knowing about it—and because he could not help her, he shook his
head. He could not bring any picture of Jack Agnew to mind.

"Tall," he said. "I believe he was on the tall side. Otherwise I cannot tell you. I am really not such a good person to
ask. I can recognize a man easily but I can't ever give much
of a physical description, even when it's someone I see on a
daily basis."

"But I thought you were the one—I heard you were the one—" she said. "Who picked him up. His head."

Arthur said stiffly, "I didn't think that you could just leave it lying there." He felt disappointed in the woman, uneasy and ashamed for her. But he tried to speak matter-of-factly, keeping reproach out of his voice.

"I could not even tell you the color of his hair. It was all—all pretty much obliterated, by that time."

She said nothing for a moment or two and he did not look at her. Then she said, "It must seem as if I am one of those people—one of those people who are fascinated by these sorts of things."

Arthur made a protesting noise, but it did, of course, seem to him that she must be like that.

"I should not have asked you," she said. "I should not have mentioned it. I can never explain to you why I did. I would like just to ask you, if you can help it, never to think that that is the kind of person I am."

Arthur heard the word "never." She could never explain to him. He was never to think. In the midst of his disappointment he picked up this suggestion, that their conversations were to continue, and perhaps on a less haphazard basis. He heard a humility in her voice, but it was a humility that was based on some kind of assurance. Surely that was sexual.

Or did he only think so, because this was the evening it was? It was the Saturday evening in the month when he usually went to Walley. He was going there tonight, he had only dropped in here on his way, he had not meant to stay as long as he had done. It was the night when he went to visit a woman whose name was Jane MacFarlane. Jane MacFarlane lived apart from her husband, but she was not thinking of getting a divorce. She had no children. She earned her living as a dressmaker. Arthur had first met her when she came to his house to make clothes for his wife. Nothing had gone on at that time, and neither of them had thought of it. In some ways Jane MacFarlane was a woman like the Librarian— good-looking, though not so young, plucky and stylish and good at her work. In other ways, not so like. He could not imagine Jane ever presenting a man with a mystery, and following that up with the information that it would never be solved. Jane was a woman to give a man peace. The submerged dialogue he had with her—sensual, limited, kind— was very like the one he had had with his wife.

The Librarian went to the switch by the door, and turned out the main light. She locked the door. She disappeared among the shelves, turning out the lights there, too, in a leisurely way. The town clock was striking nine. She must think that it was right. His own watch said three minutes to.

It was time to get up, time for him to leave, time to go to Walley.

When she had finished dealing with the lights, she came and sat down at the table beside him.

He said, "I would never think of you in any way that would make you unhappy."

Turning out the lights shouldn't have made it so dark. They were in the middle of summer. But it seemed that heavy rain clouds had moved in. When Arthur had last paid attention to the street, he had seen plenty of daylight left: country people shopping, boys squirting each other at the drinking fountain, and young girls walking up and down in their soft, cheap, flowery summer dresses, letting the young men watch them from wherever the young men congregated—the Post Office steps, the front of the feed store. And now that he looked again he saw the street in an uproar from the loud wind that already carried a few drops of rain. The girls were shrieking and laughing and holding their purses over their heads as they ran to shelter, store clerks were rolling up awnings and hauling in the baskets of fruit, the racks of summer shoes, the garden implements that had been displayed on the sidewalks. The doors of the Town Hall banged as the farm women ran inside, grabbing on to packages and children, to cram themselves into the Ladies' Rest Room. Somebody tried the Library door. The Librarian looked over at it but did not move. And soon the rain was sweeping like curtains across the street, and the wind battered the Town Hall roof, and tore at the treetops. That roaring and danger lasted a few minutes, while the power of the wind went by. Then the sound left was the sound of the rain, which was now falling vertically and so heavily they might have been under a waterfall.

If the same thing was happening at Walley, he thought, Jane would know enough not to expect him. This was the last thought he had of her for a long while.

"Mrs. Feare wouldn't wash my clothes," he said, to his own surprise. "She was afraid to touch them."

The Librarian said, in a peculiarly quivering, shamed, and determined voice, "I think what you did—I think that was a remarkable thing to do."

The rain made such a constant noise that he was released from answering. He found it easy then to turn and look at her. Her profile was dimly lit by the wash of rain down the windows. Her expression was calm and reckless. Or so it seemed to him. He realized that he knew hardly anything about her—what kind of person she really was or what kind of secrets she could have. He could not even estimate his own value to her. He only knew that he had some, and it wasn't the usual.

He could no more describe the feeling he got from her than you can describe a smell. It's like the scorch of electricity. It's like burnt kernels of wheat. No, it's like a bitter orange. I give up.

He had never imagined that he would find himself in a situation like this, visited by such a clear compulsion. But it seemed he was not unprepared. Without thinking over twice or even once what he was letting himself in for, he said, "I wish—"

He had spoken too quietly, she did not hear him.

He raised his voice. He said, "I wish we could get married."

Then she looked at him. She laughed but controlled herself.

"I'm sorry," she said. "I'm sorry. It's just what went through my mind."

"What was that?" he said.

"I thought—that's the last I'll see of him."

Arthur said, "You're mistaken."

TOLPUDDLE MARTYRS

The passenger train from Carstairs to London had stopped running during the Second World War and even the rails were taken up. People said it was for the War Effort. When Louisa went to London to see the heart specialist, in the mid-fifties, she had to take the bus. She was not supposed to drive anymore.

The doctor, the heart specialist, said that her heart was a little wonky and her pulse inclined to be jumpy. She thought that made her heart sound like a comedian and her pulse like a puppy on a lead. She had not come fifty-seven miles to be treated with such playfulness but she let it pass, because she was already distracted by something she had been reading in the doctor's waiting room. Perhaps it was what she had been reading that had made her pulse jumpy.

On an inside page of the local paper she had seen the headline LOCAL MARTYRS HONORED, and simply to put in the time she had read further. She read that there was to be some sort of ceremony that afternoon at Victoria Park. It was a ceremony to honor the Tolpuddle Martyrs. The paper said that few people had heard of the Tolpuddle Martyrs, and certainly Louisa had not. They were men who had been tried and found guilty for administering illegal oaths. This peculiar offense, committed over a hundred years ago in Dorset, England, had got them transported to Canada and some of them had ended up here in London, where they lived out the rest of their days and were buried without any special notice or commemoration. They were considered now to be among the earliest founders of the Trade Union movement, and the Trade Unions Council, along with representatives of the Canadian Federation of Labor and the ministers of some local churches, had organized a ceremony taking place today on the occasion of the hundred-and-twentieth anniversary of their arrest.

Martyrs is laying it on somewhat, thought Louisa. They were not executed, after all.

The ceremony was to take place at three o'clock and the chief speakers were to be one of the local ministers, and Mr. John (Jack) Agnew, a union spokesman from Toronto.

It was a quarter after two when Louisa came out of the doctor's office. The bus to Carstairs did not leave until six o'clock. She had thought she would go and have tea and something to eat on the top floor of Simpsons, then shop for a wedding present, or if the time fitted go to an afternoon movie. Victoria Park lay between the doctor's office and Simpsons, and she decided to cut across it. The day was hot and the shade of the trees pleasant. She could not avoid seeing where the chairs had been set up, and a small speakers' platform draped in yellow cloth, with a Canadian flag on the one side and what she supposed must be a Labor Union flag on the other. A group of people had collected and she found herself changing course in order to get a look at them. Some were old people, very plainly but decently dressed, the women with kerchiefs around their heads on the hot day, Europeans. Others were factory workers, men in clean short-sleeved shirts and women in fresh blouses and slacks, let out early. A few women must have come from home, because they were wearing summer dresses and sandals and trying to keep track of small children. Louisa thought that they would not care at all for the way she was dressed—fashionably, as always, in beige shantung with a crimson silk tam—but she noticed, just then, a woman more elegantly got up than she was, in green silk with her dark hair drawn tightly back, tied with a green-and-gold scarf. She might have been forty—her face was worn, but beautiful. She came over to Louisa at once, smiling, showed her a chair and gave her a mimeographed paper. Louisa could not read the purple printing. She tried to get a look at some men who were talking beside the platform. Were the speakers among them?

The coincidence of the name was hardly even interesting. Neither the first name nor the last was all that unusual.

She did not know why she had sat down, or why she had come over here in the first place. She was beginning to feel a faintly sickening, familiar agitation. She could feel that over nothing. But once it got going, telling herself that it was over nothing did no good. The only thing to do was to get up and get away from here before any more people sat down and hemmed her in.

The green woman intercepted her, asked if she was all right.

"I have to catch a bus," said Louisa in a croaky voice. She cleared her throat. "An out-of-town bus," she said with better control, and marched away, not in the right direction for Simpsons. She thought in fact that she wouldn't go there, she wouldn't go to Birks for the wedding present or to a movie either. She would just go and sit in the bus depot until it was time for her to go home.

Within half a block of the bus depot she remembered that the bus had not taken her there that morning. The depot was being torn down and rebuilt—there was a temporary depot several blocks away. She had not paid quite enough attention to which street it was on—York Street, east of the real depot, or King? At any rate, she had to detour, because both of these streets were being torn up, and she had almost decided she was lost when she realized she had been lucky enough to come upon the temporary depot by the back way. It was an old house—one of those tall yellow-gray brick houses dating from the time when this was a residential district. This was probably the last use it would be put to before being torn down. Houses all around it must have been torn down to make the large gravelled lot where the buses pulled in. There were still some trees at the edge of the lot and under them a few rows of chairs that she had not noticed when she got off the bus before noon. Two men were sitting on what used to be the veranda of the house, on old car seats. They wore brown shirts with the bus company's insignia but they seemed to be halfhearted about their work, not getting up when she asked if the bus to Carstairs was leaving at six o'clock as scheduled and where could she get a soft drink?

Six o'clock, far as they knew.

Coffee shop down the street.

Cooler inside but only Coke and orange left.

She got herself a Coca-Cola out of the cooler in a dirty little indoor waiting room that smelled of a bad toilet. Moving the depot to this dilapidated house must have thrown everyone into a state of indolence and fecklessness. There was a fan in the room they used as an office, and she saw, as she went by, some papers blow off the desk. "Oh, shit," said the office girl, and stamped her heel on them.

The chairs set up in the shade of the dusty city trees were straight-backed old wooden chairs originally painted different colors—they looked as if they had come from various kitchens. Strips of old carpet and rubber bathroom mats were laid down in front of them, to keep your feet off the gravel. Behind the first row of chairs she thought she saw a sheep lying on the ground, but it turned into a dirty-white dog, which trotted over and looked at her for a moment in a grave semi-official way—gave a brief sniff at her shoes, and trotted away. She had not noticed if there were any drinking straws and did not feel like going back to look. She drank Coke from the bottle, tilting back her head and closing her eyes.

When she opened them, a man was sitting one chair away, and was speaking to her.

"I got here as soon as I could," he said. "Nancy said you were going to catch a bus. As soon as I finished with the speech, I took off. But the bus depot is all torn up."

"Temporarily," she said.

"I knew you right away," he said. "In spite of—well, many years. When I saw you, I was talking to somebody. Then I looked again and you'd disappeared."

"I don't recognize you," said Louisa.

"Well, no," he said. "I guess not. Of course. You wouldn't."

He was wearing tan slacks, a pale-yellow short-sleeved shirt, a cream-and-yellow ascot scarf. A bit of a dandy, for a union man. His hair was white but thick and wavy, the sort of springy hair that goes in ripples, up and back from the forehead, his skin was flushed and his face was deeply wrinkled from the efforts of speechmaking—and from talking to people privately, she supposed, with much of the fervor and persuasiveness of his public speeches. He wore tinted glasses, which he took off now, as if willing that she should see him better. His eyes were a light blue, slightly bloodshot and apprehensive. A good-looking man, still trim except for a little authoritative bulge over the belt, but she did not find these serviceable good looks—the careful sporty clothes, the display of ripply hair, the effective expressions—very attractive. She preferred the kind of looks Arthur had. The restraint, the dark-suited dignity that some people could call pompous, that seemed to her admirable and innocent.

"I always meant to break the ice," he said. "I meant to speak to you. I should have gone in and said goodbye at least. The opportunity to leave came up so suddenly."

Louisa did not have any idea what to say to this. He sighed. He said, "You must have been mad at me. Are you still?"

"No," she said, and fell back, ridiculously, on the usual courtesies. "How is Grace? How is your daughter? Lillian?"

"Grace is not so well. She had some arthritis. Her weight doesn't help it. Lillian is all right. She's married but she still teaches high school. Mathematics. Not too usual for a woman."

How could Louisa begin to correct him? Could she say, No, your wife Grace got married again during the war, she married a farmer, a widower. Before that she used to come in and clean our house once a week. Mrs. Feare had got too old. And Lillian never finished high school, how could she be a high-school teacher? She married young, she had some children, she works in the drugstore. She had your height and your hair, dyed blond. I often looked at her and thought she must be like you. When she was growing up, I used to give her my stepdaughter's outgrown clothes.

Instead of this, she said, "Then the woman in the green dress—that was not Lillian?"

"Nancy? Oh, no! Nancy is my guardian angel. She keeps track of where I'm going, and when, and have I got my speech, and what I drink and eat and have I taken my pills. I tend toward high blood pressure. Nothing too serious. But my way of life's no good. I'm on the go constantly. Tonight I've got to fly out of here to Ottawa, tomorrow I've got a tough meeting, tomorrow night I've got some fool banquet."

Louisa felt it necessary to say, "You knew that I got married? I married Arthur Doud."

She thought he showed some surprise. But he said, "Yes, I heard that. Yes."

"We worked hard, too," said Louisa sturdily. "Arthur died six years ago. We kept the factory going all through the thirties even though at times we were down to three men. We had no money for repairs and I remember cutting up the office awnings so that Arthur could carry them up on a ladder and patch the roof. We tried making everything we could think of. Even outdoor bowling alleys for those amusement places. Then the war came and we couldn't keep up. We could sell all the pianos we could make but also we were making radar cases for the Navy. I stayed in the office all through."

"It must have been a change," he said, in what seemed a tactful voice. "A change from the Library."

"Work is work," she said. "I still work. My stepdaughter Bea is divorced, she keeps house for me after a fashion. My son has finally finished university—he is supposed to be learning about the business, but he has some excuse to go off in the middle of every afternoon. When I come home at suppertime, I am so tired I could drop, and I hear the ice tinkling in their glasses and them laughing behind the hedge. Oh, Mud, they say when they see me, Oh, poor Mud, sit down here, get her a drink! They call me Mud because that was my son's name for me when he was a baby. But they are neither of them babies now. The house is cool when I come home—it's a lovely house if you remember, built in three tiers like a wedding cake. Mosaic tiles in the entrance hall. But I am always thinking about the factory, that is what fills my mind. What should we do to stay afloat? There are only five factories in Canada making pianos now, and three of them are in Quebec with the low cost of labor. No doubt you know all about that. When I talk to Arthur in my head, it is always about the same thing. I am very close to him still but it is hardly in a mystical way. You would think as you get older your mind would fill up with what they call the spiritual side of things, but mine just seems to get more and more practical, trying to get something settled. What a thing to talk to a dead man about."

She stopped, she was embarrassed. But she was not sure that he had listened to all of this, and in fact she was not sure that she had said all of it.

"What started me off—" he said. "What got me going in the first place, with whatever I have managed to do, was the Library. So I owe you a great deal."

He put his hands on his knees, let his head fall.

"Ah, rubbish," he said.

He groaned, and ended up with a laugh.

"My father," he said, "You wouldn't remember my father?"

"Oh, yes."

"Well. Sometimes I think he had the right idea."

Then he lifted his head, gave it a shake, and made a pronouncement.

"Love never dies."

She felt impatient to the point of taking offense. This is what all the speechmaking turns you into, she thought, a person who can say things like that. Love dies all the time, or at any rate it becomes distracted, overlaid—it might as well be dead.

"Arthur used to come and sit in the Library," she said. "In the beginning I was very provoked with him. I used to look at the back of his neck and think, Ha, what if something should hit you there! None of that would make sense to you. It wouldn't make sense. And it turned out to be something else I wanted entirely. I wanted to marry him and get into a normal life.

"A normal life," she repeated—and a giddiness seemed to be taking over, a widespread forgiveness of folly, alerting the skin of her spotty hand, her dry thick fingers that lay not far from his, on the seat of the chair between them. An amorous flare-up of the cells, of old intentions. *Oh, never dies.*

Across the gravelled yard came a group of oddly dressed folk. They moved all together, a clump of black. The women did not show their hair—they had black shawls or bonnets covering their heads. The men wore broad hats and black braces. The children were dressed just like their elders, even to the bonnets and hats. How hot they all looked in those clothes—how hot and dusty and wary and shy.

"The Tolpuddle Martyrs," he said, in a faintly joking, re-signed, and compassionate voice. "Ah, I guess I'd better go over. I'd better go over there and have a word with them."

That edge of a joke, the uneasy kindness, made her think of somebody else. Who was it? When she saw the breadth of his shoulders from behind, and the broad flat buttocks, she knew who.

Jim Frarey.

Oh, what kind of a trick was being played on her, or what kind of trick was she playing on herself! She would not have it. She pulled herself up tightly, she saw all those black clothes melt into a puddle. She was dizzy and humiliated. She would not have it.

But not all black, now that they were getting closer. She could see dark blue, those were the men's shirts, and dark blue and purple in some of the women's dresses. She could see faces—the men's behind beards, the women's in their deep-brimmed bonnets. And now she knew who they were. They were Mennonites.

Mennonites were living in this part of the country, where they never used to be. There were some of them around Bondi, a village north of Carstairs. They would be going home on the same bus as she was.

He was not with them, or anywhere in sight.

A traitor, helplessly. A traveller.

Once she knew that they were Mennonites and not some lost unidentifiable strangers, these people did not look so shy or dejected. In fact they seemed quite cheerful, passing around a bag of candy, adults eating candy with the children. They settled on the chairs all around her.

No wonder she was feeling clammy. She had gone under a wave, which nobody else had noticed. You could say anything you liked about what had happened—but what it amounted to was going under a wave. She had gone under and through it and was left with a cold sheen on her skin, a beating in her ears, a cavity in her chest, and revolt in her stomach. It was anarchy she was up against—a devouring muddle. Sudden holes and impromptu tricks and radiant vanishing consolations.

But these Mennonite settlings are a blessing. The plop of behinds on chairs, the crackling of the candy bag, the meditative sucking and soft conversations. Without looking at Louisa, a little girl holds out the bag, and Louisa accepts a butterscotch mint. She is surprised to be able to hold it in her hand, to have her lips shape thank-you, then to discover in her mouth just the taste that she expected. She sucks on it as they do on theirs, not in any hurry, and allows that taste to promise her some reasonable continuance.

Lights have come on, though it isn't yet evening. In the trees above the wooden chairs someone has strung lines of little colored bulbs that she did not notice until now. They make her think of festivities. Carnivals. Boats of singers on the lake.

"What place is this?" she said to the woman beside her.

On the day of Miss Tamblyn's death it happened that Louisa was staying in the Commercial Hotel. She was a traveller then for a company that sold hats, ribbons, handkerchiefs and trimmings, and ladies' underwear to retail stores. She heard the talk in the hotel, and it occurred to her that the town would soon need a new Librarian. She was getting very tired of lugging her sample cases on and off trains, and showing her wares in hotels, packing and unpacking. She went at once and talked to the people in charge of the Library. A Mr. Doud and a Mr. Macleod. They sounded like a vaudeville team but did not look it. The pay was poor, but she had not been doing so well on commission, either. She told them that she had finished high school, in Toronto, and had worked in Eaton's Book Department before she switched to travelling. She did not think it necessary to tell them that she had only worked there five months when she was discovered to have t.b., and that she had then spent four years in a sanitorium. The t.b. was cured, anyway, her spots were dry.

The hotel moved her to one of the rooms for permanent guests, on the third floor. She could see the snow-covered hills over the rooftops. The town of Carstairs was in a river valley. It had three or four thousand people and a long main street that ran downhill, over the river, and uphill again. There was a piano and organ factory.

The houses were built for lifetimes and the yards were wide and the streets were lined with mature elm and maple trees. She had never been here when the leaves were on the trees. It must make a great difference. So much that lay open now would be concealed.

She was glad of a fresh start, her spirits were hushed and grateful. She had made fresh starts before and things had not turned out as she had hoped, but she believed in the swift decision, the unforeseen intervention, the uniqueness of her fate.

The town was full of the smell of horses. As evening came on, big blinkered horses with feathered hooves pulled the sleighs across the bridge, past the hotel, beyond the streetlights, down the dark side roads. Somewhere out in the country they would lose the sound of each other's bells.

A
REAL
LIFE

A man came along and fell in love with Dorrie Beck. At least, he wanted to marry her. It was true.

"If her brother was alive, she would never have needed to get married," Millicent said. What did she mean? Not something shameful. And she didn't mean money either. She meant that love had existed, kindness had created comfort, and in the poor, somewhat feckless life Dorrie and Albert lived together, loneliness had not been a threat. Millicent, who was shrewd and practical in some ways, was stubbornly sentimental in others. She believed always in the sweetness of affection that had eliminated sex.

She thought it was the way that Dorrie used her knife and fork that had captivated the man. Indeed, it was the same way as he used his. Dorrie kept her fork in her left hand and used the right only for cutting. She did not shift her fork continually to the right hand to pick up her food. That was because she had been to Whitby Ladies College when she was young. A last spurt of the Becks' money. Another thing she had learned there was a beautiful handwriting, and that might have been a factor as well, because after the first meeting the entire courtship appeared to have been conducted by letter. Millicent loved the sound of Whitby Ladies *College*, and it was her plan—not shared with anybody—that her own daughter would go there someday.

Millicent was not an uneducated person herself. She had taught school. She had rejected two serious boyfriends—one because she couldn't stand his mother, one because he tried putting his tongue in her mouth—before she agreed to marry Porter, who was nineteen years older than she was. He owned three farms, and he promised her a bathroom within a year, plus a dining-room suite and a chesterfield and chairs. On their wedding night he said, "Now you've got to take what's coming to you," but she knew it was not unkindly meant.

This was in 1933.

She had three children, fairly quickly, and after the third baby she developed some problems. Porter was decent— mostly, after that, he left her alone.

The Beck house was on Porter's land, but he wasn't the one who had bought the Becks out. He bought Albert and Dorrie's place from the man who had bought it from them. So, technically, they were renting their old house back from Porter. But money did not enter the picture. When Albert was alive, he would show up and work for a day when important jobs were undertaken—when they were pouring the cement floor in the barn or putting the hay in the mow. Dorrie had come along on those occasions, and also when Millicent had a new baby, or was housecleaning. She had remarkable strength for lugging furniture about and could do a man's job, like putting up the storm windows. At the start of a hard job—such as ripping the wallpaper off a whole room—she would settle back her shoulders and draw a deep, happy breath. She glowed with resolution. She was a big, firm woman with heavy legs, chestnut-brown hair, a broad bashful face, and dark freckles like dots of velvet. A man in the area had named a horse after her.

In spite of Dorrie's enjoyment of housecleaning, she did not do a lot of it at home. The house that she and Albert had lived in—that she lived in alone, after his death—was large and handsomely laid out but practically without furniture. Furniture would come up in Dorrie's conversation—the oak sideboard, Mother's wardrobe, the spool bed—but tacked onto this mention was always the phrase "that went at the Auction." The Auction sounded like a natural disaster, something like a flood and windstorm together, about which it would be pointless to complain. No carpets remained, either, and no pictures. There was just the calendar from Nunn's Grocery, which Albert used to work for. Absences of such customary things—and the presence of others, such as Dorrie's traps and guns and the boards for stretching rabbit and muskrat skins—had made the rooms lose their designations, made the notion of cleaning them seem frivolous. Once, in the summer, Millicent saw a pile of dog dirt at the head of the stairs. She didn't see it while it was fresh, but it was fresh enough to seem an offense. Through the summer it changed, from brown to gray. It became stony, dignified, stable—and strangely, Millicent herself found less and less need to see it as anything but something that had a right to be there.

Delilah was the dog responsible. She was black, part Labrador. She chased cars, and eventually this was how she was going to get herself killed. After Albert's death, both she and Dorrie may have come a little unhinged. But this was not something anybody could spot right away. At first, it was just that there was no man coming home and so no set time to get supper. There were no men's clothes to wash—cutting out the ideas of regular washing. Nobody to talk to, so Dorrie talked more to Millicent or to both Millicent and Porter. She talked about Albert and his job, which had been driving Nunn's Grocery Wagon, later their truck, all over the countryside. He had gone to college, he was no dunce, but when he came home from the Great War he was not very well, and he thought it best to be out-of-doors, so he got the job driving for Nunn's and kept it until he died. He was a man of inexhaustible sociability and did more than simply deliver groceries. He gave people a lift to town. He brought patients home from the hospital. He had a crazy woman on his route, and once when he was getting her groceries out of the truck, he had a compulsion to turn around. There she stood with a hatchet, about to brain him. In fact her swing had already begun, and when he slipped out of range she had to continue, chopping neatly into the box of groceries and cleaving a pound of butter. He continued to deliver to her, not having the heart to turn her over to the authorities, who would take her to the asylum. She never took up the hatchet again but gave him cupcakes sprinkled with evil-looking seeds, which he threw into the grass at the end of the lane. Other women—more than one—had appeared to him naked. One of them arose out of a tub of bathwater in the middle of the kitchen floor, and Albert bowed low and set the groceries at her feet. "Aren't some people amazing?" said Dorrie. And she told further about a bachelor whose house was overrun by rats, so that he had to keep his food slung in a sack from the kitchen beams. But the rats ran out along the beams and leaped upon the sack and clawed it apart, and eventually the fellow was obliged to take all his food into bed with him.

"Albert always said people living alone are to be pitied," said Dorrie—as if she did not understand that she was now one of them. Albert's heart had given out—he had only had time to pull to the side of the road and stop the truck. He died in a lovely spot, where black oaks grew in a bottomland, and a sweet clear creek ran beside the road.

Dorrie mentioned other things Albert had told her concerning the Becks in the early days. How they came up the river in a raft, two brothers, and started a mill at the Big Bend, where there was nothing but the wildwoods. And nothing now, either, but the ruins of their mill and dam. The farm was never a livelihood but a hobby, when they built the big house and brought out the furniture from Edinburgh. The bedsteads, the chairs, the carved chests that went in the Auction. They brought it round the Horn, Dorrie said, and up Lake Huron and so up the river. Oh, Dorrie, said Millicent, that is not possible, and she brought a school geography book she had kept, to point out the error. It must have been a canal, then, said Dorrie. I recall a canal. The Panama Canal? More likely it was the Erie Canal, said Millicent.

"Yes," said Dorrie. "Round the Horn and into the Erie Canal."

"Dorrie is a true lady, no matter what anybody says," said Millicent to Porter, who did not argue. He was used to her absolute, personal judgments. "She is a hundred times more a lady than Muriel Snow," said Millicent, naming the person who might be called her best friend. "I say that, and I love Muriel Snow dearly."

Porter was used to hearing that too.

"I love Muriel Snow dearly and I would stick up for her no matter what," Millicent would say. "I love Muriel Snow, but that does not mean I approve of everything she *does*."

The smoking. And saying hot damn, Chrissakes, *poop. I nearly pooped my pants.*

Muriel Snow had not been Millicent's first choice for best friend. In the early days of her marriage she had set her sights high. Mrs. Lawyer Nesbitt. Mrs. Dr. Finnegan. Mrs. Doud.

They let her take on a donkey's load of work in the Women's Auxiliary at the church, but they never asked her to their tea parties. She was never inside their houses, unless it was to a meeting. Porter was a farmer. No matter how many farms he owned, a farmer. She should have known.

She met Muriel when she decided that her daughter Betty Jean would take piano lessons. Muriel was the music teacher. She taught in the schools as well as privately. Times being what they were, she charged only twenty cents a lesson. She played the organ at the church, and directed various choirs, but some of that was for nothing. She and Millicent got on so well that soon she was in Millicent's house as often as Dorrie was, though on a rather different footing.

Muriel was over thirty and had never been married. Getting married was something she talked about openly, jokingly, and plaintively, particularly when Porter was around. "Don't you know any men, Porter?" she would say. "Can't you dig up just one decent man for me?" Porter would say maybe he could, but maybe she wouldn't think they were so decent. In the summers Muriel went to visit a sister in Montreal, and once she went to stay with some cousins she had never met, only written to, in Philadelphia. The first thing she reported on, when she got back, was the man situation.

"Terrible. They all get married young, they're Catholics, and the wives never die—they're too busy having babies.

"Oh, they had somebody lined up for me but I saw right away he would never pan out. He was one of those ones with the mothers.

"I did meet one, but he had an awful failing. He didn't cut his toenails. Big yellow toenails. Well? Aren't you going to ask me how I found out?"

Muriel was always dressed in some shade of blue. A woman should pick a color that really suits her and wear it all the time, she said. Like your perfume. It should be your signature.

Blue was widely thought to be a color for blondes, but that was incorrect. Blue often made a blonde look more washed-out than she was to start with. It suited best a warm-looking skin, like Muriel's—skin that took a good tan and never entirely lost it. It suited brown hair and brown eyes, which were hers as well. She never skimped on clothes—it was a mistake to. Her fingernails were always painted—a rich and distracting color, apricot or blood-ruby or even gold. She was small and round, she did exercises to keep her tidy waistline. She had a dark mole on the front of her neck, like a jewel on an invisible chain, and another like a tear at the corner of one eye.

"The word for you is not pretty," Millicent said one day, surprising herself. "It's *bewitching*." Then she flushed at her own tribute, knowing she sounded childish and excessive.

Muriel flushed a little too, but with pleasure. She drank in admiration, frankly courted it. Once, she dropped in on her way to a concert in Walley, which she hoped would yield rewards. She had an ice-blue dress on that shimmered.

"And that isn't all," she said. "Everything I have on is new, and everything is silk."

It wasn't true that she never found a man. She found one fairly often but hardly ever one that she could bring to supper. She found them in other towns, where she took her choirs to massed concerts, in Toronto at piano recitals to which she might take a promising student. Sometimes she found them in the students' own homes. They were the uncles, the fathers, the grandfathers, and the reason that they would not come into Millicent's house, but only wave—sometimes curtly, sometimes with bravado—from a waiting car, was that they were married. A bedridden wife, a drinking wife, a vicious shrew of a wife? Perhaps. Sometimes no mention at all—a ghost of a wife. They escorted Muriel to musical events, an interest in music being the ready excuse. Sometimes there was even a performing child, to act as chaperon. They took her to dinners in restaurants in distant towns. They were referred to as friends. Millicent defended her. How could there be any harm when it was all so out in the open? But it wasn't, quite, and it would all end in misunderstandings, harsh words, unkindness. A warning from the school board. Miss Snow will have to mend her ways. A bad example. A wife on the phone. Miss Snow, I am sorry we are cancelling— Or simply silence. A date not kept, a note not answered, a name never to be mentioned again.

"I don't expect so much," Muriel said. "I expect a friend to be a friend. Then they hightail it off at the first whiff of trouble after saying they'd always stand up for me. Why is that?"

"Well, you know, Muriel," Millicent said once, "a wife is a wife. It's all well and good to have friends, but a marriage is a marriage."

Muriel blew up at that, she said that Millicent thought the worst of her like everybody else, and was she never to be permitted to have a good time, an innocent good time? She banged the door and ran her car over the calla lilies, surely on purpose. For a day Millicent's face was blotchy from weeping. But enmity did not last and Muriel was back, tearful as well, and taking blame on herself.

"I was a fool from the start," she said, and went into the front room to play the piano. Millicent got to know the pattern. When Muriel was happy and had a new friend, she played mournful tender songs, like "Flowers of the Forest." Or:

> *"She dressed herself in male attire,*
> *And gaily she was dressed—"*

Then when she was disappointed, she came down hard and fast on the keys, she sang scornfully.

> *"Hey Johnny Cope are ye waukin' yet?"*

Sometimes Millicent asked people to supper (though not the Finnegans or the Nesbitts or the Douds), and then she liked to ask Dorrie and Muriel as well. Dorrie was a help to wash up the pots and pans afterward, and Muriel could entertain on the piano.

She asked the Anglican minister to come on Sunday, after evensong, and bring the friend she had heard was staying with him. The Anglican minister was a bachelor, but Muriel had given up on him early. Neither fish nor fowl, she said. Too bad. Millicent liked him, chiefly for his voice. She had been brought up an Anglican, and though she'd switched to United, which was what Porter said he was (so was everybody else, so were all the important and substantial people in the town), she still favored Anglican customs. Evensong, the church bell, the choir coming up the aisle in as stately a way as they could manage, singing—instead of just all clumping in together and sitting down. Best of all the words. *But thou O God have mercy upon us miserable offenders. Spare thou them, O Lord, which confess their faults. Restore thou them that are penitent, according to the Promise. . . .*

Porter went with her once and hated it.

Preparations for this evening supper were considerable. The damask was brought out, the silver serving-spoon, the black dessert plates painted with pansies by hand. The cloth had to be pressed and all the silverware polished, and then there was the apprehension that a tiny smear of polish might remain, a gray gum on the tines of a fork or among the grapes round the rim of the wedding teapot. All day Sunday, Millicent was torn between pleasure and agony, hope and suspense. The things that could go wrong multiplied. The Bavarian cream might not set (they had no refrigerator yet and had to chill things in summer by setting them on the cellar floor). The angel food cake might not rise to its full glory. If it did rise, it might be dry. The biscuits might taste of tainted flour or a beetle might crawl out of the salad. By five o'clock she was in such a state of tension and misgiving that nobody could stay in the kitchen with her. Muriel had arrived early to help out, but she had not chopped the potatoes finely enough, and had managed to scrape her knuckles while grating carrots, so she was told off for being useless, and sent to play the piano.

Muriel was dressed up in turquoise crêpe and smelled of her Spanish perfume. She might have written off the minister but she had not seen his visitor yet. A bachelor, perhaps, or a widower, since he was travelling alone. Rich, or he would not be travelling at all, not so far. He came from England, people said. Someone had said no, Australia.

She was trying to get up the "Polovtsian Dances."

Dorrie was late. It threw a crimp in things. The jellied salad had to be taken down cellar again, lest it should soften. The biscuits put to warm in the oven had to be taken out, for fear of getting too hard. The three men sat on the veranda— the meal was to be eaten there, buffet style—and drank fizzy lemonade. Millicent had seen what drink did in her own family—her father had died of it when she was ten—and she had required a promise from Porter, before they married, that he would never touch it again. Of course he did—he kept a bottle in the granary—but when he drank he kept his distance and she truly believed the promise had been kept. This was a fairly common pattern at that time, at least among farmers— drinking in the barn, abstinence in the house. Most men would have felt there was something the matter with a woman who didn't lay down such a law.

But Muriel, when she came out on the veranda in her high heels and slinky crêpe, cried out at once, "Oh, my favorite drink! Gin and lemon!" She took a sip and pouted at Porter.

"You did it again. You forgot the gin again!" Then she teased the minister, asking if he didn't have a flask in his pocket. The minister was gallant, or perhaps made reckless by boredom. He said he wished he had.

The visitor who rose to be introduced was tall and thin and sallow, with a face that seemed to hang in pleats, precise and melancholy. Muriel did not give way to disappointment. She sat down beside him and tried in a spirited way to get him into conversation. She told him about her music teaching and was scathing about the local choirs and musicians. She did not spare the Anglicans. She twitted the minister and Porter, and told about the live chicken that walked onto the stage during a country school concert.

Porter had done the chores early, washed and changed into his suit, but he kept looking uneasily toward the barnyard, as if he recalled something that was left undone. One of the cows was bawling loudly in the field, and at last he excused himself to go and see what was wrong with her. He found that her calf had got caught in the wire fence and managed to strangle itself. He did not speak of this loss when he came back with newly washed hands. "Calf caught up in the fence" was all he said. But he connected the mishap somehow with this entertainment, with dressing up and having to eat off your knees. He thought that was not natural.

"Those cows are as bad as children," Millicent said. "Always wanting your attention at the wrong time!" Her own children, fed earlier, peered from between the bannisters to watch the food being carried to the veranda. "I think we will have to commence without Dorrie. You men must be starving. This is just a simple little buffet. We sometimes enjoy eating outside on a Sunday evening."

"Commence, commence!" cried Muriel, who had helped to carry out the various dishes—the potato salad, carrot salad, jellied salad, cabbage salad, the devilled eggs and cold roast chicken, the salmon loaf and warm biscuits, and relishes. Just when they had everything set out, Dorrie came around the side of the house, looking warm from her walk across the field, or from excitement. She was wearing her good summer dress, a navy-blue organdie with white dots and white collar, suitable for a little girl or an old lady. Threads showed where she had pulled the torn lace off the collar instead of mending it, and in spite of the hot day a rim of undershirt was hanging out of one sleeve. Her shoes had been so recently and sloppily cleaned that they left traces of whitener on the grass.

"I would have been on time," Dorrie said, "but I had to shoot a feral cat. She was prowling around my house and carrying on so. I was convinced she was rabid."

She had wet her hair and crimped it into place with bobby pins. With that, and her pink shiny face, she looked like a doll with a china head and limbs attached to a cloth body, firmly stuffed with straw.

"I thought at first she might have been in heat, but she didn't really behave that way. She didn't do any of the rubbing along on her stomach such as I'm used to seeing. And I noticed some spitting. So I thought the only thing to do was to shoot her. Then I put her in a sack and called up Fred Nunn to see if he would run her over to Walley, to the vet. I want to know if she really was rabid, and Fred always likes the excuse to get out in his car. I told him to leave the sack on the step if the vet wasn't home on a Sunday night."

"I wonder what he'll think it is?" said Muriel. "A present?"

"No. I pinned on a note, in case. There was definite spitting and dribbling." She touched her own face to show where the dribbling had been. "Are you enjoying your visit here?" she said to the minister, who had been in town for three years and had been the one to bury her brother.

"It is Mr. Speirs who is the visitor, Dorrie," said Millicent. Dorrie acknowledged the introduction and seemed unembarrassed by her mistake. She said that the reason she took it for a feral cat was that its coat was all matted and hideous, and she thought that a feral cat would never come near the house unless it was rabid.

"But I will put an explanation in the paper, just in case. I will be sorry if it is anybody's pet. I lost my own pet three months ago—my dog Delilah. She was struck down by a car."

It was strange to hear that dog called a pet, that big black Delilah who used to lollop along with Dorrie all over the countryside, who tore across the fields in such savage glee to attack cars. Dorrie had not been distraught at the death; indeed she had said she had expected it someday. But now, to hear her say "pet," Millicent thought, there might have been grief she didn't show.

"Come and fill up your plate or we'll all have to starve," Muriel said to Mr. Speirs. "You're the guest, you have to go first. If the egg yolks look dark it's just what the hens have been eating—they won't poison you. I grated the carrots for that salad myself, so if you notice some blood it's just where I got a little too enthusiastic and grated in some skin off my knuckles. I had better shut up now or Millicent will kill me."

And Millicent was laughing angrily, saying, "Oh, they are not! Oh, you did *not!*"

Mr. Speirs had paid close attention to everything Dorrie said. Maybe that was what had made Muriel so saucy. Millicent thought that perhaps he saw Dorrie as a novelty, a Canadian wild woman who went around shooting things. He might be studying her so that he could go home and describe her to his friends in England.

Dorrie kept quiet while eating and she ate quite a lot. Mr. Speirs ate a lot too—Millicent was happy to see that—and he appeared to be a silent person at all times. The minister kept the conversation going describing a book he was reading. It was called *The Oregon Trail.*

"Terrible the hardships," he said.

Millicent said she had heard of it. "I have some cousins living out in Oregon but I cannot remember the name of the town," she said. "I wonder if they went on that trail."

The minister said that if they went out a hundred years ago it was most probable.

"Oh, I wouldn't think it was that long," she said. "Their name was Rafferty."

"Man the name of Rafferty used to race pigeons," said Porter, with sudden energy. "This was way back, when there was more of that kind of thing. There was money going on it, too. Well, he sees he's got a problem with the pigeons' house, they don't go in right away, and that means they don't trip the wire and don't get counted in. So he took an egg one of his pigeons was on, and he blew it clear, and he put a beetle inside. And the beetle inside made such a racket the pigeon naturally thought she had an egg getting ready to hatch. And she flew a beeline home and tripped the wire and all the ones that bet on her made a lot of money. Him, too, of course. In fact this was over in Ireland, and this man that told the story, that was how he got the money to come out to Canada."

Millicent didn't believe that the man's name had been Rafferty at all. That had just been an excuse.

"So you keep a gun in the house?" said the minister to Dorrie. "Does that mean you are worried about tramps and suchlike?"

Dorrie put down her knife and fork, chewed something up carefully, and swallowed. "I keep it for shooting," she said.

After a pause she said that she shot groundhogs and rabbits. She took the groundhogs over to the other side of town and sold them to the mink farm. She skinned the rabbits and stretched the skins, then sold them to a place in Walley which did a big trade with the tourists. She enjoyed fried or boiled rabbit meat but could not possibly eat it all herself, so she often took a rabbit carcass, cleaned and skinned, around to some family that was on Relief. Many times her offering was refused. People thought it was as bad as eating a dog or a cat. Though even that, she believed, was not considered out of the way in China.

"That is true," said Mr. Speirs. "I have eaten them both."

"Well, then, you know," said Dorrie. "People are prejudiced."

He asked about the skins, saying they must have to be removed very carefully, and Dorrie said that was true and you needed a knife you could trust. She described with pleasure the first clean slit down the belly. "Even more difficult with the muskrats, because you have to be more careful with the fur, it is more valuable," she said. "It is a denser fur. Waterproof."

"You do not shoot the muskrats?" said Mr. Speirs.

No, no, said Dorrie. She trapped them. Trapped them, yes, said Mr. Speirs, and Dorrie described her favorite trap, on which she had made little improvements of her own. She had thought of taking out a patent but had never gotten around to it. She spoke about the spring watercourses, the system of creeks she followed, tramping for miles day after day, after the snow was mostly melted but before the leaves came out, when the muskrats' fur was prime. Millicent knew that Dorrie did these things but she had thought she did them to get a little money. To hear her talk now, it would seem that she was truly fond of that life. The blackflies out already, the cold water over her boot tops, the drowned rats. And Mr. Speirs listened like an old dog, perhaps a hunting dog, that has been sitting with his eyes half shut, just prevented, by his own good opinion of himself, from falling into an unmannerly stupor. Now he has got a whiff of something nobody else can understand—his eyes open all the way and his nose quivers and his muscles answer, ripples pass over his hide as he remembers some day of recklessness and dedication. How far, he asked, and how high is the water, how much do they weigh and how many could you count on in a day and for muskrats is it still the same sort of knife?

Muriel asked the minister for a cigarette and got one, smoked for a few moments and stubbed it out in the middle of the Bavarian cream.

"So I won't eat it and get fat," she said. She got up and started to help clear the dishes, but soon ended up at the piano, back at the "Polovtsian Dances."

Millicent was pleased that there was conversation with the guest, though its attraction mystified her. Also, she thought that the food had been good and there had not been any humiliation, no queer taste or sticky cup handle.

"I had thought the trappers were all up north," said Mr. Speirs. "I thought that they were beyond the Arctic Circle or at least on the Pre-Cambrian shield."

"I used to have an idea of going there," Dorrie said. Her voice thickened for the first time, with embarrassment—or excitement. "I thought I could live in a cabin and trap all winter. But I had my brother, I couldn't leave my brother. And I know it here."

Late in the winter Dorrie arrived at Millicent's house with a large piece of white satin. She said that she intended to make a wedding dress. That was the first anybody had heard of a wedding—she said it would be in May—or learned the first name of Mr. Speirs. It was Wilkinson. Wilkie.

When and where had Dorrie seen him, since that supper on the veranda?

Nowhere. He had gone off to Australia, where he had property. Letters had gone back and forth between them.

Sheets were laid down on the dining-room floor, with the

dining table pushed against the wall. The satin was spread out over them. Its broad bright extent, its shining vulnerability cast a hush over the whole house. The children came to stare at it, and Millicent shouted to them to clear off. She was afraid to cut into it. And Dorrie, who could so easily slit the skin of an animal, laid the scissors down. She confessed to shaking hands.

A call was put in to Muriel to drop by after school. She clapped her hand to her heart when she heard the news, and called Dorrie a slyboots, a Cleopatra, who had fascinated a millionaire.

"I bet he's a millionaire," she said. "Property in Australia—what does that mean? I bet it's not a pig farm! All I can hope is maybe he'll have a brother. Oh, Dorrie, am I so mean I didn't even say congratulations!"

She gave Dorrie lavish loud kisses—Dorrie standing still for them as if she were five years old.

What Dorrie had said was that she and Mr. Speirs planned to go through "a form of marriage." What do you mean, said Millicent, do you mean a marriage ceremony, is that what you mean, and Dorrie said yes.

Muriel made the first cut into the satin, saying that somebody had to do it, though maybe if she was doing it again it wouldn't be in quite that place.

Soon they got used to mistakes. Mistakes and rectifications. Late every afternoon, when Muriel got there, they tackled a new stage—the cutting, the pinning, the basting, the sewing—with clenched teeth and grim rallying cries. They had to alter the pattern as they went along, to allow for problems unforeseen, such as the tight set of a sleeve, the bunching of the heavy satin at the waist, the eccentricities of Dorrie's figure. Dorrie was a menace at the job, so they set her to sweeping up scraps and filling the bobbin. Whenever she sat at the sewing machine, she clamped her tongue between her teeth.

Sometimes she had nothing to do, and she walked from room to room in Millicent's house, stopping to stare out the windows at the snow and sleet, the long-drawn-out end of winter. Or she stood like a docile beast in her woolen underwear, which smelled quite frankly of her flesh, while they pulled and tugged the material around her.

Muriel had taken charge of clothes. She knew what there had to be. There had to be more than a wedding dress. There had to be a going-away outfit, and a wedding nightgown and a matching dressing gown, and of course an entire new supply of underwear. Silk stockings, and a brassière—the first that Dorrie had ever worn.

Dorrie had not known about any of that. "I considered the wedding dress as the major hurdle," she said. "I could not think beyond it."

The snow melted, the creeks filled up, the muskrats would be swimming in the cold water, sleek and sporty with their treasure on their backs. If Dorrie thought of her traps, she did not say so. The only walk she took these days was across the field from her house to Millicent's.

Made bold by experience, Muriel cut out a dressmaker suit of fine russet wool, and a lining. She was letting her choir rehearsals go all to pot.

Millicent had to think about the wedding luncheon. It was to be held in the Brunswick Hotel. But who was there to invite, except the minister? Lots of people knew Dorrie, but they knew her as the lady who left skinned rabbits on doorsteps, who went through the fields and the woods with her dog and gun and waded along the flooded creeks in her high rubber boots. Few people knew anything about the old Becks, though all remembered Albert and had liked him. Dorrie was not quite a joke—something protected her from that, either Albert's popularity or her own gruffness and dignity—but the news of her marriage had roused up a lot of interest, not exactly of a sympathetic nature. It was being spoken of as a freakish event, mildly scandalous, possibly a hoax. Porter said that bets were being laid on whether the man would show up.

Finally, Millicent recalled some cousins who had come to Albert's funeral. Ordinary respectable people. Dorrie had their addresses, invitations were sent. Then the Nunn brothers from the grocery, whom Albert had worked for, and their wives. A couple of Albert's lawn-bowling friends and their wives. The people who owned the mink farm where Dorrie sold her groundhogs? The woman from the bakeshop who was going to ice the cake?

The cake was being made at home, then taken to the shop to be iced by the woman who had got a diploma in cake decorating from a place in Chicago. It would be covered with white roses, lacy scallops, hearts and garlands and silver leaves and those tiny silver candies you can break your tooth on. Meanwhile it had to be mixed and baked, and this was where Dorrie's strong arms could come into play, stirring and stirring a mixture so stiff it appeared to be all candied fruit and raisins and currants, with a little gingery batter holding it together like glue. When Dorrie got the big bowl against her stomach and took up the beating spoon, Millicent heard the first satisfied sigh to come out of her in a long while.

Muriel decided that there had to be a maid of honor. Or a matron of honor. It could not be her, because she would be playing the organ. "O Perfect Love." And the Mendelssohn.

It would have to be Millicent. Muriel would not take no for an answer. She brought over an evening dress of her own, a long sky-blue dress, which she ripped open at the waist—how confident and cavalier she was by now about dressmaking!—and proposed a lace midriff, of darker blue, with a matching lace bolero. It will look like new and suit you to a T, she said.

Millicent laughed when she first tried it on and said, "There's a sight to scare the pigeons!" But she was pleased.

She and Porter had not had much of a wedding—they had just gone to the rectory, deciding to put the money saved into furniture. "I suppose I'll need some kind of thingamajig," she said. "Something on my head."

"Her veil!" cried Muriel. "What about Dorrie's veil? We've been concentrating so much on wedding dresses, we've forgotten all about a veil!"

Dorrie spoke up unexpectedly and said that she would never wear a veil. She could not stand to have that draped over her, it would feel like cobwebs. Her use of the word "cobwebs" gave Muriel and Millicent a start, because there were jokes being made about cobwebs in other places.

"She's right," said Muriel. "A veil would be too much." She considered what else. A wreath of flowers? No, too much again. A picture hat? Yes, get an old summer hat and cover it with white satin. Then get another and cover it with the dark-blue lace.

"Here is the menu," said Millicent dubiously. "Creamed chicken in pastry shells, little round biscuits, molded jellies, that salad with the apples and the walnuts, pink and white ice cream with the cake—"

Thinking of the cake, Muriel said, "Does he by any chance have a sword, Dorrie?"

Dorrie said, "Who?"

"Wilkie. Your Wilkie. Does he have a sword?"

"What would he have a sword for?" Millicent said.

"I just thought he might," said Muriel.

"I cannot enlighten you," said Dorrie.

Then there was a moment in which they all fell silent, because they had to think of the bridegroom. They had to admit him to the room and set him down in the midst of all this. Picture hats. Creamed chicken. Silver leaves. They were stricken with doubts. At least Millicent was, and Muriel. They hardly dared to look at each other.

"I just thought since he was English, or whatever he is," said Muriel.

Millicent said, "He is a fine man anyway."

The wedding was set for the second Saturday in May. Mr. Speirs was to arrive on the Wednesday and stay with the minister. The Sunday before this, Dorrie was supposed to come over to have supper with Millicent and Porter. Muriel was there, too. Dorrie didn't arrive, and they went ahead and started without her.

Millicent stood up in the middle of the meal. "I'm going over there," she said. "She better be sharper than this getting to her wedding."

"I can keep you company," said Muriel.

Millicent said no thanks. Two might make it worse.

Make what worse?

She did not know.

She went across the field by herself. It was a warm day, and the back door of Dorrie's house was standing open. Between the house and where the barn used to be there was a grove of walnut trees whose branches were still bare, since walnut trees are among the very latest to get their leaves. The hot sunlight pouring through bare branches seemed unnatural. Her feet did not make any sound on the grass.

And there on the back platform was Albert's old armchair, never taken in all winter.

What was in her mind was that Dorrie might have had an accident. Something to do with a gun. Maybe while cleaning her gun. That happened to people. Or she might be lying out in a field somewhere, lying in the woods among the old dead leaves and the new leeks and bloodroot. Tripped while getting over a fence. Had to go out one last time. And then, after all the safe times, the gun had gone off. Millicent had never had any such fears for Dorrie before, and she knew that in some ways Dorrie was very careful and competent. It must be that what had happened this year made anything seem possible. The proposed marriage, such wild luck, could make you believe in calamity also.

But it was not an accident that was on her mind. Not really. Under this busy fearful imagining of accidents, she hid what she really feared.

She called Dorrie's name at the open door. And so prepared was she for an answering silence, the evil silence and indifference of a house lately vacated by somebody who had met with disaster (or not vacated yet by the body of the person who had met with, who had *brought about*, that disaster)—so prepared was she for the worst that she was shocked, she went watery in the knees, at the sight of Dorrie herself, in her old field pants and shirt.

"We were waiting for you," she said. "We were waiting for you to come to supper."

Dorrie said, "I must've lost track of the time."

"Oh, have all your clocks stopped?" said Millicent, recovering her nerve as she was led through the back hall with its familiar mysterious debris. She could smell cooking.

The kitchen was dark because of the big, unruly lilac pressing against the window. Dorrie used the house's original wood cookstove, and she had one of those old kitchen tables with a drawer for the knives and forks. It was a relief to see that the calendar on the wall was for this year.

Dorrie was cooking some supper. She was in the middle of chopping up a purple onion to add to the bits of bacon and sliced potatoes she had frying up in the pan. So much for losing track of the time.

"You go ahead," said Millicent. "Go ahead and make your meal. I did get something to eat before I took it into my head to go and look for you."

"I made tea," said Dorrie. It was keeping warm on the back of the stove and, when she poured it out, was like ink.

"I can't leave," she said, prying up some of the bacon that was sputtering in the pan. "I can't leave here."

Millicent decided to treat this as she would a child's announcement that she could not go to school.

"Well, that'll be a nice piece of news for Mr. Speirs," she said. "When he has come all this way."

Dorrie leaned back as the grease became fractious.

"Better move that off the heat a bit," Millicent said.

"I can't leave."

"I heard that before."

Dorrie finished her cooking and scooped the results onto a plate. She added ketchup and a couple of thick slices of bread soaked in the grease that was left in the pan. She sat down to eat, and did not speak.

Millicent was sitting too, waiting her out. Finally she said, "Give a reason."

Dorrie shrugged and chewed.

"Maybe you know something I don't," Millicent said. "What have you found out? Is he poor?"

Dorrie shook her head. "Rich," she said.

So Muriel was right.

"A lot of women would give their eyeteeth."

"I don't care about that," Dorrie said. She chewed and swallowed and repeated, "I don't care."

Millicent had to take a chance, though it embarrassed her.

"If you are thinking about what I think you may be thinking about, then it could be that you are worried over nothing. A lot of time when they get older, they don't even want to bother."

"Oh, it isn't that! I know all about that."

Oh, do you, thought Millicent, and if so, how? Dorrie might imagine she knew, from animals. Millicent had sometimes thought that if she really knew, no woman would get married.

Nevertheless she said, "Marriage takes you out of yourself and gives you a real life."

"I have a life," Dorrie said.

"All right then," said Millicent, as if she had given up arguing. She sat and drank her poisonous tea. She was getting an inspiration. She let time pass and then she said, "It's up to you, it certainly is. But there is a problem about where you will live. You can't live here. When Porter and I found out you were getting married, we put this place on the market, and we sold it."

Dorrie said instantly, "You are lying."

"We didn't want it standing empty to make a haven for tramps. We went ahead and sold it."

"You would never do such a trick on me."

"What kind of a trick would it be when you were getting married?"

Millicent was already believing what she said. Soon it could come true. They could offer the place at a low enough price, and somebody would buy it. It could still be fixed up. Or it could be torn down, for the bricks and the woodwork. Porter would be glad to be rid of it.

Dorrie said, "You would not put me out of my house."

Millicent kept quiet.

"You are lying, aren't you?" said Dorrie.

"Give me your Bible," Millicent said. "I will swear on it."

Dorrie actually looked around. She said, "I don't know where it is."

"Dorrie, listen. All of this is for your own good. It may seem like I am pushing you out, Dorrie, but all it is is making you do what you are not quite up to doing on your own."

"Oh," said Dorrie. "Why?"

Because the wedding cake is made, thought Millicent, and

the satin dress is made, and the luncheon has been ordered and the invitations have been sent. All this trouble that has been gone to. People might say that was a silly reason, but those who said that would not be the people who had gone to the trouble. It was not fair to have your best efforts squandered.

But it was more than that, for she believed what she had said, telling Dorrie that this was how she could have a life. And what did Dorrie mean by "here"? If she meant that she would be homesick, let her be! Homesickness was never anything you couldn't get over. Millicent was not going to pay any attention to that "here." Nobody had any business living a life out "here" if they had been offered what Dorrie had. It was a kind of sin to refuse such an offer. Out of mulishness, out of fearfulness, and idiocy.

She had begun to get the feeling that Dorrie was cornered. Dorrie might be giving up, or letting the idea of giving up seep through her. Perhaps. She sat as still as a stump, but there was a chance such a stump might be pulpy within.

But it was Millicent who began suddenly to weep. "Oh, Dorrie," she said. "Don't be stupid!" They both got up, and grabbed hold of each other, and then Dorrie had to do the comforting, patting and soothing in a magisterial way, while Millicent wept and repeated some words that did not hang together. *Happy. Help. Ridiculous.*

"I will look after Albert," she said, when she had calmed down somewhat. "I'll put flowers. And I won't mention this to Muriel Snow. Or to Porter. Nobody needs to know."

Dorrie said nothing. She seemed a little lost, absentminded, as if she was busy turning something over and over, resigning herself to the weight and strangeness of it.

"That tea is awful," said Millicent. "Can't we make some that's fit to drink?" She went to throw the contents of her cup into the slop pail.

There stood Dorrie in the dim window light—mulish, obedient, childish, female—a most mysterious and maddening person whom Millicent seemed now to have conquered, to be sending away. At greater cost to herself, Millicent was thinking—greater cost than she had understood. She tried to engage Dorrie in a sombre but encouraging look, cancelling her fit of tears. She said, "The die is cast."

Dorrie walked to her wedding.

Nobody had known that she intended to do that. When Porter and Millicent stopped the car in front of her house to pick her up, Millicent was still anxious.

"Honk the horn," she said. "She better be ready now."

Porter said, "Isn't that her down ahead?"

It was. She was wearing a light gray coat of Albert's over her satin dress, and was carrying her picture hat in one hand, a bunch of lilacs in the other. They stopped the car and she said, "No, I want the exercise. It will clear out my head."

They had no choice but to drive on and wait at the church and see her approaching down the street, people coming out of shops to look, a few cars honking sportively, people waving and calling out, "Here comes the bride!" As she got closer to the church, she stopped and removed Albert's coat, and then she was gleaming, miraculous, like the Pillar of Salt in the Bible.

Muriel was inside the church playing the organ, so she did not have to realize, at this last moment, that they had forgotten all about gloves and that Dorrie clutched the woody stems of the lilac in her bare hands. Mr. Speirs had been in the church, too, but he had come out, breaking all rules, leaving the minister to stand there on his own. He was as lean and yellow and wolfish as Millicent remembered, but when he saw Dorrie fling the old coat into the back of Porter's car, and

settle the hat on her head—Millicent had to run up and fix
it right—he appeared nobly satisfied. Millicent had a picture
of him and Dorrie mounted high, mounted on elephants,
panoplied, borne cumbrously forward, adventuring. A vision.
She was filled with optimism and relief and she whispered
to Dorrie, "He'll take you everywhere! He'll make you a
Queen!"

"I have grown as fat as the Queen of Tonga," wrote Dorrie
from Australia, some years on. A photograph showed that she
was not exaggerating. Her hair was white, her skin brown, as
if all her freckles had got loose and run together. She wore a
vast garment, colored like tropical flowers. The war had come
and put an end to any idea of travelling, and then when it was
over, Wilkie was dying. Dorrie stayed on, in Queensland, on
a great property where she grew sugarcane and pineapples,
cotton, peanuts, tobacco. She rode horses, in spite of her size,
and had learned to fly an airplane. She took up some travels
of her own in that part of the world. She had shot crocodiles.
She died in the fifties, in New Zealand, climbing up to look
at a volcano.

Millicent told everybody what she had said she would not
mention. She took credit, naturally. She recalled her inspiration, her stratagem, with no apologies. "Somebody had to take
the bull by the horns," she said. She felt that she was the cre-
ator of a life—more effectively, in Dorrie's case, than in the
case of her own children. She had created happiness, or something close. She forgot the way she had wept, not knowing
why.

The wedding had its effect on Muriel. She handed in her
resignation, she went off to Alberta. "I'll give it a year," she
said. And within a year she had found a husband—not the

sort of man she had ever had anything to do with in the past. A widower with two small children. A Christian minister. Millicent wondered at Muriel's describing him that way. Weren't all ministers Christian? When they came back for a visit—by this time there were two more children, their own—she saw the point of the description. Smoking and drinking and swearing were out, and so was wearing makeup, and the kind of music that Muriel used to play. She played hymns now, of the sort she had once made fun of. She wore any color at all and had a bad permanent—her hair, going gray, stood up from her forehead in frizzy bunches. "A lot of my former life turns my stomach just to think about it," she said, and Millicent got the impression that she and Porter were seen mostly as belonging to those stomach-turning times.

The house was not sold or rented. It was not torn down, either, and its construction was so sound that it did not readily give way. It was capable of standing for years and years and presenting a plausible appearance. A tree of cracks can branch out among the bricks, but the wall does not fall down. Window sashes settle at an angle, but the window does not fall out. The doors were locked, but it was probable that children got in, to write things on the walls and break up the crockery that Dorrie had left behind. Millicent never went in to see.

There was a thing that Dorrie and Albert used to do, and then Dorrie did alone. It must have started when they were children. Every year, in the fall, they—and then, she—collected up all the walnuts that had fallen off the trees. They kept going, collecting fewer and fewer walnuts, until they were reasonably sure that they had got the last, or the next-to-last, one. Then they counted them, and they wrote the final total on the cellar wall. The date, the year, the total. The walnuts were not used for anything once they were collected. They were just dumped along the edge of the field and allowed to rot.

Millicent did not continue this useless chore. She had plenty of other chores to do, and plenty for her children to do. But at the time of year when the walnuts would be lying in the long grass, she would think of that custom, and how Dorrie must have expected to keep it up until she died. A life of customs, of seasons. The walnuts drop, the muskrats swim in the creek. Dorrie must have believed that she was meant to live so, in her reasonable eccentricity, her manageable loneliness. Probably she would have got another dog.

But I would not allow that, thinks Millicent. She would not allow it, and surely she was right. She has lived to be an old lady, she is living yet, though Porter has been dead for decades. She doesn't often notice the house. It is just there. But once in a while she does see its cracked face and the blank, slanted windows. The walnut trees behind, losing again, again, their delicate canopy of leaves.

I ought to knock that down and sell the bricks, she says, and seems puzzled that she has not already done so.

THE
ALBANIAN
VIRGIN

In the mountains, in Maltsia e madhe, she must have tried to tell them her name, and "Lottar" was what they made of it. She had a wound in her leg, from a fall on sharp rocks when her guide was shot. She had a fever. How long it took them to carry her through the mountains, bound up in a rug and strapped to a horse's back, she had no idea. They gave her water to drink now and then, and sometimes *raki*, which was a kind of brandy, very strong. She could smell pines. At one time they were on a boat and she woke up and saw the stars, brightening and fading and changing places—unstable clusters that made her sick. Later she understood that they must have been on the lake. Lake Scutari, or Sckhoder, or Skodra. They pulled up among the reeds. The rug was full of vermin, which got under the rag tied around her leg.

At the end of her journey, though she did not know it was

the end, she was lying in a small stone hut that was an out-building of the big house, called the *kula*. It was the hut of the sick and dying. Not of giving birth, which these women did in the cornfields, or beside the path when they were carrying a load to market.

She was lying, perhaps for weeks, on a heaped-up bed of ferns. It was comfortable, and had the advantage of being easily changed when fouled or bloodied. The old woman named Tima looked after her. She plugged up the wound with a paste made of beeswax and olive oil and pine resin. Several times a day the dressing was removed, the wound washed out with *raki*. Lottar could see black lace curtains hanging from the rafters, and she thought she was in her room at home, with her mother (who was dead) looking after her. "Why have you hung up those curtains?" she said. "They look horrible."

She was really seeing cobwebs, all thick and furry with smoke—ancient cobwebs, never disturbed from year to year.

Also, in her delirium, she had the sensation of some wide board being pushed against her face—something like a coffin plank. But when she came to her senses she learned that it was nothing but a crucifix, a wooden crucifix that a man was trying to get her to kiss. The man was a priest, a Franciscan. He was a tall, fierce-looking man with black eyebrows and mustache and a rank smell, and he carried, besides the crucifix, a gun that she learned later was a Browning revolver. He knew by the look of her that she was a giaour—not a Muslim—but he did not understand that she might be a heretic. He knew a little English but pronounced it in a way that she could not make out. And she did not then know any of the language of the Ghegs. But after her fever subsided, when he tried a few words of Italian on her, they were able to talk, because she had learned Italian at school and had been travelling for six months in Italy. He understood so much more than anyone else around her that she expected him, at first, to understand everything.

What is the nearest city? she asked him, and he said, Skodra. So go there, please, she said—go and find the British Consulate, if there is one. I belong to the British Empire. Tell them I am here. Or if there is no British Consul, go to the police.

She did not understand that under no circumstances would anybody go to the police. She didn't know that she belonged now to this tribe, this *kula*, even though taking her prisoner had not been their intention and was an embarrassing mistake.

It is shameful beyond belief to attack a woman. When they had shot and killed her guide, they had thought that she would turn her horse around and fly back down the mountain road, back to Bar. But her horse took fright at the shot and stumbled among the boulders and she fell, and her leg was injured. Then they had no choice but to carry her with them, back across the border between the Crna Gora (which means Black Rock, or Montenegro) and Maltsia e madhe.

"But why rob the guide and not me?" she said, naturally thinking robbery to be the motive. She thought of how starved they looked, the man and his horse, and of the fluttering white rags of his headdress.

"Oh, they are not robbers!" said the Franciscan, shocked. "They are honest men. They shot him because they were in blood with him. With his house. It is their law."

He told her that the man who had been shot, her guide, had killed a man of this *kula*. He had done that because the man he had killed had killed a man of his *kula*. This would go on, it had been going on for a long time now, there were always more sons being born. They think they have more sons than other people in the world, and it is to serve this necessity.

"Well, it is terrible," the Franciscan concluded. "But it is for their honor, the honor of their family. They are always ready to die for their honor."

She said that her guide did not seem to be so ready, if he had fled to Crna Gora.

"But it did not make any difference, did it?" said the Franciscan. "Even if he had gone to America, it would not have made any difference."

At Trieste she had boarded a steamer, to travel down the Dalmatian Coast. She was with her friends Mr. and Mrs. Cozzens, whom she had met in Italy, and their friend Dr. Lamb, who had joined them from England. They put in at the little port of Bar, which the Italians call Antivari, and stayed the night at the European Hotel. After dinner they walked on the terrace, but Mrs. Cozzens was afraid of a chill, so they went indoors and played cards. There was rain in the night. She woke up and listened to the rain and was full of disappointment, which gave rise to a loathing for these middle-aged people, particularly for Dr. Lamb, whom she believed the Cozzenses had summoned from England to meet her. They probably thought she was rich. A transatlantic heiress whose accent they could almost forgive. These people ate too much and then they had to take pills. And they worried about being in strange places— what had they come for? In the morning she would have to get back on the boat with them or they would make a fuss. She would never take the road over the mountains to Cetinge, Montenegro's capital city—they had been told that it was not wise. She would never see the bell tower where the heads of Turks used to hang, or the plane tree under which the Poet-Prince held audience with the people. She could not get back to sleep, so she decided to go downstairs with the first light, and, even if it was still raining, to go a little way up the road behind the town, just to see the ruins that she knew were there, among the olive trees, and the Austrian fortress on its rock and the dark face of Mount Lovchen.

The weather obliged her, and so did the man at the hotel desk, producing almost at once a tattered but cheerful guide and his underfed horse. They set out—she on the horse, the man walking ahead. The road was steep and twisting and full of boulders, the sun increasingly hot and the intervening shade cold and black. She became hungry and thought she must turn back soon. She would have breakfast with her companions, who got up late.

No doubt there was some sort of search for her, after the guide's body was found. The authorities must have been notified—whoever the authorities were. The boat must have sailed on time, her friends must have gone with it. The hotel had not taken their passports. Nobody back in Canada would think of investigating. She was not writing regularly to anyone, she had had a falling-out with her brother, her parents were dead. You won't come home till all your inheritance is spent, her brother had said, and then who will look after you?

When she was being carried through the pine forest, she awoke and found herself suspended, lulled—in spite of the pain and perhaps because of the *raki*—into a disbelieving surrender. She fastened her eyes on the bundle that was hanging from the saddle of the man ahead of her and knocking against the horse's back. It was something about the size of a cabbage, wrapped in a stiff and rusty-looking cloth.

I heard this story in the old St. Joseph's Hospital in Victoria from Charlotte, who was the sort of friend I had in my early days there. My friendships then seemed both intimate and uncertain. I never knew why people told me things, or what they meant me to believe.

I had come to the hospital with flowers and chocolates. Charlotte lifted her head, with its clipped and feathery white hair, toward the roses. "Bah!" she said. "They have no smell! Not to me, anyway. They are beautiful, of course.

"You must eat the chocolates yourself," she said. "Everything tastes like tar to me. I don't know how I know what tar tastes like, but this is what I think."

She was feverish. Her hand, when I held it, felt hot and puffy. Her hair had all been cut off, and this made her look as if she had actually lost flesh around her face and neck. The part of her under the hospital covers seemed as extensive and lumpy as ever.

"But you must not think I am ungrateful," she said. "Sit down. Bring that chair from over there—she doesn't need it."

There were two other women in the room. One was just a thatch of yellow-gray hair on the pillow, and the other was tied into a chair, wriggling and grunting.

"This is a terrible place," said Charlotte. "But we must just try our best to put up with it. I am so glad to see you. That one over there yells all night long," she said, nodding toward the window bed. "We must thank Christ she's asleep now. I don't get a wink of sleep, but I have been putting the time to very good use. What do you think I've been doing? I've been making up a story, for a movie! I have it all in my head and I want you to hear it. You will be able to judge if it will make a good movie. I think it will. I would like Jennifer Jones to act in it. I don't know, though. She does not seem to have the same spirit anymore. She married that mogul.

"Listen," she said. "(Oh, could you haul that pillow up more, behind my head?) It takes place in Albania, in northern Albania, which is called Maltsia e madhe, in the nineteen-twenties, when things were very primitive. It is about a young woman travelling alone. Lottar is her name in the story."

I sat and listened. Charlotte would lean forward, even rock a little on her hard bed, stressing some point for me. Her puffy hands flew up and down, her blue eyes widened commandingly, and then from time to time she sank back onto the pillows, and she shut her eyes to get the story in focus again. Ah, yes, she said. Yes, yes. And she continued.

"Yes, yes," she said at last. "I know how it goes on, but that is enough for now. You will have to come back. Tomorrow. Will you come back?"

I said, yes, tomorrow, and she appeared to have fallen asleep without hearing me.

The *kula* was a great, rough stone house with a stable below and the living quarters above. A veranda ran all the way around, and there would always be an old woman sitting there, with a bobbin contraption that flew like a bird from one hand to the other and left a trail of shiny black braid, mile after mile of black braid, which was the adornment of all the men's trousers. Other women worked at the looms or sewed together the leather sandals. Nobody sat there knitting, because nobody would think to sit down to knit. Knitting was what they did while they trotted back and forth to the spring with their water barrels strapped to their backs, or took the path to the fields or to the beech wood, where they collected the fallen branches. They knitted stockings—black and white, red and white, with zigzag patterns like lightning strokes. Women's hands must never be idle. Before dawn they pounded the bread dough in its blackened wooden trough, shaped it into loaves on the backs of shovels, and baked it on the hearth. (It was corn bread, unleavened and eaten hot, which would swell up like a puffball in your stomach.) Then they had to sweep out the *kula* and dump the dirty ferns and pile up armloads of fresh ferns for the next night's sleep. This was often one of Lottar's jobs, since she was so unskilled at everything else. Little girls stirred the yogurt so that lumps would not form as it soured. Older girls might butcher a kid and sew up its stomach, which they had stuffed with wild garlic and sage and apples. Or they would go together, girls and women, all ages, to wash the men's white head scarves in the cold little river nearby, whose waters were clear as glass. They tended the tobacco crop and hung the ripe leaves to dry in the darkened shed. They hoed the corn and cucumbers, milked the ewes.

The women looked stern but they were not so, really. They were only preoccupied, and proud of themselves, and eager for competition. Who could carry the heaviest load of wood, knit the fastest, hoe the most rows of cornstalks? Tima, who had looked after Lottar when she was sick, was the most spectacular worker of all. She would run up the slope to the *kula* with a load of wood bound to her back that looked ten times as big as herself. She would leap from rock to rock in the river and pound the scarves as if they were the bodies of enemies. "Oh, Tima, Tima!" the other women cried out in ironic admiration, and "Oh, Lottar, Lottar!" in nearly the same tones, when Lottar, at the other end of a scale of usefulness, let the clothes drift away downstream. Sometimes they whacked Lottar with a stick, as they would a donkey, but this had more exasperation in it than cruelty. Sometimes the young ones would say, "Talk your talk!" and for their entertainment she would speak English. They wrinkled up their faces and spat, at such peculiar sounds. She tried to teach them words—"hand," "nose," and so on. But these seemed to them jokes, and they would repeat them to each other and fall about laughing.

Women were with women and men were with men, except at times in the night (women teased about such times were full of shame and denial, and sometimes there would be a slapping) and at meals, when the women served the men their food. What the men did all day was none of women's business. Men made their ammunition, and gave a lot of care to their guns, which were in some cases very beautiful, decorated with engraved silver. They also dynamited rocks to clear the road, and were responsible for the horses. Wherever they were, there was a lot of laughing, and sometimes singing and firing off of blanks. While they were at home they seemed to be on holiday, and then some of them would have to ride off on an expedition of punishment, or to attend a council called to put an end to some particular bout of killing. None of the women believed it would work—they laughed and said that it would only mean twenty more shot. When a young man was going off on his first killing, the women made a great fuss over his clothes and his haircut, to encourage him. If he didn't succeed, no woman would marry him—a woman of any worth would be ashamed to marry a man who had not killed—and everyone was anxious to have new brides in the house, to help with the work.

One night, when Lottar served one man his food—a guest; there were always guests invited for meals around the low table, the *sofra*—she noticed what small hands he had, and hairless wrists. Yet he was not young, he was not a boy. A wrinkled, leathery face, without a mustache. She listened for his voice in the talk, and it seemed to her hoarse but woman-ish. But he smoked, he ate with the men, he carried a gun.

"Is that a man?" Lottar said to the woman serving with her. The woman shook her head, not willing to speak where the men might hear them. But the young girls who overheard the question were not so careful. "Is that a man? Is that a man?" they mimicked Lottar. "Oh, Lottar, you are so stupid! Don't you know when you see a Virgin?"

So she did not ask them anything else. But the next time she saw the Franciscan, she ran after him to ask him her question. What is a Virgin? She had to run after him, because he did not stop and talk to her now as he had when she was sick in the little hut. She was always working when he came to the *kula*, and he could not spend much time with the women anyway—he sat with the men. She ran after him when she saw him leaving, striding down the path among the sumac trees, heading for the bare wooden church and the lean-to church house, where he lived.

He said it was a woman, but a woman who had become like a man. She did not want to marry, and she took an oath in front of witnesses that she never would, and then she put on men's clothes and had her own gun, and her horse if she could afford one, and she lived as she liked. Usually she was poor, she had no woman to work for her. But nobody troubled her, and she could eat at the *sofra* with the men.

Lottar no longer spoke to the priest about going to Skodra. She understood now that it must be a long way away. Sometimes she asked if he had heard anything, if anybody was looking for her, and he would say, sternly, no one. When she thought of how she had been during those first weeks—giving orders, speaking English without embarrassment, sure that her special case merited attention—she was ashamed at how little she had understood. And the longer she stayed at the *kula*, the better she spoke the language and became accustomed to the work, the stranger was the thought of leaving. Someday she must go, but how could it be now? How could she leave in the middle of the tobacco-picking or the sumac harvest, or during the preparations for the feast of the Translation of St. Nicholas?

In the tobacco fields they took off their jerkins and blouses and worked half naked in the sun, hidden between the rows of tall plants. The tobacco juice was black and sticky, like molasses, and it ran down their arms and was smeared over their breasts. At dusk they went down to the river and scrubbed themselves clean. They splashed in the cold water, girls and big, broad women together. They tried to push each other off balance, and Lottar heard her name cried then, in warning and triumph, without contempt, like any other name: "Lottar, watch out! Lottar!"

They told her things. They told her that children died here because of the *Striga*. Even grown-up people shrivel and die sometimes, when the *Striga* has put her spell on them. The

Striga looks like a normal woman, so you do not know who she is. She sucks blood. To catch her, you must lay a cross on the threshold of the church on Easter Sunday when everybody is inside. Then the woman who is the *Striga* cannot come out. Or you can follow the woman you suspect, and you may see her vomit up the blood. If you can manage to scrape up some of this blood on a silver coin, and carry that coin with you, no *Striga* can touch you, ever.

Hair cut at the time of the full moon will turn white.

If you have pains in your limbs, cut some hair from your head and your armpits and burn it—then the pains will go away.

The *oras* are the devils that come out at night and flash false lights to bewilder travellers. You must crouch down and cover your head, else they will lead you over a cliff. Also they will catch the horses and ride them to death.

The tobacco had been harvested, the sheep brought down from the slopes, animals and humans shut up in the *kula* through the weeks of snow and cold rain, and one day, in the early warmth of the spring sun, the women brought Lottar to a chair on the veranda. There, with great ceremony and delight, they shaved off the hair above her forehead. Then they combed some black, bubbling dye through the hair that remained. The dye was greasy—the hair became so stiff that they could shape it into wings and buns as firm as blood puddings. Everybody thronged about, criticizing and admiring. They put flour on her face and dressed her up in clothes they had pulled out of one of the great carved chests. What for, she asked, as she found herself disappearing into a white blouse with gold embroidery, a red bodice with fringed epaulets, a sash of striped silk a yard wide and a dozen yards long, a black-and-red wool skirt, with chain after chain of false gold being thrown over her hair and around her neck. For beauty, they said. And they said when they had finished, "See! She is beautiful!" Those who said it seemed triumphant, challenging others who must have doubted that the transformation could be made. They squeezed the muscles in her arms, which she had got from hoeing and wood-carrying, and patted her broad, floured forehead. Then they shrieked, because they had forgotten a very important thing—the black paint that joins the eyebrows in a single line over the nose.

"The priest is coming!" shouted one of the girls, who must have been placed as a lookout, and the woman who was painting the black line said, "Ha, he will not stop it!" But the others drew aside.

The Franciscan shot off a couple of blanks, as he always did to announce his arrival, and the men of the house fired off blanks also, to welcome him. But he did not stay with the men this time. He climbed at once to the veranda, calling, "Shame! Shame! Shame on you all! Shame!

"I know what you have dyed her hair for," he said to the women. "I know why you have put bride's clothes on her. All for a pig of a Muslim!

"You! You sitting there in your paint," he said to Lottar. "Don't you know what it is for? Don't you know they have sold you to a Muslim? He is coming from Vuthaj. He will be here by dark!"

"So what of it?" said one of the women boldly. "All they could get for her was three napoleons. She has to marry somebody."

The Franciscan told her to hold her tongue. "Is this what you want?" he said to Lottar. "To marry an infidel and go to live with him in Vuthaj?"

Lottar said no. She felt as if she could hardly move or open her mouth, under the weight of her greased hair and her finery. Under this weight she struggled as you do to rouse yourself to a danger, out of sleep. The idea of marrying the Muslim was still too distant to be the danger—what she understood was that she would be separated from the priest, and would never be able to claim an explanation from him again.

"Did you know you were being married?" he asked her. "Is it something you want, to be married?"

No, she said. No. And the Franciscan clapped his hands. "Take off that gold trash!" he said. "Take those clothes off her! I am going to make her a Virgin!

"If you become a Virgin, it will be all right," he said to her. "The Muslim will not have to shoot anybody. But you must swear you will never go with a man. You must swear in front of witnesses. *Per quri e per kruch.* By the stone and by the Cross. Do you understand that? I am not going to let them marry you to a Muslim, but I do not want more shooting to start on this land."

It was one of the things the Franciscan tried so hard to prevent—the selling of women to Muslim men. It put him into a frenzy, that their religion could be so easily set aside. They sold girls like Lottar, who would bring no price anywhere else, and widows who had borne only girls.

Slowly and sulkily the women removed all the rich clothes. They brought out men's trousers, worn and with no braid, and a shirt and head scarf. Lottar put them on. One woman with an ugly pair of shears chopped off most of what remained of Lottar's hair, which was difficult to cut because of the dressing.

"Tomorrow you would have been a bride," they said to her. Some of them seemed mournful, some contemptuous. "Now you will never have a son."

The little girls snatched up the hair that had been cut off and struck it on their heads, arranging various knots and fringes.

Lottar swore her oath in front of twelve witnesses. They

were, of course, all men, and looked as sullen as the women about the turn things had taken. She never saw the Muslim. The Franciscan berated the men and said that if this sort of thing did not stop he would close up the churchyard and make them bury their dead in unholy ground. Lottar sat at a distance from them all, in her unaccustomed clothes. It was strange and unpleasant to be idle. When the Franciscan had finished his harangue, he came over and stood looking down at her. He was breathing hard because of his rage, or the exertions of the lecture.

"Well, then," he said. "Well." He reached into some inner fold of his clothing and brought out a cigarette and gave it to her. It smelled of his skin.

A nurse brought in Charlotte's supper, a light meal of soup and canned peaches. Charlotte took the cover off the soup, smelled it, and turned her head away. "Go away, don't look at this slop," she said. "Come back tomorrow—you know it's not finished yet."

The nurse walked with me to the door, and once we were in the corridor she said, "It's always the ones with the least at home who turn the most critical. She's not the easiest in the world, but you can't help kind of admiring her. You're not related, are you?"

Oh, no, I said. No.

"When she came in it was amazing. We were taking her things off and somebody said, oh, what lovely bracelets, and right away she wanted to sell them! Her *husband* is something else. Do you know him? They are really quite the characters."

Charlotte's husband, Gjurdhi, had come to my bookstore by himself one cold morning less than a week earlier. He was pulling a wagon full of books, which he had wrapped up in a blanket. He had tried to sell me some books once before, in their apartment, and I thought perhaps these were the same ones. I had been confused then, but now that I was on my own ground I was able to be more forceful. I said no, I did not handle secondhand books, I was not interested. Gjurdhi nodded brusquely, as if I had not needed to tell him this and it was of no importance to our conversation. He continued to pick up the books one by one, urging me to run my hands over the bindings, insisting that I note the beauty of the illustrations and be impressed by the dates of publication. I had to repeat my refusal over and over again, and I heard myself begin to attach some apologies to it, quite against my own will. He chose to understand each rejection as applying to an individual book and would simply fetch out another, saying vehemently, "This, too! This is very beautiful. You will notice. And it is very old. Look what a beautiful old book!"

They were travel books, some of them, from the turn of the century. Not so very old, and not so beautiful, either, with their dim, grainy photographs. *A Trek Through the Black Peaks. High Albania. Secret Lands of Southern Europe.*

"You will have to go to the Antiquarian Bookstore," I said. "The one on Fort Street. It isn't far to take them."

He made a sound of disgust, maybe indicating that he knew well enough where it was, or that he had already made an unsuccessful trip there, or that most of these books had come from there, one way or another, in the first place.

"How is Charlotte?" I said warmly. I had not seen her for a while, although she used to visit the store quite often. She would bring me little presents—coffee beans coated with chocolate to give me energy; a bar of pure glycerine soap to counteract the drying effects, on the skin, of having to handle so much paper. A paperweight embedded with samples of rocks found in British Columbia, a pencil that lit up in the dark (so that I could see to write up bills if the lights should go out). She drank coffee with me, talked, and strolled about the store, discreetly occupied, when I was busy. Through the dark, blustery days of fall she wore the velvet cloak that I had first seen her in, and kept the rain off with an oversized, ancient black umbrella. She called it her tent. If she saw that I had become too involved with a customer, she would tap me on the shoulder and say, "I'll just silently steal away with my tent now. We'll talk another day."

Once, a customer said to me bluntly, "Who is that woman? I've seen her around town with her husband. I guess he's her husband. I thought they were peddlers."

Could Charlotte have heard that, I wondered. Could she have detected a coolness in the attitude of my new clerk? (Charlotte was certainly cool to her.) There might have been just too many times when I was busy. I did not actually think that the visits had stopped. I preferred to think that an interval had grown longer, for a reason that might have nothing to do with me. I was busy and tired, anyway, as Christmas loomed. The number of books I was selling was a pleasant surprise.

"I don't want to be any kind of character assassin," the clerk had said to me. "But I think you should know that that woman and her husband have been banned from a lot of stores in town. They're suspected of lifting things. I don't know. He wears that rubber coat with the big sleeves and she's got her cloak. I do know for sure that they used to go around at Christmastime and snip off holly that was growing in people's gardens. Then they took it round and tried to sell it in apartment buildings."

On that cold morning, after I had refused all the books in his wagon, I asked Gjurdhi again how Charlotte was. He said that she was sick. He spoke sullenly, as if it were none of my business.

"Take her a book," I said. I picked out a Penguin light verse. "Take her this—tell her I hope she enjoys it. Tell her

I hope she'll be better very soon. Perhaps I can get around to see her."

He put the book into his bundle in the wagon. I thought that he would probably try to sell it immediately.

"Not at home," he said. "In the hospital."

I had noticed, each time he bent over the wagon, a large, wooden crucifix that swung down outside his coat and had to be tucked back inside. Now this happened again, and I said, thoughtlessly, in my confusion and contrition, "Isn't that beautiful! What beautiful dark wood! It looks medieval."

He pulled it over his head, saying, "Very old. Very beautiful. Oak wood. Yes."

He pushed it into my hand, and as soon as I realized what was happening I pushed it back.

"*Wonderful* wood," I said. As he put it away I felt rescued, though full of irritable remorse.

"Oh, I hope Charlotte is not very sick!" I said.

He smiled disdainfully, tapping himself on the chest— perhaps to show me the source of Charlotte's trouble, perhaps only to feel for himself the skin that was newly bared there.

Then he took himself, the crucifix, the books, and the wagon out of my store. I felt that insults had been offered, humiliations suffered, on both sides.

Up past the tobacco field was a beech wood, where Lottar had often gone to get sticks for the fire. Beyond that was a grassy slope—a high meadow—and at the top of the meadow, about half an hour's climb from the *kula*, was a small stone shelter, a primitive place with no window, a low doorway and no door, a corner hearth without a chimney. Sheep took cover there; the floor was littered with their droppings.

That was where she went to live after she became a Virgin.

The incident of the Muslim bridegroom had taken place in the spring, just about a year after she first came to Maltsia e madhe, and it was time for the sheep to be driven to their higher pastures. Lottar was to keep count of the flock and see that they did not fall into ravines or wander too far away. And she was to milk the ewes every evening. She was expected to shoot wolves, if any came near. But none did, no one alive now at the *kula* had ever seen a wolf. The only wild animals Lottar saw were a red fox, once, by the stream, and the rabbits, which were plentiful and unwary. She learned to shoot and skin and cook them, cleaning them out as she had seen the butcher girls do at the *kula* and stewing the meatier parts in her pot over the fire, with some bulbs of wild garlic.

She did not want to sleep inside the shelter, so she fixed up a roof of branches outside, against the wall, this roof an extension of the roof of the building. She had her heap of ferns underneath, and a felt rug she had been given, to spread on the ferns when she slept. She no longer took any notice of the bugs. There were some spikes pushed into the wall between the dry stones. She did not know why they were there, but they served her well for hanging up the milk pails and the few pots she had been provided with. She brought her water from the stream, in which she washed her own head scarf, and herself sometimes, more for relief from the heat than out of concern about her dirtiness.

Everything was changed. She no longer saw the women. She lost her habits of constant work. The little girls came up in the evenings to get the milk. This far away from the *kula* and their mothers, they became quite wild. They climbed up on the roof, often smashing through the arrangement of branches which Lottar had contrived. They jumped into the ferns and sometimes snatched an armful of them to bind into a crude ball, which they threw at one another until it fell apart. They enjoyed themselves so much that Lottar had to chase them away at dusk, reminding them of how frightened they got in the beech wood after dark. She believed that they ran all the way through it and spilled half the milk on their way.

Now and then they brought her corn flour, which she mixed with water and baked on her shovel by the fire. Once they had a treat, a sheep's head—she wondered if they had stolen it—for her to boil in her pot. She was allowed to keep some of the milk, and instead of drinking it fresh she usually let it go sour, and stirred it to make yogurt to dip her bread in. That was how she preferred it now.

The men often came up through the wood shortly after the little girls had run through it on their way down. It seemed that this was a custom of theirs, in the summer. They liked to sit on the banks of the stream and fire off blanks and drink *raki* and sing, or sometimes just smoke and talk. They were not making this expedition to see how she was getting on. But since they were coming anyway, they brought her presents of coffee and tobacco and were full of competing advice on how to fix up the roof of her shelter so it wouldn't fall down, how to keep her fire going all night, how to use her gun.

Her gun was an old Italian Martini, which had been given to her when she left the *kula*. Some of the men said that gun was unlucky, since it had belonged to a boy who had been killed before he himself had even shot anybody. Others said that Martinis in general were unlucky, hardly any use at all.

Mausers were what you needed, for accuracy and repeating power.

But Mauser bullets were too small to do enough damage. There were men walking around full of Mauser holes—you could hear them whistle as they passed by.

Nothing can really compare with a heavy flintlock that has a good packing of powder, a bullet, and nails.

When they weren't talking about guns, the men spoke of

recent killings, and told jokes. One of them told a joke about a wizard. There was a wizard held in prison by a Pasha. The Pasha brought him out to do tricks in front of guests. Bring a bowl of water, said the wizard. Now, this water is the sea. And what port shall I show you on the sea? Show a port on the island of Malta, they said. And there it was. Houses and churches and a steamer ready to sail. Now would you like to see me step on board that steamer? And the Pasha laughed. Go ahead! So the wizard put his foot in the bowl of water and stepped on board the steamer and went to America! What do you think of that!

"There are no wizards, anyway," said the Franciscan, who had climbed up with the men on this evening, as he often did. "If you had said a saint, you might have made some sense." He spoke severely, but Lottar thought he was happy, as they all were, as she, too, was permitted to be, in their presence and in his, though he paid no attention to her. The strong tobacco that they gave her to smoke made her dizzy and she had to lie down on the grass.

The time came when Lottar had to think about moving inside her house. The mornings were cold, the ferns were soaked with dew, and the grape leaves were turning yellow. She took the shovel and cleaned the sheep droppings off the floor, in preparation for making up her bed inside. She began to stuff grass and leaves and mud into the chinks between the stones.

When the men came they asked her what she was doing that for. For the winter, she said, and they laughed.

"Nobody can stay here in the winter," they said. They showed her how deep the snow was, putting hands against their breastbones. Besides, all the sheep would have been taken down.

"There will be no work for you—and what will you eat?"

they said. "Do you think the women will let you have bread and yogurt for nothing?"

"How can I go back to the *kula*?" Lottar said. "I am a Virgin, where would I sleep? What kind of work would I do?"

"That is right," they said kindly, speaking to her and then to each other. "When a Virgin belongs to the *kula* she gets a bit of land, usually, where she can live on her own. But this ones doesn't really belong to the *kula*, she has no father to give her anything. What will she do?"

Shortly after this—and in the middle of the day, when visitors never came—the Franciscan climbed the meadow, all alone.

"I don't trust them," he said. "I think they will try again to sell you to a Muslim. Even though you have been sworn. They will try to make some money out of you. If they could find you a Christian, it might not be so bad, but I am sure it will be an infidel."

They sat on the grass and drank coffee. The Franciscan said, "Do you have any belongings to take with you? No. Soon we will start."

"Who will milk the ewes?" said Lottar. Some of the ewes were already working their way down the slope; they would stand and wait for her.

"Leave them," said the Franciscan.

In this way she left not only the sheep but her shelter, the meadow, the wild grape and the sumac and mountain ash and juniper bushes and scrub oak she had looked at all summer, the rabbit pelt she had used as a pillow and the pan she had boiled her coffee in, the heap of wood she had gathered only that morning, the stones around her fire—each one of them known to her by its particular shape and color. She understood that she was leaving, because the Franciscan was so stern, but she did not understand it in a way that would make her look around, to see everything for the last time. That was not necessary, anyway. She would never forget any of it.

As they entered the beech wood the Franciscan said, "Now we must be very quiet. I am going to take another path, which does not go so near the *kula*. If we hear anybody on the path, we will hide."

Hours, then, of silent walking, between the beech trees with their smooth elephant bark, and the black-limbed oaks and the dry pines. Up and down, crossing the ridges, choosing paths that Lottar had not known existed. The Franciscan never hesitated and never spoke of a rest. When they came out of the trees at last, Lottar was very surprised to see that there was still so much light in the sky.

The Franciscan pulled a loaf of bread and a knife from some pocket in his garment, and they ate as they walked.

They came to a dry riverbed, paved with stones that were not flat and easily walkable but a torrent, a still torrent of stones between fields of corn and tobacco. They could hear dogs barking, and sometimes people's voices. The corn and tobacco plants, still unharvested, were higher than their heads, and they walked along the dry river in this shelter, while the daylight entirely faded. When they could not walk anymore and the darkness would conceal them, they sat down on the white stones of the riverbed.

"Where are you taking me?" Lottar finally asked. At the start she had thought they must be going in the direction of the church and the priest's house, but now she saw that this could not be so. They had come much too far.

"I am taking you to the Bishop's house," said the Franciscan. "He will know what to do with you."

"Why not to your house?" said Lottar. "I could be a servant in your house."

"It isn't allowed—to have a woman servant in my house. Or in any priest's house. This Bishop now will not allow even an old woman. And he is right, trouble comes from having a woman in the house."

After the moon rose they went on. They walked and rested, walked and rested, but never fell asleep, or even looked for a comfortable place to lie down. Their feet were tough and their sandals well worn, and they did not get blisters. Both of them were used to walking long distances—the Franciscan in his far-flung parish and Lottar when she was following the sheep.

The Franciscan became less stern—perhaps less worried—after a while and talked to her almost as he had done in the first days of their acquaintance. He spoke Italian, though she was now fairly proficient in the language of the Ghegs.

"I was born in Italy," he said. "My parents were Ghegs, but I lived in Italy when I was young, and that was where I became a priest. Once I went back for a visit, years ago, and I shaved off my mustache, I do not know why. Oh, yes, I do know—it was because they laughed at me in the village. Then when I got back I did not dare show my face in the *madhe*. A hairless man there is a disgrace. I sat in a room in Skodra until it grew again."

"It is Skodra we are going to?" said Lottar.

"Yes, that is where the Bishop is. He will send a message that it was right to take you away, even if it is an act of stealing. They are barbarians, in the *madhe*. They will come up and pull on your sleeve in the middle of Mass and ask you to write a letter for them. Have you seen what they put up on the graves? The crosses? They make the cross into a very thin man with a rifle across his arms. Haven't you seen that?" He laughed and shook his head and said, "I don't know what to do with them. But they are good people all the same—they will never betray you."

"But you thought they might sell me in spite of my oath."

"Oh, yes. But to sell a woman is a way to get some money. And they are so poor."

Lottar now realized that in Skodra she would be in an unfamiliar position—she would not be powerless. When they got there, she could run away from him. She could find some-one who spoke English, she could find the British Consulate. Or, if not that, the French.

The grass was soaking wet before dawn and the night got very cold. But when the sun came up Lottar stopped shivering and within an hour she was hot. They walked on all day. They ate the rest of the bread and drank from any stream they found that had water in it. They had left the dry river and the mountains far behind. Lottar looked back and saw a wall of jagged rocks with a little green clinging around their bases. That green was the woods and meadows which she had thought so high. They followed paths through the hot fields and were never out of the sound of barking dogs. They met people on the paths.

At first the Franciscan said, "Do not speak to anybody—they will wonder who you are." But he had to answer when greetings were spoken.

"Is this the way to Skodra? We are going to Skodra to the Bishop's house. This is my servant with me, who has come from the mountains.

"It is all right, you look like a servant in these clothes," he said to Lottar. "But do not speak—they will wonder, if you speak."

I had painted the walls of my bookstore a clear, light yellow. Yellow stands for intellectual curiosity. Somebody must have told me that. I opened the store in March of 1964. This was in Victoria, in British Columbia.

I sat there at the desk, with my offerings spread out behind me. The publishers' representatives had advised me to stock books about dogs and horses, sailing and gardening, bird books and flower books—they said that was all anybody in Victoria would buy. I flew against their advice and brought in novels and poetry and books that explained about Sufism and relativity and Linear B. And I had set out these books, when they came, so that Political Science could shade into Philosophy and Philosophy into Religion without a harsh break, so that compatible poets could nestle together, the arrangement of the shelves of books—I believed—reflecting a more or less natural ambling of the mind, in which treasures new and forgotten might be continually surfacing. I had taken all this care, and now what? Now I waited, and I felt like somebody who had got dramatically dressed up for a party, maybe even fetching jewels from the pawnshop or the family vault, only to discover that it was just a few neighbors playing cards. It was just meat loaf and mashed potatoes in the kitchen, and a glass of fizzy pink wine.

The store was often empty for a couple of hours at a time, and then when somebody did come in, it would be to ask about a book remembered from the Sunday-school library or a grandmother's bookcase or left behind twenty years ago in a foreign hotel. The title was usually forgotten, but the person would tell me the story. It is about this little girl who goes out to Australia with her father to mine the gold claims they have inherited. It is about the woman who had a baby all alone in Alaska. It is about a race between one of the old clipper ships and the first steamer, way back in the 1840s.

Oh, well. I just thought I'd ask.

They would leave without a glance at the riches around them.

A few people did exclaim in gratitude, said what a glorious addition to the town. They would browse for half an hour, an hour, before spending seventy-five cents.

It takes time.

I had found a one-room apartment with a kitchenette in an old building at a corner called the Dardanelles. The bed folded up into the wall. But I did not usually bother to fold it up, because I never had any company. And the hook seemed unsafe to me. I was afraid that the bed might leap out of the wall sometime when I was eating my tinned soup or baked-potato supper. It might kill me. Also, I kept the window open all the time, because I believed I could smell a whiff of escaping gas, even when the two burners and the oven were shut off. With the window open at home and the door open at the store, to entice the customers, it was necessary for me to be always bundled up in my black woolly sweater or my red corduroy dressing gown (a garment that had once left its pink tinge on all my forsaken husband's handkerchiefs and underwear). I had difficulty separating myself from these comforting articles of clothing so that they might be washed. I was sleepy much of the time, underfed and shivering.

But I was not despondent. I had made a desperate change in my life, and in spite of the regrets I suffered every day, I was proud of that. I felt as if I had finally come out into the world in a new, true skin. Sitting at the desk, I made a cup of coffee or of thin red soup last an hour, clasping my hands around the cup while there was still any warmth to be got from it. I read, but without purpose or involvement. I read stray sentences from the books that I had always meant to read. Often these sentences seemed so satisfying to me, or so elusive and lovely, that I could not help abandoning all the surrounding words and giving myself up to a peculiar state. I was alert and dreamy, closed off from all particular people but conscious all the time of the city itself—which seemed a strange place.

A small city, here at the western edge of the country. Pockets of fakery for tourists. The Tudor shop fronts and double-decker buses and flowerpots and horse-drawn rides: almost insulting. But the sea light in the street, the spare and healthy old people leaning into the wind as they took their daily walks along the broom-topped cliffs, the shabby, slightly bizarre bungalows with their monkey-puzzle trees and ornate shrubs in the gardens. Chestnut trees blossom as spring comes on, hawthorn trees along the streets bear red-and-white flowers, oily-leaved bushes put out lush pink and rose-red blooms such as you would never see in the hinterlands. Like a town in a story, I thought—like the transplanted seaside town of the story set in New Zealand, in Tasmania. But something North American persists. So many people, after all, have come here from Winnipeg or Saskatchewan. At noon a smell of dinners cooking drifts out of poor, plain apartment buildings. Frying meat, boiling vegetables—farm dinners being cooked, in the middle of the day, in cramped kitchenettes.

How could I tell what I liked so much? Certainly it was not what a new merchant might be looking for—bustle and energy to raise the hope of commercial success. *Not much doing* was the message the town got across to me. And when a person who is opening a store doesn't mind hearing the message *Not much doing*, you could ask, What's going on? People open shops in order to sell things, they hope to become busy so that they will have to enlarge the shop, then to sell more things, and grow rich, and eventually not have to come into the shop at all. Isn't that true? But are there other people who open a shop with the hope of being sheltered there, among such things as they most value—the yarn or the teacups or the books—and with the idea only of making a comfortable assertion? They will become a part of the block, a part of the street, part of everybody's map of the town, and eventually of everybody's memories. They will sit and drink coffee in the middle of the morning, they will get out the familiar bits of tinsel at Christmas, they will wash the windows in spring before spreading out the new stock. Shops, to these people, are what a cabin in the woods might be to somebody else—a refuge and a justification.

Some customers are necessary, of course. The rent comes

due and the stock will not pay for itself. I had inherited a little money—that was what had made it possible for me to come out here and get the shop going—but unless business picked up to some extent I could not last beyond the summer. I understood that. I was glad that more people started coming in as the weather warmed up. More books were sold, survival began to seem possible. Book prizes were due to be awarded in the schools at the end of term, and that brought the schoolteachers with their lists and their praise and their unfortunate expectation of discounts. The people who came to browse were buying regularly, and some of them began to turn into friends—or the sort of friends I had here, where it seemed I would be happy to talk to people day after day and never learn their names.

When Lottar and the priest first saw the town of Skodra, it seemed to float above the mud flats, its domes and steeples shining as if they were made of mist. But when they entered it in the early evening all this tranquillity vanished. The streets were paved with big, rough stones and were full of people and donkey carts, roving dogs, pigs being driven somewhere, and smells of fires and cooking and dung and something terrible—like rotten hides. A man came along with a parrot on his shoulder. The bird seemed to be shrieking curses in an unknown language. Several times the Franciscan stopped people and asked the way to the Bishop's house, but they pushed by him without answering or laughed at him or said some words he didn't understand. A boy said that he would show the way, for money.

"We have no money," the Franciscan said. He pulled Lottar into a doorway and there they sat down to rest. "In Maltsia e madhe," he said, "many of these who think so well of themselves would soon sing a different tune."

Lottar's notion of running away and leaving him had vanished. For one thing, she could not manage to ask directions any better than he could. For another, she felt that they were allies who could not survive in this place out of sight of each other. She had not understood how much she depended on the smell of his skin, the aggrieved determination of his long strides, the flourish of his black mustache.

The Franciscan jumped up and said he had remembered—he had remembered now the way to the Bishop's house. He hurried ahead of her through narrow, high-walled back streets where nothing of houses or courtyards could be seen—just walls and gates. The paving stones were thrust up so that walking here was as difficult as in the dry riverbed. But he was right, he gave a shout of triumph, they had come to the gate of the Bishop's house.

A servant opened the gate and let them in, but only after some high-pitched argument. Lottar was told to sit on the ground just inside the gate, and the Franciscan was led into the house to see the Bishop. Soon someone was sent through the streets to the British Consulate (Lottar was not told this), and he came back with the Consul's manservant. It was dark by then, and the Consul's servant carried a lantern. And Lottar was led away again. She followed the servant and his lantern to the consulate.

A tub of hot water for her to bathe in, in the courtyard. Her clothes taken away. Probably burned. Her greasy black, vermin-infested hair cut off. Kerosene poured on her scalp. She had to tell her story—the story of how she came to Maltsia e madhe—and this was difficult, because she was not used to speaking English, also because that time seemed so far away and unimportant. She had to learn to sleep on a mattress, to sit on a chair, to eat with a knife and fork.

As soon as possible they put her on a boat.

Charlotte stopped. She said, "That part is not of interest."

• • •

I had come to Victoria because it was the farthest place I could get to from London, Ontario, without going out of the country. In London, my husband, Donald, and I had rented a basement apartment in our house to a couple named Nelson and Sylvia. Nelson was an English major at the university and Sylvia was a nurse. Donald was a dermatologist, and I was doing a thesis on Mary Shelley—not very quickly. I had met Donald when I went to see him about a rash on my neck. He was eight years older than I was—a tall, freckled, blushing man, cleverer than he looked. A dermatologist sees grief and despair, though the problems that bring people to him may not be in the same class as tumors and blocked arteries. He sees sabotage from within, and truly unlucky fate. He sees how matters like love and happiness can be governed by a patch of riled-up cells. Experience of this sort had made Donald kind, in a cautious, impersonal way. He said that my rash was probably due to stress, and that he could see that I was going to be a wonderful woman, once I got a few problems under control.

We invited Sylvia and Nelson upstairs for dinner, and Sylvia told us about the tiny town they both came from, in Northern Ontario. She said that Nelson had always been the smartest person in their class and in their school and possibly in the whole town. When she said this, Nelson looked at her with a perfectly flat and devastating expression, an expression that seemed to be waiting with infinite patience and the mildest curiosity for some explanation, and Sylvia laughed and said, "Just kidding, of course."

When Sylvia was working late shifts at the hospital, I sometimes asked Nelson to share a meal with us in a more informal way. We got used to his silences and his indifferent table manners and to the fact that he did not eat rice or noodles, eggplant, olives, shrimp, peppers, or avocados, and no doubt a lot of other things, because those had not been familiar foods in the town in Northern Ontario.

Nelson looked older than he was. He was short and sturdily built, sallow-skinned, unsmiling, with a suggestion of mature scorn and handy pugnaciousness laid over his features, so that it seemed he might be a hockey coach, or an intelligent, uneducated, fair-minded, and foul-mouthed foreman of a construction gang, rather than a shy, twenty-two-year-old student.

He was not shy in love. I found him resourceful and determined. The seduction was mutual, and it was a first affair for both of us. I had once heard somebody say, at a party, that one of the nice things about marriage was that you could have real affairs—an affair before marriage could always turn out to be nothing but courtship. I was disgusted by this speech, and frightened to think that life could be so bleak and trivial. But once my own affair with Nelson started, I was amazed all the time. There was no bleakness or triviality about it, only ruthlessness and clarity of desire, and sparkling deception.

Nelson was the one who first faced up to things. One afternoon he turned on his back and said hoarsely and defiantly, "We are going to have to leave."

I thought he meant that he and Sylvia would have to leave, they could not go on living in this house. But he meant himself and me. "We" meant himself and me. Of course he and I had said "we" of our arrangements, of our transgression. Now he had made it the "we" of our decision—perhaps of a life together.

My thesis was supposed to be on Mary Shelley's later novels, the ones nobody knows about. *Lodore*, *Perkin Warbeck*, *The Last Man*. But I was really more interested in Mary's life before she learned her sad lessons and buckled down to raising her son to be a baronet. I loved to read about the other women who had hated or envied or traipsed along: Harriet, Shelley's first wife, and Fanny Imlay, who was Mary's half-sister and may have been in love with Shelley herself, and Mary's stepsister, Mary Jane Clairmont, who took my own name—Claire—and joined Mary and Shelley on their unwed honeymoon so that she could keep on chasing Byron. I had often talked to Donald about impetuous Mary and married Shelley and their meetings at Mary's mother's grave, about the suicides of Harriet and Fanny and the persistence of Claire, who had a baby by Byron. But I never mentioned any of this to Nelson, partly because we had little time for talk and partly because I did not want him to think that I drew some sort of comfort or inspiration from this mishmash of love and despair and treachery and self-dramatizing. I did not want to think so myself. And Nelson was not a fan of the nineteenth century or the Romantics. He said so. He said that he wanted to do something on the Muckrakers. Perhaps he meant that as a joke.

Sylvia did not behave like Harriet. Her mind was not influenced or impeded by literature, and when she found out what had been going on, she went into a wholesome rage.

"You blithering idiot," she said to Nelson.

"You two-faced twit," she said to me.

The four of us were in our living room. Donald went on cleaning and filling his pipe, tapped it and lit it, nursed and inspected it, drew on it, lit it again—all so much the way someone would do in a movie that I was embarrassed for him. Then he put some books and the latest copy of *Macleans* into his briefcase, went to the bathroom to get his razor and to the bedroom to get his pajamas, and walked out.

He went straight to the apartment of a young widow who worked as a secretary at his clinic. In a letter he wrote to me later, he said that he had never thought of this woman except as a friend until that night, when it suddenly dawned on him what a pleasure it would be to love a kind and sensible, *unwracked-up* sort of person.

Sylvia had to be at work at eleven o'clock. Nelson usually walked her over to the hospital—they did not have a car. On this night she told him that she would rather be escorted by a skunk.

That left Nelson and me alone together. The scene had lasted a much shorter time than I had expected. Nelson seemed gloomy but relieved, and if I felt that short shrift had been given to the notion of love as a capturing tide, a glorious and harrowing event, I knew better than to show it.

We lay down on the bed to talk about our plans and ended up making love, because that was what we were used to doing. Sometime during the night Nelson woke up and thought it best to go downstairs to his own bed.

I got up in the dark, dressed, packed a suitcase, wrote a note, and walked to the phone at the corner, where I called a taxi. I took the six-o'clock train to Toronto, connecting with the train to Vancouver. It was cheaper to take the train, if you were willing to sit up for three nights, which I was.

So there I sat, in the sad, shambling morning in the day coach, coming down the steep-walled Fraser Canyon into the sodden Fraser Valley, where smoke hung over the small, dripping houses, the brown vines, the thorny bushes and huddled sheep. It was in December that this earthquake in my life had arrived. Christmas was cancelled for me. Winter with its snowdrifts and icicles and invigorating blizzards was cancelled by this blurred season of muck and rain. I was constipated, I knew that I had bad breath, my limbs were cramped, and my spirits utterly bleak. And did I not think then, What nonsense it is to suppose one man so different from another when all that life really boils down to is getting a decent cup of coffee and room to stretch out in? Did I not think that even if Nelson were sitting here beside me, he would have turned into a gray-faced stranger whose desolation and unease merely extended my own?

No. No. Nelson would still be Nelson to me. I had not changed, with regard to his skin and his smell and his forbidding eyes. It seemed to be the outside of Nelson which came most readily to my mind, and in the case of Donald it was his inner quakes and sympathies, the labored-at kindness and those private misgivings that I had got knowledge of by wheedling and conniving. If I could have my love of these two men together, and settle it on one man, I would be a happy woman. If I could care for everybody in the world as minutely as I did for Nelson, and as calmly, as uncarnally as I now did for Donald, I would be a saint. Instead, I had dealt a twofold, a wanton-seeming, blow.

The regular customers who had changed into something like friends were: a middle-aged woman who was a chartered accountant but preferred such reading as *Six Existentialist Thinkers*, and *The Meaning of Meaning*; a provincial civil servant who ordered splendid, expensive works of pornography such as I had not known existed (their elaborate Oriental, Etruscan connections seemed to me grotesque and uninteresting, compared to the simple, effective, longed-for rituals of myself and Nelson); a Notary Public who lived behind his office at the foot of Johnson Street ("I live in the slums," he told me. "Some night I expect a big bruiser of a fellow to lurch around the corner hollering 'Ste-el-la.' "); and the woman I knew later as Charlotte—the Notary Public called her the Duchess. None of these people cared much for one another, and an early attempt that I made to bring the accountant and the Notary Public into conversation was a fizzle.

"Spare me the females with the withered, painted faces,"

the Notary Public said, the next time he came in. "I hope you haven't got her lurking around anywhere tonight."

It was true that the accountant painted her thin, intelligent, fifty-year-old face with a heavy hand, and drew on eyebrows that were like two strokes of India ink. But who was the Notary Public to talk, with his stumpy, nicotined teeth and pocked cheeks?

"I got the impression of a rather superficial fellow," the accountant said, as if she had guessed and bravely discounted the remarks made about herself.

So much for trying to corral people into couples, I wrote to Donald. *And who am I to try?* I wrote to Donald regularly, describing the store, and the city, and even, as well as I could, my own unaccountable feelings. He was living with Helen, the secretary. I wrote also to Nelson, who might or might not be living alone, might or might not be reunited with Sylvia. I didn't think he was. I thought she would believe in inexcusable behavior and definite endings. He had a new address. I had looked it up in the London phone book at the public library. Donald, after a grudging start, was writing back. He wrote impersonal, mildly interesting letters about people we both knew, events at the clinic. Nelson did not write at all. I started sending registered letters. Now I knew at least that he picked them up.

Charlotte and Gjurdhi must have come into the store together, but I did not understand that they were a couple until it was time for them to leave. Charlotte was a heavy, shapeless, but quick-moving woman, with a pink face, bright blue eyes, and a lot of glistening white hair, worn like a girl's, waving down over her shoulders. Though the weather was fairly warm, she was wearing a cape of dark-gray velvet with a scanty gray fur trim—a garment that looked as if it belonged, or had once belonged, on the stage. A loose shirt and a pair of plaid wool slacks showed underneath, and there were open sandals on her broad, bare, dusty feet. She clanked as if she wore hidden armor. An arm reaching up to get a book showed what caused the clanking. Bracelets—any number of them, heavy or slender, tarnished or bright. Some were set with large, square stones, the color of toffee or blood.

"Imagine this old fraud being still on the go," she said to me, as if continuing some desultory and enjoyable conversation.

She had picked up a book by Anaïs Nin.

"Don't pay any attention," she said. "I say terrible things. I'm quite fond of the woman, really. It's him I can't stand."

"Henry Miller?" I said, beginning to follow this.

"That's right." She went on talking about Henry Miller, Paris, California, in a scoffing, energetic, half-affectionate way. She seemed to have been neighbors, at least, with the people she was talking about. Finally, naïvely, I asked her if this was the case.

"No, no. I just feel I know them all. Not personally. Well—personally. Yes, personally. What other way is there to know them? I mean, I haven't met them, face-to-face. But in their books? Surely that's what they intend? I know them. I know them to the point where they bore me. Just like anybody you know. Don't you find that?"

She drifted over to the table where I had laid out the New Directions paperbacks.

"Here's the new bunch, then," she said. "Oh, my," she said, widening her eyes at the photographs of Ginsberg and Corso and Ferlinghetti. She began reading, so attentively that I thought the next thing she said must be part of some poem.

"I've gone by and I've seen you here," she said. She put the book down and I realized she meant me. "I've seen you sitting in here, and I've thought a young woman would probably like to be outside some of the time. In the sun. I don't suppose you'd consider hiring me to sit there, so you could get out?"

"Well, I would like to—" I said.

"I'm not so dumb. I'm fairly knowledgeable, really. Ask me who wrote Ovid's *Metamorphoses*. It's all right, you don't have to laugh."

"I would like to, but I really can't afford to."

"Oh, well. You're probably right. I'm not very chic. And I would probably foul things up. I would argue with people if they were buying books I thought were dreadful." She did not seem disappointed. She picked up a copy of *The Dud Avocado* and said, "There! I have to buy this, for the title."

She gave a little whistle, and the man it seemed to be meant for looked up from the table of books he had been staring at, near the back of the store. I had known he was there but had not connected him with her. I thought he was just one of those men who wander in off the street, alone, and stand looking about, as if trying to figure out what sort of place this is or what the books are for. Not a drunk or a panhandler, and certainly not anybody to be worried about—just one of a number of shabby, utterly uncommunicative old men who belong to the city somewhat as the pigeons do, moving restlessly all day within a limited area, never looking at people's faces. He was wearing a coat that came down to his ankles, made of some shiny, rubberized, liver-colored material, and a brown velvet cap with a tassel. The sort of cap a doddery old scholar or a clergyman might wear in an English movie. There was, then, a similarity between them—they were both wearing things that might have been discards from a costume box. But close up he looked years older than she. A long, yellowish face, drooping tobacco-brown eyes, an unsavory, straggling mustache. Some faint remains of handsomeness, or potency. A quenched ferocity. He came at her whistle—which seemed half serious, half a joke—and stood by, mute and self-respecting as a dog or a donkey, while the woman prepared to pay.

At that time, the government of British Columbia applied a sales tax to books. In this case it was four cents.

"I can't pay that," she said. "A tax on books. I think it is immoral. I would rather go to jail. Don't you agree?"

I agreed. I did not point out—as I would have done with anybody else—that the store would not be let off the hook on that account.

"Don't I sound appalling?" she said. "See what this government can do to people? It makes them into *orators*."

She put the book in her bag without paying the four cents, and never paid the tax on any future occasion.

I described the two of them to the Notary Public. He knew at once who I meant.

"I call them the Duchess and the Algerian," he said. "I don't know what the background is. I think maybe he's a retired terrorist. They go around the town with a wagon, like scavengers."

I got a note asking me to supper on a Sunday evening. It was signed *Charlotte*, without a surname, but the wording and handwriting were quite formal.

My husband Gjurdhi and I would be delighted—

Up until then I had not wished for any invitations of this sort and would have been embarrassed and disturbed to get one. So the pleasure I felt surprised me. Charlotte held out a decided promise; she was unlike the others whom I wanted to see only in the store.

The building where they lived was on Pandora Street. It was covered with mustard stucco and had a tiny, tiled vestibule that reminded me of a public toilet. It did not smell, though, and the apartment was not really dirty, just horrendously untidy. Books were stacked against the walls, and pieces of patterned cloth were hung up droopily to hide the wallpaper. There were bamboo blinds on the window, sheets of colored paper—surely flammable—pinned over the light bulbs.

"What a darling you are to come," cried Charlotte. "We were afraid you would have tons more interesting things to do than visiting ancient old us. Where can you sit down? What about here?" She took a pile of magazines off a wicker chair. "Is that comfortable? It makes such interesting noises, wicker. Sometimes I'll be sitting here alone and that chair will start creaking and cracking exactly as if someone were shifting around in it. I could say it was a presence, but I'm no good at believing in that rubbish. I've tried."

Gjurdhi poured out a sweet yellow wine. For me a long-stemmed glass that had not been dusted, for Charlotte a glass tumbler, for himself a plastic cup. It seemed impossible that any dinner could come out of the little kitchen alcove, where food-stuffs and pots and dishes were piled helter-skelter, but there was a good smell of roasting chicken, and in a little while Gjurdhi brought out the first course—platters of sliced cucumber, dishes of yogurt. I sat in the wicker chair and Charlotte in the single armchair. Gjurdhi sat on the floor. Charlotte was wearing her slacks, and a rose-colored T-shirt which clung to her unsupported breast. She had painted her toenails to match the T-shirt. Her bracelets clanked against the plate as she picked up the slices of cucumber. (We were eating with our fingers.) Gjurdhi wore his cap and a dark-red silky dressing gown over his trousers. Stains had mingled with its pattern.

After the cucumber, we ate chicken cooked with raisins in golden spices, and sour bread, and rice. Charlotte and I were provided with forks, but Gjurdhi scooped the rice up with the bread. I would often think of this meal in the years that followed, when this kind of food, this informal way of sitting and eating, and even some version of the style and the untidiness of the room, would become familiar and fashionable. The people I knew, and I myself, would give up—for a while—on dining-room tables, matching wineglasses, to some extent on cutlery or chairs. When I was being entertained, or making a stab at entertaining people, in this way, I would think of Charlotte and Gjurdhi and the edge of true privation, the risky authenticity that marked them off from all these later imitations. At the time, it was all new to me, and I was both uneasy and delighted. I hoped to be worthy of such exoticism but not to be tried too far.

Mary Shelley came to light shortly. I recited the titles of the later novels, and Charlotte said dreamily, "Per-kin War-beck. Wasn't he the one—wasn't he the one who pretended to be a little Prince who was murdered in the Tower?"

She was the only person I had ever met—not a historian, not a *Tudor* historian—who had known this.

"That would make a movie," she said. "Don't you think? The question I always think about Pretenders like that is who do *they* think they are? Do they believe it's true, or what? But Mary Shelley's own life is the movie, isn't it? I wonder there hasn't been one made. Who would play Mary, do you think? No. No, first of all, start with Harriet. Who would play Harriet?

"Someone who would look well drowned," she said, ripping off a golden chunk of chicken. "Elizabeth Taylor? Not a big enough part. Susannah York?

"Who was the father?" she wondered, referring to Harriet's unborn baby. "I don't think it was Shelley. I've never thought so. Do you?"

This was all very well, very enjoyable, but I had hoped we would get to explanations—personal revelations, if not exactly confidences. You did expect some of that, on occasions like this. Hadn't Sylvia, at my own table, told about the town in Northern Ontario and about Nelson's being the smartest person in the school? I was surprised at how eager I found myself, at last, to tell my story. Donald and Nelson—I was looking forward to telling the truth, or some of it, in all its wounding complexity, to a person who would not be surprised

or outraged by it. I would have liked to puzzle over my behavior, in good company. Had I taken on Donald as a father
figure—or as a parent figure, since both my parents were
dead? Had I deserted him because I was angry at *them* for de-
serting *me*? What did Nelson's silence mean, and was it now
permanent? (But I did not think, after all, that I would tell
anybody about the letter that had been returned to me last
week, marked "Not Known at This Address.")

This was not what Charlotte had in mind. There was no
opportunity, no exchange. After the chicken, the wineglass and
the tumbler and cup were taken away and filled with an ex-
tremely sweet pink sherbet that was easier to drink than to eat
with a spoon. Then came small cups of desperately strong coffee. Gjurdhi lit two candles as the room grew darker, and I
was given one of these to carry to the bathroom, which turned
out to be a toilet with a shower. Charlotte said the lights were
not working.

"Some repairs going on," she said. "Or else they have
taken a whim. I really think they take whims. But fortunately
we have our gas stove. As long as we have a gas stove we can
laugh at their whims. My only regret is that we cannot play
any music. I was going to play some old political songs—'I
dreamed I saw Joe Hill last night,' " she sang in a mocking
baritone. "Do you know that one?"

I did know it. Donald used to sing it when he was a little
drunk. Usually the people who sang "Joe Hill" had certain
vague but discernible political sympathies, but with Charlotte
I did not think this would be so. She would not operate from
sympathies, from principles. She would be playful about what
other people took seriously. I was not certain what I felt about
her. It was not simple liking or respect. It was more like a
wish to move in her element, unsurprised. To be buoyant,
self-mocking, gently malicious, unquenchable.

Gjurdhi, meanwhile, was showing me some of the books.

How had this started? Probably from a comment I made—
how many of them there were, something of that sort—when
I stumbled over some on my way back from the toilet. He
was bringing forward books with bindings of leather or imita-
tion leather—how could I know the difference?—with mar-
bled endpapers, watercolor frontispieces, steel engravings. At
first, I believed admiration might be all that was required, and
I admired everything. But close to my ear I heard the mention
of money—was that the first distinct thing I had ever heard
Gjurdhi say?

"I only handle new books," I said. "These are marvellous,
but I don't really know anything about them. It's a completely
different business, books like these."

Gjurdhi shook his head as if I had not understood and he
would now try, firmly, to explain again. He repeated the price
in a more insistent voice. Did he think I was trying to haggle
with him? Or perhaps he was telling me what he had paid for
the book? We might be having a speculative conversation
about the price it might be sold for—not about whether I
should buy it.

I kept saying no, and yes, trying to juggle these responses
appropriately. *No*, I cannot take them for my store. *Yes*, they
are very fine. *No*, truly, I'm sorry, I am not the one to judge.

"If we had been living in another country, Gjurdhi and I
might have done something," Charlotte was saying. "Or even
if the movies in this country had ever got off the ground.
That's what I would love to have done. Got work in the movies. As extras. Or maybe we are not bland enough types to be
extras, maybe they would have found bit parts for us. I believe
extras have to be the sort that don't stand out in a crowd, so
you can use them over and over again. Gjurdhi and I are
more memorable than that. Gjurdhi in particular—you could
use that face."

She paid no attention to the second conversation that had developed, but continued talking to me, shaking her head indulgently at Gjurdhi now and then, to suggest that he was behaving in a way she found engaging, though perhaps importunate. I had to talk to him softly, sideways, nodding all the while in response to her.

"Really you should take them to the Antiquarian Bookstore," I said. "Yes, they are quite beautiful. Books like these are out of my range."

Gjurdhi did not whine, his manner was not ingratiating. Peremptory, rather. It seemed as if he would give me orders, and would be most disgusted if I did not capitulate. In my confusion I helped myself to more of the yellow wine, pouring it into my unwashed sherbet glass. This was probably a dire offense. Gjurdhi looked horridly displeased.

"Can you imagine illustrations in modern novels?" said Charlotte, finally consenting to tie the two conversations together. "For instance, in Norman Mailer? They would have to be abstracts. Don't you think? Sort of barbed wire and blotches?"

I went home with a headache and a feeling of jangled inadequacy. I was a prude, that was all, when it came to mixing up buying and selling with hospitality. I had perhaps behaved clumsily, I had disappointed them. And they had disappointed me. Making me wonder why I had been asked.

I was homesick for Donald, because of "Joe Hill."

I also had a longing for Nelson, because of an expression on Charlotte's face as I was leaving. A savoring and contented look that I knew had to do with Gjurdhi, though I hardly wanted to believe that. It made me think that after I walked downstairs and left the building and went into the street, some hot and skinny, slithery, yellowish, indecent old beast, some mangy but urgent old tiger, was going to pounce among the books and the dirty dishes and conduct a familiar rampage.

A day or so later I got a letter from Donald. He wanted a divorce, so that he could marry Helen.

I hired a clerk, a college girl, to come in for a couple of hours in the afternoon, so I could get to the bank, and do some office work. The first time Charlotte saw her she went up to the desk and patted a stack of books sitting there, ready for quick sale.

"Is this what the office managers are telling their minions to buy?" she said. The girl smiled cautiously and didn't answer.

Charlotte was right. It was a book called *Psycho-Cybernetics*, about having a positive self-image.

"You were smart to hire her instead of me," Charlotte said. "She is much niftier-looking, and she won't shoot her mouth off and scare the customers away. She won't have *opinions*."

"There's something I ought to tell you about that woman," the clerk said, after Charlotte left.

That part is not of interest.

"What do you mean?" I said. But my mind had been wandering, that third afternoon in the hospital. Just at the last part of Charlotte's story I had thought of a special-order book that hadn't come in, on Mediterranean cruises. Also I had been thinking about the Notary Public, who had been beaten about the head the night before, in his office on Johnson Street. He was not dead but he might be blinded. Robbery? Or an act of revenge, outrage, connected with a layer of his life that I hadn't guessed at?

Melodrama and confusion made this place seem more ordinary to me, but less within my grasp.

"Of course it is of interest," I said. "All of it. It's a fascinating story."

"Fascinating," repeated Charlotte in a mincing way. She made a face, so she looked like a baby vomiting out a spoonful of pap. Her eyes, still fixed on me, seemed to be losing color, losing their childish, bright, and self-important blue. Fretfulness was changing into disgust. An expression of vicious disgust, she showed, of unspeakable weariness—such as people might show to the mirror but hardly ever to one another. Perhaps because of the thoughts that were already in my head, it occurred to me that Charlotte might die. She might die at any moment. At this moment. Now.

She motioned at the water glass, with its crooked plastic straw. I held the glass so that she could drink, and supported her head. I could feel the heat of her scalp, a throbbing at the base of her skull. She drank thirstily, and the terrible look left her face.

She said, "Stale."

"I think it would make an excellent movie," I said, easing her back onto the pillows. She grabbed my wrist, then let it go.

"Where did you get the idea?" I said.

"From life," said Charlotte indistinctly. "Wait a moment." She turned her head away, on the pillow, as if she had to arrange something in private. Then she recovered, and she told a little more.

Charlotte did not die. At least she did not die in the hospital. When I came in rather late, the next afternoon, her bed was empty and freshly made up. The nurse who had talked to me before was trying to take the temperature of the woman tied in the chair. She laughed at the look on my face.

"Oh, no!" she said. "Not that. She checked out of here this morning. Her husband came and got her. We were transfer-

ring her to a long-term place out in Saanich, and he was supposed to be taking her there. He said he had the taxi outside.
Then we get this phone call that they never showed up! They
were in great spirits when they left. He brought her a pile of
money, and she was throwing it up in the air. I don't know—
maybe it was only dollar bills. But we haven't a clue where
they've got to."

I walked around to the apartment building on Pandora
Street. I thought they might simply have gone home. They
might have lost the instructions about how to get to the nursing home and not wanted to ask. They might have decided to
stay together in their apartment no matter what. They might
have turned on the gas.

At first I could not find the building and thought that I
must be in the wrong block. But I remembered the corner
store and some of the houses. The building had been changed
—that was what had happened. The stucco had been painted
pink; large, new windows and French doors had been put in;
little balconies with wrought-iron railings had been attached.
The fancy balconies had been painted white, the whole place
had the air of an ice-cream parlor. No doubt it had been ren-
ovated inside as well, and the rents increased, so that people
like Charlotte and Gjurdhi could have no hope of living there.
I checked the names by the door, and of course theirs were
gone. They must have moved out some time ago.

The change in the apartment building seemed to have some
message for me. It was about vanishing. I knew that Charlotte
and Gjurdhi had not actually vanished—they were somewhere, living or dead. But for me they had vanished. And because of this fact—not really because of any loss of them—I
was tipped into dismay more menacing than any of the little
eddies of regret that had caught me in the past year. I had lost
my bearings. I had to get back to the store so my clerk could
go home, but I felt as if I could as easily walk another way,

just any way at all. My connection was in danger—that was all. Sometimes our connection is frayed, it is in danger, it seems almost lost. Views and streets deny knowledge of us, the air grows thin. Wouldn't we rather have a destiny to submit to, then, something that claims us, anything, instead of such flimsy choices, arbitrary days?

I let myself slip, then, into imagining a life with Nelson. If I had done so accurately, this is how it would have gone.

He comes to Victoria. But he does not like the idea of working in the store, serving the public. He gets a job teaching at a boys' school, a posh place where his look of lower-class toughness, his bruising manners, soon make him a favorite.

We move from the apartment at the Dardanelles to a roomy bungalow a few blocks from the sea. We marry.

But this is the beginning of a period of estrangement. I become pregnant. Nelson falls in love with the mother of a student. I fall in love with an intern I meet in the hospital during labor.

We get over all this—Nelson and I do. We have another child. We acquire friends, furniture, rituals. We go to too many parties at certain seasons of the year, and talk regularly about starting a new life, somewhere far away, where we don't know anybody.

We become distant, close—distant, close—over and over again.

As I entered the store, I was aware of a man standing near the door, half looking in the window, half looking up the street, then looking at me. He was a short man dressed in a trenchcoat and a fedora. I had the impression of someone disguised. Jokingly disguised. He moved toward me and bumped my shoulder, and I cried out as if I had received the shock of my life, and indeed it was true that I had. For this really was Nelson, come to claim me. Or at least to accost me, and see what would happen.

We have been very happy.
I have often felt completely alone.
There is always in this life something to discover.
The days and the years have gone by in some sort of blur.
On the whole, I am satisfied.

When Lottar was leaving the Bishop's courtyard, she was wrapped in a long cloak they had given her, perhaps to conceal her ragged clothing, or to contain her smell. The Consul's servant spoke to her in English, telling her where they were going. She could understand him but could not reply. It was not quite dark. She could still see the pale shapes of roses and oranges in the Bishop's garden.

The Bishop's man was holding the gate open.

She had never seen the Bishop at all. And she had not seen the Franciscan since he had followed the Bishop's man into the house. She called out for him now, as she was leaving. She had no name to call, so she called, *"Xoti! Xoti! Xoti,"* which means "leader" or "master" in the language of the Ghegs. But no answer came, and the Consul's servant swung his lantern impatiently, showing her the way to go. Its light fell by accident on the Franciscan standing half concealed by a tree. It was a little orange tree he stood behind. His face, pale as the oranges were in that light, looked out of the branches, all its swarthiness drained away. It was a wan face hanging in the tree, its melancholy expression quite impersonal and undemanding, like the expression you might see on the face of a devout but proud apostle in a church window. Then it was gone, taking the breath out of her body, as she knew too late.

She called him and called him, and when the boat came into the harbor at Trieste he was waiting on the dock.

OPEN
SECRETS

It was on a Saturday morning
Just as lovely as it could be
Seven girls and their Leader Miss Johnstone
Went camping from the C.G.I.T.

"And they almost didn't even go," Frances said. "Because of the downpour Saturday morning. They were waiting half an hour in the United Church basement and she says, Oh, it'll stop—my hikes are never rained out! And now I bet she wishes it had've been. Then it would've been a whole other story."

It did stop raining, they did go, and it got so hot partway out that Miss Johnstone let them stop at a farmhouse, and the woman brought out Coca-Colas and the man let them take the garden hose and spray themselves cool. They were grabbing the hose from each other and doing tricks, and Frances said that Mary Kaye said Heather Bell had been the worst one, the boldest, getting hold of the hose and shooting water on the rest of them in all the bad places.

"They will try to make out she was some poor innocent, but the facts are dead different," Frances said. "It could have been all an arrangement, that she arranged to meet somebody. I mean some man."

Maureen said, "I think that's pretty farfetched."

"Well, I don't believe she drowned," Frances said. "That I don't believe."

The Falls on the Peregrine River were nothing like the waterfalls you see pictures of. They were just water falling over limestone shelves, none of them more than six or seven feet high. There was a breathing spot where you could stand behind the hard-falling curtain of water, and all around in the limestone there were pools, smooth-rimmed and not much bigger than bathtubs, where the water lay trapped and warm. You would have to be very determined to drown in there. But they had looked there—the other girls had run around calling Heather's name and peering into all the pools, and they had even stuck their heads into the dry space behind the curtain of noisy water. They had skipped around on the bare rock and yelled and got themselves soaked, finally, plunging in and out through the curtain. Till Miss Johnstone shouted and made them come back.

> There was Betsy and Eva Trowell
> And Lucille Chambers as well
> There was Ginny Bos and Mary Kaye Trevelyan
> And Robin Sands and poor Heather Bell.

"Seven was all she could get," Frances said. "And every one of them, there was a reason. Robin Sands, doctor's daughter.

Lucille Chambers, minister's daughter. They can't get out of it. The Trowells—country. Glad to get in on anything. Ginny Bos, the double-jointed monkey—she's along for the swimming and the horsing around. Mary Kaye living next door to Miss Johnstone. Enough said. And Heather Bell new in town. *And* her mother away on the weekend herself—yes, she was taking the opportunity. Getting off on an expedition of her own."

It was about twenty-four hours since Heather Bell had disappeared, on the annual hike of the C.G.I.T.—which stood for Canadian Girls in Training—out to the Falls on the Peregrine River. Mary Johnstone, who was now in her early sixties, had been leading this hike for years, since before the war. There used to be at least a couple of dozen girls heading out the County Road on a Saturday morning in June. They would all be wearing navy-blue shorts and white blouses and red kerchiefs round their necks. Maureen had been one of them, twenty or so years ago.

Miss Johnstone always started them off singing the same thing.

> *For the Beauty of the Earth,*
> *For the Beauty of the Skies,*
> *For the Love that from our Birth*
> *Over and around us lies—*

And you could hear a hum of different words going along, cautiously but determinedly, under the hymn words.

> *For the sight of Miss Johnstone's bum,*
> *Waddling down the County Road.*
> *We are the morons singing this song—*
> *Doesn't she look just like a toad?*

Did anybody else Maureen's age remember these words now? The ones who had stayed in town were mothers—they had girls old enough to go on the hike, and older. They would get into the proper motherly kind of fit about rude language. Having children changed you. It gave you the necessary stake in being grown-up, so that certain parts of you—old parts— could be altogether eliminated and abandoned. Jobs, marriage didn't quite do it—just made you *act* as if you'd forgotten things.

Maureen had no children.

Maureen was sitting with Frances Wall, having coffee and cigarettes at the breakfast table that had been wedged into the old pantry, under the high, glass-fronted cupboards. This was Maureen's house in Carstairs, in 1965. She had been living in the house for eight years, but she still felt as if she got around it on fairly narrow tracks, from one spot where she felt at home to another. She had fixed up this corner so there was a place to eat other than the dining-room table, and she had put new chintz in the sunroom. It took a long time to work her husband around to changes. The front rooms were full of valuable, heavy furniture, made of oak and walnut, and the curtains were of green-and-mulberry brocade, as in a rich-looking hotel—you could not begin to alter anything there.

Frances worked for Maureen in the house, but she was not like a servant. They were cousins, though Frances was nearly a generation older. She had worked in this house long before Maureen came into it—she had worked for the first wife. Sometimes she called Maureen "Missus." It was a joke, half friendly and half not. How much did you give for those chops, Missus? Oh, they must have seen you coming! And she would tell Maureen she was getting broad in the beam and her hair did not suit her piled and sprayed like an upside-down mixing bowl. This though Frances herself was a dumpling sort of woman with gray hair like brambles all over her head, and a plain, impudent face. Maureen did not think of herself as timid—she had a stately look—and she was certainly not incompetent, having run her husband's law office before she "graduated" (as both she and he would say) to running his house. She sometimes thought she should try for more respect from Frances—but she needed somebody around the house to have spats and jokes with. She could not be a gossip, because of her husband's position, and she didn't think it was her nature, anyway, but she let Frances get away with plenty of mean remarks, and wild, uncharitable, confident speculations.

(For example, what Frances was saying about Heather Bell's mother, and what she said about Mary Johnstone and the hike in general. Frances thought she was an authority on that, because Mary Kaye Trevelyan was her granddaughter.)

Mary Johnstone was a woman you were hardly supposed to mention in Carstairs without attaching the word "wonderful." She had had polio and nearly died of it, at the age of thirteen or fourteen. She was left with short legs, a short, thick body, crooked shoulders, and a slightly twisted neck, which kept her big head a little tilted to one side. She had studied bookkeeping, she had got herself a job in the office at Douds Factory, and she had devoted her spare time to girls, often saying that she had never met a bad one, just some who were confused. Whenever Maureen met Mary Johnstone on the street or in a store, her heart sank. First came that searching smile, the eyes raking yours, the declared delight in any weather—wind or hail or sun or rain, each had something to recommend it—then the laughing question. *So what have you been up to, Mrs. Stephens?* Mary Johnstone always made a point of saying "Mrs. Stephens," but she said it as if it was a play title and she was thinking all the time, It's only Maureen Coulter. (Coulters

were just like the Trowells that Frances had remarked on—
country. No more, no less.) *What interesting things have you
been doing lately, Mrs. Stephens?*

Maureen felt then as if she was being put on the spot and
could do nothing about it, as if a challenge was being issued,
and it had something to do with her lucky marriage and her
tall healthy body, whose only misfortune was a hidden one—
her tubes had been tied to make her infertile—and her rosy
skin and auburn hair, and the clothes she spent a lot of money
and time on. As if she must owe Mary Johnstone something,
a never specified compensation. Or as if Mary Johnstone
could see more lacking than Maureen herself would face.

Frances didn't care for Mary Johnstone, either, in the pure
and simple way she didn't care for anybody who made too
much of themselves.

Miss Johnstone had taken them on a half-mile hike before
breakfast, as she always did, to climb the Rock—the chunk of
limestone that jutted out over the Peregrine River, and was so
rare a thing in that part of the country that it was not named
anything but the Rock. On Sunday morning you always had to
do that hike, dopey as you were from trying to stay awake all
night and half sick from smoking smuggled cigarettes. Shivering, too, because the sun wouldn't have reached deep into the
woods yet. The path hardly deserved to be called one—you
had to climb over rotted tree trunks and wade through ferns
and what Miss Johnstone pointed out as Mayapples and wild
geraniums, and wild ginger. She would pull it up and nibble it,
hardly brushing off the dirt. Look what nature provides us.

I forgot my sweater, Heather said when they were halfway
up. Can I go back and get it?

In the old days Miss Johnstone would probably have said
no. Get a move on and you'll warm up without it, she would

have said. She must have felt uneasy this time, because of the waning popularity of her hikes, which she blamed on television, working mothers, laxity in the home. She said yes.

Yes, but hurry. Hurry and catch up.

Which Heather Bell never did do. At the Rock they looked at the view (Maureen recalled looking around for French safes—did they still call them that?—among the beer bottles and candy wrappers), and Heather had not caught up. On the way back they didn't meet her. She wasn't in the big tent, or in the little tent, where Miss Johnstone had slept, or between the tents. She wasn't in any of the shelters or love nests among the cedars surrounding the campground. Miss Johnstone cut that searching short.

"Pancakes," she called. "Pancakes and coffee! See if the smell of pancakes and coffee won't smoke Miss Mischief out of hiding."

They had to sit and eat—after Miss Johnstone had said grace, thanking God for everything in the woods and at home—and as they ate, Miss Johnstone called out, "Yum-*my*!

"Doesn't the fresh air give us an appetite?" she said at the top of her voice. "Aren't these the best pancakes you ever did eat? Heather better hurry up or there won't be one left. Heather? Are you listening? Not one left!"

As soon as they were finished, Robin Sands asked if they could go now, could they go and look for Heather?

"Dishes first, my lady," Miss Johnstone said. "Even if you never do pick up a dishrag around home."

Robin nearly burst out crying. Nobody ever spoke to her like that.

After they had cleaned up, Miss Johnstone let them go, and that was when they went back to the Falls. But she brought them back soon enough and made them sit in a semicircle, wet as they were, and she herself sat cross-legged in front of them and called out that anybody listening was welcome to come and join them. "Anybody hiding round here and trying to play tricks is welcome! Come out now and no questions asked! Otherwise we will just have to get along without you!"

Then she launched into her talk, her Sunday-morning-of-the-hike sermon, without any qualms or worries. She kept going and going, asking a question every now and then, to make sure they were listening. The sun dried their shorts and Heather Bell did not come back. She did not appear out of the trees and still Miss Johnstone did not stop talking. She didn't let go of them until Mr. Trowell drove into the camp in his truck, bringing the ice cream for lunch.

She didn't give them permission then, but they broke loose anyway. They jumped up and ran for the truck. They all started telling him at once. Jupiter, the Trowell's dog, jumped over the tailgate, and Eva Trowell threw her arms about him and started to wail as if he had been the one lost.

Miss Johnstone got to her feet and came over and called out to Mr. Trowell above the girls' clamoring.

"One's taken it into her head to go missing!"

Now the search parties were out. Douds was closed, so that every man who wanted to go could go. Dogs had been added. There was talk of dragging the river downstream from the Falls.

When the constable went to tell Heather Bell's mother, he found her just back from her own weekend, wearing a backless sundress and high heels.

"Well, you better find her," she said. "That's your job."

She worked at the hospital—she was a nurse. "Either divorced or never was married in the first place," Frances said. "One for all and all for one, that's her."

Maureen's husband was calling her, and she hurried away to the sunroom. After his stroke two years ago, at the age of sixty-nine, he had given up his law practice, but he still had letters to write and a bit of business to do for old clients who could never get used to anybody else. Maureen typed out all his correspondence and helped him every day with what he called his chores.

"Whaur doing out there?" he said. His speech was sometimes slurred, so she had to stay around and interpret for people who did not know him well. Alone with her he made less effort, and his tone could be testy and complaining.

"Talking to Frances," said Maureen.

"Wha' bout?"

"This and that," she said.

"Yeah."

He stretched out the word gloomily, as if to say he well knew what their talk had been about and he did not care for it. Gossip, rumor, the coldhearted thrill of catastrophe. He never went in for much talk, now or in the days when he could talk readily—even his reproofs were brief, a matter of tone and implication. He seemed to call upon a body of belief, on rules known to all decent people and maybe to all people, even those who spent their lives falling short. He seemed to be a little pained, a little embarrassed for all concerned, when he had to do this, and at the same time formidable. His reproofs were extraordinarily effective.

People in Carstairs were just growing out of the habit of calling lawyers Lawyer So-and-So, just as you would always call a doctor by his title. They no longer referred to any of the younger lawyers as Lawyer, but they always called Maureen's husband Lawyer Stephens. Maureen herself often thought of him that way, though she called him Alvin. He dressed every day just as he used to dress to go to his office—in a three-piece gray or brown suit—and his clothes, though they cost enough money, never seemed to fit well or to smooth out his long, lumpy body. Nor did they ever seem to be free of a faint sifting of cigarette ashes, crumbs, maybe even flecks of shed skin. His head wagged downward, his face sagged with preoccupation, his expression was shrewd and absentminded—you could never be sure which. People liked that—they liked that he looked a little unkempt and at a loss and then could flash out with some fearsome detail. He knows the Law, they said. He doesn't have to look it up. He's got it all in his head. His stroke hadn't shaken their faith, and it really hadn't altered his appearance or his manner much, just accentuated what was already there.

Everyone believed he could have been a judge if he had played his cards right. He could have been a senator. But he was too honorable. He wouldn't kowtow. He was a man in a million.

Maureen sat down on the hassock near him to write shorthand. His name for her, in the office, had been the Jewel, because she was intelligent and dependable, in fact quite able to draw up documents and write letters on her own. Even in the household, his wife and the two children, Helena and Gordon, had used that name for her. The children still used it sometimes, though they were grown up and lived away. Helena used it affectionately and provocatively, Gordon with a solemn, self-congratulatory kindness. Helena was an unsettled single woman who came home seldom and got into arguments when she did. Gordon was a teacher at a military college, who liked to bring his wife and children back to Carstairs, making rather a display of the place, and of his father and Maureen, their backwater virtues.

Maureen could still enjoy being the Jewel. Or at least she found it comfortable. Part of her thoughts could slip off on their own. She was thinking now of the way the night's long adventure began, at camp, with Miss Johnstone's abdicating snores, and its objective—staying awake till dawn, and all the strategies and entertainments that were relied on to achieve that, though she had never heard that they were successful.

The girls played cards, they told jokes, they smoked cigarettes, and around midnight began the great games of Truth or Dare. Some Dares were: take off your pajama top and show your boobs; eat a cigarette butt; swallow dirt; stick your head in the water pail and try to count to a hundred; go and pee in front of Miss Johnstone's tent. Questions requiring Truth were: Do you hate your mother? Father? Sister? Brother? How many peckers have you seen and whose were they? Have you ever lied? Stolen? Touched anything dead? The sick and dizzy feeling of having smoked too many cigarettes too quickly came back to Maureen, also the smell of the smoke under the heavy canvas that had been soaking up the day's sun, the smell of girls who had swum for hours in the river and run and hidden in the reeds along the banks and had to burn leeches off their legs.

She remembered how noisy she had been then. A shrieker, a dare-taker. Just before she hit high school, a giddiness either genuine or faked or half-and-half became available to her. Soon it vanished, her bold body vanished inside this ample one, and she became a studious, shy girl, a blusher. She developed the qualities her husband would see and value when hiring and proposing.

I dare you to run away. Was it possible? There are times when girls are inspired, when they want the risks to go on and on. They want to be heroines, regardless. They want to take a joke beyond where anybody has ever taken it before. To be careless, dauntless, to create havoc—that was the lost hope of girls.

From the chintz-covered hassock at her husband's side she looked out at the old copper-beech trees, seeing behind them not the sunny lawn but the unruly trees along the river—the dense cedars and shiny-leaved oaks and glittery poplars. A ragged sort of wall with hidden doorways, and hidden paths behind it where animals went, and lone humans sometimes, becoming different from what they were outside, charged with different responsibilities, certainties, intentions. She could imagine vanishing. But of course you didn't vanish, and there was always the other person on a path to intersect yours and his head was full of plans for you even before you met.

When she went to the Post Office that afternoon to send off her husband's letters, Maureen heard two new reports. A light-haired young girl had been seen getting into a black car on the Bluewater Highway north of Walley at about one o'clock on Sunday afternoon. She might have been hitchhiking. Or waiting for just one car. That was twenty miles away from the Falls, and it would take about five hours to walk it, across the country. It could be done. Or she could have got a ride in another car.

But some people tidying up family graves in a forsaken country churchyard in the swampy northeastern corner of the country had heard a cry, a scream, in the middle of the afternoon. Who was that? they remembered saying to each other. Not *what* but *who. Who was that?* But later on they thought that it might have been a fox.

Also, the grass was beaten down in a spot close to the camp, and there were fresh cigarette butts lying around. But what did that prove—people were always out there. Lovers. Young boys planning mischief.

> *And maybe some man did meet her there*
> *That was carrying a gun or a knife*
> *He met her there and he didn't care*
> *He took that young girl's life.*
>
> *But some will say it wasn't that way*
> *That she met a stranger or a friend*
> *In a big black car she was carried far*
> *And nobody knows the end.*

• • •

On Tuesday morning, while Frances was getting breakfast and Maureen was helping her husband to finish dressing, there was a knock at the front door, by someone who did not notice or trust the bell. It was not unheard-of for people to drop by this early, but it made difficulties, because Lawyer Stephens was apt to have more trouble with his speech early in the morning, and his mind, too, took a little time to get warmed up.

Through the pebbled glass in the front door Maureen saw the blurry outlines of a man and a woman. Dressed up, at least the woman was—wearing a hat. That meant serious business. But serious business, to the people involved, might still seem humdrum to others. Death threats had been issued over the ownership of a chest of drawers, and a property owner could pop a blood vessel over a six-inch overlap of a driveway. Missing firewood, barking dogs, a nasty letter—all that could fire people up and bring them knocking. *Go and ask Lawyer Stephens. Go and ask about the Law.*

Of course there was a slim chance this pair might be peddling religion.

Not so.

"We've come to see the Lawyer," the woman said.

"Well," said Maureen. "It's early." She did not know who they were right away.

"Sorry, but we got something to tell him," the woman said, and somehow she had stepped into the front hall and Maureen had stepped backward. The man shook his head as if in discomfort or apology, indicating that he had no choice but to follow his wife.

The hall filled up with the smell of shaving soap, paste deodorant, and a cheap drugstore cologne. Lily of the Valley. And now Maureen recognized them.

It was Marian Hubbert. Only, she looked different in a blue

suit—which was too heavy for this weather—and her brown cloth gloves, and a brown hat made of feathers. Usually you saw her in town wearing slacks or even what looked like men's work pants. She was a husky woman of about Maureen's age— they had been in high school together, though a year or two apart. Marian's body was clumsy but quick, and her graying hair was cut short, so that bristles showed on her neck. She had a loud voice, most of the time a rather rambunctious manner. She was toned down now.

The man with her was the man she had married not so long ago. Maybe a couple of years ago. He was tall and boyish-looking, in a cheap, cream-colored jacket with too much padding in the shoulders. Wavy brown hair, fixed with a wet comb. "Excuse us," he said in a soft voice—perhaps one that his wife was not intended to hear—as Maureen took them into the dining room. Close up, his eyes were not so young—there was a look of strain and dryness, or bewilderment. Perhaps he was not very bright. Maureen remembered now some story about Marian's getting him from an advertisement. *Woman with farm, clear title. Businesswoman with farm*, it could have been, for Marian Hubbert's other name was the Corset Lady. For years and years she had sold made-to-measure corsets and perhaps she still did, to the dwindling number of ladies who wore them. Maureen imagined her taking measurements, prodding like a nurse, bossy and professionally insulting. But she had been kind to her old parents, who lived out on the farm until they were a great age and had any number of things wrong with them. And now another story surfaced, a less malicious one, about her husband. He had driven the bus that took old folks to their therapeutic swimming session, at Walley, in the indoor pool—that was how they had met. Maureen had another picture of him, too—carrying the old father in his arms, into Dr. Sands' office. Marian charging ahead, swinging her purse by its strap, ready to open the door.

She went to tell Frances about breakfast in the dining room, and to ask her to bring extra coffee cups. Then she went to warn her husband.

"It's Marian Hubbert, or she used to be," she said. "And whatever that man's name is that she's married to."

"Slater," her husband said, the way he would dryly bring forth the particulars of a sale or lease that you wouldn't have thought he could know so readily. "Theo."

"You're more up-to-date than I am," Maureen said.

He asked if his porridge was ready. "Eat and listen," he said.

Frances brought in the porridge, and he fell to at once. Slathered with cream and brown sugar, porridge was his favorite food, winter and summer.

When she brought the coffee, Frances tried to hang about, but Marian gave her a steady look that turned her back to the kitchen.

There, thought Maureen. She can manage better than I can.

Marian Hubbert was a woman without one visible advantage. She had a heavy face, a droop to the cheeks—she reminded Maureen of some sort of dog. Not necessarily an ugly dog. Not an ugly face, really. Just a heavy and determined one. But everywhere Marian went, as now in Maureen's dining room, she would present herself as if she had absolute rights. She had to be taken account of.

She had put on a quantity of makeup, and perhaps that was another reason Maureen hadn't immediately recognized her. It was pale and pinkish and unsuited to her olive skin, her black, heavy eyebrows. It made her look odd but not pathetic. It seemed she might have put it on, like the suit and hat, to demonstrate that she could get herself up the way other women did, she knew what was expected. But perhaps she intended to look pretty. Perhaps she saw herself transformed by the pale powder that was hanging on her cheeks, the thick pink lipstick—perhaps she turned when she finished and coyly showed herself to her husband. Answering for his wife in regard to sugar for her coffee, he almost giggled when he said *lumps*.

He said please and thank you as often as possible. He said, "Thank you very much, please. Thank you. The same for me. Thank you."

"Now, we didn't know anything about this girl until after it seems like everybody else knew," Marian was saying. "I mean, we didn't even know anybody was missing or anything. Not until yesterday when we came into town. Yesterday? Monday? Yesterday was Monday. I have got my days all mixed up, because I've been taking painkiller pills."

Marian was not the sort to tell you she had been taking pills and let it go at that. She would tell you what for.

"So I had a terrible big boil on my neck, right there?" She said. She scrunched her head around, trying to show them the dressing on it. "It was giving me pain and I started getting a headache, too, and I think it was something connected. So I was feeling so bad on Sunday I just took a hot cloth and put it to my neck and I swallowed a couple of painkillers and I went and laid down. He was off work that day, but now he's working he's always got lots to do when he's home. He's working at the Atomic Energy."

"Douglas Point?" said Lawyer Stephens, with a brief look up from his porridge. There was a certain interest or respect all men showed—even Lawyer Stephens had to show it—at the mention of the new Atomic Energy Station at Douglas Point.

"That's where he works now," Marian said. Like many country women and Carstairs women, too, she referred to her husband as *he*—it was spoken with a special emphasis—rather than calling him by his name. Maureen had caught herself doing it a few times, but had corrected the habit without any-body's having to point it out to her.

"He had to take the salt out for the cows," Marian said, "and then he went back and worked on the fence. He had to go quarter of a mile, maybe, so he took the truck. But he left Bounder. He went off in the truck without him. Bounder our dog. Bounder won't go any distance unless that he can ride. He left him on guard sort of because he knew I had went and laid down. I had taken a couple of 222s, and I went into a kind of doze more than a regular sleep, and then I heard Bounder barking. It woke me right up. Bounder barking."

She got up then, and she put on her wrapper and went down-stairs. She had been lying down just in her underclothing. She looked out the front door, out the lane, and there was nobody. She didn't see Bounder, either, and by that time he had quit his barking. He quit when it was somebody he recognized. Or somebody just going by on the road. But still she wasn't sat-isfied. She looked out the kitchen windows, which gave on the side yard but not the back. Still nobody. She couldn't see the backyard from the kitchen—to do that, you had to go right out through what they called the back kitchen. It was just a sort of catchall room, like a shed tacked onto the house, all jumbled up with everything. It had a window looking out back, but you couldn't get near that or see out of it because of cardboard boxes piled up and the old couch springs stand-ing on end. You had to go right and open the back door to see out. And now she thought she could hear something at that door like a kind of clawing. Maybe Bounder. Maybe not.

It was so hot in that shut-up back kitchen packed with junk that she could barely breathe. Under her wrapper she was all sticky with sweat. She said to herself, Well, at least you haven't got a fever, you are sweating like a pig.

She was more interested in getting air to breathe than she was scared of what might be out there, so she thrust the door open. It opened outward, pushing the fellow back that was up against it. He staggered back but didn't fall. And she saw who it was. Mr. Siddicup, from town.

Bounder knew him, of course, because he often went by and sometimes cut across the property on his walks and they never stopped him. He came right through the yard, sometimes—it was just because he didn't know any better anymore. She never yelled at him, the way some people did. She had even invited him to sit on the steps and rest if he was tired, she had offered him a cigarette. He would take the cigarette, too. But he would never sit down.

Bounder was just nosing around and fawning on him. Bounder was not particular.

Maureen knew Mr. Siddicup, as everybody did. He used to be the piano tuner at Douds. He used to be a dignified, sarcastic little Englishman, with a pleasant wife. They read books from the library and were noted for their garden, especially strawberries and roses. Then, a few years ago, misfortunes started arriving. Mr. Siddicup had an operation on his throat—it must have been for cancer—and after that he could not talk, just make wheezing and growling noises. He had already retired from Douds—they had some electronic way of tuning pianos now, better than the human ear. His wife died suddenly. Then the changes came in a hurry—he deteriorated from a decent old man into a morose and rather disgusting old urchin, in a matter of months. Dirty whiskers, dribbles on his clothes, a sour smoky smell, and a look in his eyes of constant suspicion, sometimes of loathing. In the grocery store if he could not find what he wanted, or if they had changed the places of things, he would knock canned goods and boxes of cereal over on purpose. He was not welcome anymore in the café, and never went near the library. Women from his wife's church group kept going to see him for a while, bringing a meat dish or some baking. But the smell of the house was dreadful and the disorder perverse—even for a man living alone it was inexcusable—and he was the opposite of grateful. He would toss the remainders of pies and casseroles out on his front walk, breaking the dishes. No woman wanted the joke going round that even Mr. Siddicup wouldn't eat her cooking. So they left him alone. Or when you were driving along, you might spot him standing still, standing in the ditch, mostly hidden in tall weeds and grass, while cars whizzed by him. You could also run into him in a town miles away from home, and there a strange thing would happen. His face would take on something of its old expression, ready for the genial obligatory surprise, the greeting of people who lived in one place meeting in another. It did look as if he had a hope then that the moment would open out, that words would break through, in fact that perhaps the changes would be wiped out, here in a different place—his voice and his wife and his old stability in life might all be returned to him.

People were not unkind, usually. They were patient up to a point. Marian said she would never have chased him off.

She said he looked pretty wild, this time. Not just as he looked when he was trying to get his meaning out and it would not come, or when he was mad at some kids who were teasing him. His head was bobbing back and forth and his face looked swollen up, like a bawling baby's.

Now then, she said. Now, Mr. Siddicup, what's the matter? What are you trying to tell me? Do you want a cigarette? Are you telling me it's Sunday and you're all out of cigarettes?

Shook his head back and forth, then bobbed it up and down, then shook it back and forth again.

Come on, now. Make up your mind, said Marian.

Ah, ahh was all he said. He put both hands to his head, knocking off his cap. Then he backed farther off and started zigzagging around the yard in between the pump and the clothesline, still making these noises—*ah, ahh*—that would never turn into words.

Here Marian pushed back her chair so abruptly that it almost fell over. She got up and began to show them just what Mr. Siddicup had done. She lurched and crouched and banged her hands to her head, though she did not dislodge her hat. In front of the sideboard, in front of the silver tea service presented to Lawyer Stephens in appreciation of his many years' work for the Law Society, she put on this display. Her husband held his coffee cup in both hands and kept his deferential eyes on her by an effort of will. Something flashed in his face—a tic, a nerve jumping in one cheek. She was watching him in spite of her antics, and her look said, Hold on. Be still.

Lawyer Stephens, as far as Maureen could see, had not glanced up at all.

He did like that, Marian said, reseating herself. He did like that, and because she had not been feeling well herself, she got the idea that perhaps he was in pain.

Mr. Siddicup. Mr. Siddicup. Are you trying to tell me your head hurts? Do you want me to get you a pill? Do you want me to take you to the doctor?

No answer. He wouldn't stop for her. *Ah, ahh.*

In his stumbling around he found himself at the pump. They had running water in the house now, but still used the pump outside and filled Bounder's dish at it. When Mr. Siddicup took note of what it was, he got busy. He went to work on the handle and pumped it up and down like crazy. There wasn't any cup to drink from, like there used to be. But as soon as water came he stuck his head under. It splashed and stopped, because he had quit pumping. Back he went and pumped again, and stuck himself under again, and on like that, pumping and dousing, letting it pour over his head and face and shoulders and chest, soaking himself and still, when he could, making some noise. Bounder was excited and ran around bumping into him and letting out barks and whines in sympathy.

That's enough, you two! Marian yelled at them. Let go that pump! Let go and settle down!

Only Bounder listened to her. Mr. Siddicup had to keep on till he got himself so drenched and blinded he couldn't find the pump handle. Then he stopped. And he lifted one arm up, he lifted and pointed, back in the general direction of the bush and the river. He was pointing and making his noises. At the time, that didn't make any sense to her. She didn't think about it till later. Then he quit that and just sat down on the well cover, soaked and shivering, with his head in his hands.

Maybe it's something simple after all, she thought. Complaining because there isn't a cup.

If it's a cup you want, I'll go and get you one. No need to carry on like a baby. You stay there, I'll go and get you a cup.

She headed back to the kitchen and got a cup. And she had another idea. She fixed him up some graham crackers, with butter and jam. That was a kid's treat, graham crackers, but it was a thing old people liked, too, she remembered from her mother and daddy.

Back to the door she went and pushed it open with her hands full. But there was no sign of him. Nobody in the yard but Bounder, looking the way he did when he knew he'd made a fool of himself.

Where did he go, Bounder? Which way did he go?

Bounder was ashamed and fed up and wouldn't give any sign. He slunk off to his place in the house shade, in the dirt, by the foundations.

Mr. Siddicup! Mr. Siddicup! Come see what I got for you!

All silent as the dead. And her head was pounding. She

started eating the crackers herself but she shouldn't have—a couple of bites and she wanted to puke.

She took two more pills and went back upstairs. The windows up and blinds down. She wished now they'd bought a fan when the sale was on at Canadian Tire. But she slept without one, and when she woke it was nearly dark. She could hear the mower—*he*, her husband, was out finishing the grass at the side of the house. She went down to the kitchen and saw that he had cut up some cold potatoes and boiled an egg and pulled green onions to make a salad. He was not like some men—a hopeless case in the kitchen waiting for the woman to get out of a sickbed and make him a meal. She picked at the salad but couldn't eat. One more pill and up the stairs and dead to the world till morning.

We better get you to the doctor, he said then. He phoned them up at work. I got to take my wife to the doctor.

Marian said, What if she just boiled a needle and he could lance it? But he could not stand to hurt her, and anyway he was afraid he might do something wrong. So they got in the truck and drove in to see Dr. Sands. Dr. Sands was out, they had to wait. Other people waiting told them the news. Everybody was amazed they didn't know. But they hadn't had the radio on. She was the one who always turned it on and she couldn't stand the noise, the way she felt. And they hadn't noticed any groups of men, anything peculiar, on the road.

Dr. Sands fixed the boil but he didn't lance it. His way of dealing with a boil was to strike it a sharp blow, knock it on the head, when you thought he was just looking at it. There! he said, that's less fuss than the needle and not so painful overall because you didn't have time to get in a sweat. He cleaned it out and put the dressing on and said she'd soon be feeling better.

And so she was, but sleepy. She was so useless and foggy in the head that she went back to bed and slept till her husband came up around four o'clock with a cup of tea. It was then she thought of those girls, coming in with Miss Johnstone on Saturday morning, wanting a drink. She had lots of Coca-Cola and she gave it to them in flowered glasses, with ice cubes. Miss Johnstone would only take water. *He* let them play with the hose, they jumped around and squirted each other and had a great time. They were trying to skip the streams of water, and they were a bit on the wild side when Miss Johnstone wasn't looking. He had to practically wrestle the hose away from them, and give them a few squirts of water to make them behave.

She was trying to picture which girl it was. She knew the minister's daughter and Dr. Sands' daughter and the Trowells—with their little sheep eyes you would know a Trowell anywhere. But which of the others? She recalled one who was very noisy and jumping up trying to get the hose even when he took it away, and one was doing cartwheels and one was a skinny pretty little thing with blond hair. But maybe she was thinking of Robin Sands—Robin had blond hair. She asked her husband that night did he know which one, but he was worse than she was—he didn't know people here and couldn't separate out any of them.

Also she told him about Mr. Siddicup. It all came back to her now. The way he was upset, the pumping, the way he pointed. It bothered her what that could mean. They talked about it and wondered about it and got themselves into a state of wondering so they hardly got any sleep. Until she finally said to him, Well, I know what we have to do. We have to go and talk to Lawyer Stephens.

So they got up and came as soon as they could.

"Police," said Lawyer Stephens now. "Police. Who should gone to see."

The husband spoke. He said, "We didn't know if we should ought to do that or not." He had both hands on the table, fingers spread, pressed down, pulling at the cloth.

"Not accusation." Lawyer Stephens said. "Information."

He had talked in that abbreviated way even before his stroke. And Maureen had noticed, long ago, how just a few words of his, spoken in no very friendly tone—spoken, in fact, in a tone of brusque chastisement—could cheer people up and lift a weight off them.

She had been thinking of the other reason why the women stopped going to visit Mr. Siddicup. They didn't like the clothes. Women's clothes, underwear—old frayed slips and brassières and worn-out underpants and nubbly stockings, hanging from the backs of chairs or from a line above the heater, or just in a heap on the table. All these things must have belonged to his wife, of course, and at first it looked as if he might be washing and drying them and sorting them out, prior to getting rid of them. But they were there week after week, and the women started to wonder: Did he leave them lying around to suggest things? Did he put them on himself next to his skin? Was he a pervert?

Now all that would come out, they'd chalk that up against him.

Pervert. Maybe they were right. Maybe he would lead them to where he'd strangled or beat Heather to death in a sexual fit, or they would find something of hers in his house. And people would say in horrid, hushed voices that no, they weren't surprised. *I wasn't surprised, were you?*

Lawyer Stephens had asked some question about the job at Douglas Point, and Marian said, "He works in Maintenance. Every day when he comes out he's got to go through the check for X-rays, and even the rags he cleans off his boots with, they have to be buried underground."

When Maureen shut the door on the pair of them and saw

their shapes wobble away through the pebbled glass, she was not quite satisfied. She climbed three steps to the landing on the stairs, where there was a little arched window. She watched them.

No car was in sight, or truck or whatever they had. They must have left it parked on the main street or in the lot behind the Town Hall. Possibly they did not want it to be seen in front of Lawyer Stephens' house.

The Town Hall was where the Police Office was. They did turn in that direction, but then they crossed the street diagonally and, still within Maureen's sight, they sat down on the low stone wall that ran around the old cemetery and flower plot called Pioneer Park.

Why should they feel a need to sit down after sitting in the dining room for what must have been at least an hour? They didn't talk, or look at each other, but seemed united, as if taking a rest in the midst of hard shared labors.

Lawyer Stephens, when in a reminiscing mood, would talk about how people used to rest on that wall. Farm women who had to walk into town to sell chickens or butter. Country girls on their way to high school, before there was any such thing as a school bus. They would stop and hide their galoshes and retrieve them on the way home.

At other times he had no patience with reminiscing.

"Olden times. Who wants 'em back?"

Now Marian took out some pins and carefully lifted off her hat. So that was it—her hat was hurting her. She set it in her lap, and her husband reached over. He took it away, as if anxious to take away anything that might be a burden to her. He settled it in his lap. He bent over and started to stroke it, in a comforting way. He stroked that hat made of horrible brown feathers as if he were pacifying a little scared hen.

But Marian stopped him. She said something to him, she clamped a hand down on his. The way a mother might inter-

rupt the carrying-on of a simple-minded child—with a burst
of abhorrence, a moment's break in her tired-out love.

Maureen felt a shock. She felt a shrinking in her bones.

Her husband came out of the dining room. She didn't want
him to catch her looking at them. She turned around the vase
of dried grasses that was on the window ledge. She said, "I
thought she'd never get done talking."

He hadn't noticed. His mind was on something else.

"Come on down here," he said.

Early in their marriage Maureen's husband had mentioned
to her that he and the first Mrs. Stephens gave up sleeping together after Helena, the younger child, was born. "We'd got
our boy and our girl," he said, meaning there was no need to
try for more. Maureen did not understand then that he might
intend some similar cutoff for her. She was in love when she
married him. It was true that when he first put his arm around
her waist, in the office, she thought he must believe that she
was headed for the wrong door and was redirecting her—but
that was a conclusion she came to because of his propriety, not
because she hadn't longed to feel his arm there. People who
thought she was making an advantageous, though kindly, marriage, would have been amazed at how happy she was on her
honeymoon—and that was in spite of having to learn to play
bridge. She knew his power—the way he used it and the way
he held it back. He was attractive to her—never mind his age,
ungainliness, nicotine stains on his teeth and fingers. His skin
was warm. A couple of years into the marriage she miscarried
and bled so heavily that her tubes had been tied, to prevent
such a thing from ever happening again. After that the intimate part of her life with her husband came to an end. It
seemed that he had been mostly obliging her, because he felt

that it was wrong to deny a woman the chance to have a child.

Sometimes she would pester him a little and he would say, "Now, Maureen. What's all this about?" Or else he would tell her to grow up. "Grow up" was an injunction that he had picked up from his own children, and had continued to use long after they had dropped it, in fact long after they had moved away from home.

His saying that humiliated her, and her eyes would fill with tears. He was a man who detested tears above all things.

And now, she thought, wouldn't it be a relief to have that state of affairs back again! For her husband's appetite had returned—or an entirely new appetite had developed. There was nothing now of the rather clumsy ceremony, the formal fondness, of their early times together. Now his eyes would cloud over and his face would seem weighed down. He would speak to her in a curt and menacing way and sometimes push and prod her, even trying to jam his fingers into her from behind. She did not need any of that to make her hurry—she was anxious to get him into the bedroom as soon as possible, afraid that he might misbehave elsewhere. His old office had been made into a downstairs bedroom with a bathroom adjoining it, so that he would not have to climb the stairs. At least that room had a lock, so Frances could not burst in. But the phone might ring, Frances might have to come looking for them. She might stand outside the door and then she would have to hear the noises—Lawyer Stephens' panting and grunting and bullying, the hiss of disgust with which he would order Maureen to do this or that, his pounding of her right at the end and the command he let out then, a command that perhaps would be incoherent to anybody but Maureen but that would still speak eloquently, like lavatory noises, of his extremity.

"Ta' dirty! Ta' dirty!"

This came from a man who had once shut Helena in her room for calling her brother a shitty bastard.

Maureen knew enough words, but it was difficult for her in her shaken state to call up just which ones might suit, and to utter them in a tone that would be convincing. She did try. She wanted above all else to help him along.

Afterward he fell into the brief sleep that seemed to erase the episode from his memory. Maureen escaped to the bathroom. She did the first cleanup there and then hurried upstairs to replace some clothing. Often at these times she had to hang onto the bannisters, she felt so hollow and feeble. And she had to keep her mouth closed not on any howls of protest but on a long sickening whimper of complaint that would have made her sound like a beaten dog.

Today she managed better than usual. She was able to look into the bathroom mirror, and move her eyebrows, her lips and jaws, around to bring her expression back to normal. So much for that, she seemed to be saying. Even while it was going on she had been able to think of other things. She had thought about making a custard, she thought about whether they had enough milk and eggs. And right through her husband's rampage she thought of the fingers moving in the feathers, the wife's hand laid on top of the husband's, pressing down.

> So of Heather Bell we will sing our song,
> As we will till our day is done.
> In the forest green she was taken from the scene
> Though her life had barely begun.

"There is a poem already made up and written down," Frances said. "I've got it here typed out."

"I thought I'd make a custard," said Maureen.

How much had Frances heard of what Marian Hubbert had said? Everything, probably. She sounded breathless with the effort of keeping all that in. She held up the typed lines in front of Maureen's face and Maureen said, "It's too long, I don't have time." She started to separate the eggs.

"It's good," Frances said. "It's good enough to be put to music."

She read it through aloud. Maureen said, "I have to concentrate."

"So I guess I got my marching orders," said Frances, and went to do the sunroom.

Then Maureen had the peace of the kitchen—the old white tiles and high yellowed walls, the bowls and pots and implements familiar and comforting to her, as probably to her predecessor.

What Mary Johnstone told the girls in her talk was always more or less the same thing and most of them knew what to expect. They could even make prepared faces at each other. She told them how Jesus had come and talked to her when she was in the iron lung. She did not mean in a dream, she said, or in a vision, or when she was delirious. She meant that He came and she recognized Him but didn't think anything was strange about it. She recognized Him at once, though he was dressed like a doctor in a white coat. She thought, Well, that's reasonable—otherwise they wouldn't let Him in here. That was how she took it. Lying there in the iron lung, she was sensible and stupid at once, as you are when something like that hits you. (She meant Jesus, not the polio.) Jesus said, "You've got to get back up to bat, Mary." That was all. She was a good softball player, and He used language that He knew she would understand. Then He went away. And she hugged onto Life, the way He had told her to.

There was more to follow, about the uniqueness and specialness of each of their lives and their bodies, which led of course into what Mary Johnstone called "plain talk" about boys and urges. (This was where they did the faces—they were too abashed when she was going on about Jesus.) And about liquor and cigarettes and how one thing can lead to another. They thought she was crazy—and she couldn't even tell that they had smoked themselves half sick last night. They reeked and she never mentioned it.

So she was—crazy. But everybody let her talk about Jesus in the hospital because they thought she was entitled to believe that.

But suppose you did see something? Not along the line of Jesus, but something? Maureen has had that happen. Sometimes when she is just going to sleep but not quite asleep, not dreaming yet, she has caught something. Or even in the daytime during what she thinks of as her normal life. She might catch herself sitting on stone steps eating cherries and watching a man coming up the steps carrying a parcel. She has never seen those steps or that man, but for an instant they seem to be part of another life that she is leading, a life just as long and complicated and strange and dull as this one. And she isn't surprised. It's just a fluke, a speedily corrected error, that she knows about both lives at the same time. It seemed so ordinary, she thinks afterward. The cherries. The parcel.

What she sees now isn't in any life of her own. She sees one of those thick-fingered hands that pressed into her tablecloth and that had worked among the feathers, and it is pressed down, unresistingly, but by somebody else's will—it is pressed down on the open burner of the stove where she is stirring the custard in the double boiler, and held there just for a second or two, just long enough to scorch the flesh on the red coil, to scorch but not to maim. In silence this is done, and by agreement—a brief and barbaric and necessary act. So it seems. The punished hand dark as a glove or a hand's shadow, the fingers spread. Still in the same clothes. The cream-colored sleeve, the dull blue.

Maureen hears her husband moving around in the front hall, so she turns off the heat and lays down the spoon and goes in to him. He has tidied himself up. He is ready to go out. She knows without asking where he is going. Down to the Police Office, to find out what has been reported, what is being done.

"Maybe I should drive you," she says. "It's hot out."

He shakes his head, he mutters.

"Or I could walk along with you."

No. He is going on a serious errand and it would diminish him to be accompanied or transported by a wife.

She opens the front door for him and he says, "Thank you," in his stiff, quaintly repentant way. As he goes past, he bends and purses his lips at the air close to her cheek.

They've gone, there's nobody sitting on the wall now.

Heather Bell will not be found. No body, no trace. She has blown away like ashes. Her displayed photograph will fade in public places. Its tight-lipped smile, bitten in at one corner as if suppressing a disrespectful laugh, will seem to be connected with her disappearance rather than her mockery of the school photographer. There will always be a tiny suggestion, in that, of her own free will.

Mr. Siddicup will not be any help. He will alternate between bewilderment and tantrums. They will not find anything when they search his house, unless you count those old underclothes of his wife's, and when they dig up his garden the only bones they will find will be old bones that dogs have buried. Many people will continue to believe that he did something or saw something. *He had something to do with it.* When he is committed to the Provincial Asylum, renamed the Mental Health Centre, there will be letters in the local paper about Preventive Custody, and locking the stable door after the horse is stolen.

There will also be letters in the newspaper from Mary Johnstone, explaining why she behaved as she did, why in all good sense and good faith she behaved as she did that Sunday. Finally the editor will have to let her know that Heather Bell is old news, and not the only thing the town wants to be known for, and if the hikes are to come to an end it won't be the worst thing in the world, and the story can't be rehashed forever.

Maureen is a young woman yet, though she doesn't think so, and she has life ahead of her. First a death—that will come soon—then another marriage, new places and houses. In kitchens hundreds and thousands of miles away, she'll watch the soft skin form on the back of a wooden spoon and her memory will twitch, but it will not quite reveal to her this moment when she seems to be looking into an open secret, something not startling until you think of trying to tell it.

THE
JACK
RANDA
HOTEL

On the runway, in Honolulu, the plane loses speed, loses
heart, falters and veers onto the grass, and bumps to a stop. A
few yards it seems from the ocean. Inside, everybody laughs.
First a hush, then the laugh. Gail laughed herself. Then there
was a flurry of introductions all around. Beside Gail are Larry
and Phyllis, from Spokane.

Larry and Phyllis are going to a tournament of Left-handed
Golfers, in Fiji, as are many other couples on this plane. It is
Larry who is the left-handed golfer—Phyllis is the wife going
along to watch and cheer and have fun.

They sit on the plane—Gail and the Left-handed Golfers—
and lunch is served in picnic boxes. No drinks. Dreadful heat.
Jokey and confusing announcements are made from the cock-
pit. *Sorry about the problem. Nothing serious but it looks like it
will keep us stewing here a while longer.* Phyllis has a terrible

headache, which Larry tries to cure by applying finger-pressure to points on her wrist and palm.

"It's not working," Phyllis says. "I could have been in New Orleans by now with Suzy."

Larry says, "Poor lamb."

Gail catches the fierce glitter of diamond rings as Phyllis pulls her hand away. Wives have diamond rings and headaches, Gail thinks. They still do. The truly successful ones do. They have chubby husbands, left-handed golfers, bent on a lifelong course of appeasement.

Eventually the passengers who are not going to Fiji, but on to Sydney, are taken off the plane. They are led into the terminal and there deserted by their airline guide they wander about, retrieving their baggage and going through customs, trying to locate the airline that is supposed to honor their tickets. At one point, they are accosted by a welcoming committee from one of the Island's hotels, who will not stop singing Hawaiian songs and flinging garlands around their necks. But they find themselves on another plane at last. They eat and drink and sleep and the lines to the toilets lengthen and the aisles fill up with debris and the flight attendants hide in their cubbyholes chatting about children and boyfriends. Then comes the unsettling bright morning and the yellow-sanded coast of Australia far below, and the wrong time of day, and even the best-dressed, best-looking passengers are haggard and unwilling, torpid, as from a long trip in steerage. And before they can leave the plane there is one more assault. Hairy men in shorts swarm aboard and spray everything with insecticide.

"So maybe this is the way it will be getting into Heaven," Gail imagines herself saying to Will. "People will fling flowers on you that you don't want, and everybody will have headaches and be constipated and then you will have to be sprayed for Earth germs."

Her old habit, trying to think up clever and lighthearted things to say to Will.

• • •

After Will went away, it seemed to Gail that her shop was filling up with women. Not necessarily buying clothes. She didn't mind this. It was like the long-ago days, before Will. Women were sitting around in ancient armchairs beside Gail's ironing board and cutting table, behind the faded batik curtains, drinking coffee. Gail started grinding the coffee beans herself, as she used to do. The dressmaker's dummy was soon draped with beads and had a scattering of scandalous graffiti. Stories were told about men, usually about men who had left. Lies and injustices and confrontations. Betrayals so horrific—yet so trite—that you could only rock with laughter when you heard them. Men made fatuous speeches *(I am sorry, but I no longer feel committed to this marriage).* They offered to sell back to the wives cars and furniture that the wives themselves had paid for. They capered about in self-satisfaction because they had managed to impregnate some dewy dollop of womanhood younger than their own children. They were fiendish and childish. What could you do but give up on them? In all honor, in pride, and for your own protection?

Gail's enjoyment of all this palled rather quickly. Too much coffee could make your skin look livery. An underground quarrel developed among the women when it turned out that one of them had placed an ad in the Personal Column. Gail shifted from coffee with friends to drinks with Cleata, Will's mother. As she did this, oddly enough her spirits grew more sober. Some giddiness still showed in the notes she pinned to her door so that she could get away early on summer afternoons. (Her clerk, Donalda, was on her holidays, and it was too much trouble to hire anybody else.)

Gone to the Opera.
Gone to the Funny Farm.
Gone to stock up on the Sackcloth and Ashes.

Actually these were not her own inventions, but things Will used to write out and tape on her door in the early days when they wanted to go upstairs. She heard that such flippancy was not appreciated by people who had driven some distance to buy a dress for a wedding, or girls on an expedition to buy clothes for college. She did not care.

On Cleata's veranda Gail was soothed, she became vaguely hopeful. Like most serious drinkers, Cleata stuck to one drink—hers was Scotch—and seemed amused by variations. But she would make Gail a gin and tonic, a white rum and soda. She introduced her to tequila. "This is Heaven," Gail sometimes said, meaning not just the drink but the screened veranda and hedged back yard, the old house behind them with its shuttered windows, varnished floors, inconveniently high kitchen cupboards, and out-of-date flowered curtains. (Cleata despised decorating.) This was the house where Will, and Cleata too, had been born, and when Will first brought Gail into it, she had thought, This is how really civilized people live. The carelessness and propriety combined, the respect for old books and old dishes. The absurd things that Will and Cleata thought it natural to talk about. And the things she and Cleata didn't talk about—Will's present defection, the illness that has made Cleata's arms and legs look like varnished twigs within their deep tan, and has hollowed the cheeks framed by her looped-back white hair. She and Will have the same slightly monkeyish face, with dreamy, mocking dark eyes.

Instead, Cleata talked about the book she was reading, *The Anglo-Saxon Chronicle*. She said that the reason the Dark Ages were dark was not that we couldn't learn anything about them but that we could not remember anything we did learn, and that was because of the names.

"Caedwalla," she said. "Egfrith. These are just not names on the tip of your tongue anymore."

Gail was trying to remember which ages, or centuries, were

dark. But her ignorance didn't embarrass her. Cleata was making fun of all that, anyway.

"Aelfflaed," said Cleata, and spelled it out. "What kind of a heroine is Aelfflaed?"

When Cleata wrote to Will, she probably wrote about Aelfflaed and Egfrith. Not about Gail. Not *Gail was here looking very pretty in some kind of silky gray summer-pajamas outfit. She was in good form, made various witty remarks. . . .* No more than she would say to Gail, "I have my doubts about the lovebirds. Reading between the lines, I can't help wondering if disillusionment isn't setting in. . . ."

When she met Will and Cleata, Gail thought they were like characters in a book. A son living with his mother, apparently contentedly, into middle age. Gail saw a life that was ceremonious and absurd and enviable, with at least the appearance of celibate grace and safety. She still sees some of that, though the truth is Will has not always lived at home, and he is neither celibate nor discreetly homosexual. He had been gone for years, into his own life—working for the National Film Board and the Canadian Broadcasting Corporation—and had given that up only recently, to come back to Walley and be a teacher. What made him give it up? This and that, he said. Machiavellis here and there. Empire-building. Exhaustion.

Gail came to Walley one summer in the seventies. The boyfriend she was with then was a boatbuilder, and she sold clothes that she made—capes with appliqués, shirts with billowing sleeves, long bright skirts. She got space in the back of the craft shop, when winter came on. She learned about importing ponchos and thick socks from Bolivia and Guatemala. She found local women to knit sweaters. One day Will stopped her on the street and asked her to help him with the costumes for the play he was putting on—*The Skin of Our Teeth*. Her boyfriend moved to Vancouver.

She told Will some things about herself early on, in case he should think that with her capable build and pink skin and wide gentle forehead she was exactly the kind of a woman to start a family on. She told him that she had had a baby, and that when she and her boyfriend were moving some furniture in a borrowed van, from Thunder Bay to Toronto, carbon-monoxide fumes had leaked in, just enough to make them feel sick but enough to kill the baby, who was seven weeks old. After that Gail was sick—she had a pelvic inflammation. She decided she did not want to have another child and it would have been difficult anyway, so she had a hysterectomy.

Will admired her. He said so. He did not feel obliged to say, What a tragedy! He did not even obliquely suggest that the death was the result of choices Gail had made. He was en-tranced with her then. He thought her brave and generous and resourceful and gifted. The costumes she designed and made for him were perfect, miraculous. Gail thought that his view of her, of her life, showed a touching innocence. It seemed to her that far from being a free and generous spirit, she had often been anxious and desperate and had spent a lot of time doing laundry and worrying about money and feeling she owed so much to any man who took up with her. She did not think she was in love with Will then, but she liked his looks—his energetic body, so upright it seemed taller than it was, his flung-back head, shiny high forehead, springy ruff of graying hair. She liked to watch him at rehearsals, or just talking to his students. How skilled and intrepid he seemed as a director, how potent a per-sonality as he walked the high-school halls or the streets of Walley. And then the slightly quaint, admiring feelings he had for her, his courtesy as a lover, the foreign pleasantness of his house and his life with Cleata—all this made Gail feel like somebody getting a unique welcome in a place where perhaps she did not truly have a right to be. That did not matter then—she had the upper hand.

So when did she stop having it? When he got used to

sleeping with her when they moved in together, when they did so much work on the cottage by the river and it turned out that she was better at that kind of work than he was?

Was she a person who believed that somebody had to have the upper hand?

There came a time when just the tone of his voice, saying "Your shoelace is undone" as she went ahead of him on a walk—just that—could fill her with despair, warning her that they had crossed over into a bleak country where his disappointment in her was boundless, his contempt impossible to challenge. She would stumble eventually, break out in a rage—they would have days and nights of fierce hopelessness. Then the breakthrough, the sweet reunion, the jokes, and bewildered relief. So it went on in their life—she couldn't really understand it or tell if it was like anybody else's. But the peaceful periods seemed to be getting longer, the dangers retreating, and she had no inkling that he was waiting to meet somebody like this new person, Sandy, who would seem to him as alien and delightful as Gail herself had once been.

Will probably had no inkling of that, either.

He had never had much to say about Sandy—Sandra— who had come to Walley last year on an exchange program to see how drama was being taught in Canadian schools. He had said she was a young Turk. Then he had said she mightn't even have heard that expression. Very soon, there had developed some sort of electricity, or danger, around her name. Gail got some information from other sources. She heard that Sandy had challenged Will in front of his class. Sandy had said that the plays he wanted to do were "not relevant." Or maybe it was "not revolutionary."

"But he likes her," one of his students said. "Oh, yeah, he *really likes* her."

Sandy didn't stay around long. She went on to observe the teaching of drama in the other schools. But she wrote to Will, and presumably he wrote back. For it turned out that they had fallen in love. Will and Sandy had fallen seriously in love, and at the end of the school year Will followed her to Australia.

Seriously in love. When Will told her that, Gail was smoking dope. She had taken it up again, because being around Will was making her so nervous.

"You mean it's not me?" Gail said. "You mean I'm not the trouble?"

She was giddy with relief. She got into a bold and boisterous mood and bewildered Will into going to bed with her.

In the morning they tried to avoid being in the same room together. They agreed not to correspond. Perhaps later, Will said. Gail said, "Suit yourself."

But one day at Cleata's house Gail saw his writing on an envelope that had surely been left where she could see it. Cleata had left it—Cleata who never spoke one word about the fugitives. Gail wrote down the return address: 16 Eyre Rd., Toowong, Brisbane, Queensland, Australia.

It was when she saw Will's writing that she understood how useless everything had become to her. This bare-fronted pre-Victorian house in Walley, and the veranda, and the drinks, and the catalpa tree that she was always looking at, in Cleata's back yard. All the trees and streets in Walley, all the liberating views of the lake and the comfort of the shop. Useless cutouts, fakes and props. The real scene was hidden from her, in Australia.

That was why she found herself sitting on the plane beside the woman with the diamond rings. Her own hands have no rings on them, no polish on the nails—the skin is dry from all the work she does with cloth. She used to call the clothes she made "handcrafted," until Will made her embarrassed about that description. She still doesn't quite see what was wrong.

She sold the shop—she sold it to Donalda, who had wanted to buy it for a long time. She took the money, and she got herself onto a flight to Australia and did not tell anyone where she was going. She lied, talking about a long holiday that would start off in England. Then somewhere in Greece for the winter, then who knows?

The night before she left, she did a transformation on herself. She cut off her heavy reddish-gray hair and put a dark-brown rinse on what was left of it. The color that resulted was strange—a deep maroon, obviously artificial but rather too sombre for any attempt at glamour. She picked out from her shop—even though the contents no longer belonged to her— a dress of a kind she would never usually wear, a jacket-dress of dark-blue linen-look polyester with lightning stripes of red and yellow. She is tall, and broad in the hips, and she usually wears things that are loose and graceful. This outfit gives her chunky shoulders, and cuts her legs at an unflattering spot above the knees. What sort of woman did she think she was making herself into? The sort that a woman like Phyllis would play bridge with? If so, she has got it wrong. She has come out looking like somebody who has spent most of her life in uniform, at some worthy, poorly paid job (perhaps in a hospital cafeteria?), and now has spent too much money for a dashing dress that will turn out to be inappropriate and uncomfortable, on the holiday of her life.

That doesn't matter. It is a disguise.

In the airport washroom, on a new continent, she sees that the dark hair coloring, insufficiently rinsed out the night before, has mixed with her sweat and is trickling down her neck.

Gail has landed in Brisbane, still not used to what time of day it is and persecuted by so hot a sun. She is still wearing her horrid dress, but she has washed her hair so that the color no longer runs.

She has taken a taxi. Tired as she is, she cannot settle, cannot rest until she has seen where they live. She has already bought a map and found Eyre Road. A short, curving street. She asks to be let out at the corner, where there is a little grocery store. This is the place where they buy their milk, most likely, or other things that they may have run out of. Detergent, aspirin, tampons.

The fact that Gail never met Sandy was of course an ominous thing. It must have meant that Will knew something very quickly. Later attempts to ferret out a description did not yield much. Tall rather than short. Thin rather than fat. Fair rather than dark. Gail had a mental picture of one of those long-legged, short-haired, energetic, and boyishly attractive girls. *Women.* But she wouldn't know Sandy if she ran into her.

Would anybody know Gail? With her dark glasses and her unlikely hair, she feels so altered as to be invisible. It's also the fact of being in a strange country that has transformed her. She's not tuned into it yet. Once she gets tuned in, she may not be able to do the bold things she can do now. She has to walk this street, look at the house, right away, or she may not be able to do it at all.

The road that the taxi climbed was steep, up from the brown river. Eyre Road runs along a ridge. There is no sidewalk, just a dusty path. No one walking, no cars passing, no shade. Fences of boards or a kind of basket-weaving—wattles?—or in some cases high hedges covered with flowers. No, the flowers are really leaves of a purplish-pink or crimson color. Trees unfamiliar to Gail are showing over the fences. They have tough-looking dusty foliage, scaly or stringy bark, a shabby ornamental air. An indifference or vague ill will about them, which she associated with the tropics. Walking on the path ahead of her are a pair of guinea hens, stately and preposterous.

The house where Will and Sandy live is hidden by a board fence, painted a pale green. Gail's heart shrinks—her heart is in a cruel clutch, to see that fence, that green.

The road is a dead end so she has to turn around. She walks past the house again. In the fence there are gates to let a car in and out. There is also a mail slot. She noticed one of these before in a fence in front of another house, and the reason she noticed it was that there was a magazine sticking out. So the mailbox is not very deep, and a hand, slipping in, might be able to find an envelope resting on its end. If the mail has not been taken out yet by a person in the house. And Gail does slip a hand in. She can't stop herself. She finds a letter there, just as she had thought it might be. She puts it into her purse.

She calls a taxi from the shop at the corner of the street. "What part of the States are you from?" the man in the shop asks her.

"Texas," she says. She has an idea that they would like you to be from Texas, and indeed the man lifts his eyebrows, whistles.

"I thought so," he says.

It is Will's own writing on the envelope. Not a letter to Will, then, but a letter from him. A letter he had sent to Ms. Catherine Thornaby, 491 Hawtre Street. Also in Brisbane. Another hand has scrawled across it "Return to Sender, Died Sept. 13." For a moment, in her disordered state of mind, Gail thinks that this means that Will has died.

She has got to calm down, collect herself, stay out of the sun for a bit.

Nevertheless, as soon as she has read the letter in her hotel room, and has tidied herself up, she takes another taxi, this time to Hawtre Street, and finds, as she expected, a sign in the window: "Flat to Let."

But what is in the letter that Will has written Ms. Catherine Thornaby, on Hawtre Street?

Dear Ms. Thornaby,

   You do not know me, but I hope that once I have explained myself, we may meet and talk. I believe that I may be a Canadian cousin of yours, my grandfather having come to Canada from Northumberland sometime in the 1870s about the same time as a brother of his went to Australia. My grandfather's name was William, like my own, his brother's name was Thomas. Of course I have no proof that you are descended from this Thomas. I simply looked in the Brisbane phone book and was delighted to find there a Thornaby spelled in the same way. I used to think this family-tracing business was the silliest, most boring thing imaginable but now that I find myself doing it, I discover there is a strange excitement about it. Perhaps it is my age—I am 56—that urges me to find connections. And I have more time on my hands than I am used to. My wife is working with a theatre here which keeps her busy till all hours. She is a very bright and energetic young woman. (She scolds me if I refer to any female over 18 as a girl and she is all of 28!) I taught drama in a Canadian high school but I have not yet found any work in Australia.

Wife. He is trying to be respectable in the eyes of the possible cousin.

Dear Mr. Thornaby,

   The name we share may be a more common one than you suppose, though I am at present its only representative in the Brisbane phone book. You may not know that the name comes from Thorn Abbey, the ruins of which are still to be seen in Northumberland. The spelling varies—Thornaby, Thornby, Thornabbey, Thornabby. In the Middle Ages the name of the Lord

of the Manor would be taken as a surname by all the
people working on the estate, including laborers, blacksmiths,
carpenters, etc. As a result there are many people scattered
around the world bearing a name that in the strict
sense they have no right to. Only those who can trace
their descent from the family in the twelfth century are
the true, armigerous Thornabys. That is, they have the
right to display the family coat of arms. I am one
of these Thornabys and since you do not mention
anything about the coat of arms and do not trace your
ancestry back beyond this William I assume that you
are not. My grandfather's name was Jonathan.

Gail writes this on an old portable typewriter that she has bought from the secondhand shop down the street. By this time she is living at 491 Hawtre Street, in an apartment building called the Miramar. It is a two-story building covered with dingy cream stucco, with twisted pillars on either side of a grilled entryway. It has a perfunctory Moorish or Spanish or Californian air, like that of an old movie theatre. The manager told her that the flat was very modern.

"An elderly lady had it, but she had to go to the hospital. Then somebody came when she died and got her effects out, but it still has the basic furniture that goes with the flat. What part of the States are you from?"

Oklahoma, Gail said. Mrs. Massie, from Oklahoma.

The manager looks to be about seventy years old. He wears glasses that magnify his eyes, and he walks quickly, but rather unsteadily, tilting forward. He speaks of difficulties—the increase of the foreign element in the population, which makes it hard to find good repairmen, the carelessness of certain tenants, the malicious acts of passersby who continually litter the grass. Gail asks if he had put in a notice yet to the Post Office. He says he has been intending to, but the lady did not receive hardly any mail. Except one letter came. It was a strange thing that it came right the day after she died. He sent it back.

"I'll do it," Gail said. "I'll tell the Post Office."

"I'll have to sign it, though. Get me one of those forms they have and I'll sign it and you can give it in. I'd be obliged."

The walls of the apartment are painted white—this must be what is modern about it. It has bamboo blinds, a tiny kitchen, a green sofa bed, a table, a dresser, and two chairs. On the wall one picture, which might have been a painting or a tinted photograph. A yellowish-green desert landscape, with rocks and bunches of sage and dim distant mountains. Gail is sure that she has seen this before.

She paid the rent in cash. She had to be busy for a while, buying sheets and towels and groceries, a few pots and dishes, the typewriter. She had to open a bank account, become a person living in the country, not a traveller. There are shops hardly a block away. A grocery store, a secondhand store, a drugstore, a tea shop. They are all humble establishments with strips of colored paper hanging in the doorways, wooden awnings over the sidewalk in front. Their offerings are limited. The tea shop has only two tables, the secondhand store contains scarcely more than the tumbled-out accumulation of one ordinary house. The cereal boxes in the grocery store, the bottles of cough syrup and packets of pills in the drugstore are set out singly on the shelves, as if they were of special value or significance.

But she has found what she needs. In the secondhand store she found some loose flowered cotton dresses, a straw bag for her groceries. Now she looks like the other women she sees on the street. Housewives, middle-aged, with bare but pale arms and legs, shopping in the early morning or late afternoon. She bought a floppy straw hat too, to shade her face as the women do. Dim, soft, freckly, blinking faces.

Night comes suddenly around six o'clock and she must find occupation for the evenings. There is no television in the apartment. But a little beyond the shops there is a lending library, run by an old woman out of the front room of her house. This woman wears a hairnet and gray lisle stockings in spite of the heat. (Where, nowadays, can you find gray lisle stockings?) She has an undernourished body and colorless, tight, unsmiling lips. She is the person Gail calls to mind when she writes the letter from Catherine Thornaby. She thinks of this library woman by that name whenever she sees her, which is almost every day, because you are only allowed one book at a time and Gail usually reads a book a night. She thinks, There is Catherine Thornaby, dead and moved into a new existence a few blocks away.

All the business about armigerous and non-armigerous Thornabys came out of a book. Not one of the books that Gail is reading now but one she read in her youth. The hero was the non-armigerous but deserving heir to a great property. She cannot remember the title. She lived with people then who were always reading *Steppenwolf*, or *Dune*, or something by Krishnamurti, and she read historical romances apologetically. She did not think Will would have read such a book or picked up this sort of information. And she is sure that he will have to reply, to tell Catherine off.

She waits, and reads the books from the lending library, which seem to come from an even earlier time than those romances she read twenty years ago. Some of them she took out of the public library in Winnipeg before she left home, and they seemed old-fashioned even then. *The Girl of the Limberlost. The Blue Castle. Maria Chapdelaine.* Such books remind her, naturally, of her life before Will. There was such a life and she could still salvage something from it, if she wanted to. She has a sister living in Winnipeg. She has an aunt there, in a nursing home, who still reads books in Russian. Gail's grandparents came from Russia, her parents could still speak Russian, her real name is not Gail, but Galya. She cut herself off from her family—or they cut her off—when she left home at eighteen to wander about the country, as you did in those days. First with friends, then with a boyfriend, then with another boyfriend. She strung beads and tie-dyed scarves and sold them on the street.

> *Dear Ms. Thornaby,*
>
> *I must thank you for enlightening me as to the important distinction between the armigerous and the non-armigerous Thornabys. I gather that you have a strong suspicion that I may turn out to be one of the latter. I beg your pardon—I had no intention of treading on such sacred ground or of wearing the Thornaby coat of arms on my T-shirt. We do not take much account of such things in my country and I did not think you did so in Australia, but I see that I am mistaken. Perhaps you are too far on in years to have noticed the change in values. It is quite different with me, since I have been in the teaching profession and am constantly brought up, as well, against the energetic arguments of a young wife.*
>
> *My innocent intention was simply to get in touch with somebody in this country outside the theatrical-academic circle that my wife and I seem to be absorbed in. I have a mother in Canada, whom I miss. In fact your letter reminded me of her a little. She would be capable of writing such a letter for a joke but I doubt whether you are joking. It sounds like a case of Exalted Ancestry to me.*

When he is offended and disturbed in a certain way—a way that is hard to predict and hard for most people to recognize—Will becomes heavily sarcastic. Irony deserts him. He flails about, and the effect is to make people embarrassed not for themselves, as he intends, but for him. This happens seldom, and usually when it happens it means that he feels deeply unappreciated. It means that he has even stopped appreciating himself.

So that is what happened. Gail thinks so. Sandy and her young friends with their stormy confidence, their crude righteousness might be making him miserable. His wit not taken notice of, his enthusiasms out-of-date. No way of making himself felt amongst them. His pride in being attached to Sandy going gradually sour.

She thinks so. He is shaky and unhappy and casting about to know somebody else. He has thought of family ties, here in this country of non-stop blooming and impudent bird life and searing days and suddenly clamped-down nights.

Dear Mr. Thornaby,

Did you really expect me, just because I have the same surname as you, to fling open my door and put out the "welcome mat"—as I think you say in America and that inevitably includes Canada? You may be looking for another mother here, but that hardly obliges me to be one. By the way you are quite wrong about my age—I am younger than you by several years, so do not picture me as an elderly spinster in a hairnet with gray lisle stockings. I know the world probably as well as you do. I travel a good deal, being a fashion buyer for a large store. So my ideas are not so out-of-date as you suppose.

You do not say whether your busy energetic young wife was to be a part of this familial friendship. I am surprised you feel the need for other contacts. It seems I am always reading or hearing on the media about these "May-December" relationships and how invigorating they are and how happily the men are settling down to domesticity and parenthood. (No mention of the "trial runs" with women closer to their own age or mention of how those women are settling down to their lives of loneliness!) So perhaps you need to become a papa to give you a "sense of family"!

Gail is surprised at how fluently she writes. She has always found it hard to write letters, and the results have been dull and sketchy, with many dashes and incomplete sentences and pleas of insufficient time. Where has she got this fine nasty style—out of some book, like the armigerous nonsense? She goes out in the dark to post her letter feeling bold and satisfied. But she wakes up early the next morning thinking that she has certainly gone too far. He will never answer that, she will never hear from him again.

She gets up and leaves the building, goes for a morning walk. The shops are still shut up, the broken venetian blinds are closed, as well as they can be, in the windows of the front-room library. She walks as far as the river, where there is a strip of park beside a hotel. Later in the day, she could not walk or sit there because the verandas of the hotel were always crowded with uproarious beer-drinkers, and the park was within their verbal or even bottle-throwing range. Now the verandas are empty, the doors are closed, and she walks in under the trees. The brown water of the river spreads sluggishly among the mangrove stumps. Birds are flying over the water, lighting on the hotel roof. They are not sea gulls, as she thought at first. They are smaller than gulls, and their bright white wings and breasts are touched with pink.

In the park two men are sitting—one on a bench, one in a wheelchair beside the bench. She recognizes them—they live in her building, and go for walks every day. Once, she held the grille open for them to pass through. She has seen them at the shops, and sitting at the table in the tearoom window.

The man in the wheelchair looks quite old and ill. His face is puckered like old blistered paint. He wears dark glasses and a coal-black toupee and a black beret over that. He is all wrapped up in a blanket. Even later in the day, when the sun is hot—every time she has seen them—he has been wrapped in this plaid blanket. The man who pushes the wheelchair and who now sits on the bench is young enough to look like an overgrown boy. He is tall and large-limbed but not manly. A young giant, bewildered by his own extent. Strong but not athletic, with a stiffness, maybe of timidity, in his thick arms and legs and neck. Red hair not just on his head but on his bare arms and above the buttons of his shirt.

Gail halts in her walk past them, she says good morning. The young man answers almost inaudibly. It seems to be his habit to look out at the world with majestic indifference, but she thinks her greeting has given him a twitch of embarrassment or apprehension. Nevertheless she speaks again, she says, "What are those birds I see everywhere?"

"Galah birds," the young man says, making it sound something like her childhood name. She is going to ask him to repeat it, when the old man bursts out in what seems like a string of curses. The words are knotted and incomprehensible to her, because of the Australian accent on top of some European accent, but the concentrated viciousness is beyond any doubt. And these words are meant for her—he is leaning forward, in fact struggling to free himself from the straps that hold him in. He wants to leap at her, lunge at her, chase her out of sight. The young man makes no apology and does not take any notice of Gail but leans towards the old man and gently pushes him back, saying things to him which she cannot hear. She sees that there will be no explanation. She walks away.

For ten days, no letter. No word. She cannot think what to do. She walks every day—that is mostly what she does. The Miramar is only about a mile or so away from Will's street. She never walks in that street again or goes into the shop where she told the man that she was from Texas. She cannot imagine how she could have been so bold, the first day. She does walk in the streets nearby. Those streets all go along ridges. In between the ridges, which the houses cling to, there are steep-sided gullies full of birds and trees. Even as the sun grows hot, those birds are not quiet. Magpies keep up their disquieting conversation and sometimes emerge to make menacing flights at her light-colored hat. The birds with the name like her own cry out foolishly as they rise and whirl about and subside into the leaves. She walks till she is dazed and sweaty and afraid of sunstroke. She shivers in the heat—most fearful, most desirous, of seeing Will's utterly familiar figure, that one rather small and jaunty, free-striding package, of all that could pain or appease her, in the world.

> *Dear Mr. Thornaby,*
>   *This is just a short note to beg your pardon if I was impolite and hasty in my replies to you, as I am sure I was. I have been under some stress lately, and have taken a leave of absence to recuperate. Under these circumstances one does not always behave as well as one would hope or see things as rationally. . . .*

One day she walks past the hotel and the park. The verandas are clamorous with the afternoon drinking. All the trees in the park have come out in bloom. The flowers are a color that she has seen and could not have imagined on trees before—a shade of silvery blue, or silvery purple, so delicate and beautiful that you would think it would shock everything into quietness, into contemplation, but apparently it has not.

When she gets back to the Miramar, she finds the young man with the red hair standing in the downstairs hall, outside the door of the apartment where he lives with the old man. From behind the closed apartment door come the sounds of a tirade.

The young man smiles at her, this time. She stops and they stand together, listening.

Gail says, "If you would ever like a place to sit down while you're waiting, you know you're welcome to come upstairs."

He shakes his head, still smiling as if this was a joke between them. She thinks she should say something else before she leaves him there, so she asks him about the trees in the park. "Those trees beside the hotel," she says. "Where I saw you the other morning? They are all out in bloom now. What are they called?"

He says a word she cannot catch. She asks him to repeat it. "Jack Randa," he says. "That's the Jack Randa Hotel."

Dear Ms. Thornaby,

I have been away and when I came back I found both your letters waiting for me. I opened them in the wrong order, though that really doesn't matter.

My mother has died. I have been "home" to Canada for her funeral. It is cold there, autumn. Many things have changed. Why I should want to tell you this I simply do not know. We have certainly got off on the wrong track with each other. Even if I had not got your note of explanation after the first letter you wrote, I think I would have been glad in a peculiar way to get the first letter. I wrote you a very snippy and unpleasant letter and you wrote me back one of the same. The snippiness and unpleasantness and readiness to take offense seems somehow familiar to me. Ought I to risk your armigerous wrath by suggesting that we may be related after all?

I feel adrift here. I admire my wife and her theatre friends, with their zeal and directness and commitment, their hope of using their talents to create a better world. (I must say though that it often seems to me that the hope and zeal exceed the talents.) I cannot be one of them. I must say that they saw this before I did. It must be because I am woozy with jet lag after that horrendous flight that I can face up to this fact and that I write it down in a letter to someone like you who has her own troubles and quite correctly has indicated she doesn't want to be bothered with mine. I had better close, in fact, before I burden you with further claptrap from my psyche. I wouldn't blame you if you had stopped reading before you got this far. . . .

Gail lies on the sofa pressing this letter with both hands against her stomach. Many things are changed. He has been in Walley, then—he has been told how she sold the shop and started out on her great world trip. But wouldn't he have heard that anyway, from Cleata? Maybe not, Cleata was close-mouthed. And when she went into the hospital, just before Gail left, she said, "I don't want to see or hear from anybody for a while or bother with letters. These treatments are bound to be a bit melodramatic."

Cleata is dead.

Gail knew that Cleata would die, but somehow thought that everything would hold still, nothing could really happen there while she, Gail, remained here. Cleata is dead and Will is alone except for Sandy, and Sandy perhaps has stopped being of much use to him.

There is a knock on the door. Gail jumps up in a great disturbance, looking for a scarf to cover her hair. It is the manager, calling her false name.

"I just wanted to tell you I had somebody here asking questions. He asked me about Miss Thornaby and I said, Oh, she's dead. She's been dead for some time now. He said, Oh, has she? I said, Yes, she has, and he said, Well, that's strange."

"Did he say why?" Gail says, "Did he say why it was strange?"

"No. I said, She died in the hospital and I've got an American lady in the flat now. I forgot where you told me you came from. He sounded like an American himself, so it might've meant something to him. I said, There was a letter come for Miss Thornaby after she was dead, did you write that letter? I told him I sent it back. Yes, he said, I wrote it, but I never got it back. There must be some kind of mistake, he said."

Gail says there must be. "Like a mistaken identity," she says. "Yes. Like that."

Dear Ms. Thornaby,

It has come to my attention that you are dead. I know that life is strange, but I have never found it quite this strange before. Who are you and what is going on? It seems this rigamarole about the Thornabys must have been just that—a rigamarole. You must certainly be a person with time on your hands and a fantasizing turn of mind. I resent being taken in but I suppose I understand the temptation. I do think you owe me an explanation now as to whether or not my explanation is true and this is some joke. Or am I dealing with some "fashion buyer" from beyond the grave? (Where did you get that touch or is it the truth?)

When Gail goes out to buy food, she uses the back door of the building, she takes a roundabout route to the shops. On her return by the same back-door route, she comes upon the young red-haired man standing between the dustbins. If he had not been so tall, you might have said that he was hidden there. She speaks to him but he doesn't answer. He looks at her through tears, as if the tears were nothing but a wavy glass, something usual.

"Is your father sick?" Gail says to him. She has decided that this must be the relationship, though the age gap seems greater than usual between father and son, and the two of them are quite unalike in looks, and the young man's patience and fidelity are so far beyond—nowadays they seem even contrary to—anything a son customarily shows. But they go beyond anything a hired attendant might show, as well.

"No," the young man says, and though his expression stays calm, a drowning flush spreads over his face, under the delicate redhead's skin.

Lovers, Gail thinks. She is suddenly sure of it. She feels a shiver of sympathy, an odd gratification.

Lovers.

She goes down to her mailbox after dark and finds there another letter.

I might have thought that you were out of town on one of your fashion-buying jaunts but the manager tells me you have not been away since taking the flat, so I must suppose your "leave of absence" continues. He tells me also that you are a brunette. I suppose we might exchange descriptions—and then, with trepidation, photographs—in the brutal manner of people meeting through newspaper ads. It seems that in my attempt to get to know you I am willing to make quite a fool of myself. Nothing new of course in that. . . .

Gail does not leave the apartment for two days. She does without milk, drinks her coffee black. What will she do when she runs out of coffee? She eats odd meals—tuna fish spread on crackers when she has no bread to make a sandwich, a dry end of cheese, a couple of mangos. She goes out into the upstairs hall of the Miramar—first opening the door a crack, testing the air for an occupant—and walks to the arched window that overlooks the street. And from long ago a feeling comes back to her—the feeling of watching a street, the visible bit of a street, where a car is expected to appear, or may appear, or may not appear. She even remembers now the cars themselves—a blue Austin mini, a maroon Chevrolet, a family station wagon. Cars in which she travelled short distances, illicitly and in a bold daze of consent. Long before Will.

She doesn't know what clothes Will will be wearing, or how his hair is cut, or if he will have some change in his walk or expression, some change appropriate to his life here. He cannot have changed more than she has. She has no mirror in the apartment except the little one on the bathroom cupboard, but even that can tell her how much thinner she has got and how the skin of her face has toughened. Instead of fading and wrinkling as fair skin often does in this climate, hers has got a look of dull canvas. It could be fixed up—she sees that. With the right kind of makeup a look of exotic sullenness could be managed. Her hair is more of a problem—the red shows at the roots, with shiny strands of gray. Nearly all the time she keeps it hidden by a scarf.

When the manager knocks on her door again, she has only a second or two of crazy expectation. He begins to call her name. "Mrs. Massie, Mrs. Massie! Oh, I hoped you'd be in. I wondered if you could just come down and help me. It's the old bloke downstairs, he's fallen off the bed."

He goes ahead of her down the stairs, holding to the railing and dropping each foot shakily, precipitately, onto the step below.

"His friend isn't there. I wondered. I didn't see him yesterday. I try and keep track of people but I don't like to interfere. I thought he probably would've come back in the night. I was sweeping out the foyer and I heard a thump and I went back in there—I wondered what was going on. Old bloke all by himself, on the floor."

The apartment is no larger than Gail's, and laid out in the same way. It has curtains down over the bamboo blinds, which make it very dark. It smells of cigarettes and old cooking and some kind of pine-scented air freshener. The sofa bed has been pulled out, made into a double bed, and the old man is lying on the floor beside it, having dragged some of the bed-clothes with him. His head without the toupee is smooth, like a dirty piece of soap. His eyes are half shut and a noise is coming from deep inside him like the noise of an engine hope-lessly trying to turn over.

"Have you phoned the ambulance?" Gail says.

"If you could just pick up the one end of him," the manager says. "I have a bad back and I dread putting it out again."

"Where is the phone?" says Gail. "He may have had a stroke. He may have broken his hip. He'll have to go to the hospital."

"Do you think so? His friend could lift him back and forth so easy. He had the strength. And now he's disappeared."

Gail says, "I'll phone."

"Oh, no. Oh, no. I have the number written down over the phone in my office. I don't let any other person go in there."

Left alone with the old man, who probably cannot hear her, Gail says, "It's all right. It's all right. We're getting help for you." Her voice sounds foolishly sociable. She leans down to pull the blanket up over his shoulder, and to her great surprise a hand flutters out, searches for and grabs her own. His hand is slight and bony, but warm enough, and dreadfully strong. "I'm here, I'm here," she says, and wonders if she is imper-sonating the red-haired young man, or some other young man, or a woman, or even his mother.

The ambulance comes quickly, with its harrowing pulsing cry, and the ambulance men with the stretcher cart are soon in the room, the manager stumping after them, saying, ". . . couldn't be moved. Here is Mrs. Massie came down to help in the emergency."

While they are getting the old man onto the stretcher, Gail has to pull her hand away, and he begins to complain, or she thinks he does—that steady involuntary-sounding noise he is making acquires an extra *ah-unh-anh*. So she takes his hand again as soon as she can, and trots beside him as he is wheeled out. He has such a grip on her that she feels as if he is pulling her along.

"He was the owner of the Jacaranda Hotel," the manager says. "Years ago. He was."

A few people are in the street, but nobody stops, nobody wants to be caught gawking. They want to see, they don't want to see.

"Shall I ride with him?" Gail says. "He doesn't seem to want to let go of me."

"It's up to you," one of the ambulance men says, and she climbs in. (She is dragged in, really, by that clutching hand.) The ambulance man puts down a little seat for her, the doors are closed, the siren starts as they pull away.

Through the window in the back door then she sees Will. He is about a block away from the Miramar and walking towards it. He is wearing a light-colored short-sleeved jacket and matching pants—probably a safari suit—and his hair has grown whiter or been bleached by the sun, but she knows him at once, she will always know him, and will always have to call out to him when she sees him, as she does now, even trying to jump up from the seat, trying to pull her hand out of the old man's grasp.

"It's Will," she says to the ambulance man. "Oh, I'm sorry. It's my husband."

"Well, he better not see you jumping out of a speeding ambulance," the man says. Then he says, "Oh-oh. What's happened here?" For the next minute or so he pays professional attention to the old man. Soon he straightens up and says, "Gone."

"He's still holding on to me," says Gail. But she realizes as she says this that it isn't true. A moment ago he was holding on—with great force, it seemed, enough force to hold her back, when she would have sprung towards Will. Now it is she who is hanging on to him. His fingers are still warm.

When she gets back from the hospital, she finds the note that she is expecting.

Gail. I know it's you.

Hurry. Hurry. Her rent is paid. She must leave a note for the manager. She must take the money out of the bank, get herself to the airport, find a flight. Her clothes can stay behind—her humble pale-print dresses, her floppy hat. The last library book can remain on the table under the sagebrush picture. It can remain there, accumulating fines.

Otherwise, what will happen?

What she has surely wanted. What she is suddenly, as surely, driven to escape.

Gail, I know you're in there! I know you're there on the other side of the door.

Gail! Galya!

Talk to me, Gail. Answer me. I know you're there.

I can hear you. I can hear your heart beating through the keyhole and your stomach rumbling and your brain jumping up and down.

I can smell you through the keyhole. You. Gail.

Words most wished for can change. Something can happen to them, while you are waiting. *Love—need—forgive. Love—need—forever.* The sound of such words can become a din, a battering, a sound of hammers in the street. And all you can do is run away, so as not to honor them out of habit.

In the airport shop she sees a number of little boxes, made by Australian aborigines. They are round, and light as pennies. She picks out one that has a pattern of yellow dots, irregularly spaced on a dark-red ground. Against this is a swollen black figure—a turtle, maybe, with short splayed legs. Helpless on its back.

Gail is thinking, A present for Cleata. As if her whole time here had been a dream, something she could discard, going back to a chosen point, a beginning.

Not for Cleata. A present for Will?

A present for Will, then. Send it now? No, take it back to Canada, all the way back, send it from there.

The yellow dots flung out in that way remind Gail of something she saw last fall. She and Will saw it. They went for a walk on a sunny afternoon. They walked from their house by the river up the wooded bank, and there they came on a display that they had heard about but never seen before.

Hundreds, maybe thousands, of butterflies were hanging in the trees, resting before their long flight down the shore of Lake Huron and across Lake Erie, then on south to Mexico. They hung there like metal leaves, beaten gold—like flakes of gold tossed up and caught in the branches.

"Like the shower of gold in the Bible," Gail said.

Will told her that she was confusing Jove and Jehovah.

On that day, Cleata had already begun to die and Will had already met Sandy. This dream had already begun—Gail's journey and her deceits, then the words she imagined—believed—that she heard shouted through the door.

Love—forgive
Love—forget
Love—forever

Hammers in the street.

What could you put in a box like that before you wrapped it up and sent it far away? A bead, a feather, a potent pill? Or a note, folded up tight, to about the size of a spitball.

Now it's up to you to follow me.

A
WILDERNESS
STATION

I

Miss Margaret Cresswell, Matron, House of Industry, Toronto, to Mr. Simon Herron, North Huron, January 15, 1852.

Since your letter is accompanied by an endorsement from your minister, I am happy to reply. Requests of your sort are made to us frequently, but unless we have such an endorsement we cannot trust that they are made in good faith.

We do not have any girl at the Home who is of marriageable age, since we send our girls out to make a living usually around the age of fourteen or fifteen, but we do keep track of them for some years or usually until they are married. In cases such as yours we sometimes recommend one of these girls and will arrange a meeting, and then of course it is up to the two parties involved to see if they are suited.

There are two girls eighteen years of age that we are still in touch with. Both are apprenticed to a milliner and are good seamstresses, but a marriage to a likely man would probably be preferred to a lifetime of such work. Further than that cannot be said, it must be left to the girl herself and of course to your liking for her, or the opposite.

The two girls are a Miss Sadie Johnstone and a Miss Annie McKillop. Both were born legitimately of Christian parents and were placed in the Home due to parental deaths. Drunkenness or immorality was not a factor. In Miss Johnstone's case there is however the factor of consumption, and though she is the prettier of the two and a plump rosy girl, I feel I must warn you that perhaps she is not suited to the hard work of a life in the bush. The other girl, Miss McKillop, is of a more durable constitution though of leaner frame and not so good a complexion. She has a waywardness about one eye but it does not interfere with her vision and her sewing is excellent. The darkness of her eyes and hair and brown tinge of her skin is no indication of mixed blood, as both parents were from Fife. She is a hardy girl and I think would be suited to such a life as you can offer, being also free from the silly timidness we often see in girls of her age. I will speak to her and acquaint her with the idea and will await your letter as to when you propose to meet her.

11

Carstairs *Argus*, Fiftieth Anniversary Edition, February 3, 1907. Recollections of Mr. George Herron.

On the first day of September, 1851, my brother Simon and I got a box of bedclothes and household utensils together and put them in a wagon with a horse to pull it, and set out from Halton County to try our fortunes in the wilds of Huron and

Bruce, as wilds they were then thought to be. The goods were from Archie Frame that Simon worked for, and counted as part of his wages. Likewise we had to rent the house off him, and his boy that was about my age came along to take it and the wagon back.

It ought to be said in the beginning that my brother and I were left alone, our father first and then our mother dying of fever within five weeks of landing in this country, when I was three years old and Simon eight. Simon was put to work for Archie Frame that was our mother's cousin, and I was taken on by the schoolteacher and wife that had no child of their own. This was in Halton, and I would have been content to go on living there but Simon being only a few miles away continued to visit and say that as soon as we were old enough we would go and take up land and be on our own, not working for others, as this was what our father had intended. Archie Frame never sent Simon to school as I was sent, so Simon was always bound to get away. When I had come to be fourteen years of age and a husky lad, as was my brother, he said we should go and take up Crown Land north of the Huron Tract.

We only got as far as Preston on the first day as the roads were rough and bad across Nassageweya and Puslinch. Next day we got to Shakespeare and the third afternoon to Stratford. The roads were always getting worse as we came west, so we thought best to get our box sent on to Clinton by the stage. But the stage had quit running due to rains, and they were waiting till the roads froze up, so we told Archie Frame's boy to turn about and return with horse and cart and goods back to Halton. Then we took our axes on our shoulders, and walked to Carstairs.

Hardly a soul was there before us. Carstairs was just under way, with a rough building that was store and inn combined, and there was a German named Roem building a sawmill.

One man who got there before us and already had a fair-sized cabin built was Henry Treece, who afterwards became my father-in-law.

We got ourselves boarded at the inn where we slept on the bare floor with one blanket or quilt between us. Winter was coming early with cold rains and everything damp, but we were expecting hardship or at least Simon was. I came from a softer place. He said we must put up with it so I did.

We began to underbrush a road to our piece of land and then we got it marked out and cut the logs for our shanty and big scoops to roof it. We were able to borrow an ox from Henry Treece to draw the logs. But Simon was not of a mind to borrow or depend on anybody. He was minded to try raising the shanty ourselves, but when we saw we could not do it I made my way to Treeces' place and with Henry and two of his sons and a fellow from the mill it was accomplished. We started next day to fill up the cracks between the logs with mud and we got some hemlock branches so we would not be out money anymore for staying at the inn but could sleep in our own place. We had a big slab of elm for the door. My brother had heard from some French-Canadian fellows that were at Archie Frame's that in the lumber camps the fire was always in the middle of the shanty. So he said that was the way we should have ours, and we got four posts and were building the chimney on them, house-fashion, intending to plaster it with mud inside and out. We went to our hemlock bed with a good fire going, but waking in the middle of the night we saw our lumber was all ablaze and the scoops burning away briskly also. We tore down the chimney and the scoops being green basswood were not hard to put out. As soon as it came day, we started to build the chimney in the ordinary way in the end of the house and I thought it best not to make any remark.

After the small trees and brush was cleared out a bit, we set to chopping down the big trees. We cut down a big ash and split it into slabs for our floor. Still our box had not come which was to be shipped from Halton so Henry Treece sent us a very large and comfortable bearskin for our cover in bed but my brother would not take the favour and sent it back saying no need. Then after several weeks we got our box and had to ask for the ox to bring it on from Clinton, but my brother said that is the last we will need to ask of any person's help.

We walked to Walley and brought back flour and salt fish on our back. A man rowed us across the river at Manchester for a steep price. There were no bridges then and all that winter not a good enough freeze to make it easy going over the rivers.

Around Christmastime my brother said to me that he thought we had the place in good enough shape now for him to be bringing in a wife, so we should have somebody to cook and do for us and milk a cow when we could afford one. This was the first I had heard of any wife and I said that I did not know he was acquainted with anybody. He said he was not but he had heard that you could write to the Orphanage Home and ask if they had a girl there that was willing to think about the prospect and that they would recommend, and if so he would go and see her. He wanted one between eighteen and twenty-two years of age, healthy and not afraid of work and raised in the Orphanage, not taken in lately, so that she would not be expecting any luxuries or to be waited on and would not be recalling about when things were easier for her. I do not doubt that to those hearing about this nowadays it seems a strange way to go about things. It was not that my brother could not have gone courting and got a wife on his own, because he was a good-looking fellow, but he did not have the time or the money or inclination, his mind was all occupied with establishing our holding. And if a girl had parents they would probably not want her to go far away where there was little in comforts and so much work.

That it was a respectable way of doing things is shown by the fact that the minister Mr. McBain, who was lately come into the district, helped Simon to write the letter and sent word on his own to vouch for him.

So a letter came back that there was a girl that might fit the bill and Simon went off to Toronto and got her. Her name was Annie but her maiden name I had forgotten. They had to ford the streams in Hullet and trudge through deep soft snow after leaving the stage in Clinton, and when they got back she was worn out and very surprised at what she saw, since she said she had never imagined so much bush. She had in her box some sheets and pots and dishes that ladies had given her and that made the place more comfortable.

Early in April my brother and I went out to chop down some trees in the bush at the farthest corner of our property. While Simon was away to get married, I had done some chopping in the other direction towards Treeces', but Simon wanted to get all our boundaries cut clear around and not to go on chopping where I had been. The day started out mild and there was still a lot of soft snow in the bush. We were chopping down a tree where Simon wanted, and in some way, I cannot say how, a branch of it came crashing down where we didn't expect. We just heard the little branches cracking where it fell and looked up to see it and it hit Simon on the head and killed him instantly.

I had to drag his body back then to the shanty through the snow. He was a tall fellow though not fleshy, and it was an awkward task and greatly wearying. It had got colder by this time and when I got to the clearing I saw snow on the wind like the start of a storm. Our footsteps were filled in that we had made earlier. Simon was all covered with snow that did not melt on him by this time, and his wife coming to the door was greatly puzzled, thinking that I was dragging along a log.

In the shanty Annie washed him off and we sat still a while not knowing what we should do. The preacher was at the inn as there was no church or house for him yet and the inn was only about four miles away, but the storm had come up very fierce so you could not even see the trees at the edge of the clearing. It had the look of a storm that would last two or three days, the wind being from the northwest. We knew we could not keep the body in the shanty and we could not set it out in the snow fearing the bobcats would get at it, so we had to set to work and bury him. The ground was not frozen under the snow, so I dug out a grave near the shanty and Annie sewed him in a sheet and we laid him in his grave, not staying long in the wind but saying the Lord's Prayer and reading one Psalm out of the Bible. I am not sure which one but I remember it was near the end of the Book of Psalms and it was very short.

This was the third day of April, 1852.

That was our last snow of the year, and later the minister came and said the service and I put up a wooden marker. Later on we got our plot in the cemetery and put his stone there, but he is not under it as it is a foolish useless thing in my opinion to cart a man's bones from one place to another when it is only bones and his soul has gone on to Judgment.

I was left to chop and clear by myself and soon I began to work side by side with the Treeces, who treated me with the greatest kindness. We worked all together on my land or their land, not minding if it was the one or the other. I started to take my meals and even to sleep at their place and got to know their daughter Jenny who was about of my age, and we made our plans to marry, which we did in due course. Our life together was a long one with many hardships but we were fortunate in the end and raised eight children. I have seen my sons take over my wife's father's land as well as my own since my two brothers-in-law went away and did well for themselves in the West.

My brother's wife did not continue in this place but went her own way to Walley.

Now there are gravel roads running north, south, east, and west and a railway not a half mile from my farm. Except for woodlots, the bush is a thing of the past and I often think of the trees I have cut down and if I had them to cut down today I would be a wealthy man.

The Reverend Walter McBain, Minister of the Free Presbyterian Church of North Huron, to Mr. James Mullen, Clerk of the Peace, Walley, United Counties of Huron and Bruce, September 10, 1852.

I write to inform you, sir, of the probable arrival in your town of a young woman of this district, by the name of Annie Herron, a widow and one of my congregation. This young person has left her home here in the vicinity of Carstairs in Holloway Township, I believe she intends to walk to Walley. She may appear at the Gaol there seeking to be admitted, so I think it my duty to tell you who and what she is and her history here since I have known her.

I came to this area in November of last year, being the first minister of any kind to venture. My parish is as yet mostly bush, and there is nowhere for me to lodge but at the Carstairs Inn. I was born in the west of Scotland and came to this country under the auspices of the Glasgow Mission. After applying to know God's will, I was directed by Him to go to preach wherever was most need of a minister. I tell you this so you may know what sort I am that bring you my account and my view of the affairs of this woman.

She came into the country late last winter as the bride of

the young man Simon Herron. He had written on my advice to the House of Industry in Toronto that they might recommend to him a Christian, preferably Presbyterian, female suitable to his needs, and she was the one recommended. He married her straightaway and brought her here to the shanty he had built with his brother. These two young lads had come into the country to clear themselves a piece of land and get possession of it, being themselves orphans and without expectations. They were about this work one day at the end of winter when an accident befell. A branch was loosed while chopping down a tree and fell upon the elder brother so as to cause instant death. The younger lad succeeded in getting the body back to the shanty and since they were held prisoner by a heavy snowstorm they conducted their own funeral and burial.

The Lord is strict in his mercies and we are bound to receive his blows as signs of his care and goodness for so they will prove to be.

Deprived of his brother's help, the lad found a place in a neighbouring family, also members in good standing of my congregation, who have accepted him as a son, though he still works for title to his own land. This family would have taken in the young widow as well, but she would have nothing to do with their offer and seemed to develop an aversion to everyone who would help her. Particularly she seemed so towards her brother-in-law, who said that he had never had the least quarrel with her, and towards myself. When I talked to her, she would not give any answer or sign that her soul was coming into submission. It is a fault of mine that I am not well-equipped to talk to women. I have not the ease to win their trust. Their stubbornness is of another kind than a man's.

I meant only to say that I did not have any good effect on her. She stopped appearing at services, and the deterioration of her property showed the state of her mind and spirit. She would not plant peas and potatoes though they were given to her to grow among the stumps. She did not chop down the wild vines around her door. Most often she did not light a fire so she could have oat-cake or porridge. Her brother-in-law being removed, there was no order imposed on her days. When I visited her the door was open and it was evident that animals came and went in her house. If she was there she hid herself, to mock me. Those who caught sight of her said that her clothing was filthy and torn from scrambling about in the bushes, and she was scratched by thorns and bitten by the mosquito insects and let her hair go uncombed or plaited. I believe she lived on salt fish and bannock that the neighbours or her brother-in-law left for her.

Then while I was still puzzling how I might find a way to protect her body through the winter and deal with the more important danger to her soul, there comes word she is gone. She left the door open and went away without cloak or bonnet and wrote on the shanty floor with a burnt stick the two words: "Walley, Gaol." I take this to mean she intends to go there and turn herself in. Her brother-in-law thinks it would be no use for him to go after her because of her unfriendly attitude to himself, and I cannot set out because of a deathbed I am attending. I ask you therefore to let me know if she has arrived and in what state and how you will deal with her. I consider her still as a soul in my charge, and I will try to visit her before winter if you keep her there. She is a child of the Free Church and the Covenant and as such she is entitled to a minister of her own faith and you must not think it sufficient that some priest of the Church of England or Baptist or Methodist be sent to her.

In case she should not come to the Gaol but wander in the streets, I ought to tell you that she is dark-haired and tall, meagre in body, not comely but not ill-favoured except having one eye that goes to the side.

• • •

Mr. James Mullen, Clerk of the Peace, Walley, to the Reverend Walter McBain, Carstairs, North Huron, September 30, 1852.

Your letter to me arrived most timely and appreciated, concerning the young woman Annie Herron. She completed her journey to Walley unharmed and with no serious damage though she was weak and hungry when she presented herself at the Gaol. On its being inquired what she did there, she said that she came to confess to a murder, and to be locked up. There was consultation round and about, I was sent for, and it being near to midnight, I agreed that she should spend the night in a cell. The next day I visited her and got all particulars I could.

Her story of being brought up in the Orphanage, her apprenticeship to a milliner, her marriage, and her coming to North Huron, all accords pretty well with what you have told me. Events in her account begin to differ only with her husband's death. In that matter what she says is this:

On the day in early April when her husband and his brother went out to chop trees, she was told to provide them with food for their midday meal, and since she had not got it ready when they wanted to leave, she agreed to take it to them in the woods. Consequently she baked up some oatcakes and took some salt fish and followed their tracks and found them at work some distance away. But when her husband unwrapped his food he was very offended, because she had wrapped it in a way that the salty oil from the fish had soaked into the cakes, and they were all crumbled and unpleasant to eat. In his disappointment he became enraged and promised her a beating when he was more at leisure to do it. He then turned his back on her, being seated on a log, and she picked up a rock and threw it at him, hitting him on the head so that he fell down unconscious and in fact dead. She and his brother then carried and dragged the body back to the house. By that time a blizzard had come up and they were imprisoned within. The brother said that they should not reveal the truth as she had not intended murder, and she agreed. They then buried him—her story agreeing again with yours—and that might have been the end of it, but she became more and more troubled, convinced that she had surely been intending to kill him. If she had not killed him, she says, it would only have meant a worse beating, and why should she have risked that? So she decided at last upon confession and as if to prove something handed me a lock of hair stiffened with blood.

This is her tale, and I do not believe it for a minute. No rock that this girl could pick up, combined with the force that she could summon to throw it, would serve to kill a man. I questioned her about this, and she changed her story, saying that it was a large rock that she had picked up in both hands and that she had not thrown it but smashed it down on his head from behind. I said why did not the brother prevent you, and she said, he was looking the other way. Then I said there must indeed be a bloodied rock lying somewhere in the wood, and she said she had washed it off with the snow. (In fact it is not likely a rock would come to hand so easily, with all such depth of snow about.) I asked her to roll up her sleeve that I might judge of the muscles in her arms, to do such a job, and she said that she had been a huskier woman some months since.

I conclude that she is lying, or self-deluded. But I see nothing for it at the moment but to admit her to the Gaol. I asked her what she thought would happen to her now, and she said, well, you will try me and then you will hang me. But you do not hang people in the winter, she said, so I can stay here till spring. And if you let me work here, maybe you will want me to go on working and you will not want me hanged. I do not know where she got this idea about people not being hanged in the winter. I am in perplexity about her. As you may know, we have a very fine new Gaol here where the inmates are kept warm and dry and are decently fed and treated with all humanity, and there has been a complaint that some are not sorry—and at this time of year, even happy—to get into it. But it is obvious that she cannot wander about much longer, and from your account she is unwilling to stay with friends and unable to make a tolerable home for herself. The Gaol at present serves as a place of detention for the Insane as well as criminals, and if she is charged with Insanity, I could keep her here for the winter perhaps with removal to Toronto in the spring. I have engaged for a doctor to visit her. I spoke to her of your letter and your hope of coming to see her, but I found her not at all agreeable to that. She asks that nobody be allowed to see her excepting a Miss Sadie Johnstone, who is not in this part of the country.

I am enclosing a letter I have written to her brother-in-law for you to pass on to him, so that he may know what she has said and tell me what he thinks about it. I thank you in advance for conveying the letter to him, also for the trouble you have been to, in informing me as fully as you have done. I am a member of the Church of England, but have a high regard for the work of other Protestant denominations in bringing an orderly life to this part of the world we find ourselves in. You may believe that I will do what is in my power to do, to put you in a position to deal with the soul of this young woman, but it might be better to wait until she is in favour of it.

The Reverend Walter McBain to Mr. James Mullen, November 18, 1852.

I carried your letter at once to Mr. George Herron and believe that he has replied and given you his recollection of events. He was amazed at his sister-in-law's claim, since she had never said anything of this to him or to anybody else. He says that it is all her invention or fancy, since she was never in the woods when it happened and there was no need for her to be, as they had carried their food with them when they left the house. He says that there had been at another time some reproof from his brother to her, over the spoiling of some cakes by their proximity to fish, but it did not happen at this time. Nor were there any rocks about to do such a deed on impulse if she had been there and wished to do it.

My delay in answering your letter, for which I beg pardon, is due to a bout of ill health. I had an attack of the gravel and a rheumatism of the stomach worse than any misery that ever fell upon me before. I am somewhat improved at present and will be able to go about as usual by next week if all continues to mend.

As to the question of the young woman's sanity, I do not know what your Doctor will say but I have thought on this and questioned the Divinity and my belief is this. It may well be that so early in the marriage her submission to her husband was not complete and there would be carelessness about his comfort, and naughty words, and quarrelsome behaviour, as well as the hurtful sulks and silences her sex is prone to. His death occurring before any of this was put right, she would feel a natural and harrowing remorse, and this must have taken hold of her mind so strongly that she made herself out to be actually responsible for his death. In this way, I think many folk are driven mad. Madness is at first taken on by some as a kind of play, for which shallowness and audacity they are punished later on, by finding out that it is play no longer, and the Devil has blocked off every escape.

It is still my hope to speak to her and make her understand this. I am under difficulties at present not only of my wretched corpus but of being lodged in a foul and noisy place obliged to hear day and night such uproars as destroy sleep and study and intrude even on my prayers. The wind blows bitterly through the logs, but if I go down to the fire there is swilling of spirits and foulest insolence. And outside nothing but trees to choke off every exit and icy bog to swallow man and horse. There was a promise to build a church and lodging but those who made such promise have grown busy with their own affairs and it seems to have been put off. I have not however left off preaching even in my illness and in such barns and houses as are provided. I take heart remembering a great man, the great preacher and interpreter of God's will, Thomas Boston, who in the latter days of his infirmity preached the grandeur of God from his chamber window to a crowd of two thousand or so assembled in the yard below. So I mean to preach to the end though my congregation will be smaller.

Whatsoever crook there is in one's lot, it is of God's making. Thomas Boston.

This world is a wilderness, in which we may indeed get our station changed, but the move will be out of one wilderness station unto another. Ibid.

Mr. James Mullen to the Reverend Walter McBain, January 17, 1853.

I write to you that our young woman's health seems sturdy, and she no longer looks such a scarecrow, eating well and keeping herself clean and tidy. Also she seems quieter in her spirits. She has taken to mending the linen in the prison which she does well. But I must tell you that she is firm as ever against a visit, and I cannot advise you to come here as I think your trouble might be for nothing. The journey is very hard in winter and it would do no good to your state of health.

Her brother-in-law has written me a very decent letter affirming that there is no truth to her story, so I am satisfied on that.

You may be interested in hearing what the doctor who visited her had to say about her case. His belief is that she is subject to a sort of delusion peculiar to females, for which the motive is a desire for self-importance, also a wish to escape the monotony of life or the drudgery they may have been born to. They may imagine themselves possessed by the forces of evil, to have committed various and hideous crimes, and so forth. Sometimes they may report that they have taken numerous lovers, but these lovers will be all imaginary and the woman who thinks herself a prodigy of vice will in fact be quite chaste and untouched. For all this he—the doctor—lays the blame on the sort of reading that is available to these females, whether it is of ghosts or demons or of love escapades with Lords and Dukes and suchlike. For many, these tales are a passing taste given up when life's real duties intervene. For others they are indulged in now and then, as if they were sweets or sherry wine, but for some there is complete surrender and living within them just as in an opium-dream. He could not get an account of her reading from the young woman, but he believes she may by now have forgotten what she has read, or conceals the matter out of slyness.

With his questioning there did come to light something further that we did not know. On his saying to her, did she not fear hanging? she replied, no, for there is a reason you will not hang me. You mean that they will judge that you are mad? said he, and she said, oh, perhaps that, but is it not true also that they will never hang a woman that is with child? The doctor then examined her to find out if this were true, and she agreed to the examination, so she must have made the claim in good faith. He discovered however that she had deceived herself. The signs she took were simply the results of her going so long underfed and in such a reduced state, and later probably of her hysteria. He told her of his findings, but it is hard to say whether she believes him.

It must be acknowledged that this is truly a hard country for women. Another insane female has been admitted here recently, and her case is more pitiful for she has been driven insane by a rape. Her two attackers have been taken in and are in fact just over the wall from her in the men's section. The screams of the victim resound sometimes for hours at a stretch, and as a result the prison has become a much less pleasant shelter. But whether that will persuade our self-styled murderess to recant and take herself off, I have no idea. She is a good needlewoman and could get employment if she chose.

I am sorry to hear of your bad health and miserable lodgings. The town has grown so civilized that we forget the hardship of the hinterlands. Those like yourself who choose to endure it deserve our admiration. But you must allow me to say that it seems pretty certain that a man not in robust health will be unable to bear up for long in your situation. Surely your Church would not consider it a defection were you to choose to serve it longer by removing to a more comfortable place.

I enclose a letter written by the young woman and sent to a Miss Sadie Johnstone, on King Street, Toronto. It was intercepted by us that we might know more of the state of her mind, but resealed and sent on. But it has come back marked "Unknown." We have not told the writer of this in hopes that she will write again and more fully, revealing to us something to help us decide whether or not she is a conscious liar.

Mrs. Annie Herron, Walley Gaol, United Counties of Huron and Bruce, to Miss Sadie Johnstone, 49 King Street, Toronto, December 20, 1852.

Sadie, I am in here pretty well and safe and nothing to complain of either in food or blankets. It is a good stone building and something like the Home. If you could come and see me I would be very glad. I often talk to you a whole lot in my head, which I don't want to write because what if they are spies. I do the sewing here, the things was not in good repare when I came but now they are pretty good. And I am making curtains for the Opera House, a job that was sent in. I hope to see you. You could come on the stage right to this place. Maybe you would not like to come in the winter but in the springtime you would like to come.

Mr. James Mullen to the Reverend Walter McBain, April 7, 1853.

Not having had any reply to my last letter, I trust you are well and might still be interested in the case of Annie Herron. She is still here and busies herself at sewing jobs which I have undertaken to get her from outside. No more is said of being with child, or of hanging, or of her story. She has written once again to Sadie Johnstone but quite briefly and I enclose her letter here. Do you have an idea who this person Sadie Johnstone might be?

I don't get any answer from you, Sadie, I don't think they sent on my letter. Today is the First of April, 1853. But not April Fool like we used to fool each other. Please come and see me if you can. I am in Walley Gaol but safe and well.

Mr. James Mullen from Edward Hoy, Landlord, Carstairs Inn, April 19, 1853.

Your letter to Mr. McBain sent back to you, he died here

at the inn February 25. There is some books here, nobody
wants them.

III

Annie Herron, Walley Gaol, to Sadie Johnstone, Toronto.
Finder Please Post.

George came dragging him across the snow I thought it
was a log he dragged. I didn't know it was him. George said,
it's him. A branch fell out of a tree and hit him, he said. He
didn't say he was dead. I looked for him to speak. His mouth
was part way open with snow in it. Also his eyes part way
open. We had to get inside because it was starting to storm
like anything. We dragged him in by the one leg each. I pretended to myself when I took hold of his leg that it was still
the log. Inside where I had the fire going it was warm and the
snow started melting off him. His blood thawed and ran a little around his ear. I didn't know what to do and I was afraid
to go near him. I thought his eyes were watching me.

George sat by the fire with his big heavy coat on and his
boots on. He was turned away. I sat at the table, which was
of half-cut logs. I said, how do you know if he is dead?
George said, touch him if you want to know. But I would not.
Outside there was terrible storming, the wind in the trees and
over top of our roof. I said, Our Father who art in Heaven,
and that was how I got my courage. I kept saying it every
time I moved. I have to wash him off, I said. Help me. I got
the bucket where I kept the snow melting. I started on his feet
and had to pull his boots off, a heavy job. George never
turned around or paid attention or helped me when I asked.
I didn't take the trousers or coat off of him, I couldn't manage. But I washed his hands and wrists. I always kept the rag
between my hand and his skin. The blood and wet where the

snow had melted off him was on the floor under his head and shoulders so I wanted to turn him over and clean it up. But I couldn't do it. So I went and pulled George by his arm. Help me, I said. What? he said. I said we had to turn him. So he came and helped me and we got him turned over, he was laying face down. And then I saw, I saw where the axe had cut.

Neither one of us said anything. I washed it out, blood and what else. I said to George, go and get me the sheet from my box. There was the good sheet I wouldn't put on the bed. I didn't see the use of trying to take off his clothes though they were good cloth. We would have had to cut them away where the blood was stuck and then what would we have but the rags. I cut off the one little piece of his hair because I remembered when Lila died in the Home they did that. Then I got George to help me roll him on to the sheet and I started to sew him up in the sheet. While I was sewing I said to George, go out in the lee of the house where the wood is piled and maybe you can get in enough shelter there to dig him a grave. Take the wood away and the ground is likely softer underneath.

I had to crouch down at the sewing so I was nearly laying on the floor beside him. I sewed his head in first folding the sheet over it because I had to look in his eyes and mouth. George went out and I could hear through the storm that he was doing what I said and pieces of wood were thrown up sometimes hitting the wall of the house. I sewed on, and every bit of him I lost sight of I would say even out loud, there goes, there goes. I had got the fold neat over his head but down at the feet I didn't have material enough to cover him, so I sewed on my eyelet petticoat I made at the Home to learn the stitch and that way I got him all sewed in.

I went out to help George. He had got all the wood out of the way and was at the digging. The ground was soft enough, like I had thought. He had the spade so I got the broad shovel and we worked away, him digging and loosening and me shovelling.

Then we moved him out. We could not do it now one leg each so George got him at the head and me at the ankles where the petticoat was and we rolled him into the earth and set to work again to cover him up. George had the shovel and it seemed I could not get enough dirt onto the spade so I pushed it in with my hands and kicked it in with my feet any way at all. When it was all back in, George beat it down flat with the shovel as much as he could. Then we moved all the wood back searching where it was in the snow and we piled it up in the right way so it did not look as if anybody had been at it. I think we had no hats on or scarves but the work kept us warm.

We took in more wood for the fire and put the bar across the door. I wiped up the floor and I said to George, take off your boots. Then, take off your coat. George did what I told him. He sat by the fire. I made the kind of tea from catnip leaves that Mrs. Treece showed me how to make and I put a piece of sugar in it. George did not want it. Is it too hot, I said. I let it cool off but then he didn't want it either. So I began, and talked to him.

You didn't mean to do it.

It was in anger, you didn't mean what you were doing.

I saw him other times what he would do to you. I saw he would knock you down for a little thing and you just get up and never say a word. The same way he did to me.

If you had not have done it, some day he would have done it to you.

Listen, George. Listen to me.

If you own up what do you think will happen? They will hang you. You will be dead, you will be no good to anybody. What will become of your land? Likely it will all go back to the Crown and somebody else will get it and all the work you have done will be for them.

What will become of me here if you are took away?

I got some oat-cakes that were cold and I warmed them up. I set one on his knee. He took it and bit it and chewed it but he could not get it down and he spit it on to the fire.

I said, listen. I know things. I am older than you are. I am religious too, I pray to God every night and my prayers are answered. I know what God wants as well as any preacher knows and I know that he does not want a good lad like you to be hanged. All you have to do is say you are sorry. Say you are sorry and mean it well and God will forgive you. I will say the same thing, I am sorry too because when I saw he was dead I did not wish, not one minute, for him to be alive. I will say, God forgive me, and you do the same. Kneel down.

But he would not. He would not move out of his chair. And I said, all right. I have an idea. I am going to get the Bible. I asked him, do you believe in the Bible? Say you do. Nod your head.

I did not see whether he nodded or not but I said, there. There you did. Now. I am going to do what we all used to do in the Home when we wanted to know what would happen to us or what we should do in our life. We would open the Bible any place and poke our finger at a page and then open our eyes and read the verse where our finger was and that would tell you what you needed to know. To make double sure of it just say when you close your eyes, God guide my finger.

He would not raise a hand from his knee, so I said, all right. All right, I'll do it for you. I did it, and I read where my finger stopped. I held the Bible close in to the fire so I could see.

It was something about being old and gray-headed, *oh God*

forsake me not, and I said, what that means is that you are supposed to live till you are old and gray-headed and nothing is supposed to happen to you before that. It says so, in the Bible.

Then the next verse was so-and-so went and took so-and-so and conceived and bore him a son.

It says you will have a son, I said. You have to live and get older and get married and have a son.

But the next verse I remember so well I can put down all of it. *Neither can they prove the things of which they now accuse me.*

George, I said, do you hear that? *Neither can they prove the things of which they now accuse me.* That means that you are safe.

You are safe. Get up now. Get up and go and lay on the bed and go to sleep.

He could not do that by himself but I did it. I pulled on him and pulled on him until he was standing up and then I got him across the room to the bed which was not his bed in the corner but the bigger bed, and got him to sit on it then lay down. I rolled him over and back and got his clothes off down to his shirt. His teeth were chattering and I was afraid of a chill or the fever. I heated up the flat-irons and wrapped them in cloth and laid them down one on each side of him close to his skin. There was not whisky or brandy in the house to use, only the catnip tea. I put more sugar in it and got him to take it from a spoon. I rubbed his feet with my hands, then his arms and his legs, and I wrung out clothes in hot water which I laid over his stomach and his heart. I talked to him then in a different way quite soft and told him to go to sleep and when he woke up his mind would be clear and all his horrors would be wiped away.

A tree branch fell on him. It was just what you told me. I can see it falling. I can see it coming down so fast like a streak and little branches and crackling all along the way, it hardly takes longer than a gun going off and you say, what is that? and it has hit him and he is dead.

When I got him to sleep I laid down on the bed beside him. I took off my smock and I could see the black and blue marks on my arms. I pulled up my skirt to see if they were still there high on my legs, and they were. The back of my hand was dark too and sore still where I had bit it.

Nothing bad happened after I laid down and I did not sleep all night but listened to him breathing and kept touching him to see if he was warmed up. I got up in the earliest light and fixed the fire. When he heard me, he waked up and was better.

He did not forget what had happened but talked as if he thought it was all right. He said, we ought to have had a prayer and read something out of the Bible. He got the door opened and there was a big drift of snow but the sky was clearing. It was the last snow of the winter.

We went out and said the Lord's Prayer. Then he said, where is the Bible? Why is it not on the shelf? When I got it from beside the fire he said, what is it doing there? I did not remind him of anything. He did not know what to read so I picked the 131st Psalm that we had to learn at the Home. *Lord my heart is not haughty nor mine eyes lofty. Surely I have behaved and quieted myself as a child that is weaned of his mother, my soul is even as a weaned child.* He read it. Then he said he would shovel out a path and go and tell the Treeces. I said I would cook him some food. He went out and shovelled and didn't get tired and come in to eat like I was waiting for him to do. He shovelled and shovelled a long path out of sight and then he was gone and didn't come back. He didn't come back until near dark and then he said he had eaten. I said, did you tell them about the tree? Then he looked at me for the first time in a bad way. It was the same bad way his brother used to look. I never said anything more to him about what had happened or hinted at it in any way. And he never said anything to me, except he would come and say things in my dreams. But I knew the difference always between my dreams and when I was awake, and when I was awake it was never anything but the bad look.

Mrs. Treece came and tried to get me to go and live with them the way George was living. She said I could eat and sleep there, they had enough beds. I would not go. They thought I would not go because of my grief but I wouldn't go because somebody might see my black and blue, also they would be watching for me to cry. I said I was not frightened to stay alone.

I dreamed nearly every night that one or other of them came and chased me with the axe. It was him or it was George, one or the other. Or sometimes not the axe, it was a big rock lifted in both hands and one of them waiting with it behind the door. Dreams are sent to warn us.

I didn't stay in the house where he could find me and when I gave up sleeping inside and slept outside I didn't have the dream so often. It got warm in a hurry and the flies and mosquitoes came but they hardly bothered me. I would see their bites but not feel them, which was another sign that in the outside I was protected. I got down when I heard anybody coming. I ate berries both red and black and God protected me from any badness in them.

I had another kind of dream after a while. I dreamed George came and talked to me and he still had the bad look but was trying to cover it up and pretend that he was kind. He kept coming into my dreams and he kept lying to me. It was starting to get colder out and I did not want to go back in the shanty and the dew was heavy so I would be soaking when I slept in the grass. I went and opened the Bible to find out what I should do.

And now I got my punishment for cheating because the Bible did not tell me anything that I could understand, what to do. The cheating was when I was looking to find something for George, and I did not read exactly where my finger landed but looked around quick and found something else that was more what I wanted. I used to do that too when we would be looking up our verses in the Home and I always got good things and nobody ever caught me or suspected me at it. You never did either, Sadie.

So now I had my punishment when I couldn't find anything to help me however I looked. But something put it into my head to come here and I did, I had heard them talking about how warm it was and tramps would be wanting to come and get locked up, so I thought, I will too, and it was put into my head to tell them what I did. I told them the very same lie that George told me so often in my dreams, trying to get me to believe it was me and not him. I am safe from George here is the main thing. If they think I am crazy and I know the difference I am safe. Only I would like for you to come and see me.

And I would like for that yelling to stop.

When I am finished writing this, I will put it in with the curtains that I am making for the Opera House. And I will put on it, Finder Please Post. I trust that better than giving it to them like the two letters I gave them already that they never have sent.

I V

Miss Christena Mullen, Walley, to Mr. Leopold Henry, Department of History, Queen's University, Kingston, July 8, 1959.

Yes I am the Miss Mullen that Treece Herron's sister remembers coming to the farm and it is very kind of her to say

I was a pretty young lady in a hat and veil. That was my motoring-veil. The old lady she mentions was Mr. Herron's grandfather's sister-in-law, if I have got it straight. As you are doing the biography, you will have got the relationships worked out. I never voted for Treece Herron myself since I am a Conservative, but he was a colorful politician and as you say a biography of him will bring some attention to this part of the country—too often thought of as "deadly dull."

I am rather surprised the sister does not mention the car in particular. It was a Stanley Steamer. I bought it myself on my twenty-fifth birthday in 1907. It cost twelve hundred dollars, that being part of my inheritance from my grandfather James Mullen who was an early Clerk of the Peace in Walley. He made money buying and selling farms.

My father having died young, my mother moved into my grandfather's house with all us five girls. It was a big cut-stone house called Traquair, now a Home for Young Offenders. I sometimes say in joke that it always was!

When I was young, we employed a gardener, a cook, and a sewing-woman. All of them were "characters," all prone to feuding with each other, and all owing their jobs to the fact that my grandfather had taken an interest in them when they were inmates at the County Gaol (as it used to be spelled) and eventually had brought them home.

By the time I bought the Steamer, I was the only one of my sisters living at home, and the sewing-woman was the only one of these old servants who remained. The sewing-woman was called Old Annie and never objected to that name. She used it herself and would write notes to the cook that said, "Tea was not hot, did you warm the pot? Old Annie." The whole third floor was Old Annie's domain and one of my sisters—Dolly—said that whenever she dreamed of home, that is, of Traquair, she dreamed of Old Annie up at the top of the third-floor stairs brandishing her measuring stick and wearing a black dress with long fuzzy black arms like a spider.

She had one eye that slid off to the side and gave her the air of taking in more information than the ordinary person.

We were not supposed to pester the servants with questions about their personal lives, particularly those who had been in the Gaol, but of course we did. Sometimes Old Annie called the Gaol the Home. She said that a girl in the next bed screamed and screamed, and that was why she—Annie—ran away and lived in the woods. She said the girl had been beaten for letting the fire go out. Why were you in jail, we asked her, and she would say, "I told a fib!" So for quite a while we had the impression that you went to jail for telling lies!

Some days she was in a good mood and would play hide-the-thimble with us. Sometimes she was in a bad mood and would stick us with pins when she was evening our hems if we turned too quickly or stopped too soon. She knew a place, she said, where you could get bricks to put on children's heads to stop them growing. She hated making wedding dresses (she never had to make one for me!) and didn't think much of any of the men that my sisters married. She hated Dolly's beau so much that she made some kind of deliberate mistake with the sleeves which had to be ripped out, and Dolly cried. But she made us all beautiful ball gowns to wear when the Governor-General and Lady Minto came to Walley.

About being married herself, she sometimes said she had been and sometimes not. She said a man had come to the Home and had all the girls paraded in front of him and said, "I'll take the one with the coal-black hair." That being Old Annie, but she refused to go with him, even though he was rich and came in a carriage. Rather like Cinderella but with a different ending. Then she said a bear killed her husband, in the woods, and my grandfather had killed the bear, and wrapped her in its skin and taken her home from the Gaol.

My mother used to say, "Now, girls. Don't get Old Annie going. And don't believe a word she says."

I am going on at great length filling in the background but you did say you were interested in details of the period. I am like most people my age and forget to buy milk but could tell you the color of the coat I had when I was eight.

So when I got the Stanley Steamer, Old Annie asked to be taken for a ride. It turned out that what she had in mind was more of a trip. This was a surprise since she had never wanted to go on trips before and refused to go to Niagara Falls and would not even go down to the Harbor to see the fireworks on the First of July. Also she was leery of automobiles and of me as a driver. But the big surprise was that she had somebody she wanted to go and see. She wanted to drive to Carstairs to see the Herron family, who she said were her relatives. She had never received any visits or letters from these people, and when I asked if she had written to ask if we might visit she said, "I can't write." This was ridiculous—she wrote those notes to the cooks and long lists for me of things she wanted me to pick up down on the Square or in the city. Braid, buckram, taffeta—she could spell all of that.

"And they don't need to know beforehand," she said. "In the country it's different."

Well, I loved taking jaunts in the Steamer. I had been driving since I was fifteen but this was the first car of my own and possibly the only Steam car in Huron County. Everybody would run to see it go by. It did not make a beastly loud noise coughing and clanking like other cars but rolled along silently more or less like a ship with high sails over the lake waters and it did not foul the air but left behind a plume of steam. Stanley Steamers were banned in Boston, because of steam fogging the air. I always loved to tell people, I used to drive a car that was banned in Boston!

We started out fairly early on a Sunday in June. It took about twenty-five minutes to get the steam up and all that time Old Annie sat up straight in the front seat as if the show were already on the road. We both had our motoring-veils on, and long dusters, but the dress Old Annie was wearing underneath was of plum-colored silk. In fact it was made over from the one she had made for my grandmother to meet the Prince of Wales in.

The Steamer covered the miles like an angel. It would do fifty miles an hour—great then—but I did not push it. I was trying to consider Old Annie's nerves. People were still in church when we started, but later on the roads were full of horses and buggies making the journey home. I was polite as all get-out, edging by them. But it turned out Old Annie did not want to be so sedate and she kept saying, "Give it a squeeze," meaning the horn, which was worked by a bulb under a mudguard down at my side.

She must not have been out of Walley for more years than I had been alive. When we crossed the bridge at Saltford (that old iron bridge where there used to be so many accidents because of the turn at both ends), she said that there didn't used to be a bridge there, you had to pay a man to row you.

"I couldn't pay but I crossed on the stones and just hiked up my skirts and waded," she said. "It was that dry a summer."

Naturally I did not know what summer she was talking about.

Then it was, Look at the big fields, where are the stumps gone, where is the bush? And look how straight the road goes, and they're building their houses out of brick! And what are those buildings as big as churches?

Barns, I said.

I knew my way to Carstairs all right but expected help from Old Annie once we got there. None was forthcoming. I drove up and down the main street waiting for her to spot something familiar. "If I could just see the inn," she said, "I'd know where the track goes off behind it."

It was a factory town, not very pretty in my opinion. The Steamer of course got attention, and I was able to call out for directions to the Herron farm without stopping the engine. Shouts and gestures and finally I was able to get us on the right road. I told Old Annie to watch the mailboxes but she was concerned with finding the creek. I spotted the name myself, and turned us in at a long lane with a red brick house at the end of it and a couple of these barns that had amazed Old Annie. Red brick houses with verandas and key windows were all the style then, they were going up everywhere.

"Look there!" Old Annie said, and I thought she meant where a herd of cows was tearing away from us in the pasture-field alongside the lane. But she was pointing at a mound pretty well covered with wild grape, a few logs sticking out of it. She said that was the shanty. I said, "Well, good—now let's hope you recognize one or two of the people."

There were enough people around. A couple of visiting buggies were pulled up in the shade, horses tethered and cropping grass. By the time the Steamer stopped at the side veranda, a number were lined up to look at it. They didn't come forward—not even the children ran out to look close up the way town children would have done. They all just stood in a row looking at it in a tight-lipped sort of way.

Old Annie was staring off in the other direction.

She told me to get down. Get down, she said, and ask them if there is a Mr. George Herron that lives here and is he alive yet, or dead?

I did what I was told. And one of the men said, that's right. He is. My father.

Well, I have brought somebody, I told them. I have brought Mrs. Annie Herron.

The man said, that so?

(A pause here due to a couple of fainting-fits and a trip to the hospital. Lots of tests to use up the taxpayers' money. Now I'm back and have read this over, astounded at the rambling but too lazy to start again. I have not even got to Treece Herron, which is the part you are interested in, but hold on, I'm nearly there.)

These people were all dumbfounded about Old Annie, or so I gathered. They had not known where she was or what she was doing or if she was alive. But you mustn't think they surged out and greeted her in any excited way. Just the one young man came out, very mannerly, and helped first her then me down from the car. He said to me that Old Annie was his grandfather's sister-in-law. It was too bad we hadn't come even a few months sooner, he said, because his grandfather had been quite well and his mind quite clear—he had even written a piece for the paper about his early days here—but then he had got sick. He had recovered but would never be himself again. He could not talk, except now and then a few words.

This mannerly young man was Treece Herron.

We must have arrived just after they finished their dinner. The woman of the house came out and asked him—Treece Herron—to ask us if we had eaten. You would think she or we did not speak English. They were all very shy—the women with their skinned-back hair, and men in dark-blue Sunday suits, and tongue-tied children. I hope you do not think I am making fun of them—it is just that I cannot understand for the life of me why it is necessary to be so shy.

We were taken to the dining-room which had an unused

smell—they must have had their dinner elsewhere—and were served a great deal of food of which I remember salted radishes and leaf lettuce and roast chicken and strawberries and cream. Dishes from the china cabinet, not their usual. Good old Indian Tree. They had sets of everything. Plushy living-room suite, walnut dining-room suite. It was going to take them a while, I thought, to get used to being prosperous.

Old Annie enjoyed the fuss of being waited on and ate a lot, picking up the chicken bones to work the last shred of meat off them. Children lurked around the doorways and the women talked in subdued, rather scandalized voices out in the kitchen. The young man, Treece Herron, had the grace to sit down with us and drink a cup of tea while we ate. He chatted readily enough about himself and told me he was a divinity student at Knox College. He said he liked living in Toronto. I got the feeling he wanted me to understand that divinity students were not all such sticks as I supposed or led such a stringent existence. He had been tobogganing in High Park, he had been picnicking at Hanlan's Point, he had seen the giraffe in the Riverdale Zoo. As he talked, the children got a little bolder and started trickling into the room. I asked the usual idiocies . . . How old are you, what book are you in at school, do you like your teacher? He urged them to answer or answered for them and told me which were his brothers and sisters and which his cousins.

Old Annie said, "Are you all fond of each other, then?" which brought on funny looks.

The woman of the house came back and spoke to me again through the divinity student. She told him that Grandpa was up now and sitting on the front porch. She looked at the children and said, "What did you let all them in here for?"

Out we trooped to the front porch, where two straight-backed chairs were set up and an old man settled on one of them. He had a beautiful full white beard reaching down to the bottom of his waistcoat. He did not seem interested in us. He had a long, pale, obedient old face.

Old Annie said, "Well, George," as if this was about what she had expected. She sat on the other chair and said to one of the little girls, "Now bring me a cushion. Bring me a thin kind of cushion and put it at my back."

I spent the afternoon giving rides in the Stanley Steamer. I knew enough about them now not to start in asking who wanted a ride, or bombarding them with questions, such as, were they interested in automobiles? I just went out and patted it here and there as if it was a horse, and I looked in the boiler. The divinity student came behind and read the name of the Steamer written on the side. "The Gentleman's Speedster." He asked was it my father's.

Mine, I said. I explained how the water in the boiler was heated and how much steam-pressure the boiler could withstand. People always wondered about that—about explosions. The children were closer by that time and I suddenly remarked that the boiler was nearly empty. I asked if there was any way I could get some water.

Great scurry to get pails and man the pump! I went and asked the men on the veranda if that was all right, and thanked them when they told me, help yourself. Once the boiler was filled, it was natural for me to ask if they would like me to get the steam up, and a spokesman said, it wouldn't hurt. Nobody was impatient during the wait. The men stared at the boiler, concentrating. This was certainly not the first car they had seen but probably the first steam car.

I offered the men a ride first, as it was proper to. They watched skeptically while I fiddled with all the knobs and levers to get my lady going. Thirteen different things to push or pull! We bumped down the lane at five, then ten miles an hour. I knew they suffered somewhat, being driven by a woman, but the novelty of the experience held them. Next I got a load of children, hoisted in by the divinity student telling them to sit still and hold on and not be scared and not fall out. I put up the speed a little, knowing now the ruts and puddle-holes, and their hoots of fear and triumph could not be held back.

I have left out something about how I was feeling but will leave it out no longer, due to the effects of a martini I am drinking now, my late-afternoon pleasure. I had troubles then I have not yet admitted to you because they were love-troubles. But when I had set out that day with Old Annie, I had determined to enjoy myself as much as I could. It seemed it would be an insult to the Stanley Steamer not to. All my life I found this a good rule to follow—to get as much pleasure as you could out of things even when you weren't likely to be happy.

I told one of the boys to run around to the front veranda and ask if his grandfather would care for a ride. He came back and said, "They've both gone to sleep."

I had to get the boiler filled up before we started back, and while this was being done, Treece Herron came and stood close to me.

"You have given us all a day to remember," he said.

I wasn't above flirting with him. I actually had a long career as a flirt ahead of me. It's quite a natural behavior, once the loss of love makes you give up your ideas of marriage.

I said he would forget all about it, once he got back to his friends in Toronto. He said no indeed, he would never forget, and he asked if he could write to me. I said nobody could stop him.

On the way home I thought about this exchange and how ridiculous it would be if he should get a serious crush on me. A divinity student. I had no idea then of course that he would be getting out of Divinity and into Politics.

"Too bad old Mr. Herron wasn't able to talk to you," I said to Old Annie.

She said, "Well, I could talk to him."

Actually, Treece Herron did write to me, but he must have had a few misgivings as well because he enclosed some pamphlets about Mission Schools. Something about raising money for Mission Schools. That put me off and I didn't write back. (Years later I would joke that I could have married him if I'd played my cards right.)

I asked Old Annie if Mr. Herron could understand her when she talked to him, and she said, "Enough." I asked if she was glad about seeing him again and she said yes. "And glad for him to get to see me," she said, not without some gloating that probably referred to her dress and the vehicle.

So we just puffed along in the Steamer under the high arching trees that lined the roads in those days. From miles away the lake could be seen—just glimpses of it, shots of light, held wide apart in the trees and hills so that Old Annie asked me if it could possibly be the same lake, all the same one that Walley was on?

There were lots of old people going around then with ideas in their heads that didn't add up—though I suppose Old Annie had more than most. I recall her telling me another time that a girl in the Home had a baby out of a big boil that burst on her stomach, and it was the size of a rat and had no life in it, but they put it in the oven and it puffed up to the right size and baked to a good color and started to kick its legs. (Ask an old woman to reminisce and you get the whole rag-bag, is what you must be thinking by now.)

I told her that wasn't possible, it must have been a dream.

"Maybe so," she said, agreeing with me for once. "I did used to have the terriblest dreams."

SPACESHIPS
HAVE
LANDED

On the night of Eunie Morgan's disappearance, Rhea was sitting in the bootlegger's house at Carstairs—Monk's—a bare, narrow wooden house, soiled halfway up the walls by the periodic flooding of the river. Billy Doud had brought her. He was playing cards at one end of the big table and a conversation was going on at the other end. Rhea was seated in a rocking chair, over in a corner by the coal-oil stove, out of the way.

"A call of nature, then, let's say a call of nature," a man was saying, who had formerly said something about a crap. Another man had told him to watch his language. Nobody looked at Rhea, but she knew she was the reason.

"Out on the rocks to answer a call of nature. And he was thinking he'd like a piece of something, to come in handy. Though he didn't naturally expect to find it there. And what does he see? Sees this stuff laying around. Sheets of it, laying around. If that isn't the very thing! Laying all over, in sheets. So he picks it up and stuffs it in his pockets and thinks, Plenty for the next time. Doesn't think any more about it. Back to the camp."

"He was in the Army?" said a man Rhea knew—the man who shovelled the snow off the school sidewalks, through the winter.

"What made you think that? I never said that!"

"You said camp. Army camp," said the snow-shoveller. His name was Dint Mason.

"I never said Army camp. I'm talking about lumber camp. Away up north in the Province of Quebec. What would an Army camp be doing up there?"

"I thought you said Army camp."

"So somebody sees what he's got. What's that there? Well, he says, I don't know. Where'd you pick it up? It was just laying around. Well, what do you think it is? Well, I don't know."

"Sounds a lot like asbestos," said another man Rhea knew by sight, a former teacher, who now sold pots and pans for waterless cookery. He was a diabetic, and his condition was supposed to be so severe that he always had a drop of pure sugar, crystallized, at the end of his penis.

"Asbestos," said the man who was telling the story, not pleased. "And on the spot they developed the biggest asbestos mine in the entire world. And from that mine came a fortune!"

Dint Mason spoke up again. "Not for the fellow that found it, I bet you it wasn't. It never is. It never is a fortune for the fellows that found it."

"It is sometimes," said the man telling the story.

"Never is," Dint said.

"Some have found gold and got the good of it," the man

telling the story insisted. "Plenty have! They've found gold and they've got to be millionaires. Billionaires. Sir Harry Oakes, for instance. He found it. He got to be a millionaire!"

"He got himself killed," said a man who had not taken any part in the conversation till now. Dint Mason began to laugh and several others began to laugh, and the pots-and-pans man said, "Millionaires? Billionaires? What is it comes after billionaires?"

"Got himself killed, so that's how he got the good of it!" Dint Mason cried at the highest pitch of the laughter. The man who had told the story brought his flat hands down and shook the table.

"I never said he didn't! I never said he didn't get killed! We aren't talking here about whether he got killed! I said he found it, he got the good of it, he got to be a millionaire!"

Everybody had grabbed their bottles and glasses, to keep them from toppling. Even the men playing cards had stopped to laugh. Billy had his back to Rhea, his wide shoulders gleaming in a white shirt. His friend Wayne was standing at the other side of the table, watching the game. Wayne was the United Church minister's son, from Bondi, a village not far from Carstairs. He had been at college with Billy, he was going to be a journalist—he already had a job, on a newspaper in Calgary. As the conversation about asbestos proceeded, he had looked up and caught Rhea's eye, and from then on he watched her, with a slight, tight, persistent smile. This was not the first time Wayne had caught Rhea's eye, but usually he didn't smile. He would look at her and look away, sometimes when Billy was talking.

Mr. Monk pulled himself to his feet. Some illness or accident had crippled him—he walked with a stick, bent forward nearly at a right angle, from the waist. Sitting down, he looked almost normal. Standing up, he was tilted across the table, into the middle of the laughter.

The man who had told the story got up at the same time and, perhaps without meaning to, knocked his glass to the floor. It smashed, and the men began to shout, "Pay up! Pay up!"

"Pay next time," said Mr. Monk, in a voice to settle everybody down—a large and genial voice for a man so wracked and dwindled.

"There's not so many brains in this room as there is arseholes!" shouted the man who had told the story, treading on glass, kicking it aside, trotting past Rhea's chair towards the back door. His hands were clenching and unclenching and his eyes were full of tears.

Mrs. Monk brought the broom.

Ordinarily, Rhea wouldn't have been inside this house at all. She would have been sitting outside with Lucille, who was Wayne's girl, in either Wayne's car or Billy's. Billy and Wayne would go in for one drink, promising to be out in half an hour. (This promise was not to be taken seriously.) But on this night—it was early in August—Lucille was at home sick, Billy and Rhea had gone to the dance in Walley by themselves and afterward they hadn't parked, they had driven directly across country to Monk's. Monk's was on the edge of Carstairs, where Billy and Rhea lived. Billy lived in town, Rhea lived on the chicken farm just up over the bridge from this row of houses along the river.

When Billy saw Wayne's car parked outside Monk's, he greeted it as if it had been Wayne himself. "Ho-ho-ho! Wayne-the-boy!" he cried. "Beat us to it!" He gave Rhea's shoulder a squeeze. "In we go," he said. "You, too."

Mrs. Monk opened the back door to them and Billy said, "See—I brought a neighbor of yours." Mrs. Monk looked at Rhea as if Rhea were a stone on the road. Billy Doud had odd ideas about people. He lumped them together, if they were poor—what he would call poor—or "working class." (Rhea knew that term only from books.) He lumped Rhea in with the Monks because she lived up the hill on the chicken farm—not understanding that her family didn't consider themselves neighbors to the people in these houses, or that her father would never in his life have sat down to drink here.

Rhea had met Mrs. Monk on the road to town, but Mrs. Monk never spoke. Her dark, graying hair was coiled up at the back of her head, and she didn't wear makeup. She had kept a slender figure, as not many women did in Carstairs. Her clothes were neat and plain, not particularly youthful but not what Rhea thought of as housewifely. She wore a checked skirt tonight and a short-sleeved yellow blouse. Her expression was always the same—not hostile, but grave and preoccupied, as if she had a familiar weight of disillusionment and worry.

She led Billy and Rhea into this room in the middle of the house. The men sitting at the table did not look up or take any notice of Billy until he pulled out a chair. There might have been some sort of rule about this. All ignored Rhea. Mrs. Monk lifted something out of the rocking chair and made a gesture for her to sit down.

"Get you a Coca-Cola?" she said.

The crinoline under Rhea's lime-green dance dress made a noise like crackling straw as she sat down. She laughed apologetically, but Mrs. Monk had already turned away. The only person who took any notice of the noise was Wayne, who was just coming into the room from the front hall. He raised his black eyebrows in a comradely but incriminating way. She never knew whether Wayne liked her or not. Even when he danced with her, at the Walley Pavilion (he and Billy did an obligatory, one-time-a-night exchange of partners), he held her as if she were a package he was barely responsible for. He was a lifeless dancer.

He and Billy hadn't taken notice of each other as they usually did, with a growl and a punch in the air. They were cautious and reserved in front of these older men.

Besides Dint Mason and the man who sold pots and pans, Rhea knew Mr. Martin from the dry cleaners', and Mr. Boles the undertaker. Some of the others had familiar faces, and some didn't. None of these men would be exactly in disgrace for coming here—Monk's was not a disgraceful place. Yet it left a slight stain. It was mentioned as if it explained something. Even if a man flourished. "He goes to Monk's."

Mrs. Monk brought Rhea a Coca-Cola without a glass. It was not cold.

What Mrs. Monk had removed from the chair, to let Rhea sit down, was a pile of clothes that had been dampened and rolled up for ironing. So ironing went on here, ordinary housekeeping. Piecrust might be rolled out on that table. Meals were cooked—there was the woodstove, cold and spread with newspapers now, the coal-oil stove serving for summer. There was a smell of coal oil and damp plaster. Flood stains on the wallpaper. Barren tidiness, dark-green blinds pulled down to the windowsills. A tin curtain in one corner, probably concealing an old dumbwaiter.

Mrs. Monk was to Rhea the most interesting person in the room. Her legs were bare but she wore high heels. They were tapping all the time on the floorboards. Around the table, back and forth from the sideboard where the whisky bottles were (and where she would pause, to write things down on a pad of paper—Rhea's Coca-Cola, the broken glass). Tap-tap-tap down the back hall to some supply base from which she returned with a clutch of beer bottles in each hand. She was as watchful as a deaf-mute, and as silent, catching every signal around the table, responding obediently, unsmilingly, to every demand. This brought to Rhea's mind the rumors there were about Mrs. Monk, and she thought of another sort of signal a man might make. Mrs. Monk would lay aside her apron, and she would precede him out of the room into the front hall, where there must be a stairway, leading to the bedrooms. The other men, including her husband, would pretend not to notice. She would mount the stairs without looking back, letting the man follow with his eyes on her neat buttocks in her schoolteacher's skirt. Then, on a waiting bed, she arranges herself without the least hesitation or enthusiasm. This indifferent readiness, this cool accommodation, the notion of such a quick and driven and bought and paid-for encounter, was to Rhea shamefully exciting.

To be so flattened and used and hardly to know who was doing it to you, to take it all in with that secret capability, over and over again.

She thought of Wayne coming out of the front hall just as she and Billy were being brought into the room. She thought, What if he was coming from up there? (Later he told her that he had been using the phone—phoning Lucille, as he had promised. Later she came to believe those rumors were false.)

She heard a man say, "Watch your language."

"A call of nature, then, all right, a call of nature."

Eunie Morgan's house was the third one past Monk's. It was the last house on the road. Around midnight, Eunie's mother said, she had heard the screen door close. She heard the screen door and thought nothing of it. She thought of course that Eunie had gone out to the toilet. Even by 1953 the Morgans had no indoor plumbing.

Of course none of them went as far as the toilet, late at night. Eunie and the old woman squatted on the grass. The old man watered the spirea at the far end of the porch.

Then I must have gone to sleep, Eunie's mother said, but I woke up later on and I thought that I never heard her come in.

She went downstairs and walked around in the house. Eunie's room was behind the kitchen, but she might be sleeping anywhere on a hot night. She might be on the couch in the front room or stretched out on the hall floor to get the breeze between the doors. She might have gone out on the porch where there was a decent car seat that her father, years ago, had found discarded farther down the road. Her mother could not find her anywhere. The kitchen clock said twenty past two.

Eunie's mother went back upstairs and shook Eunie's father till he woke up.

"Eunie's not down there," she said.

"Where is she, then?" said her husband, as if it was up to her to know. She had to shake him and shake him, to keep him from going back to sleep. He had a great indifference to news, a reluctance to listen to what anybody said, even when he was awake.

"Get up, get up," she said. "We got to find her." Finally he obeyed her, sat up, pulled on his trousers and his boots. "Get your flashlight," she told him, and with him behind her she went down the stairs again, out onto the porch, down into the yard. It was his job to shine the flashlight—she told him where. She directed him along the path to the toilet, which stood in a clump of lilacs and currant bushes at the back of the property. They poked the light inside the building and found nothing. Then they peered in among the sturdy lilac trunks—these were practically trees—and along the path, almost lost now, that led through a sagging section of the wire fence to the wild growth along the riverbank. Nothing there. Nobody.

Back through the vegetable garden they went, lighting up the dusted potato plants and the rhubarb that was now grandly gone to seed. The old man lifted a great rhubarb leaf with his boot, shone the light under that. His wife asked whether he had gone crazy.

She recalled that Eunie used to walk in her sleep. But that was years ago.

She spotted something glinting at the corner of the house, like knives or a man in armor. "There. There," she said. "Shine it there. What's that?" It was only Eunie's bicycle, which she rode to work every day.

Then the mother called Eunie's name. She called it at the back and at the front of the house—plum trees grew as high as the house in front and there was no sidewalk, just a dirt path between them. Their trunks crowded in like watchers, crooked black animals. When she waited for an answer, she heard the gulp of a frog, as close as if it sat in those branches. Half a mile farther on, this road ended up in a field too marshy for any use, with weedy poplars growing up through the willow bushes and elderberries. In the other direction, it met the road from town, then crossed the river and climbed the hill to the chicken farm. On the river flats lay the old fairgrounds, some grandstands abandoned since before the war, when the fair here was taken over by the big fair at Walley. The racetrack oval was still marked out in the grass.

This was where the town set out to be, over a hundred years ago. Mills and hostelries were here. But the river floods persuaded people to move to higher ground. House-plots remained on the map, and roads laid out, but only the one row of houses where people lived was still there, people who were too poor or in some way too stubborn to change—or, at the other extreme, too temporary in their living arrangements to object to the invasion of the water.

They gave up—Eunie's parents did. They sat down in the kitchen without any light on. It was between three and four o'clock. It must have seemed as if they were waiting for Eunie to come and tell them what to do. It was Eunie who was in charge in that house, and they probably could hardly imagine a time when it had been otherwise. Nineteen years ago she had literally burst into their lives. Mrs. Morgan had thought she was having the change and getting stout—she was stout enough already that it did not make much difference. She thought the commotion in her stomach was what people called indigestion. She knew how people got children, she was not a dunce—it was just that she had gone on so long without any such thing happening. One day in the post office she had to ask for a chair, she was weak and overcome by cramps. Then her water broke, she was hustled over to the hospital, and Eunie popped out with a full head of white hair. She was claiming attention from the moment of her birth.

One whole summer, Eunie and Rhea played together, but they never had thought of their activity as play. Playing was what they called it to satisfy other people. It was the most serious part of their lives. What they did the rest of the time seemed frivolous, forgettable. When they cut from Eunie's yard down to the riverbank, they became different people. Each of them was called Tom. The Two Toms. A Tom was a noun to them, not just a name. It was not male or female. It meant somebody exceptionally brave and clever but not always lucky, and—just barely—indestructible. The Toms had a battle which could never end and this was with the Bannershees. (Perhaps Rhea and Eunie had heard of banshees.) The Bannershees lurked along the river and could take the form of robbers or Germans or skeletons. Their tricks and propensities were endless. They laid traps and lay in ambush and tortured the children they had stolen. Sometimes Eunie and Rhea got some real children—the McKays, who lived briefly in one of the river houses—and persuaded them to let themselves be tied up and thrashed with cattails. But the McKays could not or would not submit themselves to the plot, and they soon cried or escaped and went home, so that it was just the Toms again.

The Toms built a city of mud by the riverbank. It was walled with stones against the Bannershees' attack, and contained a royal palace, a swimming pool, a flag. But then the Toms took a journey and the Bannershees levelled it all. (Of course Eunie and Rhea had to change themselves, often, into Bannershees.) A new leader appeared, a Bannershee Queen, her name was Joylinda, and her schemes were diabolical. She had poisoned the blackberries growing on the bank, and the Toms had eaten some, being careless and hungry after their journey. They lay writhing and sweating down among the juicy weeds when the poison struck. They pressed their bellies into mud that was slightly soft and warm like just-made fudge. They felt their innards shrivel and they were shaking in every limb, but they had to get up and stagger about, looking for an antidote. They tried chewing sword grass—which, true to its name, could slice your skin—they smeared their mouths with mud, and considered biting into a live frog if they could catch one, but decided at last it was chokecherries that would save them from death. They ate a cluster of the tiny chokecherries and the skin inside their mouths puckered desperately, so that they had to run to the river to drink the water. They threw themselves down on it, where it was all silty among the waterlilies and you couldn't see the bottom. They drank and drank it, while the bluebottles flew straight as arrows over their heads. They were saved.

Emerging from this world in the late afternoon, they found themselves in Eunie's yard where her parents would be working still, or again, hoeing or hilling or weeding their vegetables. They would lie down in the shade of the house, exhausted as if they had swum lakes or climbed mountains. They smelled of the river, of the wild garlic and mint they had squashed underfoot, of the hot rank grass and the foul mud where the drain emptied. Sometimes Eunie would go into the house and get them something to eat—slices of bread with corn syrup or molasses. She never had to ask if she could do this. She always kept the bigger piece for herself.

They were not friends, in the way that Rhea would understand being friends, later on. They never tried to please or
comfort each other. They did not share secrets, except for the
game, and even that was not a secret because they let others
come and go in it. But they never let the others be Toms. So
maybe that was what they shared, in their intense and daily
collaboration. The nature, the danger, of being Toms.

Eunie never seemed subject to her parents, or even connected
to them, in the way of other children. Rhea was struck by the
way she ruled her own life, the careless power she had in the
house. When Rhea said that she had to be home at a certain
time, or that she had to do chores, or change her clothes,
Eunie was affronted, disbelieving. Every decision Eunie took
must have been on her own. When she was fifteen, she
stopped going to school and got a job in the glove factory,
and Rhea could imagine her just coming home and announcing to her parents that was what she had done. No, not even
announcing it—it would come out in an offhand way, maybe
when she started getting home later in the afternoon. Now
that she was earning money, she bought a bicycle. She bought
a radio, and listened to it in her room late at night. Perhaps
her parents would hear shots ring out then, vehicles roaring
through the streets. She might tell them things she had
heard—the news of crimes and accidents, hurricanes, ava-
lanches. Rhea didn't think they would pay much attention.
They were busy and their life was eventful, though the events
in it were seasonal and had to do with the vegetables they sold
in town to earn their living. The vegetables, the raspberries,
the rhubarb. They hadn't time for much else.

While Eunie was still in school Rhea was riding her bicycle, so they never walked together although they took the
same route. When Rhea rode past Eunie, Eunie was in the

habit of shouting out something challenging, disparaging. "Hi-oh, Silver!" And now, when Eunie had a bicycle, Rhea had started walking—there was a notion at the high school that any girl who rode a bicycle after Grade 9 looked gawky and ridiculous. But Eunie would dismount, and walk along beside Rhea, as if she was doing her a favor.

It was not a favor at all—Rhea did not want her. Eunie had always been a peculiar sight, tall for her age, with sharp, narrow shoulders, a whitish-blond crest of fuzzy hair sticking up at the crown of her head, a cocksure expression, and a long, heavy jaw. That jaw gave a thickness to the lower part of her face that seemed reflected in the thickness, the phlegmy growl, of her voice. When she was younger, none of that had mattered—her own conviction, that everything about her was the proper thing, had daunted many. But now she was five feet nine or ten, drab and mannish in her slacks and bandannas, with big feet in what looked like men's shoes, a hectoring voice, and an ungainly walk—she had gone right from being a child to being a character. And she spoke to Rhea with a proprietary air that grated, asking her if she wasn't tired of going to school, or if her bike was broken and her father couldn't afford to get it fixed. When Rhea got a permanent, Eunie wanted to know what had happened to her hair. All this she thought she could do because she and Rhea lived on the same side of town and had played together, in an era that seemed to Rhea so distant and discardable. And the worst thing was when Eunie launched into accounts that Rhea found both boring and infuriating, of murders and disasters and freakish events that she had heard about on the radio. Rhea was infuriated because she could not get Eunie to tell her whether these things had really happened, or even to make that distinction—as far as Rhea could tell—to herself.

Was that on the news, Eunie? Was it a story? Were there peo-

ple acting it in front of a microphone or was it reporting? Eunie!
Was it real or was it a play?

It was Rhea, never Eunie, who would get frazzled by these
questions. Eunie would just get on her bicycle and ride away.
"Toodeley oodeley oo! See you in the zoo!"

Eunie's job suited her, surely. The glove factory occupied
the second and third floor of a building on the main street,
and in the warm weather, when the windows were open, you
could hear not only the sewing machines but the loud jokes,
the quarrels and insults, the famous rough language of the
women who worked there. They were supposed to be of a
lower class than waitresses, much lower than store clerks.
They worked longer hours and made less money, but that
didn't make them humble. Far from it. They came jostling and
joking down the stairs and burst out onto the street. They
yelled at cars in which there were people they knew, and people they didn't know. They spread disorder as if they had every right.

People close to the bottom, like Eunie Morgan, or right at
the top, like Billy Doud, showed a similar carelessness, a
blunted understanding.

During her last year at high school, Rhea got a job, too. She
worked in the shoe store on Saturday afternoons. Billy Doud
came into the store, in early spring, and said he wanted to buy
a pair of rubber boots like the ones hanging up outside.

He was through college at last, home learning how to run
Douds piano factory.

Billy took off his shoes and displayed his feet in fine black
socks. Rhea told him that it would be better to wear woollen
socks, work socks, inside rubber boots, so that his feet
wouldn't slide around. He asked if they sold such socks and

said he would buy a pair of those, too, if Rhea would bring them. Then he asked her if she would put the wool socks on his feet.

This was all a ploy, he told her later. He didn't need either one, boots or socks.

His feet were long and white and perfectly sweet-smelling. A scent of lovely soap arose, a whiff of talcum. He leaned back in the chair, tall and pale, cool and clean—he himself might have been carved from soap. A high curved forehead, temples already bare, hair with a glint of tinsel, sleepy ivory eyelids.

"That's sweet of you," he said, and asked her to go to a dance that night, the opening dance of the season in the Walley Pavilion.

After that, they went to the dance in Walley every Saturday night. They didn't go out together during the week, because Billy had to get up early and go to the factory and learn the business—from his mother, known as the Tatar—and Rhea had to do some housekeeping for her father and brothers. Her mother was in the hospital, in Hamilton.

"There goes your heartthrob," girls would say if Billy drove by the school when they were out playing volleyball, or if he passed on the street, and in truth Rhea's heart did throb—at the sight of him, his bright hatless hair, his negligent but surely powerful hands on the wheel. But also at the thought of herself suddenly singled out, so unexpectedly chosen, with the glow of a prizewinner—or a prize—about her now, a grace formerly hidden. Older women she didn't even know would smile at her on the street, girls wearing engagement rings spoke to her by name, and in the mornings she would wake up with the sense that she had been given a great present, but that her mind had boxed it away overnight, and she could not for a moment remember what it was.

Billy brought her honor everywhere but at home. That was

not unexpected—home, as Rhea knew it, was where they cut you down to size. Her younger brothers would imitate Billy offering their father a cigarette. "Have a Pall Mall, Mr. Sellers." They would flourish in front of him an imaginary package of ready-mades. The unctuous voice, the complacent gesture made Billy Doud seem asinine. "Putty" was what they called him. First "Silly Billy," then "Silly Putty," then "Putty" by itself.

"You quit tormenting your sister," Rhea's father said. Then he took it up himself, with a businesslike question. "You aim to keep on at the shoe store?"

Rhea said, "Why?"

"Oh. I was just thinking. You might need it."

"What for?"

"To support that fellow. Once his old lady's dead and he runs the business into the ground."

And all the time Billy Doud said how much he admired Rhea's father. Men like your father, he said. Who work so hard. Just to get along. And never expect any different. And are so decent, and even-tempered, and kindhearted. The world owes a lot to men like that.

Billy Doud and Rhea and Wayne and Lucille would leave the dance around midnight and drive in the two cars to the parking spot, at the end of a dirt road on the bluffs above Lake Huron. Billy kept the radio on, low. He always had the radio on, even though he might be telling Rhea some complicated story. His stories had to do with his life at college, with parties and practical jokes and dire escapades sometimes involving the police. They always had to do with drinking. Once, somebody who was drunk vomited out a car window, and so noxious was the drink he had taken that the paint was destroyed all down the side of the car. The characters in these stories were not known to Rhea, except for Wayne. Girls' names cropped up occasionally, and then she might have to interrupt. She had seen Billy Doud home from college, over the years, with girls whose looks, or clothes, whose jaunty or fragile airs, she had been greatly taken with, and now she had to ask him, Was Claire the one with the little hat that had a veil, and the purple gloves? In church? Which one had the long red hair and the camel's-hair coat? Who wore velvet boots with mouton tops?

Usually, Billy was not able to remember, and if he did go on to tell her more about these girls, what he had to say might not be complimentary.

When they parked, and sometimes even while they drove, Billy put an arm around Rhea's shoulders, he squeezed her. A promise. There were promises also during their dances. He was not too proud to nuzzle her cheek then, or drop a row of kisses on her hair. The kisses he gave her in the car were quicker, and the speed, the rhythm of them, the little smacks they might be served up with informed her that they were jokes, or partly jokes. He tapped his fingers on her, on her knees, and just at the top of her breasts, murmuring appreciatively and then scolding himself, or scolding Rhea, saying that he had to keep the lid on her.

"You're quite the baddy," he said. He pressed his lips tightly against hers as if it was his job to keep both their mouths shut.

"How you entice me," he said, in a voice not his own, the voice of some sleek and languishing movie actor, and slipped his hand between her legs, touched the skin above her stocking—then jumped, laughed, as if she was too hot there, or too cold.

"Wonder how old Wayne is getting on?" he said.

The rule was that after a time either he or Wayne would sound a blast on the car horn, and then the other one had to answer. This game—Rhea did not understand that it was a contest, or at any rate what kind of a contest it was—came eventually to take up more and more of his attention. "What do you think?" he would say, peering into the night at the dark shape of Wayne's car. "What do you think—should I give the boy the horn?"

On the drive back to Carstairs, to the bootlegger's, Rhea would feel like crying, for no reason, and her arms, her legs, would feel as if cement had been poured into them. Left alone, she would probably have fallen fast asleep, but she couldn't stay alone because Lucille was afraid of the dark, and when Billy and Wayne went into Monk's Rhea had to keep Lucille company.

Lucille was a thin, fair-haired girl, with a finicky stomach, irregular periods, and a sensitive skin. The vagaries of her body fascinated her and she treated it as if it was a troublesome but valuable pet. She always carried baby oil in her purse and patted it on her face, which would have been savaged, a little while ago, by Wayne's bristles. The car smelled of baby oil and there was another smell under that, like bread dough.

"I'm going to make him shave once we get married," Lucille said. "Right before."

Billy Doud had told Rhea that Wayne had told him he had stuck to Lucille all this time, and was going to marry her, because she would make a good wife. He said that she wasn't the prettiest girl in the world and she certainly wasn't the smartest and for that reason he would always feel secure in the marriage. She wouldn't have a lot of bargaining power, he said. And she wasn't used to having a lot of money.

"Some people might say that was taking a cynical approach," Billy had said. "But others might say realistic. A minister's son does have to be realistic, he's got to make his own way in life. Anyway, Wayne is Wayne.

"Wayne is Wayne," he had repeated with solemn pleasure.

One time Lucille said to Rhea. "So how about you? Are you getting used to it?"

"Oh, yes," Rhea said.

"They say it's better without gloves on. I guess I'll find out once I'm married."

Rhea was too embarrassed to admit not having understood at once what they were talking about.

Lucille said that once she was married she would be using sponges and jelly. Rhea thought that sounded like a dessert, but she did not laugh, because she knew Lucille would take such a joke as an insult. Lucille began to talk about the conflict that was raging round her wedding, about whether the bridesmaids should wear picture hats or wreaths of rosebuds. Lucille had wanted rosebuds, and she thought it was all arranged, and then Wayne's sister had got a permanent that turned out badly. Now she wanted a hat to cover it up.

"She isn't a friend, even—she's only in the wedding because of being his sister and I couldn't leave her out. She's a selfish person."

Wayne's sister's selfishness had made Lucille break out in hives.

Rhea and Lucille had rolled down the car windows for air. Outside was the night with the river washing out of sight, at its lowest now, among the large white stones, and the frogs and crickets singing, the dirt roads faintly shining on their way to nowhere, and the falling-down grandstand in the old fairgrounds sticking up like a crazy skeletal tower. Rhea knew that all this was there, but she couldn't pay attention to it. More than Lucille's talk prevented her—more than the wedding hats. She was lucky: Billy Doud had chosen her, an engaged girl was confiding in her, her life was turning out perhaps better than anybody might have predicted. But at a time like this she could feel cut off and bewildered, as if she had lost something instead of gaining it. As if she had suffered a banishment. From what?

• • •

Wayne had raised his hand to her across the room, meaning, was she thirsty? He brought her another bottle of Coca-Cola and slid down to the floor beside her. "Sit down before I fall down," he said.

She understood from the first sip, or maybe from the first sniff, or even before that, that there was something else in her drink besides Coca-Cola. She thought that she would not drink all, or even half of it. She would just take a little drink now and then, to show Wayne that he had not flummoxed her.

"Is that all right?" said Wayne. "Is that the kind of drink you like?"

"It's fine," Rhea said. "I like all kinds of drinks."

"All kinds? That's good. You sound like the right kind of girl for Billy Doud."

"Does he drink a lot?" Rhea said. "Billy?"

"Put it this way," said Wayne. "Is the Pope Jewish? No. Wait. Was Jesus Catholic? No. Continue. I would not want to give you the wrong impression. Nor do I want to get clinical about this. Is Billy a drunk? Is he an alcoholic? Is he an assoholic? I mean an asshole-oholic? No, I got that wrong too. I forgot who I was talking to. Excuse please. Eliminate. Solly."

He said all this in two strange voices—one artificially high, singsong, one gruff and serious. Rhea didn't think that she had ever heard him say so much before, in any kind of voice. It was Billy who talked, usually. Wayne said a word now and then, an unimportant word that seemed important because of the tone in which he said it. And yet this tone was often quite empty, quite neutral, the look on his face blank. That made people nervous. There was a sense of contempt being held in check. Rhea had seen Billy try and try to stretch a story, twist it, change its tone—all in order to get Wayne's grunt of approval, his absolving bark of laughter.

"You must not come to the conclusion that I don't like Billy," said Wayne. "No. No. I would never want you to think that."

"But you don't like him," Rhea said with satisfaction. "You don't at all." The satisfaction came from the fact that she was talking back to Wayne. She was looking him in the eye. No more than that. For he had made her nervous, too. He was one of those people who make far more of an impression than their size, or their looks, or anything about them warrants. He was not very tall, and his compact body might have been pudgy in childhood—it might get pudgy again. He had a square face, rather pale except for the bluish shadow of the beard that wounded Lucille. His black hair was very straight and fine, and often flopped over his forehead.

"Don't I?" he said with surprise. "Do I not? How could that be? When Billy is such a lovely person? Look at him over there, drinking and playing cards with the common people. Don't you find him nice? Or do you ever think it's a little strange when anybody can be so nice all the time? *All the time.* There's only one time I've known him to slip up, and that's when you get him talking about some of his old girlfriends. Don't tell me you haven't noticed that."

He had his hand on the leg of Rhea's chair. He was rocking her.

She laughed, giddy from the rocking or perhaps because he had hit on the truth. According to Billy, the girl with the veil and the purple gloves had a breath tainted by cigarette smoking, and another girl used vile language when she got drunk, and one of them had a skin infection, a *fungus*, under her arms. Billy had told Rhea all these things regretfully, but when he mentioned the fungus he broke into a giggle. Unwillingly, with guilty gratification, he giggled.

"He does rake those poor girls over the coals," Wayne said. "The hairy legs. The hal-it-os-is. Doesn't it ever make you nervous? But then you're so nice and clean. I bet you shave your legs every night." He ran his hand down her leg, which by good luck she had shaved before going to the dance. "Or do you put that stuff on them, it melts the hair away? What is that stuff called?"

"Neet," Rhea said.

"Neet! That's the stuff. Only doesn't it have kind of a bad smell? A little moldy or like yeast or something? Yeast. Isn't that another thing girls get? Am I embarrassing you? I should be a gentleman and get you another drink. If I can stand and walk, I'll get you another drink.

"This has not got hardly any whisky in it," he said, of the next Coca-Cola he brought her. "This won't hurt you." She thought that the first statement was probably a lie, but the second was certainly true. Nothing could hurt her. And nothing was lost on her. She did not think that Wayne had any good intentions. Nevertheless, she was enjoying herself. All the bafflement, the fogged-in feeling she had when she was with Billy had burned away. She felt like laughing at everything that Wayne said, or that she herself said. She felt safe.

"This is a funny house," she said.

"How is it funny?" said Wayne. "Just how is this house funny? You're the one that's funny."

Rhea looked down at his wagging black head and laughed because he reminded her of some kind of dog. He was clever but there was a stubbornness about him that was close to stupidity. There was a dog's stubbornness and some misery, too, about the way he kept bumping his head against her knee now, and jerking it back to shake the black hair out of his eyes.

She explained to him, with many interruptions during which she had to laugh at the possibility of explaining, that what was funny was the tin curtain in the corner of the room. She said that she thought there was a dumbwaiter behind it that went up and down from the cellar.

"We could curl up on the shelf," Wayne said. "Want to try it? We could get Billy to let down the rope."

She looked again for Billy's white shirt. So far as she knew, he hadn't turned around to look at her once since he sat down. Wayne was sitting directly in front of her now, so that if Billy did turn around he wouldn't be able to see that her shoe was dangling from one toe and Wayne was flicking his fingers against the sole of her foot. She said that she would have to go to the bathroom first.

"I will escort you," Wayne said.

He grabbed her legs to help himself up. Rhea said, "You're drunk."

"I'm not the only one."

The Monks' house had a toilet—in fact a bathroom—off the back hall. The bathtub was full of cases of beer—not cooling, just stored there. The toilet flushed properly. Rhea had been afraid it wouldn't, because it looked as if it hadn't for the last person.

She looked at her face in the mirror over the sink and spoke to it with recklessness and approval. "Let him," she said. *"Let him."* She turned off the light and stepped into the dark hall. Hands took charge of her at once, and she was guided and propelled out the back door. Up against the wall of the house, she and Wayne were pushing and grabbing and kissing each other. She had the idea of herself, at this juncture, being opened and squeezed, opened and squeezed shut, like an accordion. She was getting a warning, too—something in the distance, not connected with what she and Wayne were doing. Some crowding and snorting, inside or outside of her, trying to make itself understood.

The Monks' dog had come up and was nosing in between them. Wayne knew its name.

"Get down, Rory! Get down, Rory!" he yelled as he yanked at Rhea's crinoline.

The warning was from her stomach, which was being shoved so tightly against the wall. The back door opened, Wayne said something clearly into her ear—she would never know which of these things happened first—and she was suddenly released and began to vomit. She had no intention of vomiting until she started. Then she went down on her hands and knees and vomited until her stomach felt wrung out like a poor rotten rag. When she finished, she was shivering as if a fever had hit her, and her dance dress and crinoline were wet where the vomit had splattered.

Somebody else—not Wayne—pulled her up and wiped her face with the hem of the dress.

"Keep your mouth closed and breathe through your nose," Mrs. Monk said. "You get out of here," she said either to Wayne or to Rory. She gave all of them their orders in the same voice, without sympathy and without blame. She pulled Rhea around the house to her husband's truck and half hoisted her into it.

Rhea said, "Billy."

"I'll tell your Billy. I'll say you got tired. Don't try to talk."

"I'm through throwing up," Rhea said.

"You never know," said Mrs. Monk, backing the truck out onto the road. She drove Rhea up the hill and into her own yard without saying anything more. When she had turned the truck around and stopped, she said, "Watch out when you're stepping down. It's a bigger step than a car."

Rhea got herself into the house, used the bathroom without closing the door, kicked off her shoes in the kitchen, climbed the stairs, wadded up her dress and crinoline, and pushed them far under the bed.

Rhea's father got up early to gather the eggs and get ready to go to Hamilton, as he did every second Sunday. The boys were going with him—they could ride in the back of the truck. Rhea wasn't going, because there would not be room in front. Her father was taking Mrs. Corey, whose husband was in the same hospital as Rhea's mother. When he took Mrs. Corey with him, he always put on a shirt and a tie, because they might go into a restaurant on the way home.

He came and knocked on Rhea's door to tell her they were leaving. "If you find time heavy, you can clean the eggs on the table," he said.

He walked to the head of the stairs, then came back. He called through her door, "Drink lots and lots of water."

Rhea wanted to scream at them all to get out of the house. She had things to consider, things inside her head that could not get free because of the pressure of the people in the house. That was what was causing her to have such a headache. After she had heard the truck's noise die away along the road, she got out of bed carefully, went carefully downstairs, took three aspirins, drank as much water as she could hold, and measured coffee into the pot without looking down.

The eggs were on the table, in six-quart baskets. There were smears of hen manure and bits of straw stuck to them, waiting to be rubbed off with steel wool.

What things? Words, above all. The words that Wayne had said to her just as Mrs. Monk came out the back door.

I'd like to fuck you if you weren't so ugly.

She got dressed, and when the coffee was ready she poured a cup and went outside, out to the side porch, which was in deep morning shade. The aspirins had started to work and now instead of the headache she had a space in her head, a clear precarious space with a light buzz around it.

She was not ugly. She knew she was not ugly. How can you ever be sure that you are not ugly?

But if she was ugly, would Billy Doud have gone out with her in the first place? Billy Doud prided himself on being kind.

But Wayne was very drunk when he said that. Drunkards speak truth.

It was a good thing she was not going to see her mother that day. If she ever wormed out of Rhea what was the matter—and Rhea could never be certain that she would not do that—then her mother would want Wayne chastised. She would be capable of phoning his father, the minister. The word "fuck" was what would incense her, more than the word "ugly." She would miss the point entirely.

Rhea's father's reaction would be more complicated. He would blame Billy for taking her into a place like Monk's. Billy, Billy's sort of friends. He would be angry about the *fuck* part, but really he would be ashamed of Rhea. He would be forever ashamed that a man had called her ugly.

You cannot let your parents anywhere near your real humiliations.

She knew she was not ugly. How could she know she was not ugly?

She did not think about Billy and Wayne, or about what this might mean between them. She was not as yet very interested in other people. She did think that when Wayne said those words, he used his real voice.

She did not want to go back inside the house, to have to look at the baskets full of dirty eggs. She started walking down the lane, wincing in the sunlight, lowering her head between one island of shade and the next. Each tree was different there, and each was a milestone when she used to ask her mother how far she could go to meet her father, coming home from town. As far as the hawthorn tree, as far as the beech tree, as far as the maple. He would stop and let Rhea ride on the running board.

A car hooted from the road. Somebody who knew her, or just a man going by. She wanted to get out of sight, so she cut across the field that the chickens had picked clean and paved slick with their droppings. In one of the trees at the far side of this field, her brothers had built a tree house. It was just a platform, with boards nailed to the tree trunk for you to climb. Rhea did that—she climbed up and sat on the platform. She saw that her brothers had cut windows in the leafy branches, for spying. She could look down on the road, and presently she saw a few cars bringing country children into town to the early Sunday school at the Baptist Church. People in the cars couldn't see her. Billy or Wayne wouldn't be able to see her, if by any chance they should come looking with explanations or accusations or apologies.

In another direction, she could see flashes of the river and a part of the old fairgrounds. It was easy from here to make out, in the long grass, where the racetrack used to go round.

She saw a person walking, following the racetrack. It was Eunie Morgan, and she was wearing her pajamas. She was walking along the racetrack, in light-colored, maybe pale pink, pajamas, at about half past nine in the morning. She followed the track until it veered off, going down to where the riverbank path used to be. The bushes hid her.

Eunie Morgan with her white hair sticking up, her hair and her pajamas catching the light. Like an angel in feathers. But walking in her usual awkward, assertive way—head pushed forward, arms swinging free. Rhea didn't know what Eunie could be doing there. She didn't know anything about Eunie's disappearance. The sight of Eunie seemed both strange and natural to her.

She remembered how on hot summer days, she used to think that Eunie's hair looked like a snowball or like threads of ice preserved from winter, and she would want to mash her face against it, to get cool.

She remembered the hot grass and garlic and the jumping-out-of-your-skin feeling, when they were turning into Toms.

• • •

She went back to the house and phoned Wayne. She counted on his being home and the rest of his family in church.

"I want to ask you something and not on the phone," she said. "Dad and the boys went to Hamilton."

When Wayne got there, she was on the porch cleaning eggs. "I want to know what you meant," she said.

"By what?" said Wayne.

Rhea looked at him and kept looking, with an egg in one hand and a bit of steel wool in the other. He had one foot on the bottom step. His hand on the railing. He wanted to come up, to get out of the sun, but she was blocking his way.

"I was drunk," Wayne said. "You're not ugly."

Rhea said, "I know I'm not."

"I feel awful."

"Not for that," said Rhea.

"I was drunk. It was a joke."

Rhea said, "You don't want to get married to her. Lucille."

He leaned into the railing. She thought maybe he was going to be sick. But he got over it, and tried his raising of the eyebrows, his discouraging smile.

"Oh, really? No kidding? So what advice do you have for me?"

"Write a note," said Rhea, just as if he had asked that in all seriousness. "Get in your car and drive to Calgary."

"Just like that."

"If you want, I'll ride with you to Toronto. You can drop me off and I'll stay at the Y until I get a job."

This was what she meant to do. She would always swear it was what she had meant to do. She felt more at liberty now and more dazzled by herself than she had last night when she was drunk. She made these suggestions as if they were the easiest things in the world. It would be days—weeks, maybe—before everything sank in, all that she had said and done.

"Did you ever look at a map?" said Wayne. "You don't go through Toronto on your way to Calgary. You go across the border at Sarnia and up through the States to Winnipeg and then to Calgary."

"Drop me off in Winnipeg then, that's better."

"One question," said Wayne. "Have you had a sanity test recently?"

Rhea didn't budge or smile. She said, "No."

Eunie was on her way home when Rhea spotted her. Eunie was surprised to find the riverbank path not clear, as she was expecting, but all grown up with brambles. When she pushed out into her own yard, she had scratches and smears of blood on her arms and forehead, and bits of leaves caught in her hair. One side of her face was dirty, too, from being pressed against the ground.

In the kitchen she found her mother and her father and her Aunt Muriel Martin, and Norman Coombs, the Chief of Police, and Billy Doud. After her mother had phoned her Aunt Muriel, her father had stirred himself and said that he was going to phone Mr. Doud. He had worked in Douds when he was young, and remembered how Mr. Doud, Billy's father, was always sent for in an emergency.

"He's dead," said Eunie's mother. "What if you get *her*?" (She meant Mrs. Doud, who had such a short fuse.) But Eunie's father phoned anyway and got Billy Doud. Billy hadn't been to bed.

Aunt Muriel Martin, when she'd got there, had phoned the Chief of Police. He said he would be down as soon as he got dressed and ate his breakfast. This took him a while. He disliked anything puzzling or disruptive, anything that might force him to make decisions which could be criticized later or result in his looking like a fool. Of all the people waiting in the kitchen, he might have been the happiest to see Eunie home safe, and to hear her story. It was right out of his jurisdiction. There was nothing to be followed up, nobody to be charged.

Eunie said that three children had come up to her, in her own yard, in the middle of the night. They said that they had something to show her. She asked them what it was and what they were doing up so late at night. She didn't recall what they answered.

She found herself being borne along by them, without ever having said that she would go. They took her out through the gap in the fence at the corner of the yard and along the path on the riverbank. She was surprised to see the path so nicely opened up—she hadn't walked that way for years.

It was two boys and a girl who took her. They looked about nine or ten or eleven years old and they all wore the same kind of outfit—a kind of seersucker sunsuit with a bib in front and straps over the shoulders. All fresh and clean as if just off the ironing board. The hair of these children was light brown, and straight and shiny. They were the most perfectly clean and polite and pleasant children. But how could she tell what color their hair was and that their sunsuits were made of seersucker? When she came out of the house, she hadn't brought the flashlight. They must have brought some kind of light with them—that was her impression, but she couldn't say what it was.

They took her along the path and out onto the old fairgrounds. They took her to their tent. But it seemed to her that she never saw that tent once from the outside. She was just suddenly inside it, and she saw that it was white, very high and white, and shivering like the sails on a boat. Also it was lit up, and again she had no idea where the light was coming from. And a certain part of this tent or building, or whatever it was, seemed to be made of glass. Yes. Definitely green glass, a very light green, as if panels of that were slid in between the sails. Possibly too a glass floor, because she was walking in her bare feet on something cool and smooth—not grass at all, and certainly not gravel.

Later on, in the newspaper, there was a drawing, an artist's conception, of something like a sailboat in a saucer. But flying saucer was not what Eunie called it, at least not when she was talking about it immediately afterwards. Nor did she say anything about what appeared in print later, in a book of such stories, concerning the capture and investigation of her body, the sampling of her blood and fluids, the possibility that one of her secret eggs had been spirited away, that fertilization had taken place in an alien dimension—that there had been a subtle or explosive, at any rate indescribable, mating, which sucked Eunie's genes into the life stream of the invaders.

She was set down in a seat she hadn't noticed, she couldn't say if it was a plain chair or a throne, and these children began to weave a veil around her. It was like mosquito netting or some such stuff, light but strong. All three of them moved continuously, winding or weaving it around her and never bumping into each other. By this time she was past asking questions. "What do you think you're doing?" and "How did you get here?" and "Where are the grownups?" had just slipped off to some place where she couldn't describe it. Some singing or humming might have been taking place, getting inside her head, something pacifying and delightful. And everything had got to seem perfectly normal. You couldn't inquire about anything, anymore than you would say, "What is that teapot doing here?" in an ordinary kitchen.

When she woke up there was nothing around her, nothing over her. She was lying in the hot sunlight, well on in the morning. In the fairgrounds on the hard earth.

• • •

"Wonderful," said Billy Doud several times as he watched and listened to Eunie. Nobody knew exactly what he meant by that. He smelled of beer but seemed sober and very attentive. More than attentive—you might say enchanted. Eunie's singular revelations, her flushed and dirty face, her somewhat arrogant tone of voice appeared to give Billy Doud the greatest pleasure. What a relief, what a blessing, he might have been saying to himself. To find in the world and close at hand this calm, preposterous creature. *Wonderful.*

His love—Billy's kind of love—could spring up to meet a need that Eunie wouldn't know she had.

Aunt Muriel said it was time to phone the newspapers.

Eunie's mother said, "Won't Bill Proctor be in church?" She was speaking of the editor of the Carstairs *Argus.*

"Bill Proctor can cool his heels," Aunt Muriel said. "I'm phoning the London *Free Press!*"

She did that, but she did not get to talk to the right person—only to some sort of caretaker, because of its being Sunday. "They'll be sorry!" she said. "I'm going to go over their heads right to the Toronto *Star!*"

She had taken charge of the story. Eunie let her. Eunie seemed satisfied. When she was finished telling them, she sat with a look of indifferent satisfaction. It did not occur to her to ask that anybody take charge of her, and try to protect her, give her respect and kindness through whatever lay ahead. But Billy Doud had already made up his mind to do that.

Eunie had some fame, for a while. Reporters came. A book-writer came. A photographer took pictures of the fairgrounds and especially of the racetrack, which was supposed to be the mark left by the spaceship. There was also a picture taken of the grandstand, said to have been knocked down in the course of the landing.

Interest in this sort of story reached a peak years ago, then gradually dwindled.

"Who knows what really happened?" Rhea's father said, in a letter he wrote to Calgary. "One sure thing is, Eunie Morgan never made a cent out of it."

He was writing this letter to Rhea. Soon after they got to Calgary, Rhea and Wayne were married. You had to be married then, to get an apartment together—at least in Calgary—and they had discovered that they did not want to live separately. That would continue to be the way they felt most of the time, though they would discuss it—living separately—and threaten it, and give it a couple of brief tries.

Wayne left the paper and went into television. For years you might see him on the late news, sometimes in rain or snow on Parliament Hill, delivering some rumor or piece of information. Later he travelled to foreign cities and did the same thing there, and still later he got to be one of the people who sit indoors and discuss what the news means and who is telling lies.

(Eunie became very fond of television but she never saw Wayne, because she hated it when people just talked—she always switched at once to something happening.)

Back in Carstairs on a brief visit and wandering in the cemetery, looking to see who has moved in since her last inspection, Rhea spots Lucille Flagg's name on a stone. But it is all right—Lucille isn't dead. Her husband is, and Lucille has had her own name and date of birth cut on the stone along with his, ahead of time. A lot of people do this, because the cost of stonecutting is always going up.

Rhea remembers the hats and rosebuds, and feels a tenderness for Lucille that cannot ever be returned.

At this time Rhea and Wayne have lived together for far more than half their lives. They have had three children, and between them, counting everything, five times as many lovers. And now abruptly, surprisingly, all this turbulence and fruitfulness and uncertain but lively expectation has receded and she knows they are beginning to be old. There in the cemetery she says out loud, "I can't get used to it."

They look up the Douds, who are friends of theirs, in a way, and together the two couples drive out to where the old fairgrounds used to be.

Rhea says the same thing there.

The river houses all gone. The Morgans' house, the Monks' house—everything gone of that first mistaken settlement. The land is now a floodplain, under the control of the Peregrine River Authority. Nothing can be built there anymore. A spacious parkland, a shorn and civilized riverbank—nothing left but a few of the same old trees standing around, their leaves still green but weighed down by a diffuse golden moisture that is in the air, on this September afternoon not many years before the end of the century.

"I can't get used to it," says Rhea.

They are white-haired now, all four of them. Rhea is a thin and darting sort of woman, whose lively and cajoling ways have come in handy teaching English as a second language. Wayne is thin, too, with a fine white beard and a mild manner. When he's not appearing on television, he might remind you of a Tibetan monk. In front of the camera he turns caustic, even brutal.

The Douds are big people, stately and fresh-faced, with a cushioning of wholesome fat.

Billy Doud smiles at Rhea's vehemence, and looks around with distracted approval.

"Time marches on," he says.

He pats his wife on her broad back, responding to a low grumble that the others haven't heard. He tells her they'll be going home in a minute, she won't miss the show she watches every afternoon.

Rhea's father was right about Eunie not making any money out of her experiences, and he was right too in what he had predicted about Billy Doud. After Billy's mother died, problems multiplied and Billy sold out. Soon the people who had bought the factory from him sold out in their turn and the plant was closed down. There were no more pianos made in Carstairs. Billy went to Toronto and got a job, which Rhea's father said had something to do with schizophrenics or drug addicts or Christianity.

In fact, Billy was working at Halfway Houses and Group Homes, and Wayne and Rhea knew this. Billy had kept up the friendship. He had also kept up his special friendship with Eunie. He hired her to look after his sister Bea when Bea began drinking a little too much to look after herself. (Billy was not drinking at all anymore.)

When Bea died, Billy inherited the house and made it over into a home for old people and disabled people who were not so old or disabled that they needed to be in bed. He meant to make it a place where they could get comfort and kindness and little treats and entertainments. He came back to Carstairs and settled in to run it.

He asked Eunie Morgan to marry him.

"I wouldn't want for there to be anything going on, or anything," Eunie said.

"Oh, my dear!" said Billy. "Oh, my dear, dear Eunie!"

VANDALS

I

"Liza, my dear, I have never written you yet to thank you for going out to our house (poor old Dismal, I guess it really deserves the name now) in the teeth or anyway the aftermath of the storm last February and for letting me know what you found there. Thank your husband, too, for taking you there on his snowmobile, also if as I suspect he was the one to board up the broken window to keep out the savage beasts, etc. Lay not up treasure on earth where moth and dust not to mention teenagers doth corrupt. I hear you are a Christian now, Liza, what a splendid thing to be! Are you born again? I always liked the sound of that!

"Oh, Liza, I know it's boring of me but I still think of you and poor little Kenny as pretty sunburned children slipping out from behind the trees to startle me and leaping and diving in the pond.

"Ladner had not the least premonition of death on the night before his operation—or maybe it was the night before that, whenever I phoned you. It is not very often nowadays that people die during a simple bypass and also he really did not think about being mortal. He was just worried about things like whether he had turned the water off. He was obsessed more and more by that sort of detail. The one way his age showed. Though I suppose it is not such a detail if you consider the pipes bursting, that would be a calamity. But a calamity occurred anyway. I have been out there just once to look at it and the odd thing was it just looked natural to me. On top of Ladner's death, it seemed almost the right way for things to be. What would seem unnatural would be to get to work and clean it up, though I suppose I shall have to do that, or hire somebody. I am tempted just to light a match and let everything go up in smoke, but I imagine that if I did that I would find myself locked up.

"I wish in a way that I had had Ladner cremated, but I didn't think of it. I just put him here in the Doud plot to surprise my father and my stepmother. But now I must tell you, the other night I had a dream! I dreamed that I was around behind the Canadian Tire Store and they had the big plastic tent up as they do when they are selling bedding-plants in the spring. I went and opened up the trunk of my car, just as if I were getting my annual load of salvia or impatiens. Other people were waiting as well and men in green aprons were going back and forth from the tent. A woman said to me, "Seven years sure goes by in a hurry!" She seemed to know me but I didn't know her and I thought, Why is this always happening? Is it because I did a little schoolteaching? Is it because of what you might politely call the conduct of my life?

"Then the significance of the seven years struck me and I

knew what I was doing there and what the other people were doing there. They had come for the bones. I had come for Ladner's bones, in the dream it was seven years since he had been buried. But I thought, Isn't this what they do in Greece or somewhere, why are we doing it here? I said to some people, Are the graveyards getting overcrowded? What have we taken up this custom for? Is it pagan or Christian or what? The people I spoke to looked rather sullen and offended and I thought, What have I done now. I've lived around here all my life but I can still get this look—is it the word 'pagan'? Then one of the men handed me a plastic bag and I took it gratefully and held it, thinking of Ladner's strong leg bones and wide shoulder bones and intelligent skull all washed and polished by some bath-and-brush apparatus no doubt concealed in the plastic tent. This seemed to have something to do with my feelings for him and his for me being purified but the idea was more interesting and subtle than that. I was so happy, though, to receive my load and other people were happy too. In fact some of them be-came quite jolly and were tossing their plastic bags in the air. Some of the bags were bright blue, but most were green, and mine was one of the regular green ones.

" 'Oh,' someone said to me. 'Did you get the little girl?'

"I understood what was meant. The little girl's bones. I saw that my bag was really quite small and light, to contain Ladner. I mean, Ladner's bones. What little girl? I thought, but I was already getting confused about everything and had a suspicion that I might be dreaming. It came into my mind, Do they mean the little boy? Just as I woke up I was thinking of Kenny and wondering, Was it seven years since the acci-dent? (I hope it doesn't hurt you, Liza, that I mention this— also I know that Kenny was no longer little when the accident happened.) I woke up and thought that I must ask Ladner about this. I always know even before I am awake that Ladner's body is not beside me and that the sense of him I have, of his weight and heat and smell, are memories. But I still have the feeling—when I wake—that he is in the next room and I can call him and tell him my dream or whatever. Then I have to realize that isn't so, every morning, and I feel a chill. I feel a shrinking. I feel as if I had a couple of wooden planks lying across my chest, which doesn't incline me to get up. A common experience I'm having. But at the moment I'm not having it, just describing it, and in fact I am rather happy sitting here with my bottle of red wine."

This was a letter Bea Doud never sent and in fact never finished. In her big, neglected house in Carstairs, she had entered a period of musing and drinking, of what looked to everybody else like a slow decline, but to her seemed, after all, sadly pleasurable, like a convalescence.

Bea Doud had met Ladner when she was out for a Sunday drive in the country with Peter Parr. Peter Parr was a science teacher, also the principal of the Carstairs High School, where Bea had for a while done some substitute teaching. She did not have a teacher's certificate, but she had an M.A. in English and things were more lax in those days. Also, she would be called upon to help with school excursions, herding a class to the Royal Ontario Museum or to Stratford for their annual dose of Shakespeare. Once she became interested in Peter Parr, she tried to keep clear of such involvements. She wished things to be seemly, for his sake. Peter Parr's wife was in a nursing home—she had multiple sclerosis, and he visited her faithfully. Everyone thought he was an admirable man, and most understood his need to have a steady girlfriend (a word Bea said she found appalling), but some perhaps thought that his choice was a pity. Bea had had what she herself referred to as a checkered career. But she settled down with Peter—his decency and good faith and good humor had brought her into an orderly life, and she thought that she enjoyed it.

When Bea spoke of having had a checkered career, she was taking a sarcastic or disparaging tone that did not reflect what she really felt about her life of love affairs. That life had started when she was married. Her husband was an English airman stationed near Walley during the Second World War. After the war she went to England with him, but they were soon divorced. She came home and did various things, such as keeping house for her stepmother, and getting her M.A. But love affairs were the main content of her life, and she knew that she was not being honest when she belittled them. They were sweet, they were sour; she was happy in them, she was miserable. She knew what it was to wait in a bar for a man who never showed up. To wait for letters, to cry in public, and on the other hand to be pestered by a man she no longer wanted. (She had been obliged to resign from the Light Opera Society because of a fool who directed baritone solos at her.) But still she felt the first signal of a love affair like the warmth of the sun on her skin, like music through a doorway, or the moment, as she had often said, when the black-and-white television commercial bursts into color. She did not think that her time was being wasted. She did not think it had been wasted.

She did think, she did admit, that she was vain. She liked tributes and attention. It irked her, for instance, when Peter Parr took her for a drive in the country, that he never did it for the sake of her company alone. He was a well-liked man and he liked many people, even people that he had just met. He and Bea would always end up dropping in on somebody, or talking for an hour with a former student now working at a gas station, or joining an expedition that had been hatched up with some people they had run into when they stopped at a country store for ice-cream cones. She had fallen in love with him because of his sad situation and his air of gallantry and loneliness and his shy, thin-lipped smile, but in fact he was compulsively sociable, the sort of person who could not pass a family volleyball game in somebody's front yard without wanting to leap out of the car and get into the action.

On a Sunday afternoon in May, a dazzling, freshly green day, he said to her that he wanted to drop in for a few minutes on a man named Ladner. (With Peter Parr, it was always a few minutes.) Bea thought that he had already met this man somewhere, since he called him by a single name and seemed to know a great deal about him. He said that Ladner had come out here from England soon after the war, that he had served in the Royal Air Force (yes, like her husband!), had been shot down and had received burns all down one side of his body. So he had decided to live like a hermit. He had turned his back on corrupt and warring and competitive society, he had bought up four hundred acres of unproductive land, mostly swamp and bush, in the northern part of the county, in Stratton Township, and he had created there a remarkable sort of nature preserve, with bridges and trails and streams dammed up to make ponds, and exhibits along the trails of lifelike birds and animals. For he made his living as a taxidermist, working mostly for museums. He did not charge people anything for walking along his trails and looking at the exhibits. He was a man who had been wounded and disillusioned in the worst way and had withdrawn from the world, yet gave all he could back to it in his attention to nature.

Much of this was untrue or only partly true, as Bea discovered. Ladner was not at all a pacifist—he supported the Vietnam War and believed that nuclear weapons were a deterrent. He favored a competitive society. He had been burned only on the side of his face and neck, and that was from an exploding shell during the ground fighting (he was in the Army) near Caen. He had not left England immediately but had worked for years there, in a museum, until something happened—Bea never knew what—that soured him on the job and the country.

It was true about the property and what he had done with it. It was true that he was a taxidermist.

Bea and Peter had some trouble finding Ladner's house. It was just a basic A-frame in those days, hidden by the trees. They found the driveway at last and parked there and got out of the car. Bea was expecting to be introduced and taken on a tour and considerably bored for an hour or two, and perhaps to have to sit around drinking beer or tea while Peter Parr consolidated a friendship.

Ladner came around the house and confronted them. It was Bea's impression that he had a fierce dog with him. But this was not the case. Ladner did not own a dog. He was his own fierce dog.

Ladner's first words to them were "What do you want?"

Peter Parr said that he would come straight to the point. "I've heard so much about this wonderful place you've made here," he said. "And I'll tell you right off the bat, I am an educator. I educate high-school kids, or try to. I try to give them a few ideas that will keep them from mucking up the world or blowing it up altogether when their time comes. All around them what do they see but horrible examples? Hardly one thing that is positive. And that's where I'm bold enough to approach you, sir. That's what I've come here to ask you to consider."

Field trips. Selected students. See the difference one individual can make. Respect for nature, cooperation with the environment, opportunity to see at first hand.

"Well, I am not an educator," said Ladner. "I do not give a fuck about your teenagers, and the last thing I want is a bunch of louts shambling around my property smoking cigarettes and leering like half-wits. I don't know where you got the impression that what I've done here I've done as a public

service, because that is something in which I have zero interest. Sometimes I let people go through but they're the people
I decide on."

"Well, I wonder just about us," said Peter Parr. "Just us,
today—would you let us have a look?"

"Out of bounds today," said Ladner. "I'm working on the
trail."

Back in the car, heading down the gravel road, Peter Parr
said to Bea, "Well, I think that's broken the ice, don't you?"

This was not a joke. He did not make that sort of joke. Bea
said something vaguely encouraging. But she realized—or had
realized some minutes before, in Ladner's driveway—that she
was on the wrong track with Peter Parr. She didn't want any
more of his geniality, his good intentions, his puzzling and
striving. All the things that had appealed to her and comforted
her about him were now more or less dust and ashes. Now
that she had seen him with Ladner.

She could have told herself otherwise, of course. But such
was not her nature. Even after years of good behavior, it was
not her nature.

She had a couple of friends then, to whom she wrote and
actually sent letters that tried to investigate and explain this
turn in her life. She wrote that she would hate to think she
had gone after Ladner because he was rude and testy and
slightly savage, with the splotch on the side of his face that
shone like metal in the sunlight coming through the trees. She
would hate to think so, because wasn't that the way in all the
dreary romances—some brute gets the woman tingling and
then it's goodbye to Mr. Fine-and-Decent?

No, she wrote, but what she did think—and she knew that
this was very regressive and bad form—what she did think
was that some women, women like herself, might be always
on the lookout for an insanity that could contain them. For
what was living with a man if it wasn't living inside his insan-

ity? A man could have a very ordinary, a very unremarkable, insanity, such as his devotion to a ball team. But that might not be enough, not big enough—and an insanity that was not big enough simply made a woman mean and discontented. Peter Parr, for instance, displayed kindness and hopefulness to a fairly fanatical degree. But in the end, for me, Bea wrote, that was not a suitable insanity.

What did Ladner offer her, then, that she could live inside? She didn't mean just that she would be able to accept the importance of learning the habits of porcupines and writing fierce letters on the subject to journals that she, Bea, had never before heard of. She meant also that she would be able to live surrounded by implacability, by ready doses of indifference which at times might seem like scorn.

So she explained her condition, during the first half-year.

Several other women had thought themselves capable of the same thing. She found traces of them. A belt—size 26—a jar of cocoa butter, fancy combs for the hair. He hadn't let any of them stay. Why them and not me? Bea asked him.

"None of them had any money," said Ladner.

A joke. *I am slit top to bottom with jokes.* (Now she wrote her letters only in her head.)

But driving out to Ladner's place during the school week, a few days after she had first met him, what was her state? Lust and terror. She had to feel sorry for herself, in her silk underwear. Her teeth chattered. She pitied herself for being a victim of such wants. Which she had felt before—she would not pretend she hadn't. This was not yet so different from what she had felt before.

She found the place easily. She must have memorized the route well. She had thought up a story: She was lost. She was looking for a place up here that sold nursery shrubs. That would suit the time of year. But Ladner was out in front of his trees working on the road culvert, and he greeted her in such a matter-of-fact way, without surprise or displeasure, that it was not necessary to trot out this excuse.

"Just hang on until I get this job done," he said. "It'll take me about ten minutes."

For Bea there was nothing like this—nothing like watching a man work at some hard job, when he is forgetful of you and works well, in a way that is tidy and rhythmical, nothing like it to heat the blood. There was no waste about Ladner, no extra size or unnecessary energy and certainly no elaborate conversation. His gray hair was cut very short, in the style of his youth—the top of his head shone silver like the metallic-looking patch of skin.

Bea said that she agreed with him about the students. "I've done some substitute teaching and taken them on treks," she said. "There have been times when I felt like setting Dobermans on them and driving them into a cesspit.

"I hope you don't think I'm here to persuade you of anything," she said. "Nobody knows I'm here."

He took his time answering her. "I expect you'd like a tour," he said when he was ready. "Would you? Would you like a tour of the place yourself?"

That was what he said and that was what he meant. A tour. Bea was wearing the wrong shoes—at that time in her life she did not own any shoes that would have been right. He did not slow down for her or help her in any way to cross a creek or climb a bank. He never held out a hand, or suggested that they might sit and rest on any appropriate log or rock or slope.

He led her first on a boardwalk across a marsh to a pond, where some Canada geese had settled and a pair of swans were circling each other, their bodies serene but their necks mettlesome, their beaks letting out bitter squawks. "Are they mates?" said Bea.

"Evidently."

Not far from these live birds was a glass-fronted case containing a stuffed golden eagle with its wings spread, a gray owl, and a snow owl. The case was an old gutted freezer, with a window set in its side and a camouflage of gray and green swirls of paint.

"Ingenious," said Bea.

Ladner said, "I use what I can get."

He showed her the beaver meadow, the pointed stumps of the trees the beavers had chewed down, their heaped, untidy constructions, the two richly furred beavers in their case. Then in turn she looked at a red fox, a golden mink, a white ferret, a dainty family of skunks, a porcupine, and a fisher, which Ladner told her was intrepid enough to kill porcupines. Stuffed and lifelike raccoons clung to a tree trunk, a wolf stood poised to howl, and a black bear had just managed to lift its big soft head, its melancholy face. Ladner said that was a small bear. He couldn't afford to keep the big ones, he said—they brought too good a price.

Many birds as well. Wild turkeys, a pair of ruffled grouse, a pheasant with a bright-red ring around its eye. Signs told their habitat, their Latin names, food preferences, and styles of behavior. Some of the trees were labelled too. Tight, accurate, complicated information. Other signs presented quotations.

Nature does nothing uselessly.

—Aristotle

Nature never deceives us; it is always we who deceive ourselves.

—Rousseau

When Bea stopped to read these, it seemed to her that Ladner was impatient, that he scowled a little. She no longer made comments on anything she saw.

She couldn't keep track of their direction or get any idea of the layout of the property. Did they cross different streams, or the same stream several times? The woods might stretch for miles, or only to the top of a near hill. The leaves were new and couldn't keep out the sun. Trilliums abounded. Ladner lifted a Mayapple leaf to show her the hidden flower. Fat leaves, ferns just uncurling, yellow skunk cabbage bursting out of bogholes, all the sap and sunshine around, and the treacherous tree rot underfoot, and then they were in an old apple orchard, enclosed by woods, and he directed her to look for mushrooms—morels. He himself found five, which he did not offer to share. She confused them with last year's rotted apples.

A steep hill rose up in front of them, cluttered with little barbed hawthorn trees in bloom. "The kids call this Fox Hill," he said. "There's a den up here."

Bea stood still. "You have children?"

He laughed. "Not to my knowledge. I mean the kids from across the road. Mind the branches, they have thorns."

By this time lust was lost to her altogether, though the smell of the hawthorn blossoms seemed to her an intimate one, musty or yeasty. She had long since stopped fixing her eyes on a spot between his shoulder blades and willing him to turn around and embrace her. It occurred to her that this tour, so strenuous physically and mentally, might be a joke on her, a punishment for being, after all, such a tiresome vamp and fraud. So she roused her pride and acted as if it were exactly what she had come for. She questioned, she took an interest, she showed no fatigue. As later on—but not on this day—she would learn to match him with some of the same pride in the hard-hearted energy of sex.

She did not expect him to ask her into the house. But he said, "Would you like a cup of tea? I can make you a cup of tea," and they went inside. A smell of hides greeted her, of

Borax soap, wood shavings, turpentine. Skins lay in piles, folded flesh-side out. Heads of animals, with empty eyeholes and mouth holes, were set on stands. What she thought at first was the skinned body of a deer turned out to be only a wire armature with bundles of what looked like glued straw tied to it. He told her the body would be built up with papier-mâché.

There were books in the house—a small section of books on taxidermy, the others mostly in sets. The History of the Second World War. The History of Science. The History of Philosophy. The History of Civilization. The Peninsular War. The Peloponnesian Wars. The French and Indian Wars. Bea thought of his long evenings in the winter—his orderly solitude, his systematic reading and barren contentment.

He seemed a little nervous, getting the tea. He checked the cups for dust. He forgot that he had already taken the milk out of the refrigerator, and he forgot that she had already said she did not take sugar. When she tasted the tea, he watched her, asked her if it was all right. Was it too strong, would she like a little hot water? Bea reassured him and thanked him for the tour and mentioned things about it that she had particularly appreciated. Here is this man, she was thinking, not so strange a man after all, nothing so very mysterious about him, maybe nothing even so very interesting. The layers of information. The French and Indian Wars.

She asked for a bit more milk in her tea. She wanted to drink it down faster and be on her way.

He said that she must drop in again if she was ever out in this part of the country with nothing particular to do. "And feel the need of a little exercise," he said. "There is always something to see, whatever the time of year." He spoke of the winter birds and the tracks on the snow and asked if she had skis. She saw that he did not want her to go. They stood in the open doorway and he told her about skiing in Norway, about the tramcars with ski racks on top of them and the mountains at the edge of town.

She said that she had never been to Norway but she was sure she would like it.

She looked back on this moment as their real beginning. They both seemed uneasy and subdued, not reluctant so much as troubled, even sorry for each other. She asked him later if he had felt anything important at the time, and he said yes—he had realized that she was a person he could live with. She asked him if he couldn't say wanted to live with, and he said yes, he could say that. He could say it, but he didn't.

She had many jobs to learn which had to do with the upkeep of this place and also with the art and skill of taxidermy. She would learn, for instance, how to color lips and eyelids and the ends of noses with a clever mixture of oil paint and linseed and turpentine. Other things she had to learn concerned what he would say and wouldn't say. It seemed that she had to be cured of all her froth and vanity and all her old notions of love.

One night I got into his bed and he did not take his eyes from his book or move or speak a word to me even when I crawled out and returned to my own bed, where I fell asleep almost at once because I think I could not bear the shame of being awake.

In the morning he got into my bed and all went as usual.

I come up against blocks of solid darkness.

She learned, she changed. Age was a help to her. Drink also.

And when he got used to her, or felt safe from her, his feelings took a turn for the better. He talked to her readily about what he was interested in and took a kinder comfort from her body.

On the night before the operation they lay side by side on the strange bed, with all available bare skin touching—legs, arms, haunches.

I I

Liza told Warren that a woman named Bea Doud had phoned from Toronto and asked if they—that is, Warren and Liza—could go out and check on the house in the country, where Bea and her husband lived. They wanted to make sure that the water had been turned off. Bea and Ladner (not actually her husband, said Liza) were in Toronto waiting for Ladner to have an operation. A heart bypass. "Because the pipes might burst," said Liza. This was on a Sunday night in February during the worst of that winter's storms.

"You know who they are," said Liza. "Yes, you do. Remember that couple I introduced you to? One day last fall on the square outside of Radio Shack? He had a scar on his cheek and she had long hair, half black and half gray. I told you he was a taxidermist, and you said, 'What's that?' "

Now Warren remembered. An old—but not too old—couple in flannel shirts and baggy pants. His scar and English accent, her weird hair and rush of friendliness. A taxidermist stuffs dead animals. That is, animal skins. Also dead birds and fish.

He had asked Liza, "What happened to the guy's face?" and she had said, "W.W. Two."

"I know where the key is—that's why she called me," Liza said. "This is up in Stratton Township. Where I used to live."

"Did they go to your same church or something?" Warren said.

"Bea and *Ladner*? Let's not be funny. They just lived across the road.

"It was her gave me some money." Liza continued, as if it was something he ought to know, "To go to college. I never asked her. She just phones up out of the blue and says she wants to. So I think, Okay, she's got lots."

. . .

When she was little, Liza had lived in Stratton Township with her father and her brother Kenny, on a farm. Her father wasn't a farmer. He just rented the house. He worked as a roofer. Her mother was already dead. By the time Liza was ready for high school—Kenny was a year younger and two grades behind her—her father had moved them to Carstairs. He met a woman there who owned a trailer home, and later on he married her. Later still, he moved with her to Chatham. Liza wasn't sure where they were now—Chatham or Wallaceburg or Sarnia. By the time they moved, Kenny was dead—he had been killed when he was fifteen, in one of the big teenage car crashes that seemed to happen every spring, involving drunk, often unlicensed drivers, temporarily stolen cars, fresh gravel on the country roads, crazy speeds. Liza finished high school and went to college in Guelph for one year. She didn't like college, didn't like the people there. By that time she had become a Christian.

That was how Warren met her. His family belonged to the Fellowship of the Saviour Bible Chapel, in Walley. He had been going to the Bible Chapel all his life. Liza started going there after she moved to Walley and got a job in the government liquor store. She still worked there, though she worried about it and sometimes thought that she should quit. She never drank alcohol now, she never even ate sugar. She didn't want Warren eating a Danish on his break, so she packed him oat muffins that she made at home. She did the laundry every Wednesday night and counted the strokes when she brushed her teeth and got up early in the morning to do knee bends and read Bible verses.

She thought she should quit, but they needed the money. The small-engines shop where Warren used to work had closed down, and he was retraining so that he could sell computers. They had been married a year.

. . .

In the morning, the weather was clear, and they set off on the snowmobile shortly before noon. Monday was Liza's day off. The plows were working on the highway, but the back roads were still buried in snow. Snowmobiles had been roaring through the town streets since before dawn and had left their tracks across the inland fields and on the frozen river.

Liza told Warren to follow the river track as far as Highway 86, then head northeast across the fields so as to half-circle the swamp. All over the river there were animal tracks in straight lines and loops and circles. The only ones that Warren knew for sure were dog tracks. The river with its three feet of ice and level covering of snow made a wonderful road. The storm had come from the west, as storms usually did in that country, and the trees along the eastern bank were all plastered with snow, clotted with it, their branches spread out like wicker snow baskets. On the western bank, drifts curled like waves stopped, like huge lappings of cream. It was exciting to be out in this, with all the other snowmobiles carving the trails and assaulting the day with such roars and swirls of noise.

The swamp was black from a distance, a long smudge on the northern horizon. But close up, it too was choked with snow. Black trunks against the snow flashed by in a repetition that was faintly sickening. Liza directed Warren with light blows of her hand on his leg to a back road full as a bed, and finally hit him hard to stop him. The change of noise for silence and speed for stillness made it seem as if they had dropped out of streaming clouds into something solid. They were stuck in the solid middle of the winter day.

On one side of the road was a broken-down barn with old gray hay bulging out of it. "Where we used to live," said Liza. "No, I'm kidding. Actually, there was a house. It's gone now."

On the other side of the road was a sign, "Lesser Dismal,"

with trees behind it, and an extended A-frame house painted a light gray. Liza said that there was a swamp somewhere in the United States called Great Dismal Swamp, and that was what the name referred to. A joke.

"I never heard of it," said Warren.

Other signs said "No Trespassing," "No Hunting," "No Snowmobiling," "Keep Out."

The key to the back door was in an odd place. It was in a plastic bag inside a hole in a tree. There were several old bent trees—fruit trees, probably—close to the back steps. The hole in the tree had tar around it—Liza said that was to keep out squirrels. There was tar around other holes in other trees, so the hole for the key didn't in any way stand out. "How did you find it, then?" Liza pointed out a profile—easy to see, when you looked closely—emphasized by a knife following cracks in the bark. A long nose, a down-slanting eye and mouth, and a big drop—that was the tarred hole—right at the end of the nose.

"Pretty funny?" said Liza, stuffing the plastic bag in her pocket and turning the key in the back door. "Don't stand there," she said. "Come on in. Jeepers, it's cold as the grave in here." She was always very conscientious about changing the exclamation "Jesus" to "Jeepers" and "Hell" to "help," as they were supposed to do in the Fellowship.

She went around twirling thermostats to get the baseboard heating going.

Warren said, "We aren't going to hang around here, are we?"

"Hang around till we get warmed up," said Liza.

Warren was trying the kitchen taps. Nothing came out. "Water's off," he said. "It's O.K."

Liza had gone into the front room. "What?" she called. "What's O.K.?"

"The water. It's turned off."

"Oh, is it? Good."

Warren stopped in the front-room doorway. "Shouldn't we ought to take our boots off?" he said. "Like, if we're going to walk around?"

"Why?" said Liza, stomping on the rug. "What's the matter with good clean snow?"

Warren was not a person who noticed much about a room and what was in it, but he did see that this room had some things that were usual and some that were not. It had rugs and chairs and a television and a sofa and books and a big desk. But it also had shelves of stuffed and mounted birds, some quite tiny and bright, and some large and suitable for shooting. Also a sleek brown animal—a weasel?—and a beaver, which he knew by its paddle tail.

Liza was opening the drawers of the desk and rummaging in the paper she found there. He thought that she must be looking for something the woman had told her to get. Then she started pulling the drawers all the way out and dumping them and their contents on the floor. She made a funny noise—an admiring cluck of her tongue, as if the drawers had done this on their own.

"Christ!" he said. (Because he had been in the Fellowship all his life, he was not nearly so careful as Liza about his language.) "Liza? What do you think you're doing?"

"Nothing that is remotely any of your business," said Liza. But she spoke cheerfully, even kindly. "Why don't you relax and watch TV or something?"

She was picking up the mounted birds and animals and throwing them down one by one, adding them to the mess she was making on the floor. "He uses balsa wood," she said. "Nice and light."

Warren did go and turn on the television. It was a black-and-white set, and most of its channels showed nothing but snow or ripples. The only thing he could get clear was a scene

from the old series with the blond girl in the harem outfit—
she was a witch—and the J.R. Ewing actor when he was so
young he hadn't yet become J.R.

"Look at this," he said. "Like going back in time."

Liza didn't look. He sat down on a hassock with his back
to her. He was trying to be like a grownup who won't watch.
Ignore her and she'll quit. Nevertheless he could hear behind
him the ripping of books and paper. Books were being
scooped off the shelves, torn apart, tossed on the floor. He
heard her go out to the kitchen and yank out drawers, slam
cupboard doors, smash dishes. She came back to the front
room after a while, and a white dust began to fill the air. She
must have dumped out flour. She was coughing.

Warren had to cough, too, but he did not turn around.
Soon he heard stuff being poured out of bottles—thin, splashing liquid and thick glug-glug-glugs. He could smell vinegar
and maple syrup and whisky. That was what she was pouring
over the flour and the books and the rugs and the feathers and
fur of the bird and animal bodies. Something shattered against
the stove. He bet it was the whisky bottle.

"Bull's-eye!" said Liza.

Warren wouldn't turn. His whole body felt as if it was
humming, with the effort to be still and make this be over.

Once, he and Liza had gone to a Christian rock concert and
dance in St. Thomas. There was a lot of controversy about
Christian rock in the Fellowship—about whether there could
even be such a thing. Liza was bothered by this question.
Warren wasn't. He had gone a few times to rock concerts
and dances that didn't even call themselves Christian. But
when they started to dance, it was Liza who slid under, right
away, it was Liza who caught the eye—the vigilant, unhappy
eye—of the Youth Leader, who was grinning and clapping
uncertainly on the sidelines. Warren had never seen Liza
dance, and the crazy, slithery spirit that possessed her amazed

him. He felt proud rather than worried, but he knew that whatever he felt did not make the least difference. There was Liza, dancing, and the only thing he could do was wait it out while she tore her way through the music, supplicated and curled around it, kicked loose, and blinded herself to everything around her.

That's what she's got in her, he felt like saying to them all. He thought that he had known it. He had known something the first time he had seen her at the Fellowship. It was summer and she was wearing the little summer straw hat and the dress with sleeves that all the Fellowship girls had to wear, but her skin was too golden and her body too slim for a Fellowship girl's. Not that she looked like a girl in a magazine, a model or a show-off. Not Liza, with her high, rounded forehead and deep-set brown eyes, her expression that was both childish and fierce. She looked unique, and she was. She was a girl who wouldn't say, "Jesus!" but who would, in moments of downright contentment and meditative laziness, say, "Well, *fuck*!"

She said she had been wild before becoming a Christian. "Even when I was a kid," she said.

"Wild in what way?" he had asked her. "Like, with guys?"

She gave him a look, as if to say, Don't be dumb.

Warren felt a trickle now, down one side of his scalp. She had sneaked up behind him. He put a hand to his head and it came away green and sticky and smelling of peppermint.

"Have a sip," she said, handing him a bottle. He took a gulp, and the strong mint drink nearly strangled him. Liza took back the bottle and threw it against the big front window. It didn't go through the window but it cracked the glass. The bottle hadn't broken—it fell to the floor, and a pool of beautiful liquid streamed out from it. Dark-green blood. The window glass had filled with thousands of radiating cracks, and turned as white as a halo. Warren was standing up, gasping from the liquor. Waves of heat were rising through his body. Liza stepped delicately among the torn, spattered books and broken glass, the smeared, stomped birds, the pools of whisky and maple syrup and the sticks of charred wood dragged from the stove to make black tracks on the rugs, the ashes and gummed flour and feathers. She stepped delicately, even in her snowmobile boots, admiring what she'd done, what she'd managed so far.

Warren picked up the hassock he had been sitting on and flung it at the sofa. It toppled off; it didn't do any damage, but the action had put him in the picture. This was not the first time he'd been involved in trashing a house. Long ago, when he was nine or ten years old, he and a friend had got into a house on their way home from school. It was his friend's aunt who lived in this house. She wasn't home—she worked in a jewelry store. She lived by herself. Warren and his friend broke in because they were hungry. They made themselves soda-cracker-and-jam sandwiches and drank some ginger ale. But then something took over. They dumped a bottle of ketchup on the tablecloth and dipped their fingers in, and wrote on the wallpaper, *"Beware! Blood!"* They broke plates and threw some food around.

They were strangely lucky. Nobody had seen them getting into the house and nobody saw them leaving. The aunt herself put the blame on some teenagers whom she had recently ordered out of the store.

Recalling this, Warren went to the kitchen looking for a bottle of ketchup. There didn't seem to be any, but he found and opened a can of tomato sauce. It was thinner than ketchup and didn't work as well, but he tried to write with it on the wooden kitchen wall. *"Beware! This is your blood!"*

The sauce soaked into or ran down the boards. Liza came up close to read the words before they blotted themselves out. She laughed. Somewhere in the rubble she found a Magic

Marker. She climbed up on a chair and wrote above the fake blood, *"The Wages of Sin is Death."*

"I should have got out more stuff," she said. "Where he works is full of paint and glue and all kinds of crap. In that side room."

Warren said, "Want me to get some?"

"Not really," she said. She sank down on the sofa—one of the few places in the front room where you could still sit down. "Liza Minnelli," she said peacefully. "Liza Minnelli, stick it in your belly!"

Was that something kids at school sang at her? Or something she made up for herself?

Warren sat down beside her. "So what did they do?" he said. "What did they do that made you so mad?"

"Who's mad?" said Liza, and hauled herself up and went to the kitchen. Warren followed, and saw that she was punching out a number on the phone. She had to wait a little. Then she said, "Bea?" in a soft, hurt, hesitant voice. "Oh, Bea!" She waved at Warren to turn off the television.

He heard her saying, "The window by the kitchen door. . . . I think so. Even maple syrup, you wouldn't believe it. . . . Oh, and the beautiful big front window, they threw something at that, and they got sticks out of the stove and the ashes and those birds that were sitting around and the big beaver. I can't tell you what it looks like. . . ."

He came back into the kitchen, and she made a face at him, raising her eyebrows and setting her lips blubbering as she listened to the voice on the other end of the phone. Then she went on describing things, commiserating, making her voice quiver with misery and indignation. Warren didn't like watching her. He went around looking for their helmets.

When she had hung up the phone, she came and got him. "It was her," she said. "I already told you what she did to me. She sent me to college!" That started them both laughing.

But Warren was looking at a bird in the mess on the floor. Its soggy feathers, its head hanging loose, showing one bitter red eye. "It's weird doing that for a living," he said. "Always having dead stuff around."

"They're weird," Liza said.

Warren said, "Do you care if he croaks?"

Liza made croaking noises to stop him being thoughtful. Then she touched her teeth, her pointed tongue to his neck.

III

Bea asked Liza and Kenny a lot of questions. She asked them what their favorite TV shows and colors and ice-cream flavors were, and what kind of animals they would be if they could turn into animals, and what was the earliest thing they remembered. "Eating boogers," said Kenny. He did not mean to be funny.

Ladner and Liza and Bea all laughed—Liza the loudest. Then Bea said, "You know, that's one of the earliest things I can remember myself!"

She's lying, Liza thought. Lying for Kenny's sake, and he doesn't even know it.

"This is Miss Doud," Ladner had told them. "Try to be decent to her."

"Miss Doud," said Bea, as if she had swallowed something surprising. "Bea. Bzzz. My name is Bea."

"Who is that?" Kenny said to Liza, when Bea and Ladner were walking ahead of them. "Is she going to live with him?"

"It's his girlfriend," Liza said. "They are probably going to get married." By the time Bea had been at Ladner's place for a week, Liza could not stand the thought of her ever going away.

• • •

The first time that Liza and Kenny had ever been on Ladner's property, they had sneaked in under a fence, as all the signs and their own father had warned them not to do. When they had got so far into the trees that Liza was not sure of the way out, they heard a sharp whistle.

Ladner called them: "You two!" He came out like a murderer on television, with a little axe, from behind a tree. "Can you two read?"

They were about six and seven at this time. Liza said, "Yes."

"So did you read my signs?"

Kenny said faintly, "A fox run in here." When they were driving with their father, one time, they had seen a red fox run across to the road and disappear into the trees here. Their father had said, "Bugger's living in Ladner's bush."

Foxes do not live in the bush, Ladner told them. He took them to see where the fox did live. A den, he called it. There was a pile of sand beside a hole on a hillside covered with dry, tough grass and little white flowers. "Pretty soon those are going to turn into strawberries," Ladner said.

"What will?" said Liza.

"You are a pair of dumb kids," Ladner said. "What do you do all day—watch TV?"

That was the beginning of their spending Saturdays—and, when summer came, nearly all days—with Ladner. Their father said it was all right, if Ladner was fool enough to put up with them. "But you better not cross him or he'll skin you alive," their father said. "Like he does with his other stuff. You know that?"

They knew what Ladner did. He had let them watch. They had seen him clean out a squirrel's skull and fix a bird's feathers to best advantage with delicate wire and pins. Once he was sure that they would be careful enough, he let them fit the glass eyes in place. They had watched him skin animals, scrape the skins and salt them, and set them to dry inside out before he sent them to the tanner's. Tanning put a poison in them so they would never crack, and the fur would never fall out.

Ladner fitted the skin around a body in which nothing was real. A bird's body could be all of one piece, carved of wood, but an animal's larger body was a wonderful construction of wires and burlap and glue and mushed-up paper and clay.

Liza and Kenny had picked up skinned bodies that were tough as rope. They had touched guts that looked like plastic tubing. They had squished eyeballs to jelly. They told their father about that. "But we won't get any diseases," Liza said. "We wash our hands in Borax soap."

Not all the information they had was about dead things: What does the red-winged blackbird say? *Compan-ee!* What does the Jenny wren say? *Pleasa-pleasa-please, can I have a piece of cheese?*

"Oh, can it!" said their father.

Soon they knew much more. At least Liza did. She knew birds, trees, mushrooms, fossils, the solar system. She knew where certain rocks came from and that the swelling on a goldenrod stem contains a little white worm that can live nowhere else in the world.

She knew not to talk so much about all she knew.

Bea was standing on the bank of the pond, in her Japanese kimono. Liza was already swimming. She called to Bea, "Come on in, come in!" Ladner was working on the far side of the pond, cutting reeds and clearing the weeds that clogged the water. Kenny was supposed to be helping him. Liza thought, Like a family.

Bea dropped her kimono and stood in her yellow, silky bathing suit. She was a small woman with dark hair, lightly grayed, falling heavily around her shoulders. Her eyebrows were thick and dark and their arched shape, like the sweet sulky shape of her mouth, entreated kindness and consolation. The sun had covered her with dim freckles, and she was just a bit too soft all over. When she lowered her chin, little pouches collected along her jaw and under her eyes. She was prey to little pouches and sags, dents and ripples in the skin or flesh, sunbursts of tiny purplish veins, faint discolorations in the hollows. And it was in fact this collection of flaws, this shadowy damage, that Liza especially loved. Also she loved the dampness that was often to be seen in Bea's eyes, the tremor and teasing and playful pleading in Bea's voice, its huskiness and artificiality. Bea was not measured or judged by Liza in the way that other people were. But this did not mean that Liza's love for Bea was easy or restful—her love was one of expectation, but she did not know what it was that she expected.

Now Bea entered the pond. She did this in stages. A decision, a short run, a pause. Knee-high in the water, she hugged herself and squealed.

"It's not cold," said Liza.

"No, no, I love it!" Bea said. And she continued, with noises of appreciation, to a spot where the water was up to her waist. She turned around to face Liza, who had swum around behind her with the intention of splashing.

"Oh, no, you don't!" Bea cried. And she began to jump in place, to pass her hands through the water, fingers spread, gathering it as if it were flower petals. Ineffectually, she splashed Liza.

Liza turned over and floated on her back and gently kicked a little water toward Bea's face. Bea kept rising and falling and dodging the water Liza kicked, and as she did so she set up some sort of happy silly chant. *Oh-woo, oh-woo, oh-woo.* Something like that.

Even though she was lying on her back, floating on the water, Liza could see that Ladner had stopped working. He was standing in waist-deep water on the other side of the pond, behind Bea's back. He was watching Bea. Then he, too, started jumping up and down in the water. His body was stiff but he turned his head sharply from side to side, skimming or patting the water with fluttery hands. Preening, twitching, as if carried away with admiration for himself.

He was imitating Bea. He was doing what she was doing but in a sillier, ugly way. He was most intentionally and insistently making a fool of her. See how vain she is, said Ladner's angular prancing. See what a fake. Pretending not to be afraid of the deep water, pretending to be happy, pretending not to know how we despise her.

This was thrilling and shocking. Liza's face was trembling with her need to laugh. Part of her wanted to make Ladner stop, to stop at once, before the damage was done, and part of her longed for that very damage, the damage Ladner could do, the ripping open, the final delight of it.

Kenny whooped out loud. He had no sense.

Bea had already seen the change in Liza's face, and now she heard Kenny. She turned to see what was behind her. But Ladner had dropped into the water again, he was pulling up weeds.

Liza at once kicked up a distracting storm. When Bea didn't respond to this, she swam out into the deep part of the pond and dived down. Deep, deep, to where it's dark, where the carp live, in the mud. She stayed down there as long as she could. She swam so far that she got tangled in the weeds near the other bank and came up gasping, only a yard or so away from Ladner.

"I got caught in the reeds," she said. "I could have drowned."

"No such luck," said Ladner. He made a pretend grab at her, to get her between the legs. At the same time he made a pious, shocked face, as if the person in his head was having a fit at what his hand might do.

Liza pretended not to notice. "Where's Bea?" she said.

Ladner looked at the opposite bank. "Maybe up to the house," he said. "I didn't see her go." He was quite ordinary again, a serious workman, slightly fed up with all their foolishness. Ladner could do that. He could switch from one person to another and make it your fault if you remembered.

Liza swam in a straight line as hard as she could across the pond. She splashed her way out and heavily climbed the bank. She passed the owls and the eagle staring from behind glass. The "Nature does nothing uselessly" sign.

She didn't see Bea anywhere. Not ahead on the boardwalk over the marsh. Not in the open space under the pine trees. Liza took the path to the back door of the house. In the middle of the path was a beech tree you had to go around, and there were initials carved in the smooth bark. One "L" for Ladner, another for Liza, a "K" for Kenny. A foot or so below were the letters "P.D.P." When Liza had first shown Bea the initials, Kenny had banged his fist against P.D.P. "Pull down pants!" he shouted, hopping up and down. Ladner gave him a serious pretend-rap on the head. "Proceed down path," he said, and pointed out the arrow scratched in the bark, curving around the trunk. "Pay no attention to the dirty-minded juveniles," he said to Bea.

Liza could not bring herself to knock on the door. She was full of guilt and foreboding. It seemed to her that Bea would have to go away. How could she stay after such an insult—how could she put up with any of them? Bea did not understand about Ladner. And how could she? Liza herself couldn't have described to anybody what he was like. In the secret life she had with him, what was terrible was always funny, badness was mixed up with silliness, you always had to join in with dopey faces and voices and pretending he was a cartoon monster. You couldn't get out of it, or even want to, any more than you could stop an invasion of pins and needles.

Liza went around the house and out of the shade of the trees. Barefoot, she crossed the hot gravel road. There was her own house sitting in the middle of a cornfield at the end of a short lane. It was a wooden house with the top half painted white and the bottom half a glaring pink, like lipstick. That had been Liza's father's idea. Maybe he thought it would perk the place up. Maybe he thought pink would make it look as if it had a woman inside it.

There is a mess in the kitchen—spilled cereal on the floor, puddles of milk souring on the counter. A pile of clothes from the Laundromat overflowing the corner armchair, and the dishcloth—Liza knows this without looking—all wadded up with the garbage in the sink. It is her job to clean all this up, and she had better do it before her father gets home.

She doesn't worry about it yet. She goes upstairs where it is baking hot under the sloping roof and gets out her little bag of precious things. She keeps this bag stuffed in the toe of an old rubber boot that is too small for her. Nobody knows about it. Certainly not Kenny.

In the bag there is a Barbie-doll evening dress, stolen from a girl Liza used to play with (Liza doesn't much like the dress anymore, but it has an importance because it was stolen), a blue snap-shut case with her mother's glasses inside, a painted wooden egg that was her prize for an Easter picture-drawing contest in Grade 2 (with a smaller egg inside it and a still smaller egg inside that). And the one rhinestone earring that she found on the road. For a long time she believed the rhinestones to be diamonds. The design of the earring is complicated and graceful, with teardrop rhinestones dangling from loops and scallops of smaller stones, and when hung from Liza's ear it almost brushes her shoulders.

She is wearing only her bathing suit, so she has to carry the earring curled up in her palm, a blazing knot. Her head feels swollen with the heat, with leaning over her secret bag, with her resolution. She thinks with longing of the shade under Ladner's trees, as if that were a black pond.

There is not one tree anywhere near this house, and the only bush is a lilac with curly, brown-edged leaves, by the back steps. Around the house nothing but corn, and at a distance the leaning old barn that Liza and Kenny are forbidden to go into, because it might collapse at any time. No divisions over here, no secret places—everything is bare and simple.

But when you cross the road—as Liza is doing now, trotting on the gravel—when you cross into Ladner's territory, it's like coming into a world of different and distinct countries. There is the marsh country, which is deep and jungly, full of botflies and jewelweed and skunk cabbage. A sense there of tropical threats and complications. Then the pine plantation, solemn as a church, with its high boughs and needled carpet, inducing whispering. And the dark rooms under the downswept branches of the cedars—entirely shaded and secret rooms with a bare earth floor. In different places the sun falls differently and in some places not at all. In some places the air is thick and private, and in other places you feel an energetic breeze. Smells are harsh or enticing. Certain walks impose decorum and certain stones are set a jump apart so that they call out for craziness. Here are the scenes of serious instruction where Ladner taught them how to tell a hickory tree from a butternut and a star from a planet, and places also where they have run and hollered and hung from branches and performed all sorts of rash stunts. And places where Liza thinks there is a bruise on the ground, a tickling and shame in the grass.

P.D.P.
Squeegey-boy.
Rub-a-dub-dub.

When Ladner grabbed Liza and squashed himself against her, she had a sense of danger deep inside him, a mechanical sputtering, as if he would exhaust himself in one jab of light, and nothing would be left of him but black smoke and burnt smells and frazzled wires. Instead, he collapsed heavily, like the pelt of an animal flung loose from its flesh and bones. He lay so heavy and useless that Liza and even Kenny felt for a moment that it was a transgression to look at him. He had to pull his voice out of his groaning innards, to tell them they were bad.

He clucked his tongue faintly and his eyes shone out of ambush, hard and round as the animals' glass eyes.

Bad-bad-bad.

"The loveliest thing," Bea said. "Liza, tell me—was this your mother's?"

Liza said yes. She could see now that this gift of a single earring might be seen as childish and pathetic—perhaps intentionally pathetic. Even keeping it as a treasure could seem stupid. But if it was her mother's, that would be understandable, and it would be a gift of some importance. "You could put it on a chain," she said. "If you put it on a chain you could wear it around your neck."

"But I was just thinking that!" Bea said. "I was just thinking it would look lovely on a chain. A silver chain—don't you think? Oh, Liza, I am just so proud you gave it to me!"

"You could wear it in your nose," said Ladner. But he said this without any sharpness. He was peaceable now—played out, peaceable. He spoke of Bea's nose as if it might be a pleasant thing to contemplate.

Ladner and Bea were sitting under the plum trees right behind the house. They sat in the wicker chairs that Bea had brought out from town. She had not brought much—just enough to make islands here and there among Ladner's skins and instruments. These chairs, some cups, a cushion. The wineglasses they were drinking out of now.

Bea had changed into a dark-blue dress of very thin and soft material. It hung long and loose from her shoulders. She trickled the rhinestones through her fingers, she let them fall and twinkle in the folds of her blue dress. She had forgiven Ladner, after all, or made a bargain not to remember.

Bea could spread safety, if she wanted to. Surely she could. All that is needed is for her to turn herself into a different sort of woman, a hard-and-fast, draw-the-line sort, clean-sweeping, energetic, and intolerant. *None of that. Not allowed. Be good.* The woman who could rescue them—who could make them all, keep them all, good.

What Bea has been sent to do, she doesn't see.

Only Liza sees.

I V

Liza locked the door as you had to, from the outside. She put the key in the plastic bag and the bag in the hole in the tree. She moved towards the snowmobile, and when Warren didn't do the same she said, "What's the matter with you?"

Warren said, "What about the window by the back door?"

Liza breathed out noisily. "Ooh, I'm an idiot!" she said. "I'm an idiot ten times over!"

Warren went back to the window and kicked at the bottom

pane. Then he got a stick of firewood from the pile by the tin shed and was able to smash the glass out. "Big enough so a kid could get in," he said.

"How could I be so stupid?" Liza said. "You saved my life."

"Our life," Warren said.

The tin shed wasn't locked. Inside it he found some cardboard boxes, bits of lumber, simple tools. He tore off a piece of cardboard of a suitable size. He took great satisfaction in nailing it over the pane that he had just smashed out. "Otherwise animals could get in," he said to Liza.

When he was all finished with this job, he found that Liza had walked down into the snow between the trees. He went after her.

"I was wondering if the bear was still in there," she said.

He was going to say that he didn't think bears came this far south, but she didn't give him the time. "Can you tell what the trees are by their bark?" she said.

Warren said he couldn't even tell from their leaves. "Well, maples," he said. "Maples and pines."

"Cedar," said Liza. "You've got to know cedar. There's a cedar. There's a wild cherry. Down there's birch. The white ones. And that one with the bark like gray skin? That's a beech. See, it had letters carved on it, but they've spread out, they just look like any old blotches now."

Warren wasn't interested. He only wanted to get home. It wasn't much after three o'clock, but you could feel the darkness collecting, rising among the trees, like cold smoke coming off the snow.